I0675788

The Sword of Zulfiqar

OUT OF THE DARKNESS

By *Tadek*

Copyright © 2015 by Theodore M. Gizewski

This book is copyrighted material and must not be copied, reproduced, transferred, distributed, leased, licensed, publicly performed, or used in any way
except as expressly permitted in writing by the author, or as expressly permitted by applicable United States copyright law. Any unauthorized distribution,
reproduction, transfer, lease, license, performance, or other use of this text is
expressly prohibited and may be an infringement of the author's and publish-
er's rights. Those responsible may be legally liable. The author hereby
expressly reserves any and all rights not herein explicitly granted.

Author's Note: This is a work of fiction. Names, titles, characters, institutions,
corporations, businesses, and organizations are the product of the author's imagination. or, if real, are used fictionally without any intent to describe their
actual conduct. The author does not represent the United States government
or any of its agencies or departments. Locales, situations, and events are also
the product of the author's imagination. or, if real, are used fictionally.

Book Layout © 2015 BookDesignTemplates.com

The Sword of Zulfiqar/ Tadek. -- 1st edition print.
ISBN 978-0-9967054-0-0

This book is dedicated to my beautiful and amazing wife Lynn. If not for her love and encouragement none of this would have been possible.

ACKNOWLEDGMENTS

I would like to thank my wife, Lynn who kept our home and our lives going while I was hunkered down writing this book. Still, she would always find the time to read through all of those rewrites and to help me flesh out many of the most interesting characters. She has come to know the story as well as I do and would offer thoughtful suggestions that have shaped some of the best parts of the book.

I'd also like to thank my children Ted and his wife Tonya as well as Tamara and her husband Greg for their confidence and patience. A special thanks to Tamara for helping with the cover design and to Tonya for the hours and hours of reading my early drafts.

And finally, I'd like to thank Mike Waitz of 'Sticks and Stones Freelance Editing.' He did a tremendous job of editing this book. The man is thoughtful, patient, and always willing to go the extra mile.

Mike is a real pro and has been doing this kind of work for over a decade; he's been a journalist, a teacher, and a member of the Air Force Reserve. The man even has a Masters (MA) in Homeland Security from American Military University. He knows his stuff and I'm glad I've got him in my corner.

Thanks Mike!

CONTENTS

CHAPTER ONE

Arrival

Operation Frostbite, January 18th, 0342 hours, over northern Maidan Wardak Province, Afghanistan.

After nearly two hours of flight, the muffled roar and the numbing vibration of the turbine engine had put the six men into a near hypnotic state. No one spoke. Some of the men slumped in their seats, dozing, while others just stared into space, their minds thousands of miles away. Harris, a tall, lean man awkwardly folded into the right forward cabin seat, had been thinking about the young man he had enticed to come and work for him. His name was Dawud Hawadi and he was operating under the alias Afig Hafeez when he had been sent out on a simple training exercise. It shouldn't have been any more dangerous than picking up a quart of milk at a local 7-Eleven. However, it hadn't turned out that way. Two men were dead. One was a massive, powerfully built man who had been seen fighting with Afig, and whom Afig had somehow managed to kill. The other dead man was the village Malik (headman) and a relatively well-to-do baker. He had been shot in the back and it was not clear who had shot him, or why. Then, to top it off, Afig had been taken prisoner by some mysterious character who used the name Dr. Dicos. It had turned out that this Dr. Dicos was wanted by a number of governments because of his involvement with Islamic terrorist groups that were attempting to acquire biological weapons. Interestingly, he was not particular about what brand of Islamic terrorism he supported, as long as they were certifiably fanatic and sufficiently ruthless.

Harris' headset came alive with a crackle of static, immediately followed by the pilot's voice saying, "Colonel, we're twenty minutes out.

A reconnaissance satellite passed over the landing zone seven minutes ago and shows no contacts within the three-kilometer radius."

The pilot paused for a second as he tapped on one of his several touch screens, then he continued, "Ground temperature is now a crispy...negative twenty-six degrees Celsius (-15° F), the sky is overcast, and the air is still.

Sir, I need you to give me mission go-ahead."

From this point on, operational risks began to multiply. Maidan Wardak Province was a dangerous and complicated place. Land disputes between the ethnic Hazara people in the north, and the Pashtun Kuchi nomads in the south, had again escalated. The number of local Taliban and their al-Qaeda-supplied foreign fighters was growing, and then there were the frequent incursions of Pakistani Taliban, who often included Pakistani intelligence officers and even Pakistani military personnel. And who could forget the bandits, local militias, and other Islamic insurgent groups, including bands of Islamic State fighters and the Hezb e Islami Gulbuddin, who had off-and-on alliances with the Taliban and al-Qaeda.

Their ultimate destination was the village of Sewakla, located in a high, remote valley in central Maidan Wardak Province. Sewakla and the surrounding countryside were currently under Taliban control, so it was necessary to select a landing zone on the backside of a mountain that bordered the northern side of the Sewakla valley. The approach required skirting a known Taliban winter camp and a half dozen small settlements, the occupants of which would likely include Taliban sympathizers.

What now concerned Harris was the temperature. It had dropped 4° C in the last two hours, and if it kept dropping, the cold was going to become an issue. Harris was no fan of the cold. It made men slow and clumsy, it required that they carry more gear, weapons jammed, batteries drained more quickly, and even their ammunition became less reliable. Then there was always the risk of snow blindness, frostbite, and hypothermia. Harris had almost lost an ear and two fingers to frostbite and he had once been so cold for so long that he thought he had died.

The temperatures they would experience in these mountains wouldn't qualify as "really cold," but it was cold enough and he knew their clothing and equipment wouldn't let them hang around very long. The plan was to make their way to the south side of the mountain that was part of the ridgeline that bordered the Sewakla valley. From there, they would descend to the more temperate valley floor, and then make their way to a location a few clicks outside the village of Sewakla. The planners had estimated the trek would take about six hours.

Well, Harris thought, we'll have to see about that.

After adjusting the boom mic, Harris spoke into it, saying, "Captain, continue to the landing zone. Mission is a GO. I repeat, mission is a GO."

The pilot responded, "Roger that, colonel. Mission is a GO."

A few seconds later, the chopper steeply banked left and descended into the darkness. When it finally leveled out, the chopper was less than twenty meters above the rock outcroppings and tree tops that were visible only to the pilot's instruments. There was another steep bank, this time to the right, as the chopper plunged into the mouth of a gorge that was bracketed, on both sides, by rock cliffs. The chopper repeatedly veered hard to the left and to the right as it maneuvered its way at speeds of nearly 200 knots. With one last steep right bank, the chopper shot out of the gorge, into a valley bordered on the north by high, snow-covered ridges.

The chopper, an S-97 Raider, was new and its agility and speed were impressive. Its sleek design made for a low and narrow cabin that was fitted with six folding, metal-framed, canvas seats that had become increasingly more uncomfortable with each passing minute. There were three seats on each side, facing each other across a narrow passageway. Although the cabin lights were off, there was still enough instrumentation glow for Harris to see the shadowy figures that occupied the other seats. To an outsider, he and the rest of these men would certainly cause some concern. They were lean, hard-looking men with long, scraggly beards. On their heads, several of the men wore black turbans while others wore frayed, brown pakols - flat-top woven caps with rolled rims. Over their shoulders were draped the traditional wool blanket and their clothing included the customary baggy pants, long tunics, and a hodgepodge of heavy winter jackets, including several old, Soviet army, cold-weather field jackets. Many of the garments were threadbare, and all were in need of laundering.

Atop their jackets the men wore old, Soviet-era assault vests whose pouches were stuffed with spare AK-47 magazines and grenades. To complete the image, beside each man was propped an AK-47 assault rifle that the Afghans referred to as a Kalashnikov. Like the rest of their outfits, their rifles looked old and appeared to have seen hard use.

There was little doubt that these six men looked...menacing. And it would not take much imagination to conclude that they were a band of al-Qaeda or Taliban fighters.

What an outside observer would not know was that Harris was Lieutenant Colonel Harris Bartnik, and all but one of these men were Paramilitary Operations Officers of the elite CIA, Special Operations Group. To a man, they were combat veterans who had also proved themselves to be exceptionally talented covert operators. The one non-American was an Afghan, a long-time CIA asset. His name was Housyar, and he was a Pashtun tribesman, a smart, tough old man, who was believed to be in his early seventies. Housyar knew his way around the mountains, and had the endurance and agility of a mountain goat. As importantly, he was a natural, home-spun, politician, a man who could persuade people to go barefoot in the snow.

A buzzer sounded and the five-minute countdown display lit up. All six men immediately came alert and automatically reached for their rifles, and then each reached into his canvas pouch and did a final check of his IR (infrared) night-vision goggles. The IR goggles, a ruggedized tablet computer, and their communications equipment were the only U.S. made items they carried, and even these had been specially manufactured so as to obscure all traces of their true origin.

As the chopper approached the landing zone, it slowed and began to descend. Harris could feel the tension as the men mentally prepared themselves to leave the relative security of the chopper, for a cold, hostile world where their training and their instincts would be all that would keep them alive.

These men were a specially trained, advanced unit of Operation Frostbite, and they were being deployed to gather intelligence and prepare the way for a larger contingency of Delta Force operators whose three primary objectives were to capture or kill the mysterious Dr. Dicos, neutralize whatever he was working on, and rescue Harris' young protégé, who had been given the code name "Crow."

Ever since Afig had been taken, and Dr. Dicos positively identified, more and more information was surfacing. During the last three days, Langley had determined that nine months ago, Dr. Dicos had likely come into possession of a shipment of German and Swiss lab equipment, as well as some medical supplies and chemicals. They also suspected that he had assembled a team of doctors and medical technicians, some of whom had been sprung from prisons in Egypt. Clearly, something was up, and his bosses at Langley wanted to know what, before they sent in the cavalry.

As the chopper came to a hover, less than a meter above the snow-covered mountain, the intercom came alive and the men heard the pilot say, "Good luck and good hunting gentlemen." Then the indicator light flashed green. Jerry Tuma, a wiry man of modest height, and whom they called "Blade," sprung to his feet and proceeded to slide the right cabin door open. Instantly, a blast of frigid air hit the men, and the next few seconds were a blur as the chopper bucked and twisted while the men fought to make their way to the open door. From the moment the door had been opened to when the last man had exited, was less than nine seconds, a hair-raising, tooth-jarring nine seconds during which the chopper was slammed by the most fierce wind gusts Harris had ever experienced. The men had been tossed around like pebbles in a tin can, and they didn't exactly jump out, but rather they were flung out. The winds, plus the turbulence created by the chopper blades, had churned the outside world into a swirling arctic cyclone of snow and ice. The men were hurled into this white fury, blindly falling through it and landing in the deep snow that instantly devoured them. Harris scrambled to his feet just in time to catch a glimpse of the chopper as it awkwardly rose; the right side of the fuselage was dented and the right vertical stabilizer was damaged. A second later, the chopper was gone, disappearing into the blackness.

Harris Bartnik had spent nearly three years in Afghanistan, and he had been dropped off by helicopters at least 50 times. Yet, he had never experienced anything like this. The wind had reared up out of nowhere and had hit them with the force of a Mack Truck. Although Harris didn't much believe in miracles, he had to admit that seeing all five of his men, still in one piece, was damn close to one.

Seconds after the last man had tumbled into the snow, the wind had eased and now everything had become still...eerily still. As they had trained, the men immediately donned their IR goggles and took up defensive positions. Doing a quick assessment of their situation, Harris found that their gear had been scattered and most of the men had suffered some cuts and bruises. Two of the men had injuries serious enough to require more than a Band-Aid. Connor, a tough, private man, who had been a decorated Green Beret, had been slammed against the fuselage, messing up his back, while Urbanski, who happened to have a PhD in biochemistry, but could better be described as a "smarter than average" adventurer with a strong patriotic streak, had sprained his knee. Both men were being tended to by the unit's medic, but it looked like Connor had gotten the worst of it. Although they had been on the ground less than ten minutes, the place had already taken a toll. To Harris, it seemed the mountain, itself, had tried to kill them.

Harris peered into the darkness as a feeling of uneasiness crept over him. Something was out there, he could feel it. Harris had, long ago, realized that he was able to sense some things more acutely than most other men. This went a long way in explaining why a man in his profession still had all of his appendages at the ripe old age of forty-three. Right now, his senses were telling him that something was going to happen...something bad. It was not long before the other men also sensed something was wrong. These were not amateurs; these men were alive, in large part, because they had learned to trust their instincts and, at this moment, their instincts were sounding a shrill alarm.

Harris ordered the men to close ranks and be prepared to move. They were a small, lightly armed unit and they knew that their survival depended on their ability to move quickly, to disappear before anyone could focus too much attention on them. Nonetheless, it would help to have some idea of what they were up against. After several minutes they had still not detected anything that remotely resembled a threat. Their IR goggles did not use visible light to identify objects. Instead, the goggles detected heat, or rather they detected the infrared wavelength of electromagnetic radiation emitted by an object. The warmer the object, the stronger the infrared energy it emits. In this cold environment, the heat emitted by even a small, exposed portion of a human body, say an eye, would stand out and appear as a bright image on the goggles' displays. Still, the men saw only the shadowy features of the frozen mountainside. Keeping still, they strained to listen but could hear only their breathing and the occasional creak of the shifting ice.

They had held this position for nearly 15 minutes when Harris whispered into his throat mic, "Blade, Kurt, stay where you are and stay alert. The rest of you, collect our gear...we're getting out of here."

The snow was waist deep, which was something else they had not expected. During their briefing they had been told that the snow would only be 10 to 15 centimeters (4 to 6 inches), so they had not even considered bringing snow shoes or any other deep snow equipment. After several minutes of searching, they had located what was left of their gear. Blade's pack was gone and two of the other packs had been ripped open, most of their contents blown to who knows where.

When they had collected and secured the gear that was left, Harris ordered the men to assemble. He wanted them out of there as quickly as possible. Blade would carry Connor's pack, as Connor was in a lot of pain and just barely able to walk. It took a few seconds to wrestle the packs on and then Harris gave the order to move out. The original plan was to head east and skirt around the mountain, in the general direction of Aas Pass and the village of Sheikhabad. Instead, Harris turned west. West would get them off this damn north slope and out of the deep snow in about half the time.

Forming a column, the men moved forward. The depth of the snow made progress agonizingly slow, requiring the man in front to physically plow his way through it. The effort quickly took a physical toll, and every 10 minutes the point man was rotated to the rear of the column, and the man behind him would take his place. Everyone except Connor took his turn.

Bent awkwardly, Connor trudged forward, pain evident in his face. He had not been able to straighten his back, and sensed that something was seriously wrong. Each time he lifted a leg, he would feel pain nearly sharp enough to drive him to his knees; Connor knew that he was out of the game. The cold was rapidly penetrating his clothing and he was beginning to shiver. Yet, he could feel the perspiration dripping from his forehead. Connor knew he could not go much farther, but if he went down, he knew that they would insist on carrying him.

Connor recalled once carrying a wounded man nearly eight kilometers, and would have carried him 80 more if it had been necessary. But that was not what he was thinking about now. Connor was remembering what had happened that night, eight years ago.

He had been a Special Forces operator, a 23-year-old weapons sergeant. His battalion had been deployed to Iraq to train Iraqi Army personnel in counter-insurgency techniques. It was during one of these training exercises that they received intelligence indicating that an infamous Saudi bomb maker was staying at a villa on the outskirts of Fallujah. This man had been responsible for the deaths of more than a dozen Americans, so it was decided that Connor's Special Forces 12-man A-Team, code named Viper 1, would go after the bomb maker.

Two nights later, at 0130 hours, two Special-Ops Blackhawk helicopters descended onto a deserted athletic field about four clicks from the target. The instant the choppers' skids touched down, the dark silhouettes of 12 Viper 1 operators emerged, quickly forming up and then slipping into the darkness. Their objective: A white stucco villa, in a relatively affluent Fallujah neighborhood.

It was a hot night and the men wore full combat gear. By the time they got within two city blocks of their objective, they were completely soaked with sweat. Connor remembered that he was wiping sweat from his eyes when all hell broke loose. In just eight minutes, four United States Army, Special Forces operators would be dead, and four more would be seriously wounded. But what Connor recalled most clearly was how three of these men lost their lives.

Viper 1 had stumbled onto a heavily armed Iraqi insurgent force that numbered nearly 150 fighters. Seconds after making contact, two Special Forces operators went down. One man was killed instantly while another man was seriously wounded. Unwilling to leave their wounded comrade, Viper 1 operators made three attempts to reach him. Each attempt failed and each attempt had cost the life of another operator. Connor had led the fourth attempt, and he had reached the wounded man by using the bodies of his three fallen comrades as shields. Over and over again, bullets meant for him thudded into those bodies. He had crawled through their blood, he had seen the blank stares in their dead eyes.

Connor had managed to drag the wounded man through a nearby opening in a wall, and then down a passageway between two buildings. By then, what was left of Viper 1 was running out of ammunition, their ranks had been decimated, and they had no choice but to pull back and request immediate extraction. For the next six hours, Connor carried a wounded comrade through the alleyways and back streets of Fallujah. They would travel a distance of eight kilometers, before being spotted by the Army Ranger patrol that brought them in.

It was Harris' second turn at the front of the column, when he first felt it...a deep, distant rumble that took only an instant to register.

"AVALANCHE!" He yelled the warning even as his eyes frantically searched the surrounding slope for a place that might shelter them. Spotting a narrow gap between two protruding slabs of rock, he ordered the men toward it and told them to squeeze in as far as they could. As they scrambled through the deep snow, the first chunks of ice tumbled past. A fraction of a second later, they heard a distant, deep thumping sound that shook the whole mountain. Then, suddenly, a massive boulder, the size of a bus, came hurling out of the darkness.

Connor was directly in its path and had only a second to react. Harris didn't know why Connor didn't get out of the way, why he was just standing there when the boulder smashed into him. When it had passed, all Harris could see was a gloved hand protruding from a patch of blood-stained snow.

There was no time left. The men had just reached the gap when they heard the deafening roar. Looking up, they saw a ten-meter high wall of cascading rock, ice, and snow come thundering toward them like some massive, out-of-control freight train. They all pressed themselves against the frozen rock as the avalanche thundered overhead. The mountain shook for nearly two minutes, and when it had stopped, the men's bodies ached from being pelted by rocks and ice. Snow had filled in around them, pressing against their eyes and finding its way into their ears and their mouths.

When Harris was reasonably sure that the worst was over, he tried to move but found that he was completely buried. Though it took some effort, he gradually freed his arms, and then was able to push away a block of snow that was pressing against the side of his head. As the block rolled away, it revealed a gray, early morning sky. It took nearly 20 minutes for Harris to dig himself out, and by then other men were also emerging from their would-be graves. When the last man had pulled himself to the surface, Harris could see the fatigue in the men's faces. They would need some time to recover, but the cold was also getting to them. What they really needed to do was get off this damn mountain.

Except for Connor, all of the men were accounted for. Harris had somehow managed to hang onto his pack, and now removed a package of Chinese-made chemical heat packs. As he distributed one to each man, he checked on their condition. They were exhausted and they were cold, but no one was seriously injured. On the other hand, their gear had not fared as well. Only one set of IR goggles had survived; the others had either been smashed, or ripped away and lost. Another one of their packs was missing and along with it, spare clothing, some of their climbing gear, and their medical supplies. Still, the men had managed to hang onto their rifles, a testimony to their military training.

Harris slipped an activated heat pack beneath the back of his jacket, and then used the last heat pack to heat up a canteen of water. The men were thirsty but eating snow was a bad idea. Snow would lower their body temperatures and they were already cold enough.

Rest, a drink of hot water, a few handfuls of Afghanistan's version of trail mix, which each man carried, and the heat packs soon revived the men, and they were ready to move out. As they got to their feet, Harris discovered that only one of their tactical radios worked, while the rest were completely dead or worked intermittently. For all practical purposes, they would now have to use voice commands or hand signals.

After downing what was left of the hot water, the men hoisted their remaining packs and set out for the nearby berm that had formed at the eastern boundary of the snow field. On the other side of this berm was where they had last seen Connor. No one believed that they would find him alive; they had seen the boulder hit him, they had heard the sound of bones being crushed. The best they could do was locate his body and place it somewhere from which it could later be retrieved. As the men crested the berm, they all came to a sudden stop. No one spoke, they just stared. The mountain...it was gone. Only a few meters from where they stood was a sheer drop-off. The entire north face of the mountain had collapsed and it had taken Connor's body with it. The men stared with disbelief at the empty space that had been solid rock less than an hour ago.

Ten minutes later, they were again heading west, and as they trudged through the snow, Harris thought about the mountain and what had happened to it. He thought about Connor. Connor was the seventh man Harris had lost on a mission. They had all been good, decent men, men who had died in places no one had ever heard of, on missions no one could talk about. He had long ago learned that there was no use in trying to make sense of why good, brave men died so that other men of lesser character and questionable courage could safely go about their business.

For the next three hours the men pushed themselves hard, managing to descend over a hundred meters before they finally reconnected with their original route. The depth of the snow had steadily diminished, and soon larger and larger patches of exposed rock were visible. Their route snaked around massive granite spires and down steep gorges. They were emerging from one of these gorges when Harris saw Housyar, who was leaning against the base of steep rock formation, about 50 meters in front of them. Housyar had been acting as point man and scout. They were getting close to the Sewakla turn-off, and Housyar was the only one who knew its exact location. Harris had been growing increasingly nervous as they got closer to Aas Pass. The Taliban had established an outpost at Aas Pass and it would be just a matter of time before they ran into one of their patrols.

Next to Housyar was a small, scrawny looking pine tree that grew out of a crack in the rock. A few meters past the pine tree were two rock outcroppings, and then the mountain dropped away, nearly vertically. As Harris and the other men approached, none of them could see anything that even vaguely resembled a turn-off. In fact, turning south, toward Sewakla, would mean stepping off of a high cliff. Housyar immediately spotted their doubt, and broke into a smile that displayed a prominent gold tooth and several gaps where teeth had long since gone missing. The old man's eyes were bright, energetic, and just slightly mischievous. His face was weathered with deep furrows in his brow and around his eyes. His smile was genuine, almost playful, and Harris could see the child that was still present in this old man. Without speaking, Housyar turned and walked toward the cliff's edge, where he stepped into a narrow gap between two rock outcroppings and disappeared from sight. Harris followed but it took several long seconds before he spotted Housyar again. He was about five meters to his left, and nearly completely hidden by a large, triangular rock that was cantilevered over the edge of the cliff. Harris approached, and when he peered over the rock, he saw Housyar waiting for him at what appeared to be the top of a narrow stairway that had been carved into the side of the cliff.

A few minutes later all five men were descending the crudely carved steps. They had traveled about a dozen of these steps when the distant sound of voices caught their attention. Stopping, and then keeping perfectly still, they listened. A few seconds later, the voices were close enough for Harris to hear what they were saying. They were Taliban, part of a patrol, and from the number of voices they heard, Harris guessed that there must have been 15 or 20 men. Two of the Taliban had made their way to the cliff's edge and were now standing directly above the five men, close enough that if Harris wanted to, he could reach up and touch them. Knowing that even the slightest movement could dislodge a pebble and send it noisily careening off the cliff wall, the men held their breaths.

Harris and Housyar had been responsible for selecting their route, making sure that if anyone tracked them, it would seem obvious that they were heading toward Aas Pass. There was little doubt that their trudging through the snow had left plenty of tracks, and it hadn't taken long for the Taliban to spot them. Now the Taliban were trying to figure out where the tracks had gone. After searching the area for nearly 15 minutes, they resorted to arguing and blaming each other. It took nearly 10 minutes for the headman to decide that whoever they had been following must still be heading toward Aas Pass. After all, there was simply nowhere else to go. Once this had been decided, the patrol quickly departed in what they believed was hot pursuit of the intruders.

The five men had stood on those narrow steps, nearly motionless, for more than 40 minutes. By the time the Taliban had left, the men could feel the cold again. Their legs were numb and felt like wooden stumps. They were having difficulty maintaining their balance, a dangerous condition since the steps were narrow, less than half a meter wide. The treads were worn, varied in height and depth, and tended to slope perilously downward. The inside wall was a sheer granite face, with nothing to hang onto. The outside was a vertical drop of at least a hundred meters.

They descended, slowly at first, but as the blood circulated through their legs, they picked up their pace. They had traveled for 10 or 15 minutes when Housyar said, "The Taliban are made of poor iron and they will never make a sharp sword. Many of them have lived in these mountains all of their lives, but they do not know about these steps."

Harris had known Housyar for nearly two years, and would trust the man with his life. Still, he knew very little about the man personally. Curious, he replied, "And you Housyar, where did you learn about these steps?"

Housyar did not reply immediately, and Harris was beginning to think the conversation was over. Then Housyar cleared his throat, and said, "In Lomgar, the village I come from, there was an old lady that knew about these things. Her husband had been a smuggler, and his father before him. They knew of many ways to cross these mountains, but this knowledge is now gone. The young men are full of crazy ideas and want only to fight. They have no use for the old people and think of them as ignorant.

This is how I knew the Taliban would have no knowledge of these steps."

Harris replied, "Have you ever used this stairway?"

Housyar laughed, and still grinning, said, "Harris...you...you are a funny man. No, I have not traveled these steps." Pausing for a few seconds, he then continued, "It has been sixty years, maybe more since anyone has tried to travel these steps. You see my friend, these steps are very old. Some say they were built five hundred years ago, by the Mughals, or maybe the Safavids. Yes, I think they did a good job, but that was a very long time ago. Now these steps are too old, too dangerous."

It took a moment for Harris to fully comprehend what Housyar had said.

They were descending steps that might have been built 500 years ago, and had not been used in 60 years, because they were too dangerous? Confused, Harris studied the old man for a few seconds and then said, "Housyar, these steps were your idea, why the hell did you suggest them...and, if they're so damn dangerous, why did you come with us?"

Housyar turned his head toward Harris, and Harris could see the man was still grinning. Then Housyar said, "You are American, you are CIA. You have machines that can see in the dark, you have satellites that can take pictures of me taking a shit, you have airplanes that do not need pilots. For sure, a few missing steps cannot be a problem?"

This took Harris aback. Along with confusion, he soon felt his anger building, and was about to stop their descent and...deal with Housyar, but before he could do so, Housyar spoke, "I think, maybe you have some doubts. You think Americans can do many things but you cannot fly down mountains.

Well, my friend, everything I have said is true, but I admit that I have not said everything. You see, I remember last year, I remember Wakhan Mountain and the year before that, Shandur Ridge. I remember how you and your team climbed these and how you went where even a mountain goat cannot go. This mountain is not so bad. I have seen that you still have some climbing equipment. I think these steps will not be a big problem."

Although Harris wouldn't have minded ringing Housyar's neck, just a little, he had to admit there was something about the old man that he liked.

It didn't take long before it became clear why the steps had not been used. As they rounded a corner, immediately in front of them was a gap of 10 or 12 meters where the steps had completely fallen away. Beyond the gap, were at least another 8 to 10 of the steps that did not look passable.

It was now time to demonstrate their rock-climbing skills. Blade was their designated climber, and it took him only a few seconds to retrieve a rope and some climbing gear. He then carefully examined the rock face, quickly located some strategically placed finger and toe holds, and began climbing. Blade was born to be a rock climber, and quickly made his way up and then across the gap. Almost immediately, he found a crack in the granite, sturdy enough to support a 0.75 inch tricam. A tricam was a cam-shaped device that could be wedged into a crack. A sling was attached to the tricam, which, in turn, allowed for a rope to be attached to it. Soon four tricams were in place and a rope led from one to the other. When Blade had finished setting up the rope, the men executed a Tyrolean traverse, a technique where the climbers secure themselves and their packs to the rope and then, suspended beneath the rope, pull themselves and their packs along until they reach the far side.

Harris could not help noticing Housyar's "I told you so" grin as he detached himself from the rope. Within 20 minutes, all five of the men and their gear were past the section of missing and damaged steps, and were again descending the ancient stairway.

As it turned out, their rock-climbing skills would come in handy several more times before the men reached the bottom. There was no question that the stairway had presented some serious challenges, yet, to a man, they had actually enjoyed it. This was the kind of stuff they had been trained to do, and it had boosted their confidence.

Setting out cross country, the men traveled south, using wooded ravines, stream beds, and brush-covered hillsides to conceal their presence. An hour later, Harris crested a hill and there, below him, he saw the hollow, with its thicket of small trees and brush. Barely visible was the dilapidated mud-brick structure that they would patch up and use as their Tactical Operations Center, or TOC. On the far side of the hollow was a rugged, boulder-strewn rise, from which a person could see the road that led to Sewakla and, in the distance, the village of Sewakla itself.

Before Afig had been captured, he had had enough foresight to swallow a small tracking beacon that the CIA, the NSA, and a half dozen other intelligence organizations had used to track him to the now supposedly abandoned Sewakla District Hospital, a war-ravaged structure just outside the village of Sewakla. Dr. Dicos was believed to be with Afig, and there was little doubt that Dr. Dicos was the CIA's priority target. To the higher-ups, rescuing Afig was secondary, but that wasn't exactly how Harris looked at things.

A slew of analysts had collaborated to select this hollow and, as far as Harris was concerned, they had done a particularly good job. The place was well hidden, anyone approaching could easily be spotted, it could be defended by a small group of men, and, just in case, it had multiple routes by which they could escape.

Harris immediately dispatched a two-man team to the crest of the rise, on the far side. From there, the men would have a 360° view of the countryside.

By mid-afternoon, Harris had the TOC partially operational. Chuck Hayes, the man they called Nebraska, was their radio operator, and was updating Langley on Connor's death and their current situation. Harris was down loading their latest intelligence, and the men not standing guard were working on cleaning up the mud-brick structure.

CHAPTER TWO

Preparations

In the high, icy peaks of the Hindu Kush Mountains, the winds once again gained strength and when their force could no longer be contained, they descended down the mountain into the Sewakla Valley, and slammed into the hollow just after sunset. The hollow offered little protection and the men quickly retreated to the mud-brick structure where, huddled together, they waited out the fury that swirled around them. All of that night, the wind howled through the branches, and the limbs moaned as they yielded to its force. The men could feel the wind pushing against the structure, and more than once feared it might collapse.

It had been a cold and miserable night. Having lost nearly half of their gear, keeping warm had proved to be impossible. It had become clear that if they were going to hang around much longer, they needed to upgrade their living quarters.

The mud-brick structure was square-shaped, measuring about three meters on a side. It had a dirt floor that was frozen so hard that it might as well have been concrete. The walls were just over two meters high and over half a meter thick. They had cracks in them and they had begun to crumble. Still, the walls had managed to stay upright and looked as if they would do so for at least a little while longer. Whatever roof the place once had was long gone, and judging from the smell and the amount of dung they had removed, the place must have been used as an animal shed.

As morning approached, the wind began to abate, and by the time the sky had lightened to a lead gray and then to a pale blue, the air was still. Sunrise found the men wrapped in blankets. Two men stood guard on the south rise, while the rest huddled near a small fire. Nebraska had brewed a pot of kahwah, an aromatic green tea that is a popular breakfast beverage. Unfortunately, there was no sugar. Their sugar supply had been in one of the packs that had been lost.

Like the others, Harris had pulled a blanket tightly around himself. He was sitting on the trunk of a fallen tree, hunched over a cup of hot tea, which he gripped with both hands. Inhaling the hot steam, he relished the aroma and warmth while hardly noticing Housyar, who had sat down next to him. Housyar was also wrapped in his blanket, and he was chewing, with some difficulty, a piece of dry goat meat. His right hand clasped his blanket in place, and in his left hand, he carried his Kalashnikov. For all of these men, the Kalashnikov had become part of them, something that was always within reach. Harris had already eaten a similar breakfast, and even with the hot tea, he was still cold, his neck and right shoulder were stiff, and he was tired. Looking over at the old man, he wondered how he did it. This was a hard life, even for a young man, but Housyar, who was almost twice Harris' age, had always managed to hold his own, and then some. There was little doubt that this man was driven, which made Harris recall reading Housyar's CIA dossier. It had stated that, "Housyar is intelligent, in good health, and he is considered to be trustworthy and highly motivated." It had also stated that, "Prior to 2010, Housyar was a respected Malik (headman) of a village in the southeastern province of Zabul. In January, 2010, the Taliban occupied his village and beheaded his entire family as he was forced to watch." The dossier did not describe what had precipitated the beheadings, but only that Housyar had been recruited by the CIA shortly thereafter, and that he had been working with them ever since.

The two men sat there for a few minutes, neither of them speaking, then Housyar looked over at Harris and said, "Harris, it is a good morning, yes?" Hearing Housyar say these words could not help but make him smile. Housyar had said these exact words every morning for as long as he had known the man. Looking up at the blue, early morning sky, Harris replied, "Yes, yes Housyar, I think it's a fine morning."

Housyar's expression became curious as he said, "Maybe you will answer me a question? I do not understand why a smart man like you, a man with a university diploma, comes to this place...to Afghanistan?"

Although it was phrased a bit differently, this wasn't the first time Harris had been asked this question, and, because the answer was complicated, he usually came up with a smartass reply. But Housyar was...well he was Housyar, and it seemed that he deserved an honest answer.

After a few seconds, Harris looked down at his tea and said, "I have chosen to live the life of a soldier and this is where my country has sent me. But that is not the whole story. You see Housyar, fanatics scare the hell out of me, and religious fanatics scare me doubly so. In Iraq, and now here in Afghanistan, I have seen how fanatics...Islamic fanatics have twisted the minds of so many ordinary people. They convince their followers that they are in a struggle, a jihad. But if the truth be told, this is a struggle against reason and conscience.

I think this is why Islamists fear education. They are afraid that knowledge will expose them as hateful, intolerant, zealots that feed on oppression and violence.

To me, these fanatics are like a poison...like a poison that is spreading." Harris paused for a second and then said, "Housyar, I am here because I need to do what I can to stop this poison."

Housyar had carefully listened to Harris' words, and when Harris had finished, Housyar remained silent for a moment and then he said, "I had three children, three boys. If they had lived, my first boy would now be a grown man...old like you, Harris." Housyar paused, and then continued, "Maybe it would be good if I tell you a story, my friend. You see, when the Taliban came to my village, I believed that I could talk to them. I thought I was a smart man, I had done many things in my life, and as you Americans say, I was a...'bigshot' in my village. I was sure that they would listen to me.

First, we would have a feast, and then we would give them gifts. Only then would I talk to them. I would be respectful, and I would choose my words carefully. For sure they would listen to reason. You see, many of these Taliban came from a nearby village. They were my neighbors. I had known some of them all of my life....

Harris, these men came with their weapons, they took our food, they took the gifts, they forced our young men to go with them, but they did not want to talk." Housyar paused, and Harris saw an unfamiliar hardness and anger in the old man's face, and then he said, "Yes Harris, you are right, these are fanatics and they are like a poison.

People had told me about the Taliban, they had told me about Hezb e Islami Gulbuddin, and they had told me about al-Qaeda, but I would not listen. I said it would be different, ours was a peaceful and prosperous village. We would not make trouble for the Taliban and they would leave us alone...." Housyar shook his head in disgust and then said, "This is how a stupid and foolish man thinks. This is how the poison spreads." Housyar became silent as he stared at the distant Hindu Kush Mountains. After a moment the old man rose, turned, and slowly walked away.

Harris watched the old man leave and said nothing.

Harris spent some time going over the latest radio transmissions and then met with Housyar; this time it was business. They needed to go over the latest images and discuss their plans for that day. The two of them would make their way to Sewakla. Housyar would play the role of an elderly uncle, while Harris would be the slightly dim-witted nephew. These roles had worked in the past and gave Harris a little leeway when he made cultural or language errors. On their way to Sewakla, they would pass the Sewakla District Hospital and get a feel for the layout and security. When they got to Sewakla, they would check out the town, determine how many "bad guys" they would have to deal with, and where they hung out. If the situation permitted, they would purchase some supplies and head back, being sure to again pass the Sewakla District Hospital.

Meanwhile, Urbanski would head out toward the farmland west of Sewakla District Hospital. He would reconnoiter the area and try to identify potential "overwatch" positions and places where they could pre-position the strike force.

Blade and Nebraska would hang around the TOC. Blade would man a lookout position, on the crest of the rise, while Nebraska would co-ordinate a resupply air drop, monitor the radio and continue working on their roof.

After hiking about a hundred kilometers up the south rise, Harris stopped and turned back for a look down at the hollow. He could see nothing to indicate it was now occupied. The fire was out, what was left of their gear had been concealed, and the radio had been set up inside the mud-brick structure. Satisfied, he joined up with Housyar and they continued south toward Sewakla. Both men looked tired and a little frayed around the edges. They had left their tactical vests behind but still carried their Kalashnikovs, since it would be unusual for two men to be traveling, unarmed, in these remote areas. The two men smelled of campfire smoke, sweat, and more than a little like animal dung. Except for the animal dung, they looked and smelled pretty much like any of the other traveling merchants.

As they crested the rise, the Sewakla Valley stretched out before them. It had a broad, southern exposure and, although it was at a relatively high elevation, the valley was mostly free of snow. The grade, down to the dirt road, was rugged and fairly steep, forcing the two men to carefully navigate between boulders and thickets of brush. It took them over half an hour to reach the road, and from there on, they would have to act, think, and react like Afghans. Harris' Pashto was good but tended to be too formal for the rural countryside. This combined with his six-foot-two-inch height made blending-in a bit of a challenge, but not impossible. Mullah Mohammed

Omar, the founder and spiritual leader of the Taliban, was rumored to be six feet, six inches tall, and, of course, Osama bin Laden was six feet four inches tall. Harris had taught himself to walk slightly stooped over and to round his shoulders. When spoken to, he feigned being shy, shifting nervously and avoiding eye contact. He would also be just a bit slow in responding and seem not to quite understand what was going on. These characteristics tended to make others discount him and avoid directly addressing him. And then there was his "blanket trick." Like most rural Afghans, Harris carried a blanket, but his had the distinct smell of goat shit. The odor was not overwhelming but strong enough for people to notice. It might take a couple of seconds, but people would soon step back from him and nobody was anxious to pat him down.

Housyar, on the other hand, just played Housyar, except, of course, he did not let on that he was a CIA asset, but, instead he would tell them he was a traveling merchant who was going around the countryside marketing his dried fruits and spices. Being old and not wanting to travel alone, he brought along his...nephew.

Housyar and Harris had worked together for two years and had finally tuned their ability to play off of each other's character. To Harris, it seemed that Housyar actually enjoy his role, and seemed to take a peculiar pleasure in treating Harris as if he were a simpleton. When they returned to the TOC, Harris was sure everyone would gather around, and Housyar would tell stories about their day that would have them all laughing until they were in tears – including Harris.

The terrain was nearly level but it wasn't long before they ran into their first obstacle. They had gone barely a kilometer when they came across a makeshift roadblock. Four armed men were standing in the middle of the road, their rifles at the ready. As Harris got closer, he saw that they were Hezb e Islami Gulbuddin insurgents. The Hezb e Islami Gulbuddin were the second largest insurgent group in Afghanistan, and were made up of Sunni Islamic fundamentalists who reportedly had helped Osama Bin Laden escape from Tora Bora, attacked the Coalition Forces, and carried out a number of deadly bombings in retaliation for Westerners showing films of Islam. These fruitcakes had sworn to keep fighting until all of Afghanistan was governed by Sharia Law.

Harris knew that if he and Housyar were thought to be Taliban, they would either be shot, or allowed to pass – it depended on the day. But they didn't exactly look like Taliban. Housyar was too old and Harris was just a little...too slow. If they could pass as ordinary merchants, they would probably be shaken down and then let go.

Fortunately, being Taliban or not being Taliban didn't much matter, on that day. These guys wanted money and after Housyar slipped them a couple of 100 Afghani notes, the insurgents casually waved them past.

As the two men approached the Sewakla District Hospital, they saw that the structure stood about a hundred meters up a winding, deeply rutted dirt access road. At first glance, the building seemed deserted. It had been constructed of concrete block that was now bullet-pocked and scorched by fire. Harris had studied the aerial images and knew the structure surrounded a rectangular courtyard, and that there were several out-buildings, a few of which appeared to be occupied.

The Sewakla District Hospital had been constructed by some altruistic Government Agency, with U.S. taxpayers' dollars. No doubt an attempt to win the proverbial "hearts and minds" of the local inhabitants. These people did need a hospital, but they were also quite aware that it had been built by the "invaders," the foreign "infidels," and they intensely resented it. Rural Afghanistan leaned strongly toward Islamic fundamentalism and had fierce tribal loyalties that dated back centuries. They didn't like outsiders and weren't about to change anytime soon. In the end, the Sewakla village elders came to see the Sewakla District Hospital as nothing more than a way to extract money from the Americans. It had been open less than a year before it became the battleground in a fight for land rights between Taliban-armed Kuchi Militias and the previous occupants of the area, ethnic Hazaras. The staff fled or were killed, equipment was looted, and the structures severely damaged. When the dust settled, the Infidels' hospital was in ruins and had to be abandoned. Well, at least some folks thought it had been abandoned. For the last three days, an MQ-9 Reaper drone had circled the place, capturing both photographic and IR images. That morning, one delivery vehicle and a "'technical" had entered and left the compound. A "technical" is the term used to describe a Toyota 4-wheel drive pickup with a heavy machinegun mounted atop a pedestal that was bolted to the truck's bed. The photographic images had shown four women, dressed in blue burqas, entering the hospital building, while the IR images had revealed at least 30 individual heat signatures. Three of these signatures were too hot and thought to be generators or stoves, while the remaining were human beings, presumably armed men. This meant there were a lot of people in hiding, and Harris couldn't see any of them.

Looking to the right of the access road, Harris saw the cluster of out-buildings he had seen in the aerial photographs. The buildings could best be described as the remains of several storage buildings, a machinery shed, and a dozen or more squat, flat-roofed, mud-brick structures that once housed the hospital workers and their families. Although his view was obscured, he could see that all of these structures bore the scars of a battle, and several were now little more than mounds of rubble. Still, three of the housing units were intact and looked occupied. Then Harris noticed sets of tire tracks, leading directly to what once had been the machinery shed. Two walls of the structure had collapsed, but there was still a section of the building standing. Protruding from an opening, in one of the walls, were the front grills of two technicals.

As Harris stored to memory what he was seeing, he caught movement in the corner of his eye. Turning in that direction, he saw two, rough-looking, armed men emerge from the brush. Harris immediately knew that he had screwed up; he had stood there too long. As the two men got closer, they raised their Kalashnikovs and pointed them at Harris and Housyar. Harris rarely was taken by surprise but there had been something about the place that had drawn his attention. It wasn't exactly the buildings, or at least what he could see of them. No, it was what he was not seeing. He felt that he was standing in front of an active bee hive but he couldn't see the bees. But there was even more than that. This place had a bad feeling about it. This was not the usual hideout of some high-level Islamic fanatic...there was something else going on here.

As the two men got closer, they spread out and kept the muzzles of their Kalashnikovs pointed directly at Harris and Housyar. Stopping several meters back, the two men studied them for a moment, then the taller man growled, "Put your hands on top of your heads." Housyar complied but Harris feigned confusion. Looking over at Harris, Housyar said, "Muhammad, did you not hear the man, do as he says." When working undercover, Harris frequently used the name Muhammad Kehsud. Muhammad is the name of the Islamic prophet and is believed to be the most popular given name in the world. To Muslims, the name Muhammad evoked a positive response and with it, just a little leeway.

Harris awkwardly raised his arms, seemingly trying to imitate Housyar. When both men had their hands on top of their heads, the taller man barked, "Now what do you "sons of donkeys" find so interesting in those buildings?" As the taller man spoke, the second man, who was considerably shorter, and whose most notable feature was his rather substantial beaked nose, focused on Harris...then took a step forward, shouldered his rifle, and pointed it at Harris' head. There was a cruel depravity in the man's eyes. It was as if he fed off of fear and mayhem. For a second, Harris thought it was over, as there was nothing he could do to stop this man from shooting him. Housyar had also noticed the man and subtly shifted sideways, placing himself within the man's peripheral vision. This got his attention and when he looked over at Housyar, his eyes were met by those of a man who seemed to have the ability to see right through him. The old man knew who he was, and, for just a fraction of a second, the small man felt...ashamed and vulnerable. Disoriented, he absently lowered his rifle.

The entire...confrontation had lasted no more than three seconds, during which Harris' mind had scrambled for options, none of them good. Drawing in a deep breath and then slowly releasing it, he didn't know what Housyar had done, but he was positive that the old man had just saved his life. Still, they weren't "out of the woods." Acting as if he didn't understand what was happening, Harris nervously shifted from foot to foot, then he turned to Housyar and said, "Uncle, I am thirsty...You said we would find water here." Housyar looked over at Harris and replied, "Muhammad, you must be quiet now, it is necessary that I speak to these men." Then, turning to the tall man, he asked, "Are you bandits...thieves, is that why you are pointing your guns at us? If so, you will be disappointed. We..." The tall man snapped back, "It is none of your business who we are. I have asked you a question and I give you one last chance to answer." Housyar's face took on the expression of an old man who wishes only to live out his life in peace, a man who is willing to cooperate to put this all behind him. Clearing his throat, he said, "We are merchants from Jalrez. My name...it is Housyar Kehsud, and he," pointing at Harris, "is Muhammad, my nephew. For some time now, we have heard that the people of Sewakla are prospering and thought that, perhaps, they have acquired a taste for delicacies such as our most excellent dried fruits and spices.

Yet, it seems that Allah, in his wisdom, has chosen to make our journey more...complicated. He has decided that our truck should not complete this journey. The miserable contraption has again broken and now stands alongside the road, good only for casting a shadow. Namir, my cousin, he is a mechanic and he has traveled, from Jalrez, to try and fix the thing. If Allah sees fit, Namir will be successful and we will once again have a truck.

You see, Muhammad and I know nothing about machinery and thought it would do us no good just to stand there. The distance to Sewakla was not far, so we decided to walk. Allah willing, we would soon have a cup of hot tea, we would speak with some of the merchants, and maybe we would arrange to rent a stall at the local marketplace.

Alas, I am an old man and I sometimes forget things. Today, I have forgotten to bring a flask of water." Glancing over at Harris, he continued, "Muhammad...he does not travel well and he gets thirsty quickly. I have promised to find him some water and when I saw those buildings, I thought that it was a hospital, and I thought, for sure a hospital would have water, good water." Turning, Housyar pointed to a weathered, bullet-riddled sign, and then continued, "You see, there is a sign over there. It is damaged, but it points to those buildings and it says HOSPITAL." The tall man looked past Housyar, at the sign. It wasn't clear whether he could read but both Housyar and Harris could see that he was buying the story. Trying to push things along, Harris said, "Uncle, Do these men have water? Would they let us have some of their water?" Housyar looked sternly at him and said, "Not now, Muhammad, be quiet...please." Looking a little tired and worried, Housyar faced the taller man and said, "As I have already said, Muhammad does not travel well...I think that I must find him some water, very soon."

The shorter man had regained his temerity and had impatiently listened. Stepping forward, he said, "I do not believe the old man, I do not like these two. The big one, he stinks like goat shit and I do not like the way he is always looking around. We should just shoot them both." The taller man yelled, "Shut-up Afsoon, you do not like anybody. You would shoot your own mother if you were given the chance." Then he turned to Housyar and said, "Listen to me...Housyar, I give you a warning, and I give it to you only once. This is a...very dangerous place. If you come this way again, you are not to look at these buildings, just go on past. Do you understand me, old man?" Housyar considered the man's words, and then he said, "We will do as you say." Harris' expression became worried, and he said, "Uncle, you have not asked him for water? Why..." As Harris spoke, the tall man reached into his jacket, retrieved a half-full, clear plastic bottle of water, and handed it to Housyar, saying, "Here, give him some water...He can have what is left. I have plenty." Harris reached over and grabbed the bottle from Housyar, and greedily guzzled down all of the contents. Housyar gave him a disapproving look and just shook his head. The enthusiasm with which Harris had devoured the water made the taller man actually smile, then he said, "Tell him that you will find more water and even some very good hot tea, in Sewakla, it is only a ten- or maybe a fifteen-minute walk up this road."

Afsoon, still simmering from the taller man's earlier rebuke, made his way to Harris and, without saying a word, raised his rifle and then drove the butt of it into Harris' stomach. He was not particularly fast, so Harris had a fraction of a second to prepare himself for the impact. Still, the blow managed to knock him to the ground, and a second later, Harris threw up the contents of his stomach, including the water he had just drunk. Seeing what Afsoon had done, the taller man raised his rifle and yelled, "Back away, Afsoon, or I will put a bullet in your miserable head." At first it seemed that Afsoon was going to ignore the taller man, and hit Harris a second time, but then he laughed, turned and walked away. As he did, the taller man watched him and said, "What in the name of Allah is wrong with you? Must you always hurt people? One of these days, Afsoon, someone is going to take that rifle of yours and stick it up your ass and pull the trigger."

Only partially faking the pain, Harris stood, gripped his stomach, and moaned quietly. Both Harris and Housyar knew that the confrontation, although painful for Harris, had turned out to be valuable. The taller guard, who later introduced himself as Kaihan, was a decent guy and had actually apologized for what Afsoon had done. Housyar and Kaihan were not exactly "best friends forever," but they were now...acquainted and Kaihan would find it difficult to be indifferent toward them. On the other hand, Afsoon was essentially a sociopathic asshole. In his work, Harris had come across many Afsoons and he knew the type well. Afsoon had a gaping hole where a conscience should have been. Harris believed that Afsoon was the kind of man who could be bought but never trusted.

After being told to leave, Harris and Housyar continued on their way to Sewakla. When they arrived in the squalid but bustling little village, they began their reconnaissance, covertly studying each street and each alleyway as they passed. In the marketplace, they purchased some supplies and then spent some time speaking with some of the merchants. Housyar quickly bonded with the older men and soon found out a great deal about the village. It was early afternoon when Harris and Housyar again passed by the Sewakla District Hospital. This time they both made a concerted effort to not look at the building. Kaihan and Afsoon could be seen leaning against a large sandstone boulder. Kaihan saw them first and watched them approach. A second or two later, Afsoon saw them and stood up as if preparing to intercept them, but Kaihan reached out and grabbed Afsoon's collar and pulled him back. They exchanged a few words, which Harris couldn't hear, and then Afsoon, obviously pissed, returned to his place against the boulder.

As they approached, Housyar made eye contact with Kaihan and when Afsoon wasn't looking, nodded just slightly. Kaihan nodded back.

When the two men had returned to the TOC, Harris contacted Langley and reported what they had seen and what they had encountered. He then requested that Langley contact their assets in Jalrez, a medium-sized city about 40 kilometers east of Sewakla. They were to acquire a small warehouse. All documents were to show the proprietor was Housyar Kehsud and the company name would be Jalrez Dried Fruits and Spices. Also, they would acquire a sturdy but not too pretty, used Hyundai truck and several crates of the best dried fruits and spices they could get their hands on. The truck's documentation would show Housyar Kehsud as owner for the last three years and two months. The truck, with the dried goods in the rear, was to be dropped off at a site two kilometers from the TOC. After some discussion, it was decided that acquiring the truck and the dried fruit and spices would take forty-eight hours.

That night the wind again came roaring down the mountain. On schedule, it struck the hollow just after sunset, making a resupply airdrop an impossibility. Nebraska had managed to put together a rough approximation of a roof, which would have worked just fine anywhere else in Afghanistan, but not in this particular hollow. It held together for several hours, but then, at about 0200 hours, the thing came apart, and pieces of the roof went tumbling end over end, into the night sky. It got a lot colder after that, but the extra blankets Housyar and Harris had picked up in the Sewakla helped. No one blamed Nebraska for the failure of the roof, since all he had to work with was some rope, a knife, and some dead branches. Still, he did take some teasing about a lawsuit and suspending his contractor's license.

It was becoming clear that these frickin' winds were going to be a regular thing, so Harris had to rethink their resupply strategy. At 0330 hours, he was on the radio to Langley. This time he ordered a slew of building supplies, tools, blankets, clothing, rations, medical supplies, pots and pans, a wash tub, and even a cook stove. All of which was to be added to the bed of the truck.

The road from Zarpan was mostly dirt and deeply rutted, but what made the journey even worse was that the truck, a white, 2008 Hyundai Shehzore enclosed flatbed, traveled at night and did not use its headlights. The truck and the trailing vehicle had left Jalrez at 2300 hours, got stuck twice, and arrived at its destination at 0415 hours the next day.

Wearing IR night vision goggles, Blade watched the two vehicles approach and then pull over. The driver of the Hyundai got out, walked toward the rear of the truck, and placed a magnetic key box inside the rear wheel well. He then walked over to the trailing vehicle and got in. The trailing vehicle executed a U-turn and sped away into the darkness. Blade waited. When he had first spotted the approaching vehicles, he had also spotted two additional heat sources about a click behind the trailing vehicle. These blips were too far away to identify, and at the time he had thought they may have been cattle or some kind of large, wild animals. But now, as he focused on the two blips, he saw they were getting closer and a moment later realized they were motorcycles. A few minutes later, two Honda XL 125 motorcycles came to a stop a few meters behind the truck. The riders dismounted, unslung their Kalashnikovs, and cautiously approached, one from each side of the truck. These men were bandits, men who swore their allegiance to a warlord named Hamid Moorakzai. They had probably been following the two-vehicle caravan for some time, and now that the trailing vehicle was gone, they decided to make their move. Moorakzai and his men were first-class thugs. They would rob and kill with impunity, and ran a sideline business of abducting young women and selling them. Although Moorakzai had technicals, Toyota Land Cruisers, and other vehicles, he had become known for his use of motorcycles, or more specifically Honda XL 125s. They were cheap, they were agile, and they were fast.

The guy on the left side of the truck was about to open the driver's door when suddenly his head exploded. It was too dark for the other man to see what had happened, but he sensed something had gone very wrong, and started backing away toward his motorcycle, when he too went down, a bullet punching a hole clear through his chest. Blade chambered a third round and waited. His sniper rifle had been "dead-on," the suppressor had worked as advertised, and there had been no flash to give away his position. After another 15 minutes of scanning the darkness, Blade was reasonably sure the two men were dead and no one else was coming.

It was just after 0530 hours when Blade pulled the Hyundai truck up to the base of a rise that bordered the west side of the hollow. From there, the men would have to carry the supplies to the TOC.

CHAPTER THREE

Infiltration

The truck lurched forward, thrusting Harris back against his seat, then it abruptly braked, flinging him forward and forcing him to brace himself against the dashboard. Housyar had a white-knuckled grip of the wheel and the expression of a man straddling a Brahma bull at a Texas rodeo. The vehicle precariously leaned to the left as the old man jerked the steering wheel right to avoid another massive pothole, this one deep enough to swallow the front end of the truck. It could be said that Housyar knew where the gas pedal was and where the brake was, steering was still a little iffy, while the other, more refined aspects of driving completely eluded the man. There was one more thing Harris had learned about driving with Housyar. Do not speak. Anything and everything distracted the old man. Sudden movement or just a simple comment would cause him to turn toward you and seemingly forget that he was driving.

Harris had seen Housyar face down a dozen armed Taliban insurgents with laser-like concentration. Once, the old man woke up in the middle of the night, casually picked up a venomous, half-meter-long Saw Scaled Viper that had slithered up next to him, and simply tossed it aside. Yet, he was a completely inept driver who could get rattled by nothing more than a bug hitting the windshield. Thus far, the old man had totaled a half dozen vehicles and crumpled fenders of a dozen more. He somehow found the whole thing exciting and was convinced that the..."accidents" were trivial.

As the Hyundai truck finally approached the Sewakla District Hospital, Harris, who now had his feet wedged against the dash and was gripping a nearby grab handle, spotted the turnout. Momentarily releasing the grab handle, he pointed toward it while being careful to do so slowly. Housyar grunted something unintelligible, veered around another pothole, and then jerked the steering wheel hard to the right. As the truck shot into the turnout, he slammed on the brakes, bringing it to a skidding stop. Harris yanked open the passenger door and sprang from the truck as if it were demonically possessed. Housyar followed but his exit more resembled that of a man who had miraculously subdued some wild beast. It was "show time" and they had intentionally left their Kalashnikovs behind. Housyar stood there stretching, with his back arched and his hands pressing against the small of his back. He twisted his body to one side and then the other, in an apparent effort to try and relieve the stiffness associated with a long drive. Harris played with his hands and shuffled awkwardly from one foot to another. A few seconds later, both of the men were making their way toward the Sewakla District Hospital access road. Housyar appeared thoughtful and relatively relaxed, while Harris looked as if he were unsure of himself and stayed close to, but behind Housyar. Both men were sure to keep their hands visible and appear as nonthreatening as possible. Ahead of them, two men stepped from the side of the road. As they approached, Harris saw that it was Kaihan and Afsoon, and they had their weapons at the ready.

Harris and Housyar had spent many hours preparing for this particular encounter. Several times Harris had almost nixed the whole thing because it was becoming just too damn risky. Still, Housyar was confident they could pull it off and, if the plan worked, the payoff would give them access to the hospital. In the end, Harris had given in and from there on, the two men had tirelessly worked out every detail. They had selected the best place to pull the truck over. They had practiced their posture, their gait, and even their expressions. But mostly, they went over and over the story until it seemed more real than their actual lives. Introducing the truck was necessary but it introduced its own set of problems. The moment he saw the truck pull over, Kaihan would immediately be on alert. His first thought would be "bomb." Harris and Housyar had to get them to calm down, and relax a bit. The truck was too threatening, so initial contact would have to be made at what would be considered a safe distance.

After walking about 20 paces, Harris and Housyar both stopped and waited. Sentries generally found it less threatening to approach men who are standing still than men who are walking toward them. When Kaihan saw them stop, he turned to Afsoon and told him something. Harris guessed that he told Afsoon to stay put since the man was too difficult to control when he was around Muhammad. Whatever the instructions were, Afsoon was not happy but he did stop. Kaihan continued walking toward Housyar and Harris, leaving Afsoon behind, visibly fuming. Housyar put his arms out, palms up, in a welcoming gesture. Harris, who was about a step behind Housyar, stared at the ground, his hands by his mouth, chewing nervously on his thumb nail. Kaihan stopped about three paces away and said, "Why have you come back, Housyar?...I did not think your last visit was something you wished to repeat." The old man smiled and replied, "As a Pashtun and as a Muslim, I have learned that we must value the life we have been given. I have also learned that, as human beings, we are all constantly in need of forgiveness. So I have come here, on this beautiful morning, to give you a gift. Please, Kaihan, will you come with me." Housyar turned, and began walking back toward the truck. Harris scrambled to catch up with Housyar, an expression of expectation and excitement on his face. As they approached the rear of the truck, Harris, speaking loudly enough for Kaihan to hear, said, "Uncle, are you going to give Kaihan his present now?" Housyar looked over at him and replied, "Yes Muhammad, we shall give our new friend his present." Not quite sure how he should handle this situation, Kaihan remained several steps behind, cautiously watching the two men. When they reached the rear of the truck, Kaihan stood even farther back and stepped to the side. Neither Harris nor Housyar was surprised by the man's wariness. Actually, they had worried that on seeing the truck, Kaihan might get all formal and require that they kneel on the ground with their hands behind their heads, while Afsoon called for assistance. It had all depended on how much trust Housyar had been able to establish. Smiling warmly, Housyar reached for the latch, while Harris stood nearby, brimming with anticipation. As the door began to open, Kaihan's eyes narrowed and he raised the muzzle of his Kalashnikov, pointing it directly at Housyar's chest. A moment later, the door swung completely open, releasing the sweet aroma of apples and peaches, as well as hints of mint, cinnamon, and vanilla. Inside were several stacks of shallow, cardboard boxes containing a wide assortment of dried fruits, many of which Kaihan did not recognize. Leaning against the right side wall of the truck bed were a dozen, tightly woven jute bags that Kaihan recognized as spice bags.

Reaching in, Housyar slid one of the nearest containers toward him, It had been prepared specifically for Kaihan and contained a selection of beautifully arranged dried apples, kiwi, pears, cherries, and prunes, plus five, fist-size wooden boxes containing mint, saffron, cinnamon, vanilla, and green and black cardamom. Many of the items were so rare that they could only be found in one of Kabul's most exclusive marketplaces. Seeing nothing that would suggest a threat, Kaihan lowered his Kalashnikov and approached. Housyar studied the man for a moment and then said, "Three days ago, when you stopped us, I know that you could have had us shot...no one would have questioned you. But you did not shoot us, and for that, Muhammad and I are grateful. So Kaihan, please, we ask you to take this. They are the best that I have to offer, and, when you taste them, you will understand what it is like to have tasted perfection. Maybe then, you will be kind enough to tell your friends about Housyar Kehsud and his most excellent dried fruits and spices."

Kaihan had not spoken since he had first addressed Housyar, but from the expression on his face it was clear that he was uncomfortable with the situation. After giving the array of delicacies one last look, Kaihan straightened up, looked directly at Housyar and said, "Old man, you are wasting my time. I do not accept "baksheesh" (a tip or a bribe). To do so would violate an oath I have taken. So keep your...gift and get this truck out of here."

Appearing confused, Housyar was silent for a moment and then, nodding his head, said, "Baksheesh, you think this is baksheesh. Kaihan, I am afraid that I did not make myself clear. I ask you, if this is baksheesh, what favor have I asked from you? What is it that I want you to do for me? Well, it is true that I have asked you to speak of me to your friends, if the fruits and spices please you, but that is only if you find them to your satisfaction. No, no, this is not baksheesh. My friend, I ask you to take a moment and try to see through my eyes.

Muhammad and I were strangers to you..." Kaihan interrupted, saying, "I do not have time for more of your talk. Do as I have told you or..." This time Housyar interrupted. Speaking in a patient, fatherly voice, he said, "My friend, it is early and there are no other travelers on this road, so I believe you can spare me a moment...I promise I will try to be brief." Kaihan scowled, but did not reply. Housyar continued, "You have an important job, you are a guard, and it is your duty to protect that place. You thought that we had acted suspiciously, and I now see that we may have looked suspicious. Yet, when I explained to you why we were here, you...you believed me. But that was not all that you did. Kaihan, you protected my nephew Muhammad and it is likely that you saved his life. I have now, many times, seen how my nephew can bring out the bad in some people, and how he can bring out the good in others. It was a good thing you did for Muhammad and, I am sure, Allah was watching and he will reward you. And then, when you saw that Muhammad was thirsty, you gave him your water.

I now ask you, Kaihan, is it not true that you and I are both Pashtuns, and as Pashtuns we are obligated to live by Pashtunwali traditions (an ancient, unwritten code that guides both individual and communal conduct). Well, to me, it seems that you have done two strangers a great kindness, and now Muhammad and I are indebted to you. As Pashtunwali tradition prescribes, we are obligated to repay this debt. I am not a rich man, I do not have gold or jewels, but I do have these." Gesturing to the stacks of cardboard boxes of dried fruit and the bags of spices, he then continued, "To me, these are more precious than gold or jewels. They please the eye, delight the nose, nourish the body, and the flavors will gratify the palate in ways that words cannot describe." Housyar became silent for a moment and then looked at Kaihan with the tired eyes of an old man, and said, "Kaihan, I do not know what else I can say. So I ask you one last time, please accept these, not as baksheesh, but as repayment for the kindness you have shown us."

Kaihan had no education, he had always been poor, but he did try to be a decent man, a man of honor and, to a Pashtun, honor was synonymous with adherence to Pashtunwali tradition. He was aware that kindness was to be extended without any expectation of repayment. Yet, he also knew that when one person was indebted to another, he was, in many ways, a slave to that person. To the proud and fiercely independent Pashtuns, this was not a desirable situation. So refusing to accept the repayment of a debt could be perceived as an insult, and under Pashtunwali tradition, an insult is a very serious offense that can have dire consequences.

Looking uneasy, Kaihan replied, "As you wish, Housyar, I will accept your gift and from here on you are not to think of yourself as indebted to me. But I tell you now, that I am finished with this gift business. There will be no more gifts." Housyar nodded and said, "Yes, I now understand your...situation. I know that I have made things...complicated for you, and for this I am sorry." For a moment Housyar seemed to withdraw into thought, then he spoke, saying, "Kaihan, I am an old fool, I may have made trouble for you. Afsoon will not be pleased to see that you have received a gift. This had not bothered me before, since the man has done nothing to deserve any consideration. But now that I know of your concerns, I am afraid I have given Afsoon something he can use against you. I fear the man has no loyalty and, sooner or later, it will occur to him to report you." Housyar paused for a moment as if thinking about what could be done about this situation. Then he said, "Maybe there is another way. What if you presented these, most excellent, dried fruits and spices to your superior, or, better yet, your Commander? Then there would be no question of baksheesh and you would gain favor in his eyes. Tell him that you bought them from an old merchant, for a very reasonable price. If they come to me, I will say that I sold them to you for just one quarter of the price they were really worth. They will see that I am an old man, and they will think that sometimes old men do foolish things. Yes, I think that this will make you a more important man." After pausing for just a moment, he continued, "It is possible that they will enjoy my dried fruits and spices so much that, maybe, they will give you a new partner." This caused Kaihan's lips to turn-up, just slightly, revealing the first sign of a smile, causing Housyar to break out into one of his broad, "hallelujah" grins, which, in turn, caused Harris to smile. A few seconds later, all three men were laughing loudly.

Later that morning, Harris and Housyar were, once again, on the road toward Sewakla, Harris' feet bracing against the dashboard and Housyar white-knuckling the steering wheel. Harris looked over at the old man and just shook his head.

Thanks to Housyar, they had put the second part of their plan into play, and both Harris and Housyar where reasonably sure that the dried fruits and spices would make their way to the local commander, and then to the top honcho who ran the place. Soon, maybe this afternoon, but no later than tomorrow, they would want to know how to get more.

The next morning, Harris and Housyar were approaching the Sewakla District Hospital, when they spotted five men blocking the road. As they got closer, they saw that Kaihan and Afsoon were among the men, but neither Harris nor Housyar initially recognized the others. Harris cringed at the thought of what was going to happen next. The truck veered left and then right, almost tipping onto two wheels. Finally it came to a skidding stop less than a meter from the closest man. Kaihan and Afsoon had the sense to move off to the side of the road, but the other three men had not budged. Harris didn't know why they hadn't gotten out of the way, but, to their credit, not one of them even flinched.

As it turned out, one of the three men was Farzad Aziz, Commander of the regional Hilal Jaysh, or Crescent Moon Militia (CMM). He also happened to be on the CIA's wanted list. The CMM were a small, secretive, and very disciplined group of Islamic insurgents who were unique in the sense that they offered "career opportunities" to women, albeit these careers were extraordinarily short. The women of the CMM wore blue or black burqas and were doubly certified as fanatics. This was a true Suicide Brigade since they specialized exclusively in suicide missions. The presence of the CMM baffled Harris since they weren't exactly "bodyguards" or "facility security" types. He was sure Kaihan and Afsoon were not CMM since Kaihan was a reasonable guy who would choose to live, if given the choice, while Afsoon was too flaky and unreliable. So what the hell was CMM doing here?

Farzad Aziz was in his mid-forties, a gaunt-looking character with a drawn face and long, full beard that had begun to show streaks of gray. What was most noticeable about Aziz, and the other two CMM insurgents, was their eyes. They were the dark, sunken, detached eyes of men who spent too much time praying, and who could no longer find joy in the world that surrounded them. These men thought only of shaheed (martyrdom), to die in combat for Islam. Of course it didn't hurt that in many of the Hadith collections it is said that the shaheed shall be rewarded with "seven blessings from Allah" and that one of the blessings is seventy-two virgins. Though the precise number of virgins is not defined in Qur'anic text, the Hadith, which many believe to be collections of traditions, teachings, deeds, and sayings of the Prophet, describes the seventy-two virgins in explicit detail.

There was little doubt that these men were believers and completely dedicated to their cause. They were true jihadist, fanatics determined to kill as many infidels, apostates, heretics, hypocrites, and blasphemers as possible.

Farzad studied the truck for a moment then stepped over to the driver's window, which Housyar rolled down to accommodate him. Farzad first carefully examined Housyar's face and then looked over at Harris. He took a long time studying Harris, focusing uncomfortably long on Harris' eyes. Then, he abruptly ordered both of them out of the truck. While at least three rifles were pointed at them, they were thoroughly searched and then forced to their knees and made to place their hands behind their heads. Both the cab and the bed of the truck were gone through. Their Kalashnikovs were confiscated and carefully examined. Harris was impressed, this was a reasonably well-orchestrated, "stop and search."

When they were satisfied that Harris and Housyar did not represent a threat, Farzad ordered the two men back into the vehicle and took Kaihan off to the side where, in a hushed voice, he gave him instructions that neither Harris nor Housyar could hear. Returning to the truck, Kaihan stepped up onto the running board, and ordered Housyar to drive to the Sewakla District Hospital access road, and then turn up the access road toward the hospital, which was the large building at the end. Hearing this, Harris winced and sank into his seat. He hoped that Kaihan could hang on, and that he might, one day, forgive Housyar for what he was about to do to him. The truck lurched forward, almost immediately dislodging Kaihan from his perch. After being forced to sprint alongside, he leaped back onto the running board, and hung on as if his life depended on it...which of course it did. By the time they had turned onto the Sewakla District Hospital access road, Kaihan was ready to call it a day, or maybe a whole week. But the man had his orders and Farzad was only 50 meters behind and closing. Kaihan rode it out, but not before nearly being knocked off of the running board two more times.

Both Harris and Housyar knew that high-quality dried fruit and spices were a much favored food of the Afghans and a core ingredient in many of the more exotic dishes and pastries that were craved by the wealthy and powerful. Dr. Dicos was certainly wealthy and powerful and, if he had assembled a staff, they too would likely be tired of onions, rice, and goat meat. Maidan Wardak Province was not the kind of place where you could run over to your local marketplace and pick up a hundred grams of Saffron. It would better be described as an austere place with strong undertones of bleak poverty and deprivation. If Dr. Dicos and his evil elves had been here long, they would be craving something a bit tastier.

As the truck wildly jerked, swerved, and bounced up the access road, Harris tried to survey the surrounding area, quickly discovering that the aerial images had not done a good job of revealing what was really there. It was immediately apparent that the place was more heavily fortified than they had thought. So far he had seen the gun slots of at least three, below-ground bunkers. Perpendicular to the road were what appeared to be a network of deep, narrow trenches, covered with brush and camouflage netting. About halfway up the road, Harris noticed a stack of supplies. The stack was covered with a tarpaulin and camouflage net, but Harris could see several, two-meter-long empty crates discarded off to one side. The crates were marked with the characters 9K338 Igla-S, which Harris recognized as the designation for Russian, shoulder-launched, surface-to-air missiles. As he was studying the crates, he caught movement in his peripheral vision. Looking in that direction, he saw the vague outline of two or three men standing behind some brush. A second later he saw another man, wearing a balaclava and carrying a Kalashnikov, step from behind the stack of supplies and quickly disappear into the vegetation. All of these men were dressed in full camouflage, and deliberately stayed in the shadows. These were not Taliban, nor were they CMM. These guys were bulked-up, well outfitted, and moved like professional soldiers. If Harris had to guess, he would say these guys were ex-Spetsnaz (Russian Special Forces).

Kaihan had directed Housyar to stop under the canopy of a tree and some cleverly erected camouflage netting. The spot was only 20 meters from what was once the front entry of the Sewakla District Hospital. Close-up, there was still something imposing about the place. The facade was shot-up, but there appeared to be a second, more solid inner structure.

Aziz must have radioed ahead because two men were waiting for them beneath the roof that overhung the hospital entrance. One of the men was tall, medium built, and in his early forties. The other man was shorter, heavyset, and in his fifties...late fifties. Both men were dressed in crisp, white chef uniforms, including traditional chef's hats. Looking closer, Harris saw the sagging postures and bloodshot eyes of men who weren't getting enough sleep. They both appeared uncomfortable being outside and anxiously glanced upward, into the overcast morning sky. By the time Housyar had turned off the ignition, both men had scurried over to the rear of the truck and were opening the rear doors. Neither Harris nor Housyar could see what they were doing, but it sounded like they were moving around boxes. Apparently satisfied, they began to remove the cardboard boxes and the jute bags, stacking them on a nearby concrete pad. Seeing this, Housyar stuck his head out of the driver's side window and was about to protest, when Kaihan firmly grabbed his shoulder and gestured that he should be quiet. When they had removed the last item, one of the men, the heavyset one, walked up to Housyar and handed him two sizable wads of large denomination afghanis. Housyar took the money but was unsure of whether he should count it. Glancing over at Kaihan, he saw the man shake his head just slightly. Understanding, Housyar put the money in the inside pocket of his vest and looked over at Kaihan, who said, "Go...you must now leave." As Housyar started up the truck, Kaihan wisely jumped from the running board and cautiously backed away. Then, just before Housyar put the truck into gear, the heavyset chef again appeared in Housyar's window. A vision of Housyar running over the man flashed in Harris' mind, and he reached for the key, killing the engine. As he did so, he heard the man say, "Wednesday, you will come back. Wednesday you will bring the same amount of everything, except twice as many apples and peaches. And no more vanilla....and no more black cardamom. Can you do this?" Housyar thought for a moment and then replied, "Yes, yes I can do as you ask." The man studied Housyar for a moment, seemingly trying to determine whether he could count on him. Then he nodded and stepped away from the truck.

A few minutes later, the truck was lurching toward the end of the access road, when, up ahead, one of the CMM fighters stepped from the brush, and waved for them to stop. It was no surprise that the sudden appearance of the man rattled Housyar. Overreacting, Housyar jerked the steering wheel to the right as he slammed on the brakes. The truck fishtailed, turned sideways, and skidded to a stop, still more than 50 meters from where the man was standing. Harris' face flushed and he sank deeper into his seat. He knew he shouldn't care, and he knew the man watching them was one of the "bad guys" but this was...well it was becoming really...embarrassing. The CMM fighter stared curiously, not quite sure what to do about the truck that was now cocked sideways in the road. A second later, a second CMM fighter appeared, this one was carrying their Kalashnikovs. He stared at the truck for a moment, then walked toward it, and approaching Housyar's window, he stared incredulously at the old man, and said, "I have a blind donkey that could drive better than you." Noticing Harris, he continued, "You...Goat Shit, why do you not drive?" Harris turned toward the man, but desperately avoided looking him in the face, as he struggled to reply. Then, in a nervous and halting voice he said, "Last year, I...I ran over two of our goats...and...I damaged the side of our house...Before that...I hit my neighbor lady and hurt her leg. My Uncle says I am not a good driver and I should not drive." The "odd" reply caused the CMM fighter to just shake his head in resignation. He handed Housyar their Kalashnikovs and said, "I see that it runs in the family. Now get this truck out of here and try not to kill anybody."

Housyar said little and scowled most of the drive back. On the other hand, Harris just sat there grinning. Both men knew that tonight, when the men gathered around their new stove, there would be some story-telling.

The next few days were hectic. Harris transmitted to Langley what he had seen, and then had to repeat himself several more times, as interest grew among the various agencies. Everyone wanted to know about the CMM, the Russian missiles, the ex-Spetsnaz mercenaries, and the fortifications. It was becoming clear that there was something really big happening, and it was equally clear that no one knew what it was. Afraid of what they didn't know, the decision was made to keep watching and probing.

To complicate the situation even further, Langley had recently intercepted an encrypted satellite communication that had repeatedly referred to Dr. Dicos and something called the "Zulfiqar Project." The location of one of the satellite phones was triangulated to the Abbasi Shaheed neighborhood of Karachi, Pakistan. The Taliban leader, Mullah Akhtar Mohammad Mansour, had recently been spotted in the Abbasi Shaheed neighborhood. The other satellite phone was tracked to the Mohmand Agency, a district in the Federally Administered Tribal Areas of Pakistan. Ayman al-Zawahiri, al-Qaeda's top man, was known to be hiding somewhere in or near the Mohmand Agency. The transmission implied that "top leaders" of both insurgent groups were to travel to Maidan Wardak Province later in the year. This information had Langley salivating at the prospect of getting Mullah Mansour, al-Zawahiri, and Dr. Dicos all in one strike.

More assets were assigned to Operation Frostbite and a "covert containment" strategy was to be implemented, effective immediately.

Two of these new assets, Afghan-born Boosha Sahar and Kontar Wahidi, were brought in to "turn" Afsoon. With a little digging Langley had found out that Afsoon came from a sparsely populated, mountainous area north of Bolaq. He had never been to school and was the youngest of three sons. His parents were both dead – killed in a feud over heroin transport routes. Both of his brothers had been recruited by the Taliban. One was confirmed dead and the other was in Rish Khor Prison, and was being held by the Afghan National Army

(ANA), as a terrorist. Afsoon was known to become violent at times and had a long history of getting into trouble. Based on a prison interview with his brother, Afsoon resented authority and was untrustworthy.

Using what they knew about Afsoon, Boosha and Kontar soon made contact and after a couple of friendly chats, they got down to business. Afsoon agreed to tell them everything he knew, for a Rolex watch and $2,000.00 in US currency.

According to Afsoon, the facility was large, and took up the entire basement level of the hospital. He had been allowed access to only a small part of it, the kitchen and the dining hall, but he had heard talk that there were two restricted sections that were heavily guarded. No one would talk about these sections, so Afsoon didn't know where they were or what they were for. A man who fit Dr. Dicos' description had recently arrived at the facility. Afsoon had seen him once, and then only from a distance. Still, he was able to describe him as a large man with pure white hair. He had heard that Dr. Dicos was a holy man and that Allah had blessed the man with the power to turn non-believers into ice. Afsoon went on to provide many more details about the facility and its occupants. It was at the end of their interview that Afsoon mentioned hearing about a "special guest," a young man whom they called the Chosen One. He was to be treated with reverence, but under no circumstances allowed to leave the facility. He had never seen this Chosen One and didn't know why he was called the Chosen One.

Wednesday morning found Harris and Housyar bouncing and weaving their way along the road to the Sewakla District Hospital. Just as the access road came into sight, Kaihan stepped out onto the road, but this time, he didn't stop them. Instead, he waved them onto the access road and stepped back into the brush. The absence of Afsoon was expected. It was clear that the man would sooner or later do something stupid like wear his Rolex watch, and then there would be questions. He would be taken into custody, brutally interrogated, and then beheaded or shot. There was no doubt the man would talk and then the entire operation would be put at risk. So Afsoon was given an extra $200.00 US, a ride to Jalrez, and, from there, a bus ticket to Kabul. In Kabul, he would stay at a rooming house and be watched closely until the operation was over. His sudden absence would present a problem, but Harris was reasonably sure that it wouldn't be a surprise, nor would he be missed.

A few meters into the access road, four burly men, in camouflage uniforms, stepped from the shadows and blocked the road. Predictably, Housyar performed one of his infamous maneuvers, nearly running over two of the men. When the truck finally ground to a stop, the men, in heavy Russian accents, ordered Housyar and Harris out and proceeded to roughly search both men. When finished they ordered them to stand off to the side, where two of the Russians kept their rifles pointed at them, while the other two searched the truck and checked their documents. When satisfied, they gestured to Housyar and Harris to get back into the truck, and then waved them to go ahead. Three minutes later, Housyar brought the truck to a skidding stop at the hospital entrance, where the two chefs waited for them. The men immediately went to the rear of the truck, opened the doors and proceeded to inspect the goods. Housyar could see that the heavyset man was visibly pleased as he walked up to Housyar's window. Placing his right hand over his heart, the man said, "As-salamu alaykum" (May peace be with you.) Housyar returned the greeting by saying, "Wa-Alaikum-as-salaam" (And peace to you also.) Then the man introduced himself as Chef Himsi, head chef of the Sewakla Hospital kitchen. As Chef Himsi removed two hefty rolls of afghanis from his chef uniform jacket, Harris saw the opportunity and shyly whispered, just loud enough for Chef Himsi to hear.

"Uncle, you said you would ask the man if he had a job for Faheem, you promised Faheem you would ask." Looking uncomfortable, Housyar said, "Muhammad, I am sorry but I do not think this important man needs another chef. Faheem is a skilled chef and he will soon find an opportunity to work."

Of course, the Chef heard the exchange and was silent for a moment as he seemed to be thinking, then he said, "Forgive me for listening, but did you say you know of a trained chef that is looking for work?" Housyar turned to the man and said, "Yes, Chef Himsi, my cousin's son, Faheem is an excellent chef, a good Muslim. He was trained at the Istanbul Culinary College in Turkey and has worked five years, as head chef, in a fancy Istanbul restaurant. But Faheem is a devout Muslim and the restaurant was sold to Christians. The new owner hired many Christians and soon they began to purchase meat that was not Dhabihah (prescribed Islamic method of ritual animal slaughter), and the restaurant began to serve liquor. This was unacceptable to

Faheem and he could no longer work there. His mother was ill so he returned to Afghanistan where he now lives with his mother in Jalrez. It is unfortunate, but Jalrez is a small city and there are few opportunities for a chef."

Chef Himsi listened intently while his eyes glanced between Housyar and the other man he knew was named Muhammad. When Housyar had finished, Chef Himsi looked at Housyar and said, "Housyar, the truth is I am in need of another chef. My assistant is useless, he cannot even boil water. I am working fourteen hours a day, seven days a week, and still people are not satisfied. Please, bring your cousin to see me, let us say next Wednesday when you come back with your next delivery? I will speak with him and then, we will see."

On returning to the TOC, Harris immediately advised Langley to go ahead and send for Colonel Singh. Langley analysts had come up with the idea of offering Chef Himsi some highly skilled help. Harris' initial description of Chef Himsi suggested that he was overworked and under pressure. Making available to him a skilled assistant would be like throwing a drowning man a life preserver. And, by chance, they had just the right man. His name was Atash Singh and he was the son of two Afghan physicians who had moved to Pakistan, where Atash was raised. At nineteen, he had immigrated to Canada, attended the University of Manitoba and graduated, summa cum laude in Mechanical Engineering. At twenty-five, he had immigrated to the United States and decided to try a different vocation. His passion for cooking had led him to Ferris State University, where he had earned a certificate in Culinary Management. From there, he had gone to the Istanbul Culinary College in Turkey, where he had studied to become a chef, specializing in Central and South Asian cuisine. The day he'd graduated, he had been recruited by the CIA. Atash Singh became known as Colonel Singh, but he was not exactly a colonel, at least not in the United States. While working for the CIA, he had been awarded the "honorary" rank of colonel by the British and Saudi governments. What he had done to deserve this honor was classified, but the title had stuck, and soon Atash Singh was known as Colonel Singh. The man was a true chameleon and he excelled at deep undercover work, and the man had a reputation of being a skilled assassin. Unlike most career civil servants, Colonel Singh cared about whom he worked for and what motivated that person. So, in April 2013 Colonel Singh quit the Agency. In his resignation letter, which he'd made public, he had writ-

ten that he had "become disenchanted by the Administration's deliberate disregard of the law and its pervasive assault on the individual
rights of American citizens." The Agency had been embarrassed by the
publication and they unceremoniously released Colonel Singh while
placing him on the "not for rehire" list. But things change, and now
that a politically more conservative Administration had been elected,
certain high level CIA officials had asked him to come back, and he had
agreed.

Harris did not know the man personally but knew him by reputation. In fact, when he had read Colonel Singh's resignation letter, he
too had given thought to quitting and publishing a resignation letter
with similar sentiments.

Two days later, Colonel Singh arrived at the TOC. It took three
more days to bring him up to speed and to commit to memory the
many details of his cover identity. By Tuesday night Colonel Singh was
ready. Harris was impressed with the man's ability to quickly comprehend the nuances of the relationships they had established. Colonel
Singh was now addressed as Faheem, and, in turn, he addressed
Housyar as Uncle, which was appropriate because of his age, and Harris as Muhammad or cousin.

Since the Hyundai had only two seats, Harris did not accompany
Faheem and Housyar. Instead, he watched the proceeding through
binoculars. He had spent the predawn hours finding a good spot to
hide and was in radio contact with the TOC. When Housyar pulled up
to the hospital entrance, Chef Himsi was waiting and scurried over to
the driver's side window. He and Housyar spoke for a few seconds,
then Faheem got out of the truck and walked over to where Chef
Himsi was standing. The two men exchanged greetings and then Chef
Himsi led Faheem into the building. In-between time, the assistant
chef and another man, who was dressed in a white jacket, and appeared to be a helper, unloaded the truck. Fifteen minutes later,
Faheem stepped from the hospital entrance, walked to the Hyundai,
and got in. Housyar started up the engine and the truck lurched forward. The second before Faheem had gotten into the truck, he had
scratched his head with his left hand, a signal to Harris that he had gotten the job.

As Harris prepared to leave, he took one last look at the hospital
building. With his binoculars, he paid particular attention to the vacant
windows, carefully inspecting each one individually. They were noth-

ing, just dark, gaping holes. The glass had long since been broken out. As he moved his binoculars to the last opening, he saw something. Adjusting the focus, he looked again and there, in the shadows, he saw movement. As he watched, a figure appeared, and, for just a moment, the figure stepped into the light, and Harris could see a face, Afig's face.

CHAPTER FOUR

Strapped

Four, thinly bearded, young, Afghan men lay securely bound to sturdy, stainless steel tables. Their heads had been shaved and each man wore a loose-fitting, green hospital gown that revealed lean, sinewy muscled arms that strained against the straps.

They were in a windowless basement room that had whitewashed stone walls, and a bare, concrete floor that, in places, was darkly stained. Each table was brightly illuminated by a cold beam of white light. The far reaches of the room were in shadow, punctuated by the bluish glow of monitors and instrument lights. The setting gave Afig a surreal feeling, as if he were trapped in a place that was simultaneously ancient and modern.

The room had once served as the Sewakla District Hospital morgue, but now, only the stainless steel tables remained. In an adjacent room, visible through a passageway partially screened by an oddly out-of-place tapestry, were four young women. They were robed in green, burqa-style, hospital, modesty gowns, and were also securely strapped to stainless steel tables. Their eyes, visible through the slotted head-cover openings, were wide and were staring up at the ceiling. At the edge of emotional breakdown, one by one they began to pray, hoping that quietly repeating the familiar Islamic verses would allow them to withdraw into themselves, and, in the process, preserve their sanity.

The stone walls made the rooms feel cold. In the air was the moldy smell of a basement, on top of which was the smell of human decomposition that was only partially covered by the odor of a strong hospital disinfectant.

Two men, apparently male nurses, approached and took positions around Afig's table. They varied slightly in their physiques, but in their surgical gloves, pale blue hospital scrubs, scrub caps, and surgical masks, they were nearly indistinguishable. As Afig studied the men, he couldn't help but smile. Like every other man at this facility, these men were bearded and now sizable tuffs of facial hair protruded from around the edges of their surgical masks. To Afig, they looked ridiculous and it made him wonder what was being done for show, and what was for real.

Each of the nurses had a prescribed task. One man operated an array of monitors, while the other man checked several hypodermic syringes that were displayed on the stainless steel tray next to him. Everyone was busy, yet Afig had the distinct feeling that they were waiting, and a moment later he saw whom they were waiting for. The doors opened and the esteemed Dr. Dicos marched into the room.

To those assembled, Dr. Dicos was known to be a mysterious, wise and powerful man. Among the staff, it was widely rumored that Dr. Dicos was divinely gifted and would lead those of the true faith to a great and final victory over the deniers. The Commander of the Faithful, Mullah Akhtar Mohammed Mansour, had personally blessed the Zulfiqar Project and was, even now, awaiting the word of its success.

Until that morning, the specific details of the Zulfiqar Project had been kept a secret. As they prepped the patients, Mullah Hafiz Jallah, a squat, white-bearded Imam, who was recognized as the spiritual adviser for the group, stepped forward, and as everyone became quiet, said, "With the blessing of Allah, the esteemed Dr. Dicos shall, on this glorious day, begin a solemn and sacred process. Today, the divine powers of Zulfiqar shall test four men to determine which one is the Chosen One. Only he that has been touched by the almighty himself shall pass this test. But I tell you now, my brothers, the process shall not be without pain. For those of you who do not survive this test, you need not be disheartened, for your reward shall be the paradise reserved for martyrs." With these words, everyone began chanting, "Allahu Akbar! Allahu Akbar! Allahu Akbar! (God is the greatest)" As the chanting subsided, Mullah Jallah continued, "The man that survives the mixing of his blood with that of Zulfiqar shall be given many blessings, and a great responsibility, for he shall sire a child, and that child shall be known as 'The Listener.' The Listener, and only The Listener, shall hear the Voice and the Voice shall be the Word, and the Word shall be Everything." These words again caused the assembled to chant, "Allahu Akbar! Allahu Akbar! Allahu Akbar!" Mullah Jallah continued, "Just as Imam Ali, given the mighty sword of Zulfiqar, did, with one powerful blow, cut down the great Amr ibn Abdawud, a giant, who had stood alone against a thousand men. So shall The Listener, with the blessing of Allah, once again unleash the terrible power of Zulfiqar against the enemies of the one true religion. The days of the deniers...the Zionists...and the Crusaders are soon to end. The time of a great battle is near, but this battle shall not be fought with a weapon made from mere iron, nor shall this weapon be forged from the foul and corrupt technologies of the Great Satan. Instead, this final weapon shall be made from the flesh and blood...the pure righteous flesh and blood of Zulfiqar's child, the one we will know as The Listener."

Mullah Jallah paused for a moment and then, in nearly a whisper, said, "I tell you this, my brothers, The Listener will strike great fear into the hearts of our enemies. The deniers, the infidels shall gnash their teeth and pull out their hair. There shall be great weeping as they see their grotesque monuments crumble. No denier of the true faith shall be spared, and there shall be no mercy...no pity. The time for mercy has passed and now it is time for retribution, for punishment, and for cleansing. For when this, the greatest of all Jihads, is finished, not one infidel, heretic, apostate or scoffer, shall be left breathing. All peoples of the East, West, South, and the North shall be united under one great Islamic Caliphate, and all shall submit to the laws and teachings of the true faith." The assembled, now nearly hysterical, shouted, "Allahu Akbar! Allahu Akbar! Allahu Akbar!"

Aaban, Sahla, and Barr, three of the young men now strapped to the stainless steel tables, were deeply honored and excited that the powerful Dr. Dicos had selected them as candidates for this "most holy endeavor." Afig, the fourth man, was not of this mind set. He had been...forcefully "drafted" and still only had a vague idea of what was going on. But there was no doubt that he did not want to be strapped to the table, nor was he looking forward to what they were going to do to him.

Afig had arrived at this place a week ago...or maybe three weeks ago, he could no longer be sure. He remembered being handcuffed and shoved into the back seat of a black car or SUV. Sometime later, he woke up and found himself lying in a bed, dressed only in a green hospital gown. He had been hooked up to an IV bag and when he had tried to move, he'd realized his wrists were handcuffed to the metal frame of the bed. Turning caused his head to ache so he had studied the room using as little head movement as possible. The place was large and had no windows. It had once been painted a dingy yellow that was given a sickening hue by the bluish white light cast by the two rows of fluorescent ceiling fixtures. Afig remembered that two of the ceiling fixtures were dark and one of the fixtures, the one off to his right, had been flickering, which threatened to bring on a throbbing headache. He was surrounded by a dozen or more empty, metal-framed beds, all identical to his except the stained mattresses were bare. There was no one around and, except for a faint background hum, the room had been completely silent.

Wakened by the sound of voices, Afig had had no idea if it was an hour later or if it was the next day. Blinking, he had tried to focus on the two men standing beside his bed. The man on the right wore a white lab coat and had a stethoscope slung around his neck. Afig had dismissed this man as his attention had turned to the man standing next to him. Without realizing it, he had begun straining against his handcuffs, the metal cutting into his wrists. There, standing over him, was Dr. Dicos, the man Afig's father called Thalj Shayton. Afig had felt his body stiffen and he had begun to sweat, yet he had not felt hot; actually, he had begun to feel...cold. An icy coldness had washed over him as if someone had opened a door to a frigid outside world, but there had been no such door...the coldness had emanated from Dr. Dicos. The man standing next to Dr. Dicos had also felt the cold, and had tactfully tried to move farther away from the man.

When Dr. Dicos had seen the alarm and apprehension in Afig's face, he had spoken, saying, "It is good that you are awake, my friend. I have been looking for you for some time now, and here...you have come to me. Allah be praised."

Dr. Dicos had paused as he studied Afig's eyes, then he continued, "Ah yes, you...you think you know who I am. Well, we shall see about that." Apparently satisfied, Dr. Dicos had turned and walked away.

The days that followed had been busy and Afig had not had any further contact with Dr. Dicos. He had often thought about the man, and he had thought about his father's description of Thalj Shayton. Some of it had fit, but some of it hadn't. After a while, Afig's more rational mind took over and he had begun to doubt the Thalj Shayton connection. Dr. Dicos was, as Harris would aptly describe him, one of the "bad guys," nothing more and nothing less. The coldness he had experienced had been his imagination, or maybe someone had opened a door to the outside and he hadn't seen it. Anyway, he had been taken prisoner, and he had been under constant guard by half a dozen armed men.

Afig had been subjected to days of unexpectedly mild questioning. His...interrogators had smiled frequently and listened, with great interest, as he had responded to their questions. He had studied Afig Hafeez's dossier, but the information had not included much in the way of descriptive detail. So he had had to make things up, and then he'd had to remember what he had made up so as not contradict anything he had already said. Several of the men asking questions had been older, and Afig had soon been able to deduce that they were senior al-Qaeda and Taliban emissaries. They had traveled to this place specifically to see him.

After repeating this story for what seemed like the hundredth time, the subject matter had abruptly changed, and they had begun asking him his opinion on religious issues. This had caught Afig off guard even though, as a youth, he had successfully completed all the required Islamic instruction and had memorized large sections of the Qur'an. He had attended many hours of Qur'anic tafseer classes that were supposed to "reveal the will of Allah," as it was conveyed in the text of the Qur'an. Yet, after less than a day of religious questions, he had come to realize that his responses had conveyed a tone of skepticism. Afig was...a doubter and it would only be a matter of time before he would have said something that would have given him away. As the questions dragged on, Afig had become uncomfortably anxious, when he remembered an old American film. In it, a simple gardener was mistakenly thought to be a wealthy businessman. His simple gardening metaphors were interpreted to be profound, allegorical insights into business and the economy. Afig didn't know much about gardening, but he knew a little about orchards, so, for the next two days, Afig had recited a litany of axioms pertaining to the planting and maintenance of an orchard. He had not been sure whether his interrogators thought he was insolent, mad, or wise beyond their ability to comprehend. Either way, the religious questions had soon come to a stop and Afig had been allowed some free time. Two things had then happened. First, he had expelled the transmitter beacon and had been unable to retrieve it. It hadn't mattered, since he was reasonably sure the battery was dead, and if someone hadn't tracked him by then, they probably would never track him. The second thing that had happened was that he was allowed to take in some fresh air. To do so, they had blindfolded and handcuffed him and then escorted him through two sets of doors, down a long corridor and up a flight of stairs. At the top of the stairs, they had removed his blindfold and walked him down an outer corridor, whose walls were singed black and bullet-pocked. Near the end of the corridor, there was a window, or what was left of a window. The glass pane had been shattered, and now lay as jagged shards on the floor. A guard had stood on each side of him and two more waited nearby. Afig had stared out through the opening. He knew that he would be allowed only a few seconds, so he inhaled and savored the cold, fresh air. It was morning, and he had wanted to feel the sunlight, so he had leaned out into the opening. It had been a long time since he had felt the warmth of the sun and it felt good. As he was taking in the scene, a glint of reflected light caught his attention. Turning toward its source, he had seen that the terrain was steep scrub brush. Initially, he had thought the sun had been reflected off of a piece of broken glass, but this particular hillside wasn't the kind of place you would expect to find broken glass. As he studied the spot closely, he saw the reflection reappear and this time he would have sworn that it had moved. He immediately knew it must have been a rifle scope or binoculars. Although he had not actually seen anyone, Afig was convinced that someone had been watching the building, and may have spotted him. Hoping he had been right, Afig remained leaning, through the opening, as long as he could. It had taken less than a minute for the guards to become impatient. They had grabbed Afig's shoulders, forcefully pulling him back inside.

CHAPTER FIVE

Black Snake

Afig had finished Isha (evening prayers) when two guards approached him. He was told to sit on the edge of his bed. They then proceeded to handcuff both of his wrists to the heavy metal bed frame, and then they chained his ankles to a ring cemented into the floor. Afig did not know how to respond since, up until now, he had been treated civilly, and he had not offered any resistance.

Once secured, the guards backed away and stood on both sides of the door, apparently waiting for someone. It was not long before an elderly man, one of his interrogators, entered the room. The man had never been introduced, but the others had referred to him as the Imam. Afig remembered him well for he was an unusually tall, thin man, slightly stooped, and thought to be in his seventies. His graying hair protruded from beneath a black turban and his beard was long, disheveled, and heavily streaked with grey. The beard, and the half glasses he wore, initially gave him a wise grandfatherly look. But as Afig studied him more closely, he became aware of his eyes. The half glasses were a distraction, a prop. When the Imam peered over them, Afig saw a hardness, an unmistakable cruelty in the dark pupils. During his questioning, those eyes had focused in on Afig's every expression, every gesture, every movement – they seemed to miss nothing. After a time, Afig had come to suspect that this man was capable of reading his thoughts – or at least making one think he could.

The Imam's eyes took in the room before settling on Afig. Seeing him securely cuffed seemed to please the man as the slightest hint of a smile emerged at the corners of his mouth. Removing his half glasses, he took a moment to study Afig. His expression was now a mixture of curiosity and distaste, as if he were looking at some kind of odd but disgusting creature. Not taking his eyes off of Afig, the Imam waved the guards away. After giving them enough time to leave, he stepped toward Afig and, when he was about a meter away, he stopped. Then, in almost a whisper, the Imam said, "Dr. Dicos has warned me to be careful around you. He said that you are more powerful than you look...and that you might be dangerous. He also believes that you may be the "special" one that he has been waiting for." This statement got Afig's attention. In his short career as a spy, he had killed a man, he had caused another man to be "executed," he had been kidnapped, and was now thought to be someone "special" by the very person who had kidnapped him? Searching the Imam's eyes, he tried to determine whether the man was serious or whether this was some kind of inter-rogation trick. Seeing only a dark cruelty, he turned away and as he did, the Imam said, "Afig Hafeez,...or whoever you are, I do not know whether you are "special" but I can assure you this: When I am fin-ished with you, we will know how special you are. You see, we already know that you are a liar, a heretic, and an imposter, yet these things are insignificant. What matters is what you are."

Not understanding what he was talking about, Afig feigned fear and confusion. He had been told about interrogation techniques, where the interrogator pretends he knows all about you, hoping that you will be-lieve that there is no point in continuing to deceive him. Still, the Imam had been convincing and Afig suddenly had doubts. Knowing he had to do something, he adopted the air of disbelief that he thought would be consistent with an innocent man being accused of a crime he did not commit, or even understand. Afig looked up, directly into the Imam's face and pleaded, "Sir, I...I am an honest man, a good Muslim. I am not a liar....I dream only of being a jihadist...to follow in..." Before Afig could finish, the Imam drew back his hand and slapped Afig with such force that it jerked his head sideways and caused blood to spatter onto both men's tunics. There was a jagged cut in Afig's upper lip, and he could taste the blood seeping into his mouth. As Afig tried to shake off the blow, he could hear the Imam say, "If you are not silent, I will have your tongue cut out, marinated in your piss, and then served to you on a stick. Now let me continue. Yes, yes, I was saying that you are a liar, or maybe you are a spy. Yet, after so many days of listening to your mindless babble, I do not think you are intelligent enough to be a spy. You are, more likely, a common criminal, a scoundrel who stum-bled into something you do not understand and have no control over."

It sounded as if the Imam had made up his mind, and there was nothing left to discuss. Yet, if that were true, then what did this man want? Afig remained silent and just stared at the Imam. Feeling the blood pool in his mouth, he gathered it and spat it at the Imam's feet.

Seemingly pleased by Afig's defiance, the Imam took a moment to visually inspect the restraints and then gestured for the guards to return. As the two guards approached, the Imam spoke, without turning away from Afig, "It is time to introduce this young man to the 'black snake.' Now, would you please go and fetch it for me." The men did not immediately respond, but instead glanced at each other, with an expression that Afig interpreted as confusion. When the Imam noticed their hesitation, he turned and glared at the two men, with such ferocity that they immediately left the room.

A minute or two later, the guards returned with what appeared to be two, meter-and-a-half-long, sections of heavy, black rubber hose. Seeing the black hoses, Afig immediately understood what was going to happen, and began struggling to free himself. This reaction amused the Imam and he watched with some interest, but, after a moment, he became bored at the sight and ordered the men to proceed. Stepping toward Afig, the two men raised their sections of hose, but still hesitated striking Afig. Their reluctance outraged the Imam, and he screamed at them, "Do it, you fools, do it now, or you will take his place!"

Afig successfully deflected the first blow, but the second one caught him squarely across his shoulder. It felt like someone had lashed him with a steel cable. After that, the blows continued to find their mark, until Afig could do nothing but scream in pain. When the guards stopped, the Imam yelled at them to continue, and to strike even harder. Whenever a particularly punishing blow registered, the Imam could be heard laughing and ordering his men to do it again. The blows kept coming until Afig could no longer scream, he could not even whimper, he desperately prayed for unconsciousness or even death.

He did not know when they stopped the beating. He did not remember the Imam standing over him, sadistically poking at the shredded flesh and at the massive purple and red welts.

When Afig regained consciousness, he found himself in his bed, and the only sensation he felt were the waves of pain, excruciating pain that washed over him. Everything hurt, it hurt to open his eyes and it hurt to breathe. Raising just one finger immediately brought tears to his eyes. He closed his eyes and the blackness mercifully engulfed him.

The next time he became conscious, Afig immediately sensed the pain had largely subsided. It was not gone completely but it was now only a small fraction of what it had been. He didn't know how long he had been unconscious but found himself lying in a bed whose sheets were blood-stained and sweat-soaked. Cursing, he realized that he needed to urinate. As he struggled to sit, a hand reached out to help him. Squinting through eyes that were still swollen, Afig saw a man, whom he did not recognize. Pushing the hand away, Afig tried to stand up, on his own. He did manage to get to his feet but immediately felt dizzy. Sensing that he was about to fall, he reluctantly reached out, and grabbed the man's arm. The two of them stood there for a long moment as Afig fought a wave of nausea that had engulfed him. Gradually it subsided and Afig slowly shuffled toward the toilet.

Before he was finished, Afig nearly passed out twice, but the man had been there and each time he had steadied him. As Afig looked into the man's face, he saw the shame in his eyes. The man deliberately did not meet Afig's eyes, but, instead looked away. As the two men made their way back to Afig's bed, the man awkwardly cleared his throat and, in an apologetic voice, said, "Efendi (Sir), my name is Merzad....I come from a very small village near Delaram...Forgive me, these things are not important, what is important is that you know I did not have anything to do with your... your beating." Afig was taken aback by first being addressed as Efendi, an honorific title usually reserved for those of a learned profession, or of high-ranking social status, and then being addressed in an apologetic tone. Even so, he did not reply. He was not in an understanding or a forgiving mood, nor did he feel talkative. As they approached the bed, Merzad gestured toward a chair and said, "Efendi, Perhaps you could sit for a few minutes. This will allow me to make you a clean bed, and then I will get you some clothes and help you wash." Looking down, Afig saw that his tunic and pants were tattered and caked in dry blood. When he looked at the bed, and saw that it too was blood-stained. Suddenly, the thought of bathing and lying in a clean bed seemed to be an unimaginable luxury.

Afterward, as Afig, now freshly scrubbed, lay down onto a clean bed, Merzad said, "I see that you are healing quickly, Efendi. This is very good news for the guards. They were under strict orders to see that no harm came to you. I think, maybe, the Imam has gone mad. But, Allah be praised, you have refused to die. No man has ever survived such a beating, and yet, here you are...alive and only four days have passed and you are nearly healed....Maybe they are right." It had not been easy for Afig to concentrate, but this last statement had drawn him in and he said, "What?...What did you mean when you said – Maybe they are right?"

Merzad seemed to struggle to answer, but after looking away for a moment, he turned to Afig and said, "I am a simple man and I do not understand these things, but everyone now knows that you have been selected as a "candidate." Many believe that you are the one that is most likely to pass the test." Seeing the confusion in Afig's eyes, he continued, "You see, Efendi, for some time now, Dr. Dicos has been selecting four young men, men who have proven themselves to be...special. Most of the time, these men are known to be fierce fighters, but sometimes he selects very bright students and once he even selected a doctor. You, Efendi, you have been selected as one of these men. It is a great honor and your family will receive a large reward." Afig waited for more information but it seemed that Merzad had finished speaking. Turning toward Merzad, he asked, "You have spoken of a test. What is this test?"

Merzad seemed to hesitate, and then he answered, saying, "I do not know what the test is, but I have heard that it is very difficult to pass. The test has been given many times, yet...no one has passed it. Forgive me, Efendi, I do not wish to tell you bad things. But...I have heard that if you fail the test, it means that you are... dead." Merzad paused for a moment and then said, "Efendi, there is something else, but I do not know if it is important. I have heard that, each year, Dr. Dicos also selects four young and very beautiful women. They are kept isolated, in a separate area, and I know nothing about them. I am sorry."

As Afig tried to process this information, he shifted to find a more comfortable position, but failing to do so, resigned himself to just lie there.

Slowly, consciousness gave way to a deep sleep. Afig dreamt but the dreams were chaotic and confusing. He had had these same dreams before and in them he was always hunting someone. This time, the dream was more vivid and, for just a fraction of a second, he thought he might understand, but then Afig felt a coldness wash over him and his eyes sprang open. Scanning the room, his eyes came to rest on a dark figure, sitting in a far corner. Seeing Afig stir, the man stood and stepped into the light. Dr. Dicos gestured to someone past Afig, and when Afig turned, he saw one of Dr. Dicos' bodyguards stepping out of the room. A moment later he returned, gripping the back collar of the...Imam as he shoved him into the room. Afig immediately stiffened, he would never forget that man's face, nor would he forget the voice demanding that they "hit him harder." By now, Afig was sitting upright, his body tense as he stared at his torturer. Seeing this, Dr. Dicos spoke, saying, "Afig Hafeez, it appears that the great and merciful Allah has spared your life and through his compassion he has restored you to health. But now, my young friend, it is time for justice." Afig turned to Dr. Dicos and seeing the man's pale skin, pure white hair, and those spectacled, ice-blue eyes, he felt a sense of dread and...revulsion. Dr. Dicos continued, "Afig Hafeez, I ask you, did this man," pointing toward the Imam, "order that you be beaten?" For a moment, Afig was confused and then he realized that Dr. Dicos was playing the role of...judge and wanted him to accuse the Imam. Afig took a breath and said, "I may be mistaken, but are you not the man in charge of this place? If the Imam had me beaten, was he not acting on your orders?" Afig could see Dr. Dicos' eyes harden and there was a moment of awkward silence. Then, in a voice that was artificially tolerant and increasingly impatient, he replied, "It is true that I hold the 'scepter,' but it is also true that not everyone submits to my authority. So I ask you again, did this man order your beating?" Knowing that it would be fruitless to continue taunting Dr. Dicos, he replied, "Yes, yes it was the Imam that had me beaten."

As far as Afig was concerned, both men could take the first available bus to hell, but what happened next surprised him. On hearing Afig's answer, Dr. Dicos nodded at the guard, who swiftly removed the heavy, burlap bag he had tucked into his waistband, and pulled it over the Imam's head. He then drew his pistol, pressed the muzzle next to where the Imam's temple would be, and pulled the trigger. The blast was deafening, and the Imam's head jerked to the side. The burlap bag contained most of the blood and brain tissue, but a fine, red mist escaped and, for a moment, was suspended in the air. The Imam's knees buckled and his lifeless body collapsed to the floor.

As Afig watched the scene unfold, he was at once horrified and yet glad the sadistic bastard was dead. It was at that moment that he realized the Imam's expression had never changed. The man had looked indifferent to the whole proceeding, almost as if he were not aware of what was happening.

Afig's ears were still ringing when he heard Dr. Dicos say, "You see, Afig Hafeez, you can trust me, I am your friend. All I ask in return is your...obedience."

CHAPTER SIX

Student

Three years earlier.

Kabul was always hot in September and this year was no exception. Dawud Hawadi didn't much like the heat and found it really hard to study. His saving grace was that it started cooling down after 8:00 PM, which meant Dawud would spend another late night buried in his books. He didn't mind. It was quiet, no one bothered him, and he was actually interested in the material he was studying. Still, there were challenges. The power would go out on a regular basis, and the textbooks as well as much of the library reference materials, could be better thought of as museum relics. He desperately needed to get onto the internet, but that wasn't an option. Since most of the "Foreigners" had left, internet access had become more and more spotty. And now, thanks to the growing influence of Islamic fundamentalism, the internet had been proclaimed the source of every conceivable evil known to mankind. Under pressure, the National Assembly, which was made up of "honest, intellectual giants, and independent thinkers," naturally capitulated. Now, barring any technical difficulties, the internet would be turned on at 7:30 AM, then shut down, for an hour, during each prayer period, and then turned off at 7:00 PM. On top of that, download speeds had slowed to a crawl and thousands of sites were blocked or made off-limits. The only place left to get real, high-speed internet that wasn't monopolized by Islamic cartoonish programming and Imams pontificating on the latest fatwa (legal opinion or learned interpretation of Islamic Law), was the University library. And even there, you were assigned a monitor to ensure you were not viewing sites that were un-Islamic. This meant that Dawud would have to drag himself out of bed at 7:00 AM to get to the library by 7:30 AM. If he was late, it meant he would have to queue up and wait his turn for a computer to open up.

For the third time in a week, Dawud slept in and didn't make it to the library until 8:20 AM. He would now have to wait in line, and it was almost 10:00 AM before he got his turn. It was just after 1:00 PM when he timed out and one of the monitors asked him to leave. It was the same guy who periodically looked over his shoulder and wrote down the URL he was visiting. Dawud wasn't sure of what they did with this information, but sometimes imagined a room full of old, stern-looking men, with long, white beards. They would type, using only one finger, and they would systematically bring up each site and then carefully review it to verify that it did not contain any un-Islamic material. This made Dawud smile since he spent most of his time reviewing technical papers that were usually written in English. Though he knew English fairly well, he still needed to use his English to Pashto dictionary and his technical dictionary, at least three or four times before he got through the first page. Although his current love was Fluid Mechanics, he too found it a bit numbing to have to read through some of the PDF documents.

More likely, the monitors simply put the list of URLs in his file, and if, at some future time, he was suspected of behaving un-Islamic, they would go over the list to try and build a case against him. Dawud was not an activist, and hoped only to be left alone. Still, he knew this was naive, and he knew that, one day, he would have to stand up against these Islamic thugs.

Dawud was eighteen years old. He was a tall, athletically built young man with thick, reddish brown hair that seemed to be permanently disheveled. He had his mother's light skin; large, curious, green eyes; and a broad, easy smile. He was thought to be a good-looking kid, but not in the Hollywood, "pretty boy" way. He had his father's high forehead, a nose that looked as if it had once been broken, and a strong, square jaw. He had also inherited his father's broad shoulders and height. Standing 191 cm (6 ft, 2 inches), he already had a presence. Combined, these features gave Dawud an easygoing, intelligent, yet distinctly masculine air that offered him a number of advantages, advantages that Dawud did not seem to recognize. Instead, Dawud found himself worrying about things and he had a habit of second-guessing himself. These were traits that he had exhibited since he was a small boy, and his mother had always wanted him to relax and lighten up. His father was less concerned, saying, "The boy has a good head on his shoulders and he will figure out a way to live that will be right for him."

Dawud lived at home but spent over 12 hours a day on campus. He had a part-time job at the Engineering Lab, and he was carrying a full load of classes. The job was not particularly challenging but the pay was OK, and it made him feel part of the institution. He also got to know people like Professor Feda Bakkali, who kept him abreast of campus politics, and who had encouraged him to continue studying English. He had said, "English is the key to unlock the secrets of the modern world. No matter how smart you are, without English, you can never become a first tier Scientist, Engineer, or Medical Doctor."

Dawud got good grades, loved his major, and he felt comfortable at the University. It was not long before several of the faculty members noticed these things and were impressed with his fluency in English. Soon he was invited to participate in the English Conversational Club. Dawud accepted immediately. He eagerly joined in and soon found himself being asked to tutor other club members. English was as natural to Dawud as Pashto, and he spoke it with a curious blend of British and American accents. At home, English was easily spoken as often as Pashto. Actually, his mother seemed to prefer English and would switch to Pashto only after Dawud's father had come into the house. This was not that his father would disapprove, but more because she wanted him to relax and feel comfortable. His father was one of those men everyone was drawn to, a man people naturally followed. This was true even though Morad Hawadi Pasha was a very private man and really preferred to be in the company of his family. His father spoke Pashto eloquently, more eloquently than anyone Dawud knew. But foreign languages were altogether another thing. It was not that he did not try to speak English. In fact, for as long as Dawud could remember, his father had made a sincere effort to learn the language. He diligently worked at developing his vocabulary, grammar, and pronunciation, but the process had never become natural.

Looking at the wall clock, Dawud saw it was just after five. He was running a little late but would still have plenty of time to catch the next bus. Dawud's parents had not limited his foreign language studies to English. He had also been "encouraged" to study Arabic and his Arabic class was at 5:30 PM. His instructor was an elderly Saudi man by the name of Mawlawi Ahmed Abdel. He had earned the honorific religious title of Mawlawi for his scholarship of Sunni religious matters. The Mawlawi had a large, beaklike nose and deeply creased face and hands. His gray beard was long but neatly trimmed and he wore thick, black, horn-rimmed glasses that partially obscured his eyes. Eyes that seemed permanently fixed in a curious squint. But what bothered

Dawud about the man was his breath. It always smelled of garlic, stale cigarettes, and something that reminded him of decay. The Mawlawi was a very formal and serious man who was in his mid-seventies or maybe late seventies. He was a firm believer in the "old ways" and had nothing but scorn for television, smart phones, and computers – computers being synonymous with the internet. To him, the indiscriminate use of these technologies, or more specifically the deluge of mindless advertising that exploited them, polluted and corrupted the mind and soul. This contempt of the modern extended to dress, and he refused to teach any student who wore Western or non-traditional clothing. This meant Dawud would have to go home and change out of his tee shirt, jeans, and tennis shoes, and into the traditional baggy pants that were called tombann, the long over-shirt that was called a payraan, and sandals. Dawud wasn't thrilled about having to change but he wasn't about to upset the Mawlawi. Once Dawud had complained to his father, who had told him that the Mawlawi had once been a professor at a prestigious university in Saudi Arabia. He had left his position as Wahhabism grew in strength. Wahhabis began taking over classrooms. Good professors were fired while incompetent ones replaced them. Soon you were declared to be a "denier" or an "apostate" if you dared to challenge their fanatical views. The Mawlawi was also internationally recognized as an Arabic linguist, and was sought after to translate ancient documents. Dawud's father had said, "One should not be distracted by the superficial peculiarities of this man. He is a wise man, a strong, independent thinker. He has learned a great deal in his lifetime and has much to teach if you are willing to listen."

As Dawud left the Mechanical Engineering building, he began walking south toward Seh Aqrab Road. There he would catch the Millie Bus heading toward Wazir Akbar Khan, the neighborhood where he lived. The state-run Millie Bus system was inexpensive but there were far too few buses and far too many people who wanted to ride. No matter, it was cheap, and these days Dawud was traveling back and forth to the University so often, that paying for a taxi would be out of the question.

Ahead of him, he saw a small crowd of 10 or 12 people who had gathered alongside the narrow gravel path. As Dawud approached, he could see they were watching a practice session of the Agriculture Faculty Cricket Team. Stopping, his eyes took in the group of spectators and immediately saw that the group was really two groups. A group of young male students, and a separate group of young female students. What bothered him was the fact that four of the female students wore burqas and all but one of the male students wore beards. A year ago, the group would have been a mix of male and female students, and to have worn a beard or a burqa would have seemed out of place.

Dawud turned his attention to the cricket field. This year's team was supposed to be very good and everyone expected they would win the Peace Cricket League. As he was watching the batsman coolly step into position, Dawud was suddenly knocked backward by a thunderous blast that caused dust to rise up from the field, and windows in nearby buildings to shatter. It took a second for Dawud to regain his balance, and when he did he tried to determine where the blast had come from. Instinctively, he looked east, and there he saw a column of smoke and dust rising from somewhere around Artal Bridge, about a kilometer away.

No one had any doubt that it was a bomb, in fact it was the second bomb they had heard that week. Dawud could hear gasps and cries of fear from those around him. He saw people begin running for the shelter of buildings and doorways; others were frozen, staring in the direction of the explosion with expressions of astonishment and confusion.

It was then that he heard the chatter of automatic gunfire, followed at once by a smaller explosion, and then more automatic gunfire. Now, more and more Dawud could hear cries of anguish. Two young women, both wearing stylish jackets, their heads covered with hijabs, were stopped nearby, seemingly paralyzed by the rising column of smoke that was quickly spreading across a large part of the sky. He remembered seeing them earlier. They had been walking side by side, arms entwined. Brimming with energy, they had seemed young and happy as they spoke to one another and laughed. Now, both were quiet, and the taller, the one in the white print hijab and with the large dark eyes, had turned a ghostly white color. As the seconds passed, Dawud could see that this girl had begun to shake. When it seemed that she was going to collapse, her friend put her arms around her, and eased her to the gravel path. Once there, both girls held each other, their eyes swelled with tears and they wept.

A feeling of anger and frustration swept over Dawud. As far back as he could remember, Kabul had been a violent place. It was here that the struggle for the future of Afghanistan was taking place. But still,

Dawud had hoped that, somehow, he could just be a student, worry about grades and what to say to that pretty girl he always saw reading, on the concrete steps of the Computer Science Building.

Turning his eyes to the cricket field, Dawud could see that the cricket players had all left. A group of them had gathered near the door to the locker room and were pressing cell phones against their ears.

The sound of gunfire had been replaced with the sound of converging sirens. People slowly began to re-emerge from doorways, while others began to migrate toward the campus entrance at Seh Aqrab Road.

The sound of blasting horns drew Dawud's attention to the growing number of the pedestrians stepping out into the street. They were trying to wave down a taxi or a passing car that might give them a ride. Most of these people needed to check up on families and friends, while others just wanted to be away from here, get away from the horrific scene that was still unfolding only a 15-minute walk from where they stood. Dawud flinched as he saw two cars honk, one of them forced to swerve to avoid hitting a short, heavyset man who had frantically run out in front of it. This scene had the effect of refocusing Dawud. He too had people – a mother, a father, and a little sister whom he cared about and now wondered if they were safe.

As Dawud left the campus, his head turned toward the approaching sirens. A short convoy of ANP (Afghan National Police) patrol cars and six ANA (Afghan National Army) armored hummers sped by. These were soon followed by three ambulances, lights flashing, and sirens screaming. All were speeding east, speeding toward the smoke and the terrible scene that awaited them.

Like most people who lived in Kabul, Dawud had experienced this scene before. He knew by the strength of the first explosion, it was a car bomb, or maybe even a truck bomb. The second explosion was much smaller and was probably a suicide bomber, intent on killing the rescuers, the people coming out to help those hurt and maimed. Car and truck bombs were particularly horrendous since they were powerful enough to level nearby buildings, toss cars into the air as if they were toys, and totally obliterate human beings. It was late in the afternoon and the explosions appeared to have been located near Artal Bridge and Abne Cina Hospital. There would have been a lot of people on the street and a lot of traffic, maybe even school buses at this time of the day. It was likely that, in an instant, many lives had been permanently and savagely altered.

Twice before, Dawud had seen, close-up, the aftermath of such an explosion. The sight of all those shattered and dismembered bodies was forever etched into his mind. He would never forget the blast, the deafness and ringing in his ears that followed. The smell of pulverized concrete and burning fuel mixed with the smell of burning flesh. Smoldering fragments of the bomber's car, its engine, sections of its suspension system, and even the seats had been hurled 50 meters or more in different directions. Nearby cars had been flipped onto their sides, or onto their roofs. They were ablaze, their occupants hopelessly trapped inside. Parts of bodies, pieces of shredded clothing, shoes, and blood, lots of blood were everywhere. It would take a moment for the shock to wear off then there would be the moaning of the hurt and dying, the screaming and the crying of those who somehow survived and those frantically trying to find someone they knew – a child, a mother, a friend. Someone who had been standing next to them only moments ago...and was now gone. Dawud remembered seeing one man, his clothes shredded and still smoldering, looking under a pile of twisted metal for his severed arm.

People, faces darkened by dust and blood, could be seen stumbling around aimlessly. Others would be sitting up, rocking back and forth, staring blankly at nothing.

Both times Dawud had been unfortunate enough to have witnessed these horrible scenes, they had been much the same. He had helped put people into the backs of trucks and back seats of cars, so they could be rushed to the hospital. He had helped people find someone in the smoke and dust. He remembered how grateful he was when a soldier told him to leave, as they began the gruesome job of collecting bodies. He would never forget these sights, even though he would try very hard to never remember.

Dawud's home was in North Kabul, the Wazir Akbar Khan neighborhood, which was about five kilometers northeast of the University. He was reasonably sure his mother and sister were staying home today, but he was not sure what his father was doing. His father operated a successful export business and had offices near Shahre Now Park, well north of where the bombing took place. However, Dawud's father, Morad Hawadi Pasha, was also a friend and adviser to the Foreign Ministry. Dawud vaguely remembered that his father had meetings scheduled at the Ministry of Foreign Affairs, but was not sure if it was today. Even so, the Ministry was still two kilometers northeast of the explosions, and he should be safe.

Dawud cursed to himself. It would have been so easy to just call and check up on everyone, but he had dropped his cell phone once too often and it had quit working. Reluctant to tell his father, he had planned to buy a new one with the money he was earning. His only consolation was the inevitability of the system to crash during any kind of an emergency. Sure enough, a moment later, Dawud could see the frustrated expressions as people frantically dialed their numbers, but were not being connected.

Fearing the chaos that followed this kind of attack, Dawud decided to walk home, a decision quickly validated when he saw the traffic grind to a complete stop. He would have to be careful and take side streets, alleys, and even cut through a couple of abandoned warehouses, to avoid the police and military checkpoints. These checkpoints scooped up anyone who fit a certain profile, and Dawud was quite aware that he fit the profile in at least two ways. He was male and he was the right age. Lately, being a University student had also become a liability. The police were well aware of the secretive Taliban political cell at the University, and they knew that it had strong support among students in the Islamic Studies Department.

CHAPTER SEVEN

Car Bomb

The trip home took Dawud nearly an hour and a half. This meant that he would miss Mawlawi Ahmed Abdel's Arabic class, but under these circumstances, it could not be helped. Turning the corner onto his street, Dawud could see the front of his house and immediately noticed the ANP patrol car parked at the curb. His stomach suddenly clenched, and every terrible scenario he could imagine flashed through his mind. Had his father been hurt in the bombing – had he been killed? Had his mother changed her mind and gone out? What about his sister? He sprinted the last block, praying all the way that Allah in his mercy had spared his family. Rushing past the empty police car and into the house, Dawud almost collided with Captain Mustafa, who was standing in the entry to their living room. Breathing heavily, Dawud apologized and greeted the Captain. The man was a highly respected Kabul police officer and headed one of the most effective intelligence units in the department. The man was also a close family friend, and was like an uncle to Dawud and his sister Afrah.

Seeing Captain Mustafa heightened Dawud's anxiety, since this was the man who would bring them bad news. Yet, when he entered the living room, his mother and sister turned toward him, and he could see the relief in their eyes. Confused, Dawud walked over to where they were standing, but before he made it halfway across the room, his mother came to him and pulled him into her embrace. As she did so, he could hear her say, "I have been praying to Allah that he would spare you, and he has answered my prayers. Allah be praised, for you are safe, my son." Dawud could see the tears form in his mother's eyes and then felt his sister step up close to him and take his hand. There were tears in her eyes, as well, and it was then that he realized they had been worried about him. After all, he had been the closest to the bombings, and the bus, the one he would have normally taken, drove directly by the detonations.

Captain Mustafa cleared his throat and said, "I was just reassuring your mother that you would be safe, and here you are, Allah be praised. And yes, your father is also safe. I have visited with him only twenty minutes ago and he has been worried about you." The man paused for a moment, his expression became solemn, and then he continued, "Regrettably...the bombings that occurred this afternoon have taken the lives of General Jawid Sajadi, his two bodyguards, and six civilians. In the events that followed, two of my officers were killed. A car, loaded with explosives, rammed General Sajadi's motorcade, just north of the Artal Bridge. My men were in the lead car, providing a police escort. They tried to reach the General but were fired upon by two men, one of whom wore an explosive vest, which he detonated. The explosion killed the police officers as well as the suicide bomber. The other gunman survived the blast and fired on people that were trying to help. In the confusion, he slipped away, but his injuries were serious and he will not get far."

Captain Mustafa paused for a second before saying, "I have had the sad duty to inform General Sajadi's wife, Madame Huma, of this tragedy. A police woman is with her and I have assigned a patrol car to be stationed outside her home...It is still possible that al-Qaeda will want to kill Madame Huma, as a warning to others.

Your husband was made aware of this tragedy and has been summoned to the Ministry. He worried that he could not be here, so he asked me to provide a police escort for you, Madame. He thought that you would want to pay your respects to your friend Madame Huma." Dawud's mother interrupted, saying, "Yes, Captain Mustafa, I am very grateful for your offer, but you have lost two of your men, and I am sure you have far more important things to do. I am quite capable of taking a taxi, as I have done many times before." Captain Mustafa replied, saying, "I beg you, Madame Nikoo, reconsider. I am already here and it is no bother. And, Madame Nikoo, you know your husband. I personally do not have the courage to tell him that I have failed to persuade you." This brought a brief smile to Dawud's mother's face, as she considered Captain Mustafa's words. Dawud was sure she was thinking of all those times Captain Mustafa had singlehandedly taken on every kind of thug, murderer, rapist, and crazed insurgent imaginable. They all knew that Captain Mustafa, for all practical purposes, was unfamiliar with the concept of fear. After a moment of careful thought, Madame Nikoo replied.

"Captain Mustafa, if there is one thing you do not lack, it is courage. Please forgive me, I am being stubborn, and it is not the right time to be stubborn. I know my husband wishes for me to be safe and I know that you, too, are trying to protect me. Yes...yes of course I will accept you as my police escort, and I thank you for your kindness." Madame Nikoo was again silent as her expression turned sad, and she looked toward the window and said, "I must not forget how sad a day this is. I cannot imagine how Madame Huma feels....how lost she must be. I must do whatever I can to comfort my friend."

Dawud's mother turned toward Captain Mustafa and asked, "Please excuse me for a moment?"

Captain Mustafa straightened and immediately replied, "Yes Madame, of course."

As they waited for Dawud's mother to return, Dawud looked over at Captain Mustafa, who seemed immersed in thought. He was of modest height and had a solid, stocky build. He wore a neatly trimmed mustache and kept his hair very short. Dawud noticed that he had become greyer since he had last seen him. His facial features were best described as rugged and his expressions could change from hard as steel to soft as a puppy. His small eyes took in everything at once. The man was quick to smile and had a good-natured sense of humor. Over the years, he had become a bit fleshier, but his barrel chest, thick neck, and beefy hands could not help but remind you of a powerful bull.

Dawud would never forget the day he saw Captain Mustafa fight off two larger men, swinging metal pipes. They were going to teach him a lesson and made the mistake of attacking him in his own home. Dawud was only 10 and had persuaded his mother to let him spend the day with Captain Mustafa. Captain Mustafa had promised to show him around the police station, and take him for a ride in his police car. His mother had reluctantly agreed and had dropped him off at the Captain's house. It was still early, so he and Captain Mustafa sat around a table, discussing what they planned to do. He had just finished his tea when they heard a heavy thud, then Dawud remembered seeing wood splintering as the front door flew open. Two men, carrying metal pipes, burst in, and seeing Captain Mustafa, they immediately charged directly at him. Ten seconds later, the two men lay unconscious and bleeding from their noses and mouths. Captain Mustafa was inspecting the door frame and bemoaning the damage. Dawud had not completely escaped unscathed. When Captain Mustafa had delivered his final fusillade of blows, one attacker had been thrown sideways, slamming into the table with such force, it disintegrated. Pieces of wood and glass were flung in all directions. One piece of glass struck Dawud on the back of his right hand, leaving a fairly small but deep cut. It had not hurt much, and Dawud was proud of the injury and the scar that would follow. For years, he thought of Captain Mustafa as a kind of superhero. Unfortunately, Dawud's mother was not as pleased. That was the last time she had allowed Dawud to stay with Captain Mustafa. It was not that his parents blamed the Captain – on the contrary, both his father and mother had only the greatest respect for the man and thought of him as a dear friend. He was almost a member of the family. But they were also quite aware of the constant attempts on his life, and thought it would be too dangerous to have a child around him.

Only a few minutes had passed when Dawud's mother returned wearing a black Hijab and a long, black coat. These were familiar to Dawud, these were his mother's mourning clothes. She had worn these many times before and had once told him that she had lost almost all of her friends, and wondered when it would be her turn.

Madame Nikoo looked at Captain Mustafa, and then at Dawud and his sister, Afrah. Dawud could see the sadness in her eyes. He knew his mother felt a deep sorrow for Madame Huma, but, he also knew that his mother was thinking how she would feel if Captain Mustafa had come to tell her that her husband was...dead.

Dawud's mother's voice trembled, just slightly, as she asked, "Please, my friend, would you take me to Madame Huma now?"

Captain Mustafa subtly gestured to Dawud to accompany them to the patrol car. Once Madame Nikoo had been seated in the back, and the door was closed, Captain Mustafa looked up at Dawud and spoke.

"Dawud, your father and General Jawid had both served as Lieutenant Generals in the ANA, and, prior to that, as Major Generals in the United Islamic Front. We know al-Qaeda targeted General Jawid. They killed him because General Jawid had many secular views that he openly espoused. Now you may ask, where did he get these...dangerous ideas? Well Dawud, he got them from your father." Captain Mustafa paused for a moment and then continued, "It is truly a miracle that your father is still alive. In the last twelve months, there have been fourteen attempts on his life."

Captain Mustafa looked away for a moment as he struggled with what he should say. Then, looking at Dawud with a grave expression, he continued, "My informants have told me that al-Qaeda is planning to detonate another bomb. This time it will be at General Jawid's funeral, and your father is the target. I have spoken with him, but he dismisses the threat and insists on attending.... He has said that not attending the funeral would dishonor General Jawid's memory and it would be an insult to his grieving widow.

Your father has asked me not to mention the threat to your mother and I have not. But I ask you to speak with your father, and persuade him to stay away. There are many ways he can show his respect without becoming a martyr." Captain Mustafa again paused and then said, "Dawud, these are again, dangerous times. Too many of our people have closed their eyes, but the day is coming when they will be forced to open their eyes, and when they do, they will find their heads on the chopping block.

Sadly, there are too few of us left, so it will be necessary for your father to be very careful...your whole family must be careful. The ANP cannot be trusted and the Army is not much better."

Captain Mustafa's words kept repeating in Dawud's head as he watched the patrol car drive away. He had never before been asked to intervene in such a way. Was it his place to tell his father what to do?

CHAPTER EIGHT

Mujahideen

In December, 1979, the Soviet Army invaded Afghanistan and two months later, a young, idealistic, college graduate named Morad Hawadi began his life as a mujahid. After nearly a decade of fighting the Soviets, on February 15th, 1989 the Soviets were driven from Afghanistan, and the country almost immediately fell into a violent civil war. Mujahideen factions that had once been allied, turned on each other. One of these factions was the Taliban and with Pakistan providing weapons, training, and financial support they soon came to dominate the battlefield.

Sometime between 1988 and 1989 the Maktab al-Khidamat, which was known as the "Afghan Services Bureau," remade itself into what was to be called al-Qaeda ("the Base"). Though al-Qaeda's focus was a global Jihad, it and the Taliban shared many of the same fundamentalist Islamic tenets. Being natural allies, al-Qaeda established a headquarters in the country and funneled money and foreign fighters to the Taliban.

Morad Hawadi had rejected the religious fundamentalism of both groups and had fought with a band of mujahideen opposing the Taliban onslaught. Then, in September of 1993, Morad Hawadi was leading a raiding party that was ambushed, and he was wounded. Though his wounds were not life-threatening, he needed some time to recover. He was taken to a remote mountain camp, where he encountered a beautiful and spirited young woman, who was named Nikoo. He immediately fell in love and they were soon married. A year later, Morad Hawadi and Nikoo would have a son, whom they would name Dawud.

When Morad Hawadi returned to the fighting, he was given command of a small, highly skilled unit that specialized in infiltration and assassination. This unit became so effective that al-Qaeda commanders targeted him specifically, and placed a substantial bounty on his head. Soon, attempts on his life became frequent, and on four separate occasions, suicide bombers had killed his entire security detail, but had left him with only minor injuries. With each attempt, his reputation grew and soon he had become a legend. Commander Morad Hawadi's popularity both pleased and worried his commanders. He had managed to instill discipline, and a feeling of pride, camaraderie, and loyalty in a bunch of illiterate farmers. But they lost many Commanders and feared that if he were to be killed, it would demoralize his unit, and possibly the entire army. So Commander Morad Hawadi was ordered to take some time off. He was told to disappear for a little while, and let things calm down.

Morad Hawadi and Nikoo had very little money, they had a 3-year-old son, and she was pregnant again. Still, Nikoo managed to stretch what they had, and put together at least one decent meal every day. It was winter, and this sometimes meant there would be no money for heating oil. Nikoo would always say that she did not mind, because it gave her a good excuse to cuddle up to her husband, and to hold her little boy close to her.

It was on one of these wintery afternoons when Jawid Sajadi came by. Jawid Sajadi and Morad Hawadi where both young mujahideen Commanders and close friends.

Jawid Sajadi was having a family problem and wanted some advice from his friend, but when he saw the conditions under which the Hawadi family lived, he had an idea, and after a moment, said, "My friend, I have a proposition for you. We, that is my wife Huma and our little girl Mitra, live on a small, but prosperous farm that had belonged to Huma's grandfather. The house is large, we have plenty of wood to keep it warm, and we have plenty of chickens and goats. He explained that, "As you know, Hawadi, I am also a Commander and I will be away for long periods of time. My wife, Huma, she is precious to me, but she is a city girl and knows nothing about the farm. My little daughter, Mitra, is three years old, but she is not well. Huma is having some...difficulty caring for her, and the farm. So my friend, would you and Nikoo do me a kindness, and move in with us?" Jawid Sajadi paused, but before Morad Hawadi could say anything, he continued, "I see that Nikoo is pregnant and will have the baby soon. Would it not be better for Nikoo to have Huma there to help her? You know as well as I do that we both will soon return to the field and rejoin our units. Would it not be better that Nikoo and Huma have each other?

Morad Hawadi and Nikoo accepted but were initially unsure about the arrangement. When they arrived at the farm, and first saw Huma and Mitra, they immediately knew how desperate things had become.

Huma was far too thin, there were dark circles beneath her eyes, and she was at the edge of physical exhaustion. Their little girl, Mitra, was bedridden, her skin was pale, and she had a terrible cough. The farm was also in need of help. From what Morad Hawadi could see, the goats had not been milked nor had the chickens been fed. Minutes after Huma had been introduced to Nikoo, the woman broke down into tears.

Three days would pass and then Jawid Sajadi would be called back to his unit. He would leave the next morning, but before departing, he had taken Morad Hawadi off to the side, and, holding back tears, told him that Huma and Mitra were the most important things in the world to him. For weeks, he had not been able to sleep or eat, worrying about them. But now that he and Nikoo were there, he was sure that everything would be all right.

At first, everything was all right. It had taken them a few days to get things in order, and then they had settled into a busy, but pleasant routine. About a month after Jawid Sajadi had left, Nikoo had her baby. She wept for hours, not because she was sad, but rather because she was happy that her husband could be with her. A week later, Morad Hawadi was also ordered back. It was only a few days after Morad Hawadi had left, that Huma became ill, and then late on a cold February night, Mitra coughed one last time and slipped away. Nikoo desperately tried to revive the child, but it was no use. Allah had chosen to take the little girl.

Her daughter's death devastated Huma. She blamed herself for being ill, for not being a good mother. Huma refused to eat, and she would not sleep, or even speak. Days went by, and the days turned into weeks. Nikoo took care of the farm, her son, her new baby girl, and Huma. There had been no word from Morad Hawadi nor from Jawid Sajadi. This was to be expected, but she had still hoped. It was the beginning of March when Huma showed her first sign of recovering, and it would take another three weeks before the woman would again "join the living." During the next two months, Nikoo and Huma became good friends, as close as sisters. But Huma would never quite recover. The petite, frail young women would seem cheerful and full of energy, but then late at night, Nikoo would hear her weeping.

Commander Morad Hawadi spent that spring fighting the Taliban in Daghlan and Nurestan Provinces. In late summer, he was called back to the United Islamic Front Headquarters in Taleqan, where he was promoted to Senior Commander, and made an "Aide" to Amad Shah Massoud, himself. The posting was in Taleqan, and Taleqan was about two hours north of Jawid Sajadi's farm. Commander Morad Hawadi was given a living allowance that was large enough to have his family come live with him. But Nikoo could not abandon Huma. Huma had always been kind and generous to them. And, of course, Morad Hawadi would never forget how Jawid Sajadi and Huma had made it possible for his family to have full stomachs and to be warm and comfortable, even on the coldest winter nights. The farm was a good place, a place where his wife was happy and his children had thrived. It had also become clear that Huma would never be completely well. Her frequent bouts of illness had eventually damaged her heart and she had little strength. By herself, she would not be able to take care of the farm. So, Morad Hawadi used his housing allowance to buy an old car, which he used to drive to the farm. There, Nikoo would always be waiting for him and they would be a family, if only for a few hours.

The war had come to a stalemate, with neither the United Islamic Front nor the Taliban making any headway, and then on September 9th 2001, Amad Shah Massoud – The Lion of Panjshir, was assassinated by two al-Qaeda suicide bombers. This was a major blow to the United Islamic Front, since Amad Shah Massoud was the only man who was able to hold the alliance together. Then, two days later, on September 11th, 2001, al-Qaeda terrorists hijacked four passenger planes, crashing two of them into the Twin Towers of the World Trade Center, and another one into the Pentagon. A fourth plane crashed into a field, in the state of Pennsylvania, after a group of brave passengers attacked the hijackers, keeping them from completing their mission. By October, 2001, the stalemate was completely smashed. The United States, United Kingdom, and Australia, in an alliance with the United Islamic Front (Northern Alliance), launched what the Americans called Operation Enduring Freedom. In a matter of weeks, the Taliban regime had collapsed and the Taliban leadership had fled to Pakistan.

Eventually, the United Islamic Front would become part of the Afghanistan National Army (ANA) and Morad Hawadi would be promoted to Brigadier General. As he became more senior in rank, he was assigned to the National Military Command Center in Kabul, where he and his family were united. Jawid Sajadi had also moved up in rank, and he and Huma returned to Kabul, where they lived in the house that Huma had grown up in. Huma's father had died and Huma had inherited the house, the farm, and numerous other properties, as well as a significant amount of money.

Much of Kabul was severely damaged, and it was still infested with al-Qaeda cells, Taliban, and other insurgent groups. Given General Morad Hawadi's experience and reputation, he was put in command of a unit whose task was to hunt down and destroy the largest and the most dangerous of these groups. He became known as "the Scorpion of Kabul," for his men struck unexpectedly, often at night, and their attacks were always lethal.

Soon, the Hawadi family had enough money to purchase a home in Northern Kabul, in the relatively wealthy Wazir Akbar Khan neighborhood. Jawid Sajadi and Huma lived less than a kilometer away, and Nikoo and Huma would speak with each other nearly every day.

By the time General Morad Hawadi retired, he had achieved the rank of Lieutenant General. On the day of his retirement, General Jawid Sajadi was promoted to Lieutenant General and was assigned to Morad Hawadi's command. The two men had remained close and it was General Jawid Sajadi who had insisted that his friend become an adviser to the Ministry of Defense.

In addition to being a Ministry of Defense adviser, Morad Hawadi started a wholesale fruit and nut distributorship and an export business, which quickly flourished, and now he could provide his family a few luxuries. Nikoo could buy whatever she wanted. Dawud and his sister Afrah could have fashionable clothing, new tennis shoes, and even a computer and cell phone. The children attended good schools and they could afford tutors, to polish their skills. They even had money for a new car.

Even in his late fifties, retired General Morad Hawadi was still a tall, handsome man. His tanned and ruddy complexion testified to the many years he had spent out of doors. His face bore several scars, old battle wounds that, rather than disfiguring him, made him look more authoritative...more masculine. To both his external enemies and his internal adversaries, the scars had caused hesitation, and a reluctance to act too rashly.

Over the years, his hair had become thinner, but was still mostly a deep, brown color that was now highlighted with grey. He wore a thick, neatly trimmed beard that was the same color as his hair. There was a military bearing about the man, a sense of confidence and authority that was further accentuated by his trim physique, broad shoulders, and a straight back. Even to Dawud, there was something about his father that made you want to stand at attention and salute.

Remarkably, even after decades of war and hardship, he had been left whole. His mind was sharp and clear, and he was still strong and physically robust. Yet, Morad Hawadi had undergone a change. He had lost his taste for battle, or more accurately, his taste for killing. Now, his only true passions were his wife, Nikoo, and his two children. There was something else that had changed. Though Morad Hawadi still thought of himself as a Muslim, he did not have the faith of his youth. These days, Morad Hawadi worried about his religion. He worried that far too many Muslims had turned a blind eye to the intolerance and savagery perpetrated in the name of Islam. Something was very wrong.

CHAPTER NINE

Funeral

Dawud was in his room, waiting, when he finally heard the sound of the front door opening and his father's voice. In his mind, Dawud could picture his mother and father as they greeted each other. It was always the same, for as far back as he could remember. As his father came through the door, his mother would be waiting. She would approach her husband and they would reach for each other and embrace. For a few seconds, neither would speak, they would just hold each other, as if the outside world didn't exist. His mother's eyes would search her husband's face and she would immediately know if something was troubling him. Years later, Dawud would think of his parents and the way they would greet each other. He would ache to see them just one more time.

The news of General Jawid's death would have brought sadness to both of his parents, and Dawud was sure they would want to speak about it. But he could wait no longer, and burst from his room. He needed to talk to his father.

Morad Hawadi was putting on his slippers as Dawud approached him and said, "Father, may I speak with you?" Morad Hawadi raised his head and looked at his son curiously. Dawud could see the sadness in his eyes, as the man replied, "My son, what is troubling you?"

Dawud had spent hours rehearsing what he would say, but now, it all seemed...so awkward. Nevertheless, he continued, "I'm sorry Father, it cannot wait. It is important, but I must speak with you.... privately."

Morad Hawadi studied Dawud's face for a moment and then replied, "Yes, yes I see, of course."

He then turned to his wife and gripped her hand, as he said, "Nikoo, would you please excuse us, I believe our son has something he wishes to discuss...in private." Curious, Dawud's mother studied him for a moment, but seeing the seriousness in her son's expression, she did not pursue her curiosity, but instead smiled and replied, "Of course, speak to our son." She then went up, onto her tip toes, and kissed her husband softly on his cheek. Morad Hawadi smiled at his wife, released her hand, and he and Dawud walked to the modest sized room that Morad Hawadi had used as an office.

When the door was closed, Dawud's father stepped back from him, studied him for a brief moment, and then said, "Son, am I correct to assume you have spoken with Captain Mustafa?" Dawud suddenly felt that his father knew what he was going to ask, or at least part of it. Replying, he said, "Yes sir." Morad Hawadi then continued, "Then you are aware that, this afternoon, my friend, General Jawid, was killed?" Dawud replied, "Yes Father." Morad Hawadi paused, momentarily, as he thought of his friend and the last time they had spoken. General Jawid had tried to persuade him to enter politics. He had said the National Assembly was dominated by miserable, narrow-minded men who would be more adept at herding goats, than governing a nation. Realizing that he had been distracted, Morad Hawadi said, "I am sorry Dawud. I... I have not let you speak. Now Son, what is it that you wanted to say?" Dawud replied, "Sir, Captain Mustafa said that al-Qaeda planned to attack the funeral procession and that you would be a target." Morad Hawadi did not immediately reply. Instead, he looked toward his bookshelves. Then, after nearly a minute, he said, "Ah yes, my dear friend Captain Mustafa. He is a good man. Did he mention that two of his men were also killed?" Dawud replied, "Yes, Father. He said they were killed by the second suicide bomber, while trying to reach General Jawid's car." Morad Hawadi continued, "Yes...that is also what I have been told. These were good men. Two of Captain Mustafa's best. He was close to their families. He had attended the agiqah (the welcoming celebration) for their children. Of course, Captain Mustafa intends to attend the funerals of these two men, and it is only natural and right that he do so. But I suspect Captain Mustafa did not mention that al-Qaeda has also targeted him, and that at least two men have already been selected to ...martyr themselves. As we now speak, these men are being prepared. They will be wearing explosive vests and they will try to infiltrate the funeral procession. One man will work his way toward Captain Mustafa, and when he is as close as he can get, he will detonate the explosives. The second man will be some distance away, and after the first detonation he will move in, and if Captain Mustafa has survived the initial detonation, the second bomber will try to finish him off. As I understand it, these threats have not dissuaded Captain Mustafa from attending. Now why is it that he is willing to risk his life to attend this funeral?"

Morad Hawadi paused for a moment and then continued.

"Yes, of course he would not tell you these things, and why should he...Captain Mustafa was here to try to protect me.

Now, please forgive me, Son, I have been rambling while you have something you wish to tell me." Dawud wasn't quite sure how to reply. He knew his father well and realized that he had once again been "set up." He had just been provided what his father called "context"...information that would influence what he had to say. This was one of his favorite tactics, one Dawud was familiar with, and one that tended to frustrate him, because it almost always made something that was black and white, suddenly seem grey. It took Dawud a moment to reply, but when he did he looked directly into his father's eyes with as much determination and confidence as he could gather, and said, "Sir, I...I will be accompanying you to General Jawid's funeral."

Dawud's father was momentarily taken aback, and, as he processed what his son had said, he realized that he had been outmaneuvered. This immediately made him feel intensely proud of his son, and, just as quickly, frightened as to where it would lead. It took Morad Hawadi a long time to reply, and when he did, he said, "Yes...I can see what you are thinking, but I do not believe that me attending the funeral, and you attending it, are equivalent...Still, I can already hear your arguments, and I imagine my responses would not be as credible as I had once hoped. Unfortunately, it seems that I do not have a choice.... We shall attend General Jawid's funeral...together, as father and son...Allah have mercy on me, for I fear your mother is going to kill me, and I fear her far more than I fear al-Qaeda."

Leaving his father's office, Dawud saw his mother patiently waiting for them. As Nikoo always did, she studied her husband's face and immediately saw the worry in his eyes. She would wait until they were in bed, before she would query her husband and he would tell her that their son would be attending the funeral with him.

Morad Hawadi did not tell her about the threats. It was not necessary. People were always trying to kill Morad Hawadi, and somehow, he always survived. It was true that he was a careful man, but it was just as true that her husband was a ferocious fighter, a man who did not hesitate putting himself at risk. Nikoo had heard many stories about her husband, how it was a miracle that he was still alive. How suicide bombers had detonated themselves near him, killing everyone but him. His enemies had thought of him as being bewitched, while his friends thought that Allah considered him as special and was watching over him. But Nikoo knew there was something else. She had sensed it when she had first met him, and she sensed it now. If Morad Hawadi had been an ordinary man, she would have been a widow long ago. But did this...specialness extend to their son? She did not know, and that now troubled her greatly. Nikoo became silent for a long time. Later, while lying nestled in her husband's arms, she would ask, "When will this end? Will there ever be a day that I will not have to worry about someone trying to kill you?" Nikoo paused, and then continued, "My husband, will you be able to protect our son?" Morad Hawadi did not answer...He did not know the answer.

Over a thousand people turned out for General Jawid's funeral. Many were high-ranking officers, important politicians, and men who had served beneath the General. No snipers, no suicide bombers attacked their procession, probably because security had been so tight. Both police and military were present and lined the route. Many plainclothes officers mingled with the crowd and dozens of checkpoints had been set up. No one got near the procession without first being searched. Later, it would be learned that 37 men had been turned away, and another 14 had been arrested. Dozens more were observed turning around before they reached the check points.

The funeral for the two ANP officers had not gone as smoothly. ANP officers were using their newly acquired IR Bomb Detection device. They were scanning a group of men approaching the funeral precession, when the machine began "beeping." It had detected the IR signatures of explosive vests on two different men. They were walking about 30 meters apart and both had attached themselves to group of mourners who were heading directly toward the heart of the procession. Fortunately, they would have to pass through a gate in a concrete barricade, which was immediately ordered closed. Loudspeakers announced that there had been an accidental gasoline spill, and another access gate was being opened at Wazir Road, three blocks west. This directed the mourners through a mostly industrial area and gave the ANP time to isolate the bombers.

Plainclothes ANP officers infiltrated the group of mourners who were now walking west, and through some clever maneuvering, directed one of the bombers into an alleyway. It took the man a few seconds to realize that he had been cut off from the other mourners, and was now alone. At first he was confused, then he saw the armored vehicle rumbling toward him. The man raised his arms, he cried out Allahu Akbar, Allahu Akbar, Allahu Akbar, and detonated the explosives. Hearing the explosion, the second man stopped and looked around. Seeing several plainclothes ANP officers approaching, his hand clamped around a detonator, but before he could press the button, a 7.62 mm round smashed through the base of his skull, dropping him like a rag doll. There would be no one to interrogate, but there was also no one hurt, thanks to Sergeant Rahim, the ANP sniper who had made the shot. However, Sergeant Rahim was not particularly happy about what he had done. Everything had happened too fast, so he had not had time to think. If he had chosen not to fire or if he had missed, and the bomber had blown himself up, Sergeant Rahim would have anonymously received a package of ten, one-hundred Euro bills. Now, all he was likely to get was some meaningless commendation, and he would be lucky if he didn't get a bullet in his own head.

After the funeral, Dawud and his father were given a ride home in an unmarked ANP car. They didn't speak much. Dawud was high on adrenalin, and had heard about how the ANP had averted an attack. At 18, this had been the first time he had intentionally placed himself in this kind of danger. Surprisingly, he had not been afraid. Of course, he knew his courage had been small, or even insignificant, when compared to his father's courage or the courage of Captain Mustafa. These men had proven themselves a thousand times over. But still, Dawud was glad he had walked by his father's side. Being there had made him feel proud; it had made him feel like a man.

These days, Dawud's father gave no thought to his personal courage; he had been fighting in wars for much of his life, faced numerous enemies, and he had been the one who had survived. Certainly courage was part of it, and so were skill, strength, and intelligence, but he had killed, and he had seen men die who were braver, more skilled, stronger, and more intelligent than he was. Early on, Morad Hawadi had suspected that other forces were at play, and that his survival had as much to do with things that were far beyond his understanding, not to mention his control. A stray bullet was just as lethal as a well-aimed one. He, and many of his war-weary comrades, no longer exhibited the classical symptoms of fear, but, instead had come to accept that their fate was, in large part, predetermined. It was not so much that some invisible hand shielded them, but rather that some sequence of events, set in motion long ago, had caused them to be precisely who they were, what they were, and where they were. He had often wondered how differently things would have turned out, if he had been born one fraction of a second earlier, or later. For one fraction of a second had often been all that had separated him from death, and that same fraction had permitted him to kill another human being. However, on this day, Morad Hawadi had felt fear, not for himself, but for his son.

As they approached the house, Dawud could see his mother standing in their doorway, her arms crossed and with an anxious expression on her face. Seeing her husband and son exit the vehicle, her relief was almost palpable, and she could be seen straightening up as if a great weight had been lifted from her shoulders. From her nervous restlessness, it was obvious that she desperately wanted to run to them and take them both in her arms, but she held back, knowing that decorum prescribed that she not publically embarrass them with such a physical display of emotion. But as they approached, her false composure disintegrated and she rushed toward them, reaching out. They reached for her as well and she finally embraced both of them as tightly as she could. A moment later a second set of arms embraced them. It was Afrah, she was sobbing quietly, and held onto them so tightly that Dawud was actually having trouble holding back his own tears.

CHAPTER TEN

Acid

Dawud's mother, Nikoo, was an attractive, slim, middle-aged woman with fine features and long, shiny, chestnut-colored hair that was now showing traces of grey. She had the slim, well-proportioned physique of an athletic woman. Her eyes were bright and intelligent and she was known to be highly spirited, and had an endless supply of energy.

Nikoo Hawadi had brought Dawud's father immeasurable joy and comfort, as well as occasional consternation. He often, albeit half-heartedly, blamed the latter on his wife's mother, who had been half Scottish and had insisted on sending Nikoo to an English boarding school, for what she called a good primary education. While there, Nikoo had perfected her English and had developed a strong academic foundation. By the time she had returned to Afghanistan, she had been irreversibly Westernized. She spoke English fluently, loved reading – mostly American and British authors, and loved geology and architecture. Although the opportunities to promote her views were limited, she campaigned for what she called "Natural Feminism."

This was not an American, or even a European feminism. Nikoo expected equal opportunity and equal pay for equal performance. But she also demanded that the genders be recognized as fundamentally different from one another. She would always say, "A thousand good women will always be better than a thousand good men, at certain things, while a thousand good men will always be better than a thousand good women, at certain other things. To not recognize these differences is to ignore Nature itself."

Dawud's father and mother would have many lively and thoughtful discussions on this subject. It would usually start with Dawud's mother presenting a recent insight she had, or a concept she was forming. Since these ideas tended to incorporate many philosophically Western notions, and, because she believed that to master a language, one must be able to use the language effectively and rapidly articulate complex and abstract arguments, she used English rather than Pashto. Although

Dawud's father's English was decidedly inferior to his wife's, he went along, knowing that the exercise would improve his English. More importantly, he knew his children would benefit from observing what he hoped were amiable and thoughtful exchanges, on important subjects that were often too sensitive or controversial to be discussed outside of their home. Morad Hawadi hoped they would eventually want to participate and have their own opinions.

Often the discussions became quite lively and Dawud's father would break the "English only" rule and unconsciously switch between English and Pashto. This would bring a howl of protest from Dawud and his sister, who rarely had the opportunity to correct their father. On other occasions, Dawud and his sister would be delighted by their father's mispronunciation of a word or his misusage of a phrase. There was a quasi-formal process to these debates. First Dawud's mother would present her position as concisely and eloquently as she could, then Dawud's father would present his supposedly brilliant, albeit bilingually botched opposing view point, doing his best to appear confident and superior. Then they would argue back and forth until their points were made and nothing new was being offered. At this point, they would attempt to summarize their positions...but more often than not, Dawud's father would simply succumb to his wife's intelligence and quick wit, not to mention her boundless energy, irrepressible spirit, and advanced preparation. Inevitably he would make an exaggerated gesture of surrender, all the while smiling with a clear sense of pride. It was obvious Morad Hawadi absolutely loved his wife and he would not want her to change in any way. On those occasions when Dawud's mother would win a particularly important concession, she would pump her fists into the air and do a victory dance around the room. This would never fail to bring laughter from Dawud, his sister, and even from their father. Her lighthearted gloating would last only seconds before she would playfully stroll over to her husband and they would put their arms around each other, holding each other as if they were two halves of something that was drawn together by a force of nature.

Of course, these physical displays of affection were relatively rare in a religiously conservative country like Afghanistan, and were considered un-Islamic and vulgar by many people. However, in their home, these displays of affection were common and acted as a kind of nourishment and a source of comfort. This was one of those Western behaviors that Nikoo had observed while at boarding school in England, and had deliberately chosen to adopt and weave deeply into the fabric of the home she would build for her family. At first, her husband had not been comfortable with these open displays, but gradually her tenderness and the gentle touching of his hand and his arm as they sat next to each other, became something he expected and actually began to crave. He missed her not sitting next to him, he missed the warmth of her skin, the smell of her hair, and soon he was reaching for her, holding her hand, and touching her arm as she passed. Now he was hooked, and nothing felt more natural than holding his wife's hand, gently brushing her hair away from her eyes, and putting his arms around her.

As time passed, Dawud would recall these days as some of the best of his life. He loved the University and was getting good grades. His father now only traveled occasionally and the trips had to do with his business, not war. His sister Afrah was becoming a beautiful young woman, and had her mother's spirit and boundless energy. And his mother was almost glowing with happiness and pride in her family. It was as if they lived separate from the world around them.

Afghanistan was slowly disintegrating. The Islamists were growing more powerful, suicide bombings had increased, and Taliban religious leaders had issued a decree that banned girls above the age of 8 from receiving an education. In their view, "Female education is against Islamic teachings and spreads vulgarity in Society." They threatened to blow up schools, poison their water, poison their air, and do physical harm to those young girls attending school, and to those who would teach them.

Then, on a crisp, sunny October day, a young, disheveled looking, bearded man wearing a filthy brown jacket, pulled his motorcycle alongside two young girls on their way to school. Studying them with a dark, menacing expression, he barked, "You...you girls are you going to school?" At first the girls were too frightened to answer and just looked down, being sure not to make eye contact. When it looked like the man was starting to get off of his motorcycle, one of the girls answered.

"Yes...yes sir...We are late so we must go now."

In what seemed like blur of motion, the man yanked off the hijab of one of the girls, and with his other hand, splashed the girl's face with a burning acid. The girl was Dawud's sister, Afrah; she had just turned 15 years old, and now her beautiful, flawless skin was blistering as the acid, now beginning to foam, ate its way deeper. Afrah, whose name meant "happiness," screamed and tried to protect herself but it was too late. The man, satisfied with what he had done, mounted his motorcycle and sped off.

Dawud's father was out of town, on one of his now infrequent business trips. Afig had been studying, for a test in his Thermodynamics class, while his mother had just finished folding laundry, and was settling into her favorite chair to read a book, when they were interrupted by a loud knocking at their front door. As Dawud opened the door, he saw that it was Madame Gulnar, the lady from next door. He could see something was wrong. Normally, the woman appeared well-groomed, quite composed, and even a bit formal. However, Dawud had known her for many years, and knew her to be kind and generous, though she could be a little fearful, when it came to her two daughters. The Madame Gulnar now standing in front of him looked frantic, her hair was a mess, and her eyes were red...as if she had been crying. At first, Madame Gulnar couldn't speak and Dawud was sure something had happened to one of her daughters, but then she managed to pull herself together, and in a quiet, trembling voice said, "Dawud...I...I...need to speak to your mother."

Before Dawud could answer, his mother had come up beside him and when she saw the woman she said, "Gulnar, what is it, what has happened?" Madame Gulnar reached out to Dawud's mother and replied, "Nikoo, I am so sorry, something terrible has happened. Please, Nikoo, may I come in?" Madame Gulnar was the mother of the other girl, the girl who had been walking with Afrah to school that morning. When she had entered the house, it would take her only a few moments to convey what she knew, what her daughter had told her had happened to Afrah. Dawud's mother had listened carefully, her hand covering her mouth, her eyes widening with each word. He could see a growing wave of shock, anger, and...fear wash over his mother. Dawud felt his face flush, as what had happened to his sister sank in. It was at that moment that something clicked inside of him, and he immediately knew that their world had changed. Dawud hardly noticed his fingernails digging into his palms as he clenched his fists.

When Madame Gulnar had finished, it took a moment for Dawud's mother to speak, then she looked up at Madame Gulnar and, in a controlled, but very urgent tone of voice, asked, "Gulnar, would...would you be kind enough to drive us to the hospital?" Grateful to be able to do something, and, grateful that, somehow, her friend, Nikoo, had not chosen to blame her or her daughter for this terrible thing, Madame Gulnar replied, "Yes, yes please. I have my car and we can go immediately."

During the drive, no one spoke. Dawud's mother sat up-front, with Madame Gulnar. He could see the tension in her face and her body tremble as she tried to hold in her desperate desire to be at her daughter's side. Dawud's thoughts drifted to his sister. Afrah meant "happiness" and she had truly lived up to her name. She was a sweet, quiet girl, who was curious about everything. Afrah laughed easily and she was smart. But what drew everyone to her most was her patience and her kindness. To the dismay of their parents, she would give away her lunches, her pencils, her notebooks, and once she had even given away her new shoes. Worried that she was not eating, their mother had finally started making her two lunches, and had her promise that she would eat one of them. Afrah had once told him that she never forgot how hard it was when they had lived in the North. Their farm had produced enough food for their family, but many of their neighbors were less fortunate. She remembered when she was only three and her one playmate, Nahal, a little girl about her age, always wanted to play at her house. Afrah's mother would always make them a hot lunch and gave them a piece of bread with jam as a snack. Then one day Nahal stopped coming over. Later she had learned that her friend's mother had died from pneumonia, complicated by severe malnutrition. Nahal was the second youngest of seven children. The children had been split up and sent off to different homes. Nahal, who had been better nourished than her siblings, had been taken in by a couple who would hire her out to a brick making factory, as soon as she was five. Afrah had also learned that her mother had been regularly sending food packages to the family, an extra piece of cheese, a loaf of bread, and even some eggs – when they could be spared. But it was not enough. They had seven children, plus their grandparents lived with them.

On the other side of their farm, was a family of ten. During a particularly cold winter, three of the younger children died from influenza that was again complicated by malnutrition. No one had any money and there just was not enough food to go around. Dawud could also remember these families and had remembered how emaciated everyone had looked. He had only been 7 or 8 but he had felt guilty and sad. Somehow, his family had managed to survive those hard times.

Afrah had told him that she now had more food than she could eat, but many of the "scholarship" girls at her school were not so fortunate. Their tuition had been paid for by a European aid group, but they were usually from poor families and food could be scarce. Dawud had attended a prestigious boys' high school and everyone he knew seemed to be well fed. He knew it was a bubble, and that the daily struggles of too many Afghans were still terribly difficult. So a couple of years ago, he had begun to slip most of his lunch into Afrah's lunch box, so she would have more to give away. About a year later, Dawud's mother had caught him slipping a sandwich into his sister's box, but instead of scolding him she had smiled at him, as her eyes teared up, and she quickly turned away without saying a word.

Afrah was a good student and was liked by her teachers and her classmates. She was really smart and quicker at languages than even Dawud. Like her mother, she loved to read and she would enthusiastically devour book after book. Each evening, Afrah and her mother would go into the kitchen, where they would sit at the breakfast table and talk about her books. One day, Dawud had asked why they went into the kitchen. Why didn't they talk in the living room or dining room? Her mother had told him that she was sure no one would bother them there, since the men in the family seemed to have a natural aversion to the kitchen.

Afrah had once told Dawud that her secret dream was to be a physicist or maybe a chemist, and that she wanted to go to university in the West. Dawud didn't know if that would be possible, but he had promised her that he would do everything he could to make that happen. Now Dawud wondered what would happen to his little sister. How would this...this barbaric act, change her?

As they pulled to a stop, Dawud's mother sprang from the car, with Dawud and Madame Gulnar trailing right behind. The three of them rushed through the dingy, poorly lit corridors in search of someone who could direct them to Afrah's bed. Finally, a nurse pointed them to a ward off of the Receiving Area. At first, they did not recognize Afrah. She was wearing a green hospital gown, her left arm was hooked up to an IV bottle, and her face and right hand were wrapped with heavy gauze bandages. When Dawud realized he was looking at his sister, his heart sank and tears welled up in his eyes. Looking at his mother, he saw, for just a fraction of a second, the pain. Nikoo immediately regained control and bent over her daughter, carefully wrapping her arms around her, and held her. Afrah was awake, but she must have been given a sedative, because her voice was weak and her words were slow to come. When she felt her mother's arms, she began to quietly sob. Dawud could hear Afrah asking over and over again.

"Why did he do this to me? We were wearing our hijabs and we were both respectful. Why momma? Why...why was he so mean?"

At hearing these words, Dawud turned away, placing his hands over his face, and began to weep quietly, hoping Afrah would not hear him. Dawud's mother gently rocked Afrah back and forth in her arms, softly whispering to her that it was not her fault and that everything would be all right. Grief and rage swelled up inside Dawud and he could not even imagine the pain his mother was feeling. After a few minutes or maybe half an hour, Afrah dozed off and her mother gently laid her back down, carefully brushing her hair aside and kissing her forehead, for a long time. Her expression had changed. Dawud had never before seen his mother this angry; her jaw was clenched tightly, flexing the muscles in her cheeks and neck. Her eyes were ablaze with a mixture of grief and raw fury. Dawud was also angry, no he was beyond angry. He wanted to hunt this animal down, and when he found him, he would beat him to death with his bare hands. This animal was surely not human, no human could do such a thing. Dawud felt his grip tightening on the metal frame of Afrah's bed. When he looked down, he saw he had made deep indents in the metal in the form of his fingers. This surprised Dawud since he had never been particularly strong, and had always thought of himself as a student or maybe, someday, an engineer. The rage he was feeling and the display of brute strength were new to him and momentarily confused him.

Dawud's mother slowly stood and turned to Dawud, saying, "Dawud, please, please do not let your sister wake up alone." She then turned to leave, but immediately stopped, turned back, and raised her hand to touch Dawud's face. Stroking his cheek and running her fingers through his hair, she said, "I love you Dawud, you must watch your sister for me...please. I will be back soon."

She then hesitantly turned and walked away, gesturing to Madame Gulnar to follow her.

CHAPTER ELEVEN

Hospital

Dawud anxiously paced, as he watched Afrah for any sign that she was awake. As the minutes ticked by, he became growingly concerned about his mother, and chided himself for not asking where she was going. Nearly an hour had passed, when Dawud noticed a doctor walking toward him. He was a middle-aged man, of medium height, and graying hair. He wore thick glasses; a crisp, white coat; and the obligatory stethoscope hung from around his neck. The man introduced himself as Dr. Usman. Dawud immediately explained that he was Afrah's brother and began to query the doctor about his sister's condition.

Dr. Usman studied Dawud and, at first, he was unsure whether Dawud was the right person to talk to. Still, there was something about this unassuming young man that intrigued him. Actually, he had felt the same way when he had first seen the girl. There was something about both of these young people that was at first captivating, and then, strangely...disturbing. He had been a doctor for over 20 years, and he had treated prime ministers, warlords, tribal chieftains, and dozens of prominent Clerics, yet, he had never once been impressed by these men. So why did these two have such an effect on him? After a moment, Dr. Usman brought up the clipboard he was carrying, and began to read:

"The patient arrived at the hospital at 10:05 AM." Dr. Usman paused reading, and said, "I was the admitting physician, and I performed the initial assessment of your sister's condition." Then he continued, "The patient, who identified herself as Afrah Hawadi, was conscious and alert. She was suffering from moderate to severe acid burns to the left side of her face and her left eye. She also had several minor acid burns on her right hand. The affected areas were subjected to immediate and prolonged irrigation, and an intravenous infusion of Ringer's lactate solution was begun. Following irrigation, antibiotic ointments were applied and the injuries were bandaged. The patient was given acetaminophen with oxycodone, for pain." Dr. Usman stopped reading, looked up at Dawud, and said, "The burns are not life-threatening – that is, if we can keep the infections under control. However, burns like these can cause significant scarring, which, in turn, can have a psychological effect on the patient. I am sorry, but there will be some difficult times ahead." These words burnt into Dawud's heart, like red-hot irons. His little sister did not deserve this. This was not right.

The doctor went on to explain that the damage would have been much more severe if it had not been for the young girl who had been with Afrah. Dawud knew this girl was Madame Gulnar's daughter, Sarah. It appeared that Sarah had had the presence of mind to immediately flush Afrah's eye and face with water, from a water bottle she was carrying.

When Dawud could think of nothing more to ask, the doctor excused himself and went over to Afrah, where he removed the bandages and examined the injured eye and skin. When he had finished, he looked over at Dawud and said, "The damage to your sister's eye is less severe than I thought. Allah willing, she will again be able to see." It was then that Dawud heard a commotion and saw Madame Gulnar rushing toward him. Stopping directly in front of him, he saw that the woman was sweating, her body was shaking, and her eyes were huge. Dawud looked around for his mother, but could not see her. Turning to Madame Gulnar, he asked, "Madame Gulnar, where is my mother?" The woman was now swaying back and forth and Dawud was sure the woman was going to collapse. As he reached out to support her, the doctor appeared and both men helped her to a chair. Dawud could hear her repeating his mother's name, "Nikoo...Nikoo." Kneeling directly in front of her, Dawud took a breath and then quietly asked, "Madame Gulnar, please, where is my mother...where is Nikoo?"

The mention of Nikoo's name seemed to bring her around, and she looked across at Dawud with such fear in her eyes that he was taken aback. Then in a distant voice, said, "Dawud, I...I should have helped her...I am so sorry." Dawud was now absolutely sure something terrible had happened. It took him a moment before he could speak, then he said, "Please...Please tell me what happened to my mother...to...Nikoo." It took Madame Gulnar a moment, then she began to speak, "Nikoo wanted me to drive to where Afrah had been attacked. She was angry. You know she was angry, you remember, don't you?"

Dawud did remember the expression on his mother's face and nodded to Madame Gulnar, so she would continue. "I was angry too. What kind of person could be so cruel? Nikoo...Nikoo wanted to know who had hurt her daughter. She wanted to know why someone would do such a terrible thing. So I drove her to the place. She got out of the car and started asking people questions. What had they seen and did they know the man that had attacked her daughter? She demanded to know who he was, and where he had gone. Most people did not know anything, and those that had seen what had happened were too afraid to talk. But then one of the women shopkeepers called her over, and they talked for a minute or two. I could not hear what they were saying, but I could see her pointing south toward Zargona Road. When Nikoo...your mother, returned to the car, she told me that the lady had seen the motorcycle go south and turn right at the intersection. She had also told your mother that the motorcycle was red, and it had a broken headlight. Nikoo made me drive up and down Zargona Road three times. The whole time, I was praying to Allah that we would not see anyone. I was afraid, I was afraid what Nikoo might do."

Madame Gulnar was silent for a long moment, and Dawud noticed several other nurses and another doctor were now standing nearby and listening. Then, in a quiet, trembling voice, Madame Gulnar continued, "On the third time we saw him, we both saw him...even though I did not want to see him. There he was, the bearded man in that old, dirty, brown jacket. He...he was standing next to a red motorcycle, and Allah have mercy, the motorcycle had a broken head light.

I told your mother not to get out of the car, we could call the police...they had guns. This was a very bad situation, much too dangerous for a woman. He was an evil man...a man who would hurt little girls. From where I had stopped the car, I could see he was smoking a cigarette. He had such mean eyes, for a young man.

Your mother didn't listen to me, Dawud..... why didn't she listen to me? She said the police would not come, they did not care about this kind of thing...She was right; they never come for things like this. I know Nikoo was very angry. I was angry too, but Dawud, she should have stayed in the car. I told her to stay in the car...maybe we could find someone to help us. I did...I...I really did. But she didn't listen to me. When she saw the man was getting ready to leave, your mother got out of the car. She crossed the street and walked over to the man. I could hear her talking to him, but I could not hear the words. He got very angry and started yelling at her, very loudly – calling her bad names. Your mother did not back away, she kept asking him something. I think she was saying, 'Why did you do such a thing? Why did you hurt my little girl?'

I could now hear her, from in the car. I wanted to get out and bring her back. People stopped and watched like it was a show. The man then raised his hand and he hit your mother across the face. He hit her hard because she fell down and I could see blood on her face. She was trying to get up when I saw another man step toward your mother. I don't know where he came from, he must have come out of one of the shops. I thought he was going to help your mother. I thought every-thing would be all right. But then I saw he had a gun in his hand. Even then I thought maybe he was going to stop this man, even arrest him......
Instead he...he put the gun to your mother's forehead and said some-thing. She just stared at him, and then she spit at him. I could not believe my eyes, she was on her knees, looking up at a man holding a gun to her head, and she spit at him. She was not afraid of him, she would not say what he wanted. Dawud...Dawud I'm sorry....He pulled the trigger...he pulled it twice. The back of your mother's head explod-ed. No, No, forgive me Dawud. I should not have told you that. It is just that I cannot forget what I saw. I see it in my mind, over and over again. I'm sorry, please forgive me......They were like animals. They just looked at her lying at their feet. I think the man...the man in that dirty brown jacket, may have kicked at her body, but I don't know this for sure. I was across the street and could not see very well. The two men just stood there, one of them lit another cigarette, and they talked to each other, like they had done nothing wrong and had nothing to fear. Then, after a few minutes, both of them got on the motorcycle and they drove off. I called the police, but you know how they are, it took them a long time to come. I stayed by your mother till they took her body away. I'm sorry Dawud, I did not do anything to stop them. I...I was afraid, these were very bad men and I thought they would kill me too."

Dawud did not know what to say, but even if he had, he could not speak, he could hardly breathe.

The news of what had happened spread fast, and most people re-acted with shock and outrage, but there were also many others who saw the killing of Nikoo and the assault on Afrah as the work of dedi-cated jihadists, men who were true soldiers of Allah. There were a growing number of powerful Imams and Clerics who supported the Taliban decree banning the education of girls. In their minds, it was necessary to make an example of a few, in order to discourage the many from choosing the wrong path.

When the news had reached Captain Mustafa, the tough, old policeman had broken down and wept. With all the mayhem and death he had seen, he thought it could no longer affect him, but he was wrong.

Meanwhile, a military helicopter had been sent to Charikar, to transport Morad Hawadi back to Kabul, and three hours after Nikoo had been shot, the helicopter carrying Morad Hawadi touched down at an ANA airbase just outside of Kabul. Captain Mustafa was waiting for him. The two men embraced, exchanged a few words, and then, Captain Mustafa led him to one of the three waiting patrol cars. The moment their doors closed, the sirens and lights were turned on, and the three cars sped off toward the Kabul CURE Hospital.

As they rode along, sirens screaming, Captain Mustafa did not know what to say to his old friend. He had always been much more elegant with his fists than he had been with his tongue. They had been speeding along for several minutes when Morad Hawadi said, "My friend, can you update me on my daughter's condition?" Captain Mustafa told him what he knew, and then explained that the Director of the hospital was standing by to provide more details. Morad Hawadi then asked about Dawud. Captain Mustafa told him that Dawud had not left his sister's side. On hearing this, Morad Hawadi quietly nodded his head.

As they came to a stop, Morad Hawadi could see the hospital in front of them. He could also see his escorts, a police officer, a doctor, and a nurse. The two men got out of the patrol car, and Captain Mustafa said, "I am sorry, my friend, but I cannot go in with you. I have some serious hunting to do." Morad Hawadi knew what he meant. He knew that Captain Mustafa would not stop until he had tracked down the two men and...dealt with them. But, Morad Hawadi also knew that Captain Mustafa, as good as he was, would not find these men. That job would be his.

As Captain Mustafa drove away, Morad Hawadi turned to his escorts, who introduced themselves, offered their condolences, and then led him to Afrah's room. When it had become known that Afrah was Morad Hawadi's daughter, she had been transferred to a second-floor, private room. The Kabul CURE Hospital was as good as Afghanistan had to offer and Morad Hawadi was grateful his daughter had been taken there. As they got off of the elevator and turned toward Afrah's room he saw another police officer, one of Captain Mustafa's most trusted men, standing guard. He wore body armor, and had a pistol holstered at his waist. The man also had a sub-machinegun slung across his chest, and looked quite proficient at using it. The guard saw them approach and saluted as Morad Hawadi passed. Morad Hawadi opened the door and as he entered, he saw Afrah lying in the hospital bed, the left side of her face bandaged, and an IV inserted in her right arm. Dawud was sitting by her side, holding her hand, and softly speaking to her. The sight caused Morad Hawadi's chest to tighten as his worry for his children and his grief nearly overwhelmed him. Morad Hawadi steeled himself and approached Afrah's bed. When Dawud saw his father, he rose and the two of them embraced, both feeling the other shudder as they tried to hold back their already tattered emotions. They both held each other tightly, without speaking. After several moments, they heard a woman clear her throat and say, "Pasha Hawadi, sir, I apologize for disturbing you, but would you please follow me. The Director is waiting to give you his report." Releasing his father, Dawud saw a nurse standing there. She was the same one who had come into the room with his father. She was young, probably new to nursing, and she seemed a little unsure of herself, and embarrassed at having to disturb them.

Morad Hawadi went over to his daughter's side and gently touched her cheek. She looked up at him, and he could hear her say, "Daddy...It was my fault. I am sorry." Tears welled up in his eyes and he bent over and kissed her cheek softly and whispered, "My little Afrah, you have nothing to be sorry about. It is I that am sorry. I am sorry that I was not there to protect you and your mother. But 'little one,' we must not let this evil defeat us. While we mourn our dead, while we tend to our wounds...while we blame ourselves, they celebrate." After a moment, he straightened up, nodded at the nurse, and he and Dawud followed her out of the room.

The Director was a distinguished man. He was sitting behind a large, highly polished wooden desk. As soon as he saw them enter, he stood up and rushed over to greet them, saying, "Pasha Hawadi, I am Doctor Bachour and am so very honored to meet you, but regret it has to be under such tragic circumstances. I have heard so many...."

Dawud was always impressed by his father's celebrity status. Certainly, he was a famous warrior, but, more than that, he had become a sort of "folk hero," a man whose courage and integrity were beyond question. However, on this day, his father was in no mood for accolades or niceties. Interrupting Dr. Bachour, Morad Hawadi said, "Doctor Bachour, I am sure that you can appreciate my situation, so you will understand that it is necessary for me to speak directly to the doctor that is treating my daughter."

Dr. Bachour's expression hardened, and Dawud could see that the man was disappointed. Yet, as Dr. Bachour considered Morad Hawadi's request, his features again softened and Dawud could see a mixture of understanding and sympathy fill the man's eyes. Dr. Bachour cleared his throat and replied, "Yes, yes, of course, I understand. I will summon Doctor Usman immediately."

Dawud remembered speaking with Dr. Usman and was glad he would be the one to describe Afrah's condition.

A few minutes later, Dr. Usman entered the room. He was obviously nervous as he shuffled through a file folder he had brought with him. Finally, he found what he had been looking for, and looked up at Dr. Bachour, who gestured that he address Pasha Hawadi.

"Sir, the patient arrived at the hospital at about 10:05 AM." Dr. Usman paused reading, and said, "As I have told your son, I was the admitting physician, and I performed the initial assessment of your daughter's condition." Then he continued, "The patient, who identified herself as Afrah Hawadi, was conscious and alert. She suffered from moderate to severe acid burns to the left side of her face and her left eye...."

Dr. Usman's description of Afrah's condition was pretty much the same as he had conveyed to Dawud, except for his latest entries, which read, "The patient is responding exceptionally well and there is evidence that some tissue regeneration has already occurred. For example, ocular surface damage to the left eye had included total epithelial loss, stromal haze, and obscuring of iris detail. When the patient was re-examined three hours later, much of the epithelial tissue had regenerated, stromal haze was clearing, and iris detail was visible. There is no known explanation for the rapidity of recovery." This did not surprise Morad Hawadi nor Dawud. Morad Hawadi and his children had always healed quickly and generally seemed to avoid getting sick. Obviously, this did not mean they didn't get hurt nor did it mean they didn't get sick, but rather that they "bounced back" more quickly than most people. Nikoo, on the other hand, had managed to catch most childhood diseases, got sick to her stomach in the back seat of cars, and seemed to catch colds and the occasional flu on a regular basis. Although she had been glad her family had been so...robust, she often complained that they didn't really appreciate how miserable even a simple cold could make you feel.

As Dr. Usman completed his report, Morad Hawadi said, "Doctor Usman, would you be kind enough to give us your opinion of my daughter's prognosis?"

Dr. Usman momentarily seemed unsure of what to say, then he carefully closed his folder, and then looked directly at Morad Hawadi, and replied, "Sir, I cannot explain why, but your daughter is recovering far more quickly than any of us had expected. If this continues, she will be fully healed in two or maybe three weeks; however, there is still the danger of infection and the likelihood of scarring. I believe we can control the risk of infection, but we can do little to prevent the scarring." Dr. Usman paused, as he allowed this information to be processed, and then he continued, "As I have already told your son, the young lady that was with your daughter did a great deal to minimize the damage. She had the foresight to quickly flush your daughter's face and eye with water, preventing more serious injury. Although I had neglected to mention it earlier, it has also come to my attention that a passerby, a man, had thought to quickly to pull away the acid-soaked fabric from around your daughter's neck. If he had not, the burns would have been much deeper and more widespread. This same man had generously paid a taxi driver to rush your daughter to this specific hospital.... There was no way for him to have known, but I am one of only four doctors in Kabul who have had formal training in the treatment chemical burns, and I was the only one on duty."

Morad Hawadi was silent for a moment, as he thought of this day. His wife had been brutally murdered and his daughter had intentionally been splashed with acid. Yet, there had also been acts of kindness. He would have to try, very hard, to remember these acts of kindness, over the days that were to follow.

After a protracted moment of silence, Dr. Usman said, "Pasha Hawadi, I have heard the story of your wife's senseless and tragic death. May I offer my sincere condolences. I cannot imagine how great the sorrow you and your children must feel."

Morad Hawadi looked away, his eyes glistening with the tears he refused to let flow. It took a moment for him to regain his composure and then he said, "Thank you Doctor Usman...Thank you for caring for my daughter and thank you for your kind words."

Turning to look at Dr. Bachour, Morad Hawadi asked, "Doctor Bachour, I understand my wife's body is here. May I please see her?"

Dr. Bachour replied, "Yes, Pasha Hawadi, of course...Sir, I have been told that the damage to your wife's skull was quite severe...it...it may not be...suitable for your son to see his mother that way."

Morad Hawadi turned to Dawud and studied him, and then said, "You are now a grown man, Dawud, and you have the right to make your own decision." Dawud immediately replied, "Father, I would like to see my mother...To see her one last time."

As Morad Hawadi and Dawud turned to leave, Dr. Bachour said, "Sir, before I have someone escort you, there is something that has been bothering me, and perhaps, you can help?" Morad Hawadi replied, "Yes, what is it?" Dr. Bachour continued, "I have witnessed two violent attacks on this hospital, and each of these attacks has taken several lives, including nurses and doctors. So you must forgive me if I have become a bit paranoid. Nonetheless, hospital security has notified me that there are three men standing on the far side of Char-Qala Road. They have been there since about the time you arrived. I would not have bothered you with this matter, except, I thought these men might be associated with you...possibly your security detail?" Morad Hawadi replied, "I do not have my own security, but, perhaps the ANP have provided security that I am not aware of." Dr. Bachour did not look convinced as he said, "These men do not look like ANP officers. Perhaps you would be kind enough to take a look and give me your opinion?" Now curious, Morad Hawadi replied, "Yes, yes of course." Dr. Bachour then said, "Excellent, we should be able to see them from my window." Dr. Bachour stood and accompanied Morad Hawadi to the modest, double windows that looked east, giving them a decent view of Char-Qala Road. It took only a second for Morad Hawadi to spot the three men, and what he saw caused his blood to instantly run cold. Dawud, Dr. Bachour, and Dr. Usman all noticed Morad Hawadi's shocked expression, and it was Dr. Usman who spoke first, saying, "Pasha Hawadi, are you all right? Is something wrong?" Morad Hawadi did not reply, but thought Dr. Usman had no idea how wrong everything had suddenly become. There, on the far side of Char-Qala Road, stood three men, but only one interested Morad Hawadi – the one with pure white hair and an equally white, neatly trimmed beard. He was unusually tall, well-dressed, and powerfully built. The other two men were nothing more than his bodyguards. As Morad Hawadi watched, the white-haired man seemed to sense him and slowly turned his head to look up, straight at him. In that instant, Morad Hawadi knew, for certain, whom he was looking at. Shocked by the realization, he pulled back from the window. It was only a second, but when he returned, the white-haired man and his two bodyguards were gone.

They had all been watching Morad Hawadi's reactions and it was Dr. Bachour who asked, "Pasha Hawadi, do you know these men? Is there some kind of problem?" Morad Hawadi replied, "No...no, I do not know these men, but I would like to take some precautions." Doctor Bachour replied, "We have an excellent security department. I am sure we can handle them." Morad Hawadi was more than certain they could not. In fact, he was not sure if the entire Afghan National Army could handle these men. Still, he would prefer not to cause a commotion, so he replied, "Yes, I am sure that is true, still, there are a few simple things we could do...They are not intrusive and they will not significantly disrupt the operations of your hospital." Doctor Bachour was not convinced, but the tone of Pasha Hawadi's voice now conveyed the authority of a "commanding general" and he had never been good at standing up against that kind of authority. So, reluctantly he agreed to cooperate – as long as he was sure the operation of the hospital would not be disrupted.

Over the next hour, Afrah was quietly moved to another room, and registered under a different name. A lock was installed on the inside of her door, and the officer guarding her room was repositioned across the corridor, where it would not be obvious which room he was guarding. Then Morad Hawadi contacted Captain Mustafa and arranged to have a female officer assigned to Afrah. She would guard the door from the inside, and unlock it only after receiving radio confirmation from the guard outside. Morad Hawadi knew this would have to do. He could not acquire the force it would take to be effective, so he would have to rely on subterfuge.

When everyone was finally in place and after he had again spoken with Afrah, Morad Hawadi called Dr. Bachour. A few minutes later, a stout, middle-aged nurse appeared, and escorted Dawud and Morad Hawadi down two flights of stairs to the basement level. There, the nurse guided them down a long, dreary corridor, to the hospital's morgue. A female attendant was waiting for them. She had placed Nikoo's body on a stainless steel examining table and had covered her with a crisp, white sheet. Once Morad Hawadi and Dawud had entered the small room, she folded the sheet back, exposing Nikoo's face and neck, and then she quietly stepped out of the room. A white hijab had been wrapped tightly around her head, revealing only her face. Her eyes were closed and someone had applied makeup in an attempt to cover the bruising on her cheek. Morad Hawadi was grateful for this gesture, for his Nikoo did almost look like she was asleep. The two of them spent over an hour beside Nikoo's body. Morad Hawadi gently stroked her cheek, but neither he nor Dawud spoke. Both men were clearly struggling to deal with their grief, to deal with their anger, and to deal with their regrets. Slowly, a dark, cold emptiness washed over them as they fully came to realize that Nikoo was really gone and she would never again warm them with her smile, and with her touch. Finally Morad Hawadi kneeled and Dawud followed. The two of them prayed. After a long while the two of them rose and prepared to leave, but Morad Hawadi found leaving very difficult to do. He did not want to be separated from his Nikoo, he wanted to stay by her side, to hold her in his arms. How could he go on without her? That was when the tears came. They came in a torrent and it seemed he would never be able to stop. Yet, as the minutes passed, Morad Hawadi somehow regained a semblance of control. His body trembling, he slowly bent down and gave his Nikoo, his beautiful Nikoo, a last kiss. As he did so, several of his tears dropped onto the cold skin of her face.

CHAPTER TWELVE

Revelation

Dawud sat in a straight-backed, metal chair, next to Afrah's bed. It was nearly 10:30 PM and he was exhausted, and found himself staring at the speckled blue tile on the floor, as he struggled to make sense of what had happened.

The sedatives Afrah had been given, had now worn off and Afrah was awake. Her injured eye and the left side of her face were covered with a fresh, white gauze bandage. She had been silent for hours, and was still struggling to hold back her tears. She had been told about her mother, and the general circumstances of her death, but it didn't seem possible, none of it seemed possible. Her mother was the kindest, gentlest, and most generous person she had ever known. Her friend Saba's mother, Madame Uzma was a mean woman. She had once beaten Saba so badly that she had left bruises on her arms and legs, yet Madame Uzma was still alive. If someone had to die, why couldn't it have been Madame Uzma? Although she didn't want to think this way, she could not help it. Then, just in the last few minutes, Afrah began to fully appreciate that what had happened was intentional, and that someone was responsible for doing these...these terrible things. They were the ones who had chosen to splash her with acid, and they were the ones who had chosen to kill her mother. Afrah was suddenly ashamed of her weakness, her submissiveness. She had blamed herself, she had even contemplated trading Madame Uzma's life for her mother's, while, all along, those who were truly guilty were still out there, free to harm others. Afrah swore to herself that she would never again be so...so pathetic.

There was a vacant room next door, and Morad Hawadi had told the female officer to go there and get some rest. He was armed and would stand in for her. Besides, he needed to be alone with his children. Since he and Dawud had returned from the hospital morgue, Morad Hawadi had seemed distant, preoccupied in thought. Much of it was mourning the loss of his Nikoo, but there was also something else. Morad Hawadi had something to say and he didn't know how to say it.

Although both Dawud and Afrah were both deeply immersed in their own grief, they had been observant enough to notice their father's anxiousness. It was Dawud who finally spoke, saying, "Father, the men in front of the hospital, did they have anything to do with our mother's death?" It took a moment for Afrah to register her brother's words, and when she did, her eyes became larger and she looked over at her father with a growing alertness. Her day had been a sequence of terrible events, and then she had been drugged. When her drugs wore off, and her mind began to clear, she would be overcome by the pain, and overwrought with grief. Afrah cleared her throat, and then said, "Father, what is Dawud talking about? What men in front of the hospital?"

Morad Hawadi's ears heard his daughter's words, and for just a moment, his daughter's voice and the voice of Nikoo were one. The sound was sweet to his ears and it squeezed at his heart. He could not look in her direction; he could not bear to have his children see him so...wounded. After what seemed like several minutes, Morad Hawadi once again pulled himself together, and began to speak, "I....I do not believe the men Dawud refers to had anything to do with what happened to you or your mother. It is not their way. But I do believe that one of those men is particularly dangerous, and now that he has found me, I am afraid that I owe you both an explanation.

It is not by chance that I have told you so little about my childhood, and I have told you even less about my...our ancestry. This was, in part, because there are many things that I do not understand and cannot explain, but mostly, it was because I had hoped it was behind me and was best forgotten. Unfortunately, this does not seem to be the case."

These words captured Afrah's and Dawud's attention, and they studied their father with great interest. Morad Hawadi slowly turned in their direction, and they could see the redness in his eyes and the deep sadness they conveyed. But Dawud and Afrah could also see the worry and even something that might have been fear. Moving with the stiffness of a man 20 years older, Morad Hawadi eased himself into a chair. At first, he did not say anything, he just looked down at his hands, which were clasped in his lap. And when Morad Hawadi spoke, his voice was almost a whisper, and Dawud and Afrah had to strain to hear the words. "The man, Farzam Hawadi is not your...biological grandfather. He was a good man, but Farzam Hawadi was my adoptive father."

This revelation surprised Dawud and Afrah. Although they knew little about Farzam Hawadi – he had died long before they were born – they had always imagined him to be this kindly old man, who, had he lived, would have coddled them and indulged them as small children, and who would have offered charming anecdotes and timely wisdom as they grew. Now, with only these few words, Farzam Hawadi had become a stranger.

Morad Hawadi continued, "I know there will be things...things that I will now tell you, that will confuse you, or that you may find very hard to believe, but I ask you to be patient and hear me out.

Let me begin by saying I loved and admired Farzam Hawadi very much. He gave me his name and treated me as his own son. But I also loved and admired my real parents and have never forgotten them.

To have you better understand, I must take you back a little further...to Saudi Arabia, to a time before I met Farzam Hawadi.

I remember my father...let us call him Asim Rahman, for that is the name he last used, and I honestly do not know his or my mother's true name. Asim was always a very...cautious and vigilant man, a person that one might consider to be paranoid. By this, I mean he would always be armed, and he would take extraordinary precautions with our safety. Sometimes, he would leave the house through the back door, so he could reconnoiter our street before my mother and I would be permitted to leave the house. He would get up in the middle of the night to check the doors and windows, and then he would stand alone, in the dark, and watch our street from an upstairs window. By the time I was five, we had moved and we had changed our names twice. It would be reasonable to say that we lived as if we were being hunted. It was not because my father feared the police or the Government. On the contrary, my father was an educated man and a successful merchant. He had a number of friends in very important positions.

Some time later, I would learn that my father had been a soldier, and then an officer in the Mabahith – the Saudi secret police. It seems that he gradually became disenchanted with the Saudi Theocracy, or maybe he had problems with the Saudi Monarchy. Whatever the reason, he left the Mabahith and become a merchant. Several years later, he met my mother, and they were married. At first, their lives were relatively normal. Then everything changed. My father received a telephone call from the Jeddah police. My grandfather lived in Jeddah, and the police wanted to report that he was missing. My grandmother had died, several years earlier, so my father was my grandfather's only living relative. The police wanted to know if my father knew where he was. When my father said he did not, the police asked him if he recognized the name 'Thalj Shayton.' The name 'Thalj Shayton' had been hastily written across a piece of paper that was found lying on the floor of my grandfather's office. My father immediately recognized this name and knew what it meant. My grandfather was gone and he would never be found.

My grandfather's disappearance and the name Thalj Shayton were the catalyst that triggered my father's...paranoia. You see, stories of Thalj Shayton and disappearances are like a pattern that reappears over and over again in the fabric of our family's history. I recall reading a story that dated back over two hundred years. It went something like this:

It was the time of Abd al-Wahhab and the early days of the Emirate of Diriyah. Abbas and his young son Mirsab, (distant ancestor of ours) came across an old woman being dragged through the streets of their village. She was a known mystic and the Islamic Council had convicted her of practicing witchcraft. Under the law, she had been sentenced to death. When the woman saw Abbas and his son, her eyes grew large and her face was distorted with fear as she cried out to her guards:

'Be afraid of them, not of me. I am nothing, it is their blood that is cursed. They will cause your children's children great misfortune, no one will be spared.

The mighty fallen angel, Thalj Shayton, hunts them, he is nearby, and is coming for them.'

Abbas had once been a soldier, but was now a tabib (a doctor). During his life, he had come across many people that he considered to be...mad. He had encountered them in war and, sometimes, they lived in his own village – just as this old lady did. Still, it bothered him that she knew the name Thalj Shayton, the 'ice devil.' He had thought the name Thalj Shayton was known only to him and his father.

This was a time of myth, a time of demons, devils, and possession. Although Abbas was not inclined to be superstitious, he had experienced the mysterious before, more often than he would have liked. So it was understandable that he wanted to put this experience behind him.

However, his son Mirsab believed the old woman and became deeply disturbed by what she had said.

Many hours later Abbas and his son returned to their home, only to

*discover Abbas' mother standing in the path, staring at the sky, and unable
to speak. Abbas soon discovered that his father was missing. Worried, Abbas went to his neighbors to ask if they knew where the man had gone. The
neighbors knew nothing about his father's disappearance; however, two of
his neighbors, who had been working in a nearby field, remembered seeing
a large man with white hair and a white beard. He had been standing in
front of Abbas' house. When Mirsab heard what his neighbors had seen,
he reminded his father about what the old woman had said. That night
Abbas could not sleep. He recalled the many stories he had heard about
Thalj Shayton. He remembered that Thalj Shayton hunted those of his lineage, for those of his lineage had been both blessed and cursed. The next
day, Abbas and his son left his village and went into hiding in the distant
Hijaz Mountains.*

*It is said that several years later, a herder, tending his sheep, had spo-
ken with Mirsab. Mirsab had told him that his father had been missing for
many months, and that he, Mirsab, was being pursued by someone he described as a tall, powerfully built man, with white hair and a white beard.
Years later, travelers reported seeing Mirsab in Yanbu Hunayn, and then
in Badr Hunayn, and finally in Rabigh. It is believed that Mirsab married,
and had a son.'*

Mirsab's son would be a grandfather of yours, ten generations past.
Stories like this have been told for generations. The fallen angel known
as Thalj Shayton is always portrayed as the same character – a large,
powerfully built man, with pure white hair and a white beard. Every so
often, someone will also describe him as having 'empty blue eyes' and
skin 'colder than ice.' They would say he could cause the wind to blow
and the snow to fall. From everything that I have heard and read, Thalj
Shayton appears to be pursuing only those of our lineage. You see,
your great, great, great, great grandfather came from the town of
Rabigh, and was told this story by his grandfather...the year before he
disappeared.

Forgive me, for I am digressing, and I still have much more to tell.

My grandfather disappeared only weeks before I was born, and my
father, much as Abbas had done, went into a kind of hiding."

Morad Hawadi paused for a moment, seemingly trying to order
what he would say next, and then he continued. "I was born in Saudi
Arabia, in the city of Al Madinah. As with almost everything in our
lives, my birth was kept a secret and there are no documents recording
it. My father operated a profitable, antique tapestry business, but I be-

lieve that he was also involved in something else, something that took him away for three or four days every month. I never discovered what this was, but my mother would always worry about him, and I was left with the impression he was doing something dangerous. At night, I could hear her praying for his safety, and sometimes I could hear her asking that Allah, in His mercy, forgive my father.

Anyway, it turned out that his preoccupation with secrecy...and our security, gave him an air of mystery. Although I do not think it was intentional, this air of mystery transferred to his tapestry business, making the tapestries somehow more exotic, which translated into more expensive. There were rumors that the tapestries came from the Royal Family's collection and were once owned by famous people like Saladin, Al-Zarqali, and others. I do not think this was true and my father did not hesitate trying to dispel these rumors. But human beings believe what they want and the more he denied the rumors, the more people believed they were true.

When I look back on it, I see that his life was a bit of an enigma.

My parents were very much in love, and were always kind and generous with each other. I was their only child and they showed me a great deal of affection. Those were good years...happy years. Unfortunately, this happiness was not to last.

It was on one of those hot, dusty August afternoons; the heat was relentless, and the sun hung low in a dusty sky. It was my mother's birthday, and I remembered my father teasing her about being older than him, if only by nine days. My mother had insisted that she and I accompany my father on an errand, after which my father promised we would all go out to dinner – a rare and special event in our home. My father had to pick up a payment for some tapestries he had delivered earlier that week. The money was waiting for him, and it was not supposed to take long.

The customer was a wealthy merchant whose shop was across from the old bazaar. My mother did not have the opportunity to get out much, so the drive through the bustling streets, and the chance to observe the crowded bazaar, were a treat for her. As he always did, my father carefully scanned the street, and he would always make us wait in our walled courtyard while he started up the van. When he was sure it was safe, he would drive to the gate, and we would hurry to get into the vehicle. This was routine and we did not think much of it. We were used to him constantly watching his rearview mirrors, and turning his head to quickly inspect the drivers in the nearby cars. As far back as I can remember my father had the practice of driving past his destination, and then turning back, and that day was no exception. When he was satisfied everything was safe, he found a parking place, directly across the street from the merchant's shop. He was pleased with the location because it let him keep an eye on us. Checking the glove box, he verified that the pistol was still there and that it was loaded. My mother knew what to do. She was to take the pistol out of the glove box if she noticed anything suspicious, and then she was to shoot anyone that she thought represented a danger. Before walking away, he checked the doors, and then looked around one more time. Satisfied, he hurried off, and I can still see him looking back at the van, and seeing my mother wave at him. The errand would take only a few minutes and he was expecting to collect a substantial amount of money. I remember that it was a relatively new van, but it got very hot when the air conditioning was off. I was playing in the back, in a space between two stacks of tapestries. My mother was up front, in the passenger seat. She was watching the bustling crowds while softly humming one of my favorite melodies. I loved to hear the sound of my mother's voice, and I would often stop playing to just listen. This was one of those times, and I can still remember how clear and sweet it sounded. Then, suddenly, she stopped humming. I did not want her to stop, and was about to register my complaint, when I heard her whisper.

'Babba, hide, hide right now.'

I knew what that meant, I knew the drill, but this time it seemed different. This time it felt real. My mother had not turned her head, which I knew meant someone was watching her and she did not want to give away my presence. A moment later I heard her whisper.

'I love you Babba, you wait here. Do not show yourself. Please, Babba, do exactly as I say.'

Her voice was strained, and I could tell that she was frightened. Next, I heard the glove box open and then the van's door open. The last thing I heard her say was, 'Stay hidden, Babba, I will be right back...I love you Babba.'

I felt the van move as she got out. Then the door closed. A second or two later, I heard brakes screech and a heavy thump. People began to yell, but I did not move. I had buried myself beneath several of the tapestries, and was staying as still and as quiet as I could, just as I had always practiced. I remember being very hot, when I heard the van door open and then close, a few seconds later. It seemed like a long time had passed, when I heard the van door open again and my father's voice. He was frantically calling out my name. At first, I could not speak, I was dizzy, and my throat was dry, so nothing would come out. It was only after I heard my name the third time, that I responded. The tapestries covering me were pulled back and I saw my father's face. His eyes were wide, and there were tears in them. He pulled me into his arms and held me tightly against his chest. We stayed this way for several minutes, and then he put me in the passenger seat while he stepped away from the van to speak to a man. In front of me, I saw that the glove box was open and empty. When I looked out through the side window, I could see something covered by a blanket. It took me a second to notice the shoe lying next to the blanket. It was my mother's shoe – she had chosen to wear that pair especially for this day's outing. I was staring at the blanket, as my father spoke with a man that I now know was a Mabahith agent, an old friend of his.

Anyway, I stared at that blanket for a long time, hoping I would see movement, but there was nothing. Eventually, two men placed my mother's body on a stretcher, and they took her away in an ambulance.

Later that day, I heard my father speaking to someone. They were discussing what had happened, and I heard him say a large, black car had intentionally swerved to hit my mother. It stopped for a moment, and then drove away quickly, disappeared into traffic.

I do not remember much about the funeral, except that it was small.

By the end of the week, my father had become convinced that...Thalj Shayton was responsible for my mother's death. Not long after that, our neighbor reported seeing a strange man with white hair, white beard, and wire-rimmed spectacles, standing out in front of our house. That afternoon, my father told me that we were moving away, and two days later, we were on an airplane to Kabul. We moved into a small, but comfortable house in northwest Kabul, the Share Naw neighborhood. My father told me that we should be safe now. Afghanistan was a big country and it was far away from Saudi Arabia. Thalj Shayton would have great difficulty finding us, in such a remote and isolated place.

During the next few years, my father told me all he knew about Thalj Shayton. He would read me old letters that had been written by my grandfather, great grandfather, and many before him. In those letters, they wrote about Thalj Shayton, they had tried to pass on all they knew about the man.

To my shame, growing up, I did not always show a great deal of empathy, nor was I a particularly cooperative child. I had a rebellious nature, and gradually found Thalj Shayton lessons to be boring. To me, it seemed that my father was obsessed with some mythical character, and more than once, I questioned whether he was completely sane. In short, I made life unnecessarily difficult for my father...a behavior that I regret to this day.

When I was about nine years old, I had already become proficient at sneaking out of our house, usually to play with my friend Jawid, but sometimes I would just want to get away. This was not as nefarious as it sounds, if you consider that I had spent almost all of my young life in hiding. I was taught to be suspicious of everyone, and to be as invisible as possible. I knew these precautions were my father's way of protecting me, but it had been nearly five years since my mother had been killed. Unlike my father, I had doubts as to who had killed my mother. Make no mistake, I missed my mother every day, but years had come and gone, and, sadly, I had begun to forget many things about her.

As time had passed, my father did become less vigilant but he also became more withdrawn. He had never stopped mourning the loss of my mother, and if anything, his grief had become even deeper. He would never forgive himself for leaving her in that van. A deep depression had consumed him, and it permeated the entire house. It sometimes seemed to suck the life out of him and everything around him. I tried to cheer him up. Once I took some of the money I had saved, and bought a book of jokes. Every day I would tell him three jokes. He would listen, smile, and sometimes he would affectionately mess up my hair, with his large hand. But the smile never extended to his eyes, and it would not be long before he would retreat back into his silence. This was about the same time that I got it into my head that going to school was what I needed to do, so I relentlessly argued, cajoled, connived, and begged, until my father finally relented. It was not that I lacked for learning. I had been homeschooled for years, and that year, my father and an old man, a retired university professor, had somehow become acquainted. The old man had agreed to instruct me in more advanced mathematics and science. But I wanted more, I wanted to have my own friends, I wanted to play sports, and...I wanted to be away from the house, away from the sadness. My father's decision to let me go to school presented its own set of problems. He was a Muslim, but a very progressive Muslim, who believed verses from the Qur'an may be interpreted allegorically, or even set aside. He detested the growing orthodoxy, and the radicalization of Islam, and made it quite clear that he was not about to have his son's mind polluted by some fanatical Cleric. Madrassas (Islamic schools) were quickly becoming hot-beds of extremism, and the roots of the Taliban movement were already well-established. Soviet influence in the government was growing and there was talk of another coup d'état, or even a full-scale rebellion. The choices were few, but he finally settled on one of the few International Schools that could be found in Kabul. It was supported by the German government and had a good academic reputation. From the very first day, I loved that school. For me, school meant I could relax my guard, I could freely mingle with other children, and I could make friends. It seemed that I was now officially 'normal,' although 'normal' had a skewed meaning in a place like Afghanistan.

Playing with my friend Jawid became the highlight of the week, and on that particular Saturday afternoon, I had once again snuck out of the house. Jawid and I had a kite fight planned. Both of us had spent many hours toughening the lines of our kites with tiny, razor-sharp shards of crushed glass. I was positive my efforts were superior. I would easily slice his line and I would rule the day.

Jawid's apartment was two blocks from my house, and the two of us climbed up onto the roof of his two-story building. From there, we planned to launch our latest kite designs. High roofs were a good place to fly kites – no power lines, no trees, no building to get in the way, and there was usually a good steady breeze.

We were getting our kites assembled when something drew my attention to the street below. That was when I saw him, a large man, wearing loose fitting clothing, a pakol (Afghan cap), and wire-rimmed glasses. Although the clothing helped conceal his physique, it was obvious that the man was big, and powerfully built. From beneath the pakol, I could see strands of pure white hair – instantly, I knew I was looking at Thalj Shayton. At first, I thought I must be mistaken. How could I know what Thalj Shayton looked like? I had never actually seen the man. Yet, as I watched him, all my doubts slipped away. He stood nearly a head taller than the other men he passed. His shoulders were broad, his neck was thick, and his arms were larger than most men's thighs. And, of course, there was his hair. I had never seen such pure white hair, but I think it was the way he moved that confirmed his identity. His movements were too...easy for a man his size. There was also something alien about him, something that did not belong.

As I was watching him, he slowed, and then stopped. It was then that I noticed he was with two other men, one standing on each side of him. As I watched, I noticed that he began to turn in my direction. Scared that I would be seen, I dropped to the roof and stayed as low as I could, hoping I had been quick enough. Jawid noticed what I had done and asked me what was wrong. I did not reply; too many thoughts were cascading through my mind, and I had barely heard him. It took me a moment to realize that Thalj Shayton was heading in the direction of my house...I had to warn my father. I carefully peeked over the edge of the roof, and I saw the man was gone. It took me only a few seconds to scramble down to the street, and set off running toward home.

Fifty meters into my sprint, I heard gunfire. People around me had also heard it, and they began running for cover. There was a short pause, before a second burst of gunfire could be heard. Then everything became quiet and all I could hear was a distant dog barking. I knew there was now no need to warn my father – he and Thalj Shayton had made contact, and whatever had happened was now over.

Getting home quickly now seemed less urgent. Actually, I began to dread it, I dreaded what I would find...or not find. The street was now empty and I could see the corner, up ahead. Once I turned that corner, I would be able to see my house. As I got closer, an odd feeling washed over me, a strange, almost alien sense of peace...I was now certain that my father was...gone, and I began to feel a deep sadness, but this sadness was accompanied by relief. My father's grieving was over. For years, I had known that the only thing that had kept his heart beating, was his need to protect me. Turning the corner, I was able to see my house and immediately saw that the heavy, reinforced front door was gone, and now lay in the street, nearly ten meters away. As I studied the gaping hole where the door had been, I saw movement, the silhouette of a man...a large man. Retreating back around the corner, I pressed myself against the side of a building and watched. The man could be seen moving around the house, as if he were looking for something...or someone. It was then that it occurred to me, that he was looking for me. At that same moment, the silhouette froze, turned, and stepped into the doorway. He was in the shadows but I could still see that he was not wearing his wire-rimmed glasses, and for just a second, I was able to see that where his eyes should have been, were two...black holes that seemed to extend farther back than the man's skull did. Although the sight would have disturbed anyone, it triggered in me a reaction that is difficult to describe.

For just a moment, I understood who Thalj Shayton was, and I remember wanting, very badly, to kill him. A second later, the wire-rimmed glasses were back on and the appearance of eyes returned. Thalj Shayton moved through the doorway, heading in my direction. I cannot tell you what he did after that, because I was running, and I kept running. When I could run no farther, I stopped, and I can still remember how hard my heart was beating as I turned to see if anyone had followed. I saw no one, but not seeing Thalj Shayton did not give me comfort. I could still feel his presence and I knew he was still hunting me. Tired and thirsty, I hid in an old, abandoned car, from which I watched and I waited. The minutes turned to an hour, then two hours. I think I fell asleep, because when I next stared out at the street, it was afternoon. I knew I would have to go back, I needed to see...to confirm that my father was...gone.

The shadows were long by the time I found my way back to that corner. The street was quiet, and after watching for several long minutes, I finally thought it was safe enough, and approached the house. Someone had leaned the heavy front door back up against the opening, but entering that way would have put me in plain view. Instead, I used the small window at the side of the house. I knew how to release the iron grate and how to swing it out of the way. I knew this because I had used that very window to sneak out of the house that morning.

The rooms were lit only by the beams of late afternoon sunlight that came through the small windows. Two of the living room chairs had been overturned, and the drawers in my father's desk had been removed, and the contents dumped onto the floor. Books had been scattered around the room, and some, those in English and German, had their pages torn out. I had seen the police cause this kind of damage. If someone did not watch them, they would pretend to look for evidence, but would actually search for money and jewelry, which would quickly disappear into their pockets. Often, the police felt it was their duty to enforce Islamic tenets against pornography and blasphemy, and they would destroy anything they did not understand. This included documents they could not read, foreign language books, and any material that depicted the female form.

As I looked around, I saw the bullet holes. The walls were pocked with dozens of holes, and I could still smell the acrid scent of gunpowder. There was no blood, just dozens of empty shell casings. When I went to my room, I saw the wooden door had been smashed inward, and there were more shell casings. That must have been where my father had made his last stand, since the door had been locked from the inside. I am sure he would have come to my room...to protect me. To this day, I imagine his surprise at not finding me there.

I stood there for a long time, just staring...trying to comprehend what I was seeing. Eventually my thoughts turned to my situation, and I wondered what would happen to me. The sound of approaching footsteps drew me back. Turning, I saw the dark silhouette of what appeared to be a frail man, walking toward me. He had somehow squeezed by the heavy front door while I had been distracted. The light was getting dimmer and it took me several seconds before I realized that I was looking at Farzam Hawadi. Farzam Hawadi was the retired university professor my father had engaged to tutor me. He was not a large man and his back was a little hunched, due to his age. His hair had thinned, and had long ago turned white. To me, it seemed his face was permanently set in a scowl, a scowl that had far more to do with aging skin than disposition. Farzam Hawadi wore thick, black horn-rimmed glasses that magnified his intelligent and mischievous green eyes. I remember how, at first, I was confused by the man's sour expression, and how it contradicted those eyes and boundless humor, wit, and sarcasm. Now, when I saw him, my body relaxed. He slowly reach out and put his hand on my shoulder. For a moment, he said nothing, and then the old man quietly said, "I am sorry." The words struck me like a hammer, my stomach clenched, I doubled over, and I vomited. As I retched, I felt the grief washing over me, and I began to weep. Between the retching and sobbing, I told the old man everything. I told him about the disappearances, about Thalj Shayton, and about my mother. The old man was silent for a long time, and then he told me to pack some of my clothing and a few keepsakes, because I would be going home with him. I am not certain why, but I trusted this old man; maybe it was because he and my father had been friends, or maybe it was because I had no one else. All I know is that this old man had believed me, and he took me in, treated me as if I were his son. He gave me the name Morad Hawadi and I lived with him for over five years before he became ill, and had to be hospitalized. Farzam Hawadi had a little money and some property. Anticipating his decline, he had made arrangements for me to attend a prestigious military academy, and when he died, he left me his estate. Most of it was used to pay for my schooling and my room and board. The rest of the money was used to pay for my university education, and lawyers, and an array of corrupt bureaucrats managed to steal the little that remained.

I never saw Thalj Shayton again, not until today. Over time, I had begun to think he had been just a figment of my imagination. Yet, he was so thoroughly tied to the memory of my real parents that I could not dismiss one without dismissing the other." Morad Hawadi grew silent for a moment, and then continued, "Well, now I suspect you may have a few questions. I will try to answer them as best I can."

Dawud and his sister stared at their father with expressions of shock and disbelief. Their minds were spinning as they tried to absorb the implications of his...bizarre story. It was Dawud who was able to speak first. He knew he would have a thousand questions, yet he was having difficulty putting the words together. Still, he managed to ask, "Do you have any idea who this Thalj Shayton is, or why he is hunting us?" Morad Hawadi shook his head and replied, "I honestly do not know whether he is a man, an angel, or a demon...but I do know that he is persistent. Some have speculated that he is some kind of supernatural spirit that one of our ancestors offended. Others say he is Cerberus, the mythical dog that guarded the gate to the inferno. Nobody knows who he is or why he is hunting us. Still, there is some good news. You see, he takes his...prey in order of their birth, which means he will be coming after me first, and I will not be easy to catch." Afrah's eyes were wide and alert, as she asked, "Father, does he kill the people? How do they just disappear?" Morad Hawadi thought about the question and then said, "I do not know if he kills those whom he hunts, but I can tell you he looks as if he is capable of killing. What I know is that they are gone, there are no bodies, no blood, and I am reasonably sure that no one ever comes back." Dawud then asked, "Has anyone spoken with him, tried to reason with him, or to stop him?" Morad Hawadi answered, "From time to time, there have been people who were convinced that Thalj Shayton could be reasoned with. Unfortunately, none of these people have ever returned from such a conversation.

When it comes to resistance, I believe my father...your grandfather resisted. Our home was a fortress, and my father was not inexperienced in mortal combat. There was plenty of evidence that he had fired at Thalj Shayton, and that a battle had ensued. Even so, minutes later, when I saw him, Thalj Shayton did not look injured or even bothered by the encounter. This is further supported by the writings. They contained stories about people setting traps, ambushes, and even organizing man-hunts for Thalj Shayton, but it seems that he is illusive, indestructible, and possibly...immortal, at least as we understand it."

Just as Morad Hawadi had finished speaking, his cell phone vibrated. Very few people had this number and they called it only when they had something important to say. The call lasted several minutes and Morad Hawadi made no effort to conceal the conversation. He had spent too much of his time keeping secrets, and now that would end. His children needed to know everything, if they were to survive.

Morad Hawadi stared at his cell phone for a moment, and then slipped it back into his pocket, and said, "It seems that I am becoming very popular among the wrong kind of people. One of Captain Mustafa's informants has reported that my name has come up during a secret meeting of the Taliban Leadership Council. It seems they are trying to decide whether to elevate me to the top of their assassination list. They believe I intend to retaliate for their attacks on Afrah and Nikoo. Apparently, the assailants were Taliban foot soldiers, and did not know who their victims were. The Council does not want me to make this personal, but if I do, they too will make it personal, and they will make my death their top priority."

Dawud and his sister were now being confronted with yet another crisis. So much had happened, that they were having difficulty keeping up.

Worried for her father, Afrah said, "What are you going to do, father? You know what they did to General Jawid Sajabi...he was at the top of their list, but now you have Thalj Shayton also hunting you."

Morad Hawadi was surprised that Afrah knew of General Jawid Sajabi's position on the list, or even that the list existed, but then he reminded himself that his daughter would put the fictional, British James Bond to shame when it came to acquiring secrets. Morad Hawadi replied, "It is too soon for me to say, but it seems that I will soon have a decision to make."

Dawud had been silent, and Morad Hawadi wondered what the boy was thinking, when Dawud said, "Father, do you still have those 'letters'...the letters that spoke of Thalj Shayton?"

Morad Hawadi seemed hesitant to answer. His expression was a mixture of regret and worry. Finally, after several long seconds, he replied, "I was wondering when you would ask me about those letters. One of those letters dated back nearly eight hundred years, and in it, it spoke of an ancestor being hunted by Thalj Shayton, nearly a thousand years prior. These letters had but one purpose...to convey to future generations what the writer knew about Thalj Shayton. They had been passed from father to son, for all that time." Looking at Afrah, he continued, "It is not that our ancestors objected to passing the letters to a daughter, but until now...until you, Afrah, there has never been a female child born to our lineage. When your mother had become pregnant, and then when I discovered you were a girl, I thought the spell had been broken, and I, and my descendants, would once and for all be free of Thalj Shayton.

Well, that does not seem to be the case.... My father kept the letters in a copper lockbox. I knew how important the letters were, and I looked for the box, the evening I went to live with Farzam Hawadi. Unfortunately, the box was gone..... I am sorry, Dawud, I know the letters would have made my story more believable and much more real."

CHAPTER THIRTEEN

Nikoo

Morad Hawadi left the hospital about midnight. He had work to do, and even at that late hour, planned to meet with Captain Mustafa. Dawud stayed behind with Afrah. He could still hear his mother's words, "Dawud, please, please do not let your sister wake up alone." As long as Afrah was in the hospital, he would honor his mother's request.

Afrah wanted her mind to be clear, so she had refused pain medication. It was nearly 1:30 AM when finally the pain, the loss of her mother, and the strange revelations her father had made, seemed to overwhelm her, and in her mind, she saw faces of people she had never met, she saw unfamiliar landscapes and buildings, and she saw a child. The images caused Afrah to feel alone and frightened, and she began to weep quietly. Dawud saw his sister's body tremble, and asked if there was something he could do. Afrah just shook her head and said, "It will pass...this all will pass." Dawud did not know what she meant, but he sensed this was not the time to ask. So he took her hand and held it until the weeping stopped and her body quieted.

When Afrah was finally asleep and everything was quiet, Dawud placed his face into his hands and he too wept. He wept for his sister, he wept for his mother, and he wept for his father.

Morad Hawadi had no time for sleep and little time to mourn. Much had to be done. Nikoo's funeral would be the next day, and he had to arrange for security. He also had to do some longer-term planning. In some ways, he was grateful to be busy, grateful to be able to subdue his grief, to be able to place it in some back corner of his mind, at least for now.

The funeral was kept very private. Morad Hawadi, Dawud, Captain Mustafa, and only a few of the Hawadis' closest friends attended. Afrah demanded to attend and was allowed to leave the hospital for Salat al-Janazah, the funeral prayers. She would return to the hospital as the funeral procession left the mosque. This was acceptable since traditionally, only men are allowed in the procession and at the gravesite.

Two days later, Afrah was discharged from the hospital. Her injuries were freshly bandaged and she was given clean clothing to wear. As she was leaving the hospital, Dr. Usman approached her and handed her a small brown paper bag containing a bottle of antibiotics capsules, eye drops, and a jar of medicated salve. After giving her some last-minute instructions, he cleared his throat and said, "Afrah, I know that this has been a very difficult time for you, but I want you to know that it has been an honor...yes an honor for me to have been the one to treat you. You are very special, Afrah, and I know this with absolute certainty." Afrah did not reply, but instead smiled at Dr. Usman. As Dr. Usman watched her drive away, he replayed her smile in his mind. It was not the smile of a sixteen-year-old girl; no, this smile was the same, exact smile his mother had given him, the day he told her he would become a doctor.

Captain Mustafa drove the three of them to their home, where they were greeted by a burly looking man, with a sub-machinegun slung across his chest. Dawud and Afrah were introduced to Thabit, the man Morad Hawadi had hired to guard them. Thabit was well-known to both Morad Hawadi and to Captain Mustafa. He had many years of experience and he was smart; still, Morad Hawadi knew that this would be only a temporary situation. If either Thalj Shayton or the Taliban decided to come after him, one man, even a good man, would not be able to stop them.

For Dawud, entering the house turned out to be much more agonizing than he had expected. Everything was exactly as he had left it. His mother's scent was still in the air, and memories of her were everywhere. Her slippers lay by the door, just where she had left them. That was just three or maybe four days ago...it seemed like a thousand years ago. Neither his father nor Afrah spoke, but rather they chose to just solemnly go about their business. Dawud saw Afrah automatically walk toward the kitchen and then hesitate. They all knew that would be the first place her mother would go. She would always ask Afrah to come help her, then she would say, "There are men in the house and if we do not feed them something, they will starve to death." Then, like clockwork, Afrah would grumble, "Mother...you must stop spoiling them. They know where the food is kept and they can help themselves."

Morad Hawadi had also been watching Afrah, and when he saw her hesitate, he went to her and put his arms around her, and whispered to her, "You will not be preparing food on this day or anytime soon. You are going to rest." Pausing for a second, he then continued, "Maybe it is time Dawud and I learned to feed ourselves."

The next few days were difficult, as grief and loss permeated every thought, and for a little while, the Taliban and Thalj Shayton seemed only to be a distant threat.

It had been almost two weeks since Afrah had been attacked, and their mother had been murdered. Afrah's injuries were healing quickly. The blisters were gone but there was still a considerable amount of redness in the area, and some swelling around her eye. The vision in her injured eye had completely returned. Yet, as the days passed, Afrah had become more withdrawn. She was angry, she was determined to return to school, and she refused to make any effort to conceal her injuries. School had once been a place where she had learned new things, where she had friends, where she played sports, and where she gossiped and shared stories. Now, those things seemed unimportant. Afrah wanted to go to school because the Taliban, al-Qaeda, and all those other religious nut-cases, did not want her to go to school...they feared education, and they particularly feared educating girls. She would show them that they had good reason to be afraid. School would become her weapon and she was determined to make it a fierce weapon, one that she would wield at them at every opportunity.

Conversations were few and subdued in tone, as it seemed that music and laughter no longer had a place beneath their roof. It was on one such somber evening that Morad Hawadi's handheld radio buzzed. Dawud's father answered, and Dawud could hear Thabit's voice explain that there was a man wanting to speak to him. He claimed to be an assistant to Mullah Kaihan Mohammad, and wanted to personally deliver a letter to Pasha Hawadi. Morad Hawadi instructed Thabit to first search the man, and only then show him to the door. When Dawud's father stood up, Dawud could see him reach into his desk and remove his pistol, which he then tucked into the waistband of his pants. The pistol was clearly visible when Morad Hawadi opened the door and came face to face with a thinly bearded young man, in his early twenties. The young man identified himself as Waleed and said he was the personal assistant to Mullah Kaihan Mohammad. He explained that he was there to deliver a letter from the Mullah to Pasha Hawadi.

Dawud knew Mullah Kaihan Mohammad was the head Cleric at one of the largest and most influential mosques in northern Kabul. His father did not like this man. As he put it, the man was a pompous, lying ass, and was widely believed to support the Taliban insurgency, and was likely one of its spiritual leaders. Morad Hawadi did not accept the letter outright, but instead he made the young man open it first, remove the enclosed sheet of paper, unfold it, and then hand it to him. This made Thabit, who was standing nearby, smile just slightly, while it made the young man's face grow red with anger. Once Morad Hawadi held the letter, he dismissed the young man, with a flick of his wrist – a simple and clearly demeaning gesture. Dawud watched as Waleed hesitated, unsure of what he should do. A moment later, Thabit's large hand gripped the young man's shoulder, and he was sent scurrying on his way.

After the door was closed, Morad Hawadi just stood there, and then after what seemed like a minute or two, he brought the sheet of paper up to eye level and began to read it. Dawud could see his father's eyes narrow and his lips press together tightly, both signs that the letter did not please him. Turning abruptly, Morad Hawadi hurried to his room, where he disappeared from Dawud's sight. About 30 minutes later, Morad Hawadi reemerged and Dawud saw he had changed clothes, and was carrying his heavy wool coat and a large, black duffel bag.

Morad Hawadi paused for a moment, glancing down at his duffle bag as if he had just now fully realized the significance it represented. He then bent over and put down his duffle bag and placed his coat on top of it. Standing up again, Morad Hawadi's eyes met Dawud's, and they stared at each other for a long moment before he walked over to where Dawud was sitting, and sat down in the chair across from him. Dawud had studied him as he had approached, noticing his father's shoulder holster, just visible beneath his open sports jacket. His father's appearance was unsettling to Dawud, it was as if something very serious was about to happen.

Morad Hawadi looked into his son's eyes for a moment, and then spoke in the quiet, resolute tone of a man who had something difficult to say, and had every intention of saying it.

"Allah willing, one day you will have a wife and children. Then you will understand how great such gifts can be... Your mother...she loved you both in a way that is beyond us, as men, to comprehend. She celebrated every little event, your first smiles, your first steps...your first words. She thought of them as nothing less than miracles and they filled her with immeasurable joy and pride. She constantly worried about the two of you, every little bump, every bruise. She worried whether you were eating right, whether you were warm enough, whether you were getting enough sleep, how you would do on a test, your friends, even whom the two of you would one day marry. You see, my son, when that man attacked your sister, your mother had no choice but to go out and find him. Every cell in her body demanded that she do it. She needed to confront this man, she needed to understand why he would do such a thing. Your mother had always believed that people, deep down inside, were good and, if given a chance, they could be reasoned with." Morad Hawadi looked down at the table and slowly shook his head as if he were still having difficulty accepting what had happened. Finally, Morad Hawadi gave a heavy sigh and looked up at Dawud, with eyes that were sad and very serious, then he said, "Our institutions are corrupt...our laws are not enforced, but what is worse is that our resolve to be a nation of free men and women, is weak and it is failing us. The Taliban, and their many allies, are getting stronger; they see the corruption, they see our petty divisions, they see our incompetence, and it pleases them. They can disfigure an innocent young girl, they can murder a decent and good woman, all in broad daylight, on a busy public street, and fear no retribution. This is not...not acceptable." Morad Hawadi became quiet. He looked like a man who was alone and bore a heavy burden. After a long moment, he again spoke, saying, "You live in a country that has many hard edges, it is determined to rip itself apart...It wallows in ignorance and too many of its people gladly embrace tribalism and a theocracy that bathes them in blood.

I have lived my life believing that most Afghans, deep down inside, would want to be citizens of the twenty-first century, they would want to experience the advances made by science and medicine. I believed there was an intrinsic human desire for people to want to be free, free to think... to choose...to act. But it turns out that I have been wrong. People of Afghanistan, and those in much of the Middle East, willingly subordinate themselves to a brutal, oppressive theology that make them more suited for the seventh century than the twenty-first century." Shaking his head in frustration and disappointment, he continued, "It is not Afghanistan that I wish to speak to you about. I have only a little time before I must leave, and I...I may not have another chance to tell you some things, some things about your mother. I believe you and your sister deserve to know...to know who she was.

Now, Dawud, would you please go and get your sister."

Dawud got up and went to his sister's door. Knocking lightly, he announced, "Afrah, father is going away and he wishes to speak to us."

The door opened almost immediately, and Dawud could see the confused and frightened expression on Afrah's face as she said, "What are you saying, Dawud, father is not going away! He's...he's not going anywhere." Glancing over Dawud's shoulder, she saw her father sitting at their dining room table. She also saw the black duffel bag and the coat. Now seriously worried, Afrah stepped past Dawud and walked toward her father, as she said, "You are going away!...Why?" Hearing his daughter's words, Morad Hawadi's eyes teared. Dawud would be all right. He was a man and he was much stronger than he thought he was. But Afrah, she was his wonderful little mystery. She could be stronger than Dawud, yet, she could be as fragile as a piece of burnt paper. Knowing time was short, he called, "Come here, Afrah. You too, Dawud, please come, sit by me. I wish to tell you some things. Once his two children had sat down across from him, Morad Hawadi began to speak, saying, "I have been a soldier for almost all of my adult life, I have seen a great deal of death, and yet I have learned that memories of a person live long past their death. This, of course, is something that you already know, but I have learned something else. For memories to be...real, to be almost alive, it is important to really know who the person was, to know what they had to struggle with, to know the difficult choices they made, to know how they lived. Otherwise your memories are incomplete and represent only a two-dimensional image of the person. Your mother was...a very special person and you deserve to remember her for who she truly was.

Yes, for certain, she was a wonderful mother and you will have those memories, for the rest of your life. But there was much more."

Both Dawud and Afrah were still trying to process their father's imminent departure, but they had also been drawn in by his words. At the same time, they clearly remembered the CURE Hospital and the last time their father had a story to tell them. Not sure what to expect, they tried to prepare themselves for the revelations that were sure to come.

Morad Hawadi continued, "You probably know that your grandparents, on your mother's side, were educated people, both university graduates. Your mother grew up in a relatively prosperous home, I understand that your grandparents were good Muslims, and were kind, generous to everyone they knew. But what you may not know is that your mother was an unusually bright and strong-willed child. For her age, she was very thoughtful and insightful. She had a strong sense of right and wrong and was not afraid to express herself, particularly if she felt something was wrong or someone was being unjustly treated. By the time she was four years old, she had learned how to read, but most of her reading materials were religious in nature, since they came from a small library at their mosque. This did not satisfy your mother and she persuaded her parents to get her different books on every subject imaginable. She devoured this material and soon was reading books published in Turkey, Jordan, Egypt and even Western Europe and America. By the time she was eleven years old, she had already read several books that offered different perspectives of Islam. She had even read two books that compared other religions to Islam, including Christianity, Judaism, and Buddhism. She had once told me that those books had been a revelation to her, and that it had influenced her perception of religion. By the time she was twelve, she had formed some strong opinions including the outright rejection of Islamic fundamentalism. She had come to despise the religious fanatics that advocated hate, intolerance, and violence. A week before her thirteenth birthday, she managed to disrupt her Islamic studies class by daring to argue with the Cleric. In many ways, she was more informed than he was and she could not understand why, in Islam, under traditional Sharia interpretation, women were generally considered less than men, and why it took the testimony of two women to equal the testimony of one man. Why was it permitted for a man to have four wives and a woman could marry only one man, and why was it that a man was permitted to beat his wife? For a young Muslim girl, this was very dangerous thinking. The Cleric called her insolent and implied she was becoming a kufrul-kurh (a non-believer who detests any of Allah's or Muhammad's commands). These were serious charges, but your grandparents were prosperous, well-respected in their mosque, and generous in their giving to sadaqah (charity). There were many aspects of their faith that troubled them and they were not about to punish their daughter for what they believed was not a rejection of Allah's or Muhammad's commands, but reasonable questions for any young Muslim woman. Disturbed by the Cleric's fierce reaction, your grandfather privately rebuked the Cleric and challenged him to address their daughter's questions. Unfortunately, this did not work out well. The

Cleric was offended and saw your grandfather, and his entire family, as heretics. It was soon clear that they were in danger of losing their lives. So your grandparents took your mother, and they fled to Mazar-i-Sharif. Your grandparents saw religious extremism growing and they feared for their daughter, so they sent her to a boarding school in England, the same boarding school your grandmother had attended.

You and Afrah knew that she had gone to boarding school, but I do not think you knew the circumstances. No matter, your mother studied very hard and by the end of her first term, she had already climbed to the middle of her class, and was steadily moving up. She enjoyed school, but mostly, she enjoyed the freedom to ask questions and to explore any subject she wanted. No one told her she must think one way or another. By the end of her second term, your mother was in the top of her class, and was no longer thought of as that shy, simple Muslim girl from that strange, faraway land. Her tuition costs were high and she worried about the financial strain it put on her parents. When she was fifteen, she began to work, part-time, as a nurse's aide in a nearby public health clinic. Soon, a young English woman doctor, a woman your mother called Doctor Betty, had taken an interest in her. She began to assist her with medical procedures, she gave shots, cleaned wounds, applied casts, and even learned how to suture. By the time your mother was sixteen, she was in training as a nurse. I believe if circumstances had been different, your mother would have stayed in England and studied to become a doctor. But that was not to be. Two weeks after your mother had turned seventeen, she was notified that her parents were seriously ill and would likely die. She immediately returned to Afghanistan. Her parents were in the Mazar-i-Sharif Hospital in Mazar-i-Sharif, and she was at once appalled by the condition of the place. The hospital was dirty, fly-infested, understaffed, and over-crowded. Both of her parents were in comas and lay in their own excrement. They had not been expected to live, so the staff had placed them in a ward for the dying, where they had provided them only minimal attention. The place smelled like sweat, vomit, decay, and human waste. Your mother immediately tried to give them water and clean them up but it was too late – your grandparents died early the next morning, within two hours of each other. The one doctor who had originally examined them said they had both ingested some kind of strong poison, and that there was no cure. Because he was busy, and because she was a woman, he offered no other explanation or assistance.

Your mother managed to get the hospital to report the poisoning to the police, but it did not matter. At this same time, Afghanistan was in the middle of the Soviet occupation and a civil war was heating up. Tens of thousands of people had been displaced by the fighting, gun battles in the streets were common, many were starving, and many others were injured. There was little official interest in the poisoning of two relatively anonymous individuals, and there would be no investigation.

Your grandparents' estate quickly became prey to the usual corrupt government officials. Your mother was young and a woman, she had few rights, and in the end, she was left with only enough money to live on for about a year. She never found out why or who had murdered her parents, and was now surviving alone, as a single woman, in a society of growing Islamic militancy.

Your mother's nursing skills helped her get a job in the very hospital where her parents had died. The work was terrible because your mother had been hired to assist in surgery where doctors did little to save limbs, but rather quickly resorted to amputation. Each day she would watch a dozen or more limbs be amputated. It was a job none of the other nurses would take.

With the civil war raging, the Taliban were moving swiftly to consolidate their hold on Afghanistan. Mazar-i-Sharif was poised to fall and then there would be the inevitable slaughter. A fellow nurse persuaded your mother to run away while she could. The Taliban would surely kill her, if for no other reason than that she had been educated by the infidels. Your mother fled to Asabadab, Kunar Province, where she worked in a small maternity clinic. As you can imagine, life in Asabadab was difficult; nearly half of the city had been destroyed by the Soviets. By then, the Taliban had taken control of over two thirds of Afghanistan, and the United Front for the Salvation of Afghanistan was the only significant force standing in their way. When your mother heard the United Front was desperately short of doctors and medical supplies, she organized a group of women to collect food, bandages, and any medicine they could find. Then, she somehow gathered together a party that included herself, two fifteen-year-old boys, two old men, and four donkeys. They would hike for four days over a high, desolate mountain pass and down into a remote, narrow valley bordered on both sides by steep rock cliffs. One of the old men knew of an isolated United Front outpost, near the Pakistan border, and that became their destination.

When Nikoo's, your mother's, party arrived at our remote camp, everyone was surprised to see them, particularly to see your mother – a woman. There were no women in the camp and most of the men had not seen a woman in months. Many of the men wanted her to go, afraid she would be a distraction and she would not be safe there. The men also questioned what kind of a woman would travel such a long distance, with only the company of men, men that were not her relatives. Our camp was very primitive, no toilets – just slit trenches and some rough wood planks, there was nowhere to bathe, and the men slept together in an odd assortment of tattered tents, mud-brick sheds, and a few timber structures. To further complicate things, your mother's manner was direct and not particularly deferential to the notoriously chauvinistic males. When someone started scolding her for what he perceived as an impropriety, Nikoo would simply turn and walk away, an act that infuriated the man even more. Many of the men refused to let her treat their wounds, preferring to risk infection and death over having this young woman touch them. Some fools actually began talking about having her beaten and then turning her away.

During much of this time, I was unaware of what was going on. Although I was technically second in command, I had been temporarily disabled and was recovering from some minor but painful wounds. The Commander was too busy to be concerned with this matter, so he ordered the men to take their complaints to me. Later, I would come to suspect he had heard the story of Nikoo and had gotten a look at her. Impressed, he decided to do some matchmaking. If so, I will forever be grateful.

Anyway, as the situation got more serious, Merzad, one of my immediate subordinates, came to me for instructions. Merzad was a fair and thoughtful man, he explained to me what this woman had done and the men's reaction to her. I was immediately impressed with the courage of this young woman, not to mention the physical stamina needed to travel, on foot, almost fifty kilometers, and climbing over a thousand meters through rugged and dangerous country. And she did this just to bring medical supplies to a wretched group of fighters, and then she offered to provide them desperately needed medical attention. I had never heard of such a thing. But what then got my attention was the hostile reception this young woman was receiving. I tell you honestly, I was disappointed in my men. We had been fighting these religious fanatics for years, over and over again, we had seen what they had done to women, we had avenged these women's deaths, and now they behaved like this. I gave my aide fifteen minutes to assemble the men. The men knew I was displeased, though some of them thought I was angry with the woman, while others were not so sure. Finally, everyone was there; I could even see the Commander had opened his tent flap so he could watch. I threw my shoulder back, stood as straight as I could, and then attempted to stridently march up to the platform.

Unfortunately, the best I could do was awkwardly hobble, and I actually needed assistance to get up onto the platform. This was not the image I intended to project, but I think it did get me some sympathy. When I was finally in position, I cleared my throat and gave the assembled men the best scowl I could muster, and everyone went quiet. I had previously arranged for two of my men to find and then escort this young woman to me. I intended to address the men with her standing beside me. Now, seeing her for the first time, I was nothing less than dumbfounded. She was so young, and she was the most beautiful thing I had ever seen. Strands of hair had come away from beneath her hijab and hung across her forehead, her face was smeared with sweat and dirt, and her clothing was spattered with mud, ripped in places, and smeared with the blood of the men she had been treating. She looked exhausted, but she stood tall and defiant. Her expression was proud, and yet, in her eyes I could see this young woman was terrified. She would later tell me that she was sure that she was going to be publicly humiliated and sent away. She even thought she might be beaten. This fear had been reinforced when the two of my more brawny fighters had come to fetch her and escort her to the platform. She thought they were guards, there to ensure she would not try to escape. What then happened had been a total surprise to her.

I do not remember exactly what I said in my speech, I just remember constantly wanting to look over at that young lady. But when I had finished, I had told everyone of her courage and her compassion, I had told them that no man had thought to organize and lead such an expedition. No, it had taken the heart of a woman to conceive of this act, and it had taken a very brave woman to see it through. Finally, I told them that this brave young woman was our unit's personal heroine, a gift directly from Allah. I also made it very clear that if any man treated her with disrespect, he would answer to me, and would soon after answer directly to Allah himself. This was a rough group of men, known for their coarseness, irreverence, and ferocity in battle. But I have found that these men can sometimes have large hearts, and they are capable of a unique kind of compassion and kindness. It is as if they suppressed these sentiments, in order to function as warriors in a harsh and brutal environment. For many of the men, my speech had managed to resonate, and I could sense a change take place. At first everyone was silent and I was starting to worry that I had not gotten through to them, but then I heard someone murmur the name Nikoo, it was repeated, then others followed and soon the entire unit was chanting Nikoo, Nikoo, Nikoo! The Commander had listened to my speech and would let it be known that he would turn over his own sleeping tent, cot, and blankets to Nikoo. This gesture gave her the status of an honored guest, an important person. She was now shielded by both authority and custom, but to these men, that made little difference, they had taken her into their hearts and they would be sure no harm would come to her...regardless of what any custom or authority figure may dictate. In the end, your mother had become widely recognized as the unit's personal heroine...actually it was more than that. She was thought of as a kind of saint and was treated with a reverence few, if any, had seen before. For her part, Nikoo treated our wounds, fed us when we were ill, and insisted we clean up our garbage, bathe, and wash our clothing. Eventually, we built a small hospital building, where the sick and wounded could be kept warm and dry. Your mother ran that little hospital for over a year, and because of her efforts, many men survived who otherwise would have died.

I had fallen in love with your mother the moment I saw her, but soon, her newfound status as a 'Saint' complicated things. It did not seem appropriate for me, or anyone else, to approach her romantically. Thankfully, my injuries still required attention and Nikoo never failed to stop by to clean my wounds and change my bandages. As spring arrived, the fighting resumed. I would always find a reason to stop by before I would go out into the field. Sometimes, I would be gone for a few days, while other times, I would be gone for a week or more, but she would always be waiting for me. The fighting was becoming more intense; we were coming across more and more Taliban, and they were better armed and better trained. We were sending many of them to hell, but there were always more to replace them, and they were growing stronger. It was just a matter of time before they would find our base, and when they did, they would attack. This meant it was becoming too dangerous for Nikoo, and I had begun making plans for her to escape, when I was ordered to report to my Commander. I was told that our unit had proven itself, and that we had done more than our share of the fighting. It had been nearly a year since we had had our last reinforcement. Desertions and casualties had reduced our numbers by more than half, and we were no longer an effective fighting force. Starting the next day, we were to be integrated into a larger unit, which he would command. Meanwhile, I would be given my own unit, which was to be based near Lake Shiva. He then suggested that I *get off of my ass* and ask Nikoo to marry me, for if she were my wife I could take her with me. The Taliban had not gotten as far north as Lake Shiva, and she should be safe there...at least for a while. Less than five minutes later, I asked your mother to marry me...and, Allah be praised, she said yes."

CHAPTER FOURTEEN

Blame

Morad Hawadi's eyes hardened. He was silent for a long time, and then he stood up, placed his fists on the table, bent over, and looked directly at his two children as he said, "I am going to find these...these animals, and when I do, I will kill them. I will have no mercy. When these men attacked Afrah and murdered my Nikoo, they sealed their fate and they may have sealed my fate as well."

Pasha Hawadi reached into his inside jacket pocket and pulled out the folded Mullah Kaihan Mohammad's letter, and placed it on the table. Staring at it, he said, "My decision to go after these men was made when I received this letter. You see, we face two enemies, the fanatics and...the mysterious Thalj Shayton. But I am getting ahead of myself.... Please, Dawud, would you read this letter out loud...so your sister can hear."

Dawud picked up the letter and began to read.

"Dear Brother Hawadi:

It has deeply saddened me to hear of your recent troubles. Nonetheless, I find it my solemn duty to advise you that these unfortunate events would not have occurred, if you had been more devout in your faith and more diligent in your responsibilities as a father and husband.

As a father, you have failed to adequately supervise your daughter. You have permitted her to leave your home without a suitable mahram (a male escort that is a certain male blood relative or in-law). Furthermore, you have ignored the prohibition against educating young girls. By sending her to school, a place where she is taught to be willful and wicked, you have recklessly placed her in danger.

As a husband, you have also failed. You have not required that your wife be accompanied by a mahram, nor have you taught her humility and submission. Witnesses have described your wife's demeanor and her tone of voice as insolent. She had publically harassed and attempted to demean a man, a complete stranger, and when given the opportunity to atone, she refused.

It is the duty of every good Muslim to act when he is confronted with someone who flagrantly violates the teachings of the Prophet, may peace be upon him. Since you had failed as both a husband and a father, it was appropriate and necessary that others act.

As the appointed Qadi (judge) in this matter, I have completed a thorough investigation into the role of the two men involved and have found that both of them acted righteously and in accordance with the law. Therefore, they have been found completely innocent of any wrongdoing. To further emphasize this judgment, I have issued a 'fatwa' (decree, legal opinion) declaring that these two men have been absolved of all guilt in this matter. Additionally, any attempt at retribution will be viewed as an attempt to harm two righteous and innocent men, and shall be dealt with accordingly.

My brother, I say this from my heart. Accept what has happened, accept it as a hard but necessary lesson, a lesson that is meant to teach you not to stray from the doctrines of the true faith.

Assalaam alaikum
Mullah Kaihan Mohammad"

It was Morad Hawadi who spoke first. His eyes were dark and his voice was low, almost a growl, as he said, "To understand this letter better, you must understand that Kaihan Mohammad has been a spiritual adviser to the Taliban and a member of the inner council. This letter is actually from the Taliban, and it is their way of admonishing me and yet appearing to give me an opportunity to atone. Of course, they do not expect me to 'atone,' but having publically issued a warning, they have claimed the 'high ground.' Now, when they try to kill me, it will be because I have not repented and continue to defy religious authority. Those that know me will know this is all nonsense, but there are many others who believe these Clerics, people that will now question my character...my faith.

No matter, it simply comes down to this. If I stay, I will be putting the both of you in very serious danger. The Taliban know that I will try to hunt down the people who are responsible for splashing acid on my daughter and killing my wife. They will try to stop me and these people have no qualms about killing the innocent. So, one day, when we are eating a meal at this table, or sleeping in our beds, a car will turn onto our street, pull over in front of this house, and a second later, there will be a flash of light, a thundering boom, and this house and its occupants will instantly be blown to pieces. Neither Captain Mustafa nor Thabit will be able to stop this from happening.

And let us not forget the mysterious Thalj Shayton. He was at the hospital, and I have no doubt he will soon discover who I am and where I live. As I have already said, he hunts us in the order of our birth, which means you are safe, as long as he does not get his hands on me. This, in turn, means I must disappear."

Pasha Hawadi looked down at the table. He had said what he needed to, and now it was time to go. Still, leaving was going to be difficult and he knew that life would soon become very hard for his children. They were so young and they were smart, but was that going to be enough?

Morad Hawadi looked up from the table, and said, "I know that you both still grieve for your mother, and I wish it were within my power to undo what has happened to her and what has happened to Afrah, but it is not. Therefore, we must deal with the situation at hand. From now on, the decisions you make will likely make the difference between life and death. It will not be long before the Taliban make their move. When they find I am gone, they will come for the two of you. They will try to use you to get to me, and then they will kill all of us. You have a week, maybe ten days, but no more. It will be necessary for you to leave this house, to leave Kabul. I have begun to make arrangements and when they are final, I will pass you this information, through Captain Mustafa."

Morad Hawadi paused for a moment, and then cleared his throat as he looked directly at Dawud and spoke.

"Dawud, in my absence, you will be responsible for your sister. Tomorrow, you must go to Efandi Fahir's office, where you will be required to sign some papers, and then he will give you a brown leather briefcase. The briefcase's combination is 5-8-3. Inside the briefcase are two money belts with about 150,000 afghanis in each. This should be enough to get you by for a few months. You will also have access to my bank account, but I suggest you access it very carefully. There are many ways to trace transactions and to locate you. The documents will provide further proof of who you are and your authority to withdraw money from my account."

Morad Hawadi paused for a moment, as he quickly thought through the detailed arrangements he and Efandi Fahir had made. Efandi Fahir was a competent lawyer, an honest man, and still it had taken several days to work out all the contingencies.

Morad Hawadi then continued, "Although we are comfortable, we are not rich, so there is only a modest amount of money in the bank. Maybe enough for the two of you to live frugally for two or three years.

I have made arrangements to have the house rented, and Efandi Fahir will see that our belongings are packed and stored. He will also oversee the tenants and ensure the rent is deposited. My young associate Ubald will take over my business. Allah willing, the house and the business will provide you some extra money, but I would not count on this. As soon as it is known that I am not available to protect my interests, the buzzards will begin circling, and it will only be a matter of time before someone figures out how to get their hands on everything we own."

Afrah interrupted, asking, "Father, what about you? You will need money too." Morad Hawadi was touched by his daughter's concern, and for just a second, a smile appeared at the corners of his mouth. Then, just as quickly, his seriousness returned and he replied, "Do not worry about me. I have kept some money, and long ago, I learned how to...live off of my enemies. It is a skill similar to living off the land, but considerably more lucrative. Also, I have many close allies and I know people that owe me great favors."

Dawud asked, "Will we be able to contact you?" Hawadi replied, "That will not be easy. For now, you will have to leave word with Captain Mustafa or Efandi Fahir. Neither of them will know how to reach me, but I will be checking in with them, when I can do so safely. No matter, for now it is best that you and Afrah just disappear, and the better you do this, the better your chances are of surviving."

He would delay no longer. It was time to go, and Morad Hawadi stood up and walked around the table, stopping behind where Dawud and Afrah sat. There, he gently touched each of his children, savoring the scent of their hair, the feel of their skin, and the warmth of their bodies. After a moment, Dawud and Afrah stood, turned, and embraced their father. No one knew what to say. Their father was going away and they may never see him again. After a long moment, Morad Hawadi kissed both of his children and then released them. His eyes glistened with tears. No longer able to look at them, his eyes were drawn to the green, wingback chair. The one Nikoo had picked out, the one he had bought her for her birthday, and the one she had immediately made her favorite. Was what had happened a punishment? There was little doubt that he had earned a bullet many times over, but not his Nikoo. For a fraction of a second, he could see Nikoo sitting there, looking back at him. Had she really been so beautiful? As quickly as she had appeared, she was gone. Morad Hawadi would stare at that chair for several more seconds before his eyes looked back at his children. He could see Nikoo in both of them and he studied their faces, determined to memorize even the smallest detail. Gradually, Morad Hawadi gathered enough courage to turn and then walk away.

Dawud and Afrah watched as their father picked up his coat and bag, and walked to the door. He turned one last time and looked at them, his eyes were wet with tears, and he quietly said, "As-salamu alaykum (May peace be with you)." In voices that were choked with emotion, Dawud and Afrah replied, "Wa-Alaikum-as-salaam (And peace to you also). After a moment, he turned, opened the door, and walked through it, away from his children, away from his home, away from the life that he had so carefully assembled and once shared with his Nikoo. A minute or two later Dawud and Afrah heard the door of their father's grey Camry close and the engine start. They rushed to the window, hoping for a last glimpse of his familiar face, but all they saw were the car's tail lights as it pulled out of their driveway and turned up their street. In seconds the car had disappeared and they were alone.

Morad Hawadi stared straight ahead as he drove away. Was he abandoning his children? Had he given his options enough thought?....Yes, he thought he had, and, as the distance grew, he became more and more convinced that leaving was his only option. He would draw the attention and the hate of his enemies to him. He hoped they would be so busy counting their dead and trying to hide that they would not have time to dwell on his children. The night was dark and cold. The streets were empty, but Pasha Hawadi did not notice. There was work to be done.

Dawud could not remember how long he had stared out of that window, hoping to see his father's car returning. Sunlight was now streaming through that same window and Dawud found himself in his mother's chair. He only vaguely remembered deciding to sit in it, and then it was only supposed to be for a few minutes. As his mind cleared, he looked around, he saw Afrah lying on the couch, breathing deeply and still asleep. He stared at her for a long time as he thought, "It's you and me, little sister, just the two of us."

Dawud's father had been gone for nearly four days when Captain Mustafa's patrol car pulled up in front of their house. As Captain Mustafa got out of his car, Dawud rushed over and greeted him. He and his sister had been starving for news about their father, news about what would happen next. Captain Mustafa appeared particularly vigilant and there was a sense of urgency in his expression. As he and Dawud walked toward the house, his eyes darted up and down the street, stopping momentarily at each parked car and gateway.

As they entered the house, Captain Mustafa seemed to relax, just slightly, and said, "Dawud, I have spoken to your father, he...contacted me early this morning." His eyes scanned the room and then guided Dawud and Afrah, who had just joined them, away from the front window and into a hallway.

Once there, Captain Mustafa took a moment to study the two of them and then said, "Your father sends his greetings and is praying for your wellbeing. He has given me instructions and it appears that you will have to leave sooner than either of us had expected.

But first, Dawud, did you go to Efandi Fahir's office as your father instructed?"

Dawud replied, "Yes sir." Captain Mustafa continued, "Good, then we can proceed. However, I need to update you on what is happening. Two hours ago, I was notified that the bodies of three suspected Taliban insurgents, and the body of a wanted al-Qaeda operative had been found in the Char Qala neighborhood. It is likely that one of these men is the man that assaulted Afrah."

Turning to Afrah, Captain Mustafa reached into his jacket and removed a stack of photographs, which he handed to her, and then said, "Afrah, would you please look at these photos and tell me if you recognize the man that assaulted you?"

Afrah accepted the photographs but was, at first, hesitant to look at them, thinking they would show grotesque pictures of bloody, mutilated bodies, but when she finally looked at the first photograph, she saw it was a picture of a man's face, taken from the shoulders, up. The man's eyes were open and stared blankly, straight ahead. He had a slack expression that seemed void of any emotion. It took her only a moment to realize the man was dead. She carefully studied all of the photographs, stopping at number four, studying it for a long time. When she had finished looking at all six images, she returned to the fourth one, placed it on the top, and then handed the stack back to Captain Mustafa. Afrah, gesturing to the top photograph, said, "This is him, this is the man who threw the acid at me. I recognized him immediately." Captain Mustafa replied, "Yes, thank you Afrah. That is the one I suspected as well."

Afrah asked, "Did my father kill him,...kill all four men?" Captain Mustafa was reluctant to answer. He was quite sure this was Pasha Hawadi's work. Each man had been killed by a narrow, sharp blade penetrating the base of their skulls, severing their spinal cords, and puncturing their brains. There had been no evidence of a struggle, little blood, and the men had died instantly. Years ago, when Pasha Hawadi was a fighter for the United Islamic Front, he was renowned for his ability to penetrate enemy camps, and to kill quickly and silently. Captain Mustafa now suspected this was how he had done it. Still, he was not sure it had been Pasha Hawadi, nor would he ever ask him. Afrah was young, did she need to know everything? Then he thought of what this young girl had gone through, and wondered that if she believed her father had administered this....justice, it might help put these horrible things, behind her. Not knowing what was the right answer, he decided to simply be honest, and replied, "I do not know."

Afrah was quiet for a moment as she stared down at the floor, then she straightened up, looked Captain Mustafa directly in the eyes and said, "I hope he did this, and I hope he finds the man that killed my mother."

Captain Mustafa had known Afrah since she was only three or four years old, and she had always been a curious, sweet, and innocent child. It now saddened him to see this kind of hardness growing in her, yet, as he studied her, he realized that this was a much more complicated young woman than he had previously thought.

After a moment, Captain Mustafa said, "These...killings did not go unnoticed. The Taliban suspect your father and will soon declare him to be a fajir (wicked evil-doer). They will condemn him to death, a penalty they will extend to anyone that assists him. Both your father and I are convinced that the two of you will also be targeted, possibly as soon as tomorrow."

Captain Mustafa paused for a moment so that Dawud and Afrah could fully digest these words, and then continued, "Before coming here, I spoke with Mawlawi Ahmed Abdel, who I believe is Dawud's Arabic teacher?" Dawud replied, "Yes sir."

Captain Mustafa then continued, "Well, your father has contacted him and he has offered you a place to stay. It is a modest house, in the town of Farkhar, which is in Takhar Province. The house was left to him by a distant relative and he says it is an old, but solid mud brick structure. He says it has a good roof, a good well, and a good stove, but no electricity. He has been paying an old, widow lady, living next door, to keep an eye on the place, but would welcome having someone live in it, and the Mawlawi can be trusted to keep this arrangement confidential.

He will notify the widow lady that you are coming, and he will tell her that you are his niece and nephew." Dawud interrupted, "Sir, Farkhar is over 200 kilometers from Kabul. I have heard that the Taliban routinely stop the buses and question the passengers. Several of my class mates have been stopped, and they say the Taliban even checked their cell phones, to see if they contained any 'undesirable' phone numbers, pornography, or even un-Islamic ringtones. If the Taliban are looking for us, I don't think we would get very far." Captain Mustafa replied, "You are right Dawud. The highway to Charikar is still secure, but north of Charikar, the highway is controlled by the insurgents. This has made it necessary to arrange for other transportation.

Now listen carefully. A yellow taxi, driven by an old friend of mine, will be here, to pick you up, at 2:30 PM this afternoon. That is less than three hours from now, be packed and ready to go. The taxi will take you by way of the Najeeb Market, to the Kabul Airport, the North Side Military Encampment. There, you will board a routine ANA helicopter flight to Taleqan, which is north/west of Farkhar. The helicopter will depart at exactly 3:30 PM. It will not wait for you, so do not be late."

Captain Mustafa then took a few seconds to focus on their appearance. Neither was showy, but there was a certain understated opulence in what they wore. They also looked so,... so contemporary, almost Western. In Kabul, they passed as the children of the growing affluent class, but in Farkhar, they would stand out like a tree in the desert.

After giving this some thought, Captain Mustafa continued, "Dawud, I want you to switch clothes with Thabit. He is a little shorter and a little wider than you are, but I think the look will be good. And maybe Afrah can cut your hair,...make you look more like Thabit.

Now you Afrah, your appearance can be concealed much more easily. You will wear a burqa."

Afrah immediately began to protest but stopped when Captain

Mustafa gave her one of his... disapproving looks.

Captain Mustafa then said, "Afrah, if you are to survive, you must become an actress. Whenever you interact with others, whether it be a neighbor, a friend, a taxi driver, or just a stranger passing you on the street, you must appear and behave as if you were a simple woman of modest means. Do this well, and, Allah willing, a day will come when you can show them who you really are.

There is one more thing. You are each permitted one, modest, suitcase. I need not remind you to take plain, durable clothing, the kind worn in the countryside. The snow will soon come, so be sure to take warm garments, preferably those made of wool. Oh yes, take only sturdy walking shoes – a pair of good boots, if you have them. The terrain, around Farkhar, can get very rugged and you may need to travel long distances, on foot."

Afrah said, "Captain Mustafa, we will do as you ask, but I am still very worried about my father. Will you be watching out for him? Can you protect him?" Captain Mustafa hesitated, then replied, "Honestly, I do not know where your father is or even how to contact him. However, Pasha Hawadi is a natural and an extraordinarily capable predator. He can disappear at will, and then reappear standing behind you, as you brush your teeth. This is how he appeared to me this morning, and I tell you, I was rattled,...yes your tough old Captain Mustafa was taken completely by surprise and I still do not know how he did it.

But to answer your question, yes, yes of course, I will do everything I can to help your father, but it will not be simple. Our relationship is well known and I am under constant surveillance. By this afternoon, I doubt I will be able to visit the men's room without being accompanied by someone who is watching me.

But this is not of immediate concern. It is now time for the two of you to get busy. You must pack your suitcases, change your clothing, and you must prepare yourselves to leave this house...to leave Kabul."

Finished with his instructions, Captain Mustafa took one last look at these two kids. They had become his family and he would worry about them. He wished he could do more for them, but he knew that one day his enemies would get to him and he did not want Dawud and Afrah anywhere nearby. Dawud had grown to be a man, and Captain Mustafa could see Pasha Hawadi in him. Although Dawud did not know it yet, he would, one day, become a formidable warrior. It was in his eyes, and in the way he moved. He was like a young bear that had not yet realized he was a bear. But it was Afrah that had always puzzled him. In many ways, she looked so young, so innocent, yet Afrah was special. She had the best of both Nikoo and Pasha Hawadi, and yet, somehow there was so much more to her.

Clearing his throat, Captain Mustafa said, "You have good blood in your veins, and I believe courage will come naturally to you. You are both well-read, intelligent young people; however, I caution you not to rely too heavily on reasoning. The people coming for you do not care about books and have no interest in your reasoning. In one way or another, they have come to subscribe to a great and malevolent deception. Your reasoning or anything else that might challenge their....delusions, in effect, challenges their character and even their...intelligence. For them to entertain the possibility that one brick, in their elaborately constructed artifice, was a deception...a lie, would throw suspicion onto the entire construct. It would mean that they had been duped, they had permitted themselves to be manipulated. More importantly, it would mean that the misery and pain they have inflicted on others was needless, cruel, and barbaric.

To avoid having to address any contradictory evidence or inconvenient truths, these fanatics wish only to think of the world as being populated by believers – those that unquestionably subscribe to the great deception, or by deniers – those who question or do not accept their delusions, and therefore represent a threat that must be eliminated.

Live long enough, and this world will reveal itself to you. You will see the ignorance and the mindless brutality that lies just beneath the facade of what we call civilization. In the end, it is fear, not reason, that we all respond to."

Captain Mustafa paused and his eyes looked away, as if he was remembering something. Then he continued, "It was my father that once said 'Good men can be persuaded to do terrible things, if they are afraid. And it is equally true that evil men can be persuaded to do wonderful things, if they are afraid.'

Well, I think that is enough of my philosophy. You are both young and you will find your own way, and you will discover your own truths."

Dawud had politely listened to the wisdom that this older man had tried to convey. However, Captain Mustafa had given this lecture before, and Dawud had nearly memorized the words. Still, on this particular day, the words did seem to be more salient. Even so, Dawud's mind quickly became distracted. He thought of all that had happened, how his life had changed, and how it would soon change even more. With hope and concern in his voice, Dawud asked, "How long must we stay away?"

Captain Mustafa thought for a moment, and then replied, "That is a difficult question to answer. However, if you rephrase your question, you might be able to answer it for yourselves. For example, what if you had asked, 'How long will it take for your father to hunt down and... deal with those who are responsible for attacking Afrah and killing your mother?' Then you might ask, 'When will the Taliban and al-Qaeda put aside what your father has done to them?'

Of course, there is the issue of the law. So you might ask, 'Will the Government look the other way as your father systematically executes some of Kabul's most prominent Clerics and Imams?'

And finally there is the matter of that peculiar man...the one your father calls Thalj Shayton. How long will it be before he loses interest in hunting your father?"

In his not-so-subtle way, Captain Mustafa had managed to show Dawud how...stupid his question had been, and Dawud immediately felt embarrassed. But it did not take long for the embarrassment to be overshadowed by the realization that he and Afrah would likely never return to this house, or their lives. The semblance of normality that they had become so comfortable with, was now in their past. They were fugitives, and those hunting them were determined to find them and kill them. He had known this, but suddenly, it now seemed much more real.

Captain Mustafa had noticed that Afrah, too, had been listening to his rephrasing of her brother's question, and now saw the blood drain from her face. It was their moment of realization, their coming to grips with the reality that their old life had ended, and that there would be no going back. Soon it would be the simple things that would become important, things like keeping warm, finding a place to sleep, and finding something to eat.

Sensing that time had run out, Captain Mustafa glanced at his watch and saw that he had been there for nearly an hour. He had disconnected the patrol car's GPS transponder, and had taken precautions to be sure no one had followed him. Still, he had not checked in with the dispatcher, and had now been "off the radar" nearly 30 minutes too long. Someone would come looking for him, and Pasha Hawadi's home would be near the top of their list.

This would have to be his goodbye. Approaching Dawud, he reached out and firmly squeezed his shoulders, and then he kissed him on his checks. Next, he stepped in front of Afrah and gently cupped her chin in his hand, as he said, "I pray that Allah will have mercy on you, little one. Listen to your brother...but also listen to your heart...I have the feeling that it will guide you well."

Captain Mustafa stepped back and quietly said, "Assalaam alaikum."

Dawud and Afrah, both responded, "Waalalkum assalaam."

Captain Mustafa turned and walked away.

After Captain Mustafa left, Dawud and Afrah hardly spoke. They began packing, and in some strange way, the effort soothed them. It kept them from thinking about their mother, their father, and about what was ahead.

CHAPTER FIFTEEN

Leaving

Dawud and Afrah were both staring out of their front window when they saw a yellow taxi slow, and then stop. Checking the wall clock, Dawud saw that it was 2:23 PM, the taxi was early.

Except for the head cover, Afrah had on the blue burqa that Captain Mustafa had told her to wear. She despised the thing and winced when she saw her reflection in the window. Reluctantly, Afrah slipped on her head cover, and when it was properly adjusted, she nodded at Dawud. A moment later, she and her brother had picked up their suit-cases and were passing, for what might be the last time, through the front door of their home. Dawud wore Thabit's trousers, shirt, and windbreaker. Afrah had tried her best to cut his hair, and had, mostly, succeeded. Neither of them spoke, neither of them looked back, but instead they headed directly toward the taxi and the new life that was ahead of them.

Thabit, now dressed in a set of Pasha Hawadi's fancy slacks, shirt, and sports jacket, was at the side of the house, checking the windows, when he saw the taxi arrive. A quick look at his watch confirmed that it was early, seven minutes early. This immediately alarmed him since Captain Mustafa was a stickler for punctuality, and he demanded that everyone who worked for him be the same. As he was making his way back toward the front of the house, Thabit saw Dawud approach the taxi and open the back door. Afrah, who was several steps behind Dawud, seemed to hesitate as she studied the driver.

This was not good. Dawud and Afrah should have waited for him. It was his job to check out the taxi before they even got close to it.

Breaking into a sprint, Thabit raced toward his charges, his mind flooding with all the things that could go wrong. He had only made it about halfway to where Afrah was standing, when he saw that the driver had a pistol in his hand and was swinging it toward the girl. Not having a clear shot and still being too far away, Thabit's stomach clenched in anticipation of watching the young girl being shot down right in front of him. But instead of hearing a gunshot, he saw an arm reach out from behind the driver, grab the man's face, and then yank the man's head sideways so hard that Thabit could hear his neck snap. Less than a second later, Thabit was positioned between the taxi and Afrah, his sub-machinegun leveled at the driver, whose body was now slumped forward and whose head faced, unnaturally, back over his right shoulder.

Stunned by what had just happened, Afrah could only stare. The moment she had seen the driver, she had known something was very wrong. The taxi had been recently washed and polished, yet the driver's appearance was quite the opposite. His hair was dirty and unkempt, his jacket and shirt were frayed at the collar and sleeves, and he reeked of cigarette smoke. It was also apparent that the man had recently shaved. His skin, where a beard had grown, was noticeably paler than the rest of his face. On top of that, the driver was in his early or mid-thirties, and Captain Mustafa had described the driver as an "'old friend," someone whom he "trusted." This man was too young and he certainly did not look like a man Captain Mustafa, or anyone else, would trust.

By the time she had come to these conclusions, Dawud had already gotten into the back seat. It was then that she had noticed the man's eyes lock onto her, and she could see that he was smiling as if something pleased him. In the next instant, Afrah had seen the pistol in the driver's hand. He had been trying to aim it at her when Dawud's arm had suddenly appeared, from behind the driver, grabbing the man's face, and then yanking the man's head to the right. The sound of the driver's neck...snapping, had sickened Afrah and she'd had to look away. A moment later, Thabit lunged between her and the taxi. He was pointing his sub-machinegun at the driver, but Afrah knew that was no longer necessary.

Afrah stood there staring at the ground, as Thabit approached the vehicle, his sub-machinegun at the ready. He only momentarily glanced toward Dawud, as Dawud stepped out of the taxi and turned toward his sister.

Dawud hardly noticed Thabit, but instead his eyes searched the mesh screen of the burqa, hoping to see some indication of what Afrah was feeling. Failing to do so, he said, "I am sorry, Afrah, I know I should have acted more quickly."

But what Dawud did not say was that he had somehow known what was going to happen. The moment he'd stepped out of the house, he had known the driver was going to try and kill them. And that was just the beginning. Dawud had known the driver's name...Lashkar. He also had known this man had blood on his hands...innocent blood, and that he would have to be...killed. The rest had been simple, as if he had practiced it a thousand times.

Until now, Dawud had never thought about killing anyone, and then, in the matter of a few seconds, he had not only thought about it, but had actually done it. Struggling to try and make sense of every-thing, Dawud was uncertain as to how he was supposed to be feeling. Was he supposed to feel sorry for the man? Was he supposed to feel guilty? Not feeling either of these emotions, he wondered if he was some kind of "psycho," or was he...something else.

Afrah did not think her brother had acted slowly; in fact, it seemed that he had known exactly what to do and had acted extraordinarily fast. Yet, she was sad for him, sad that he had been forced to take the man's life. When she saw the troubled expression in her brother's eyes, she pulled off her head cover and ran to him, wrapping her arms around him, and hugging him as tightly as she could.

Dawud hugged his sister back, and in doing so, felt relieved. He felt that he had acted correctly and had done what needed to be done. There was no reason to feel guilty, in fact he was certain that not only his sister, but others would now live because he had killed this man. He wondered if this was how his father had felt when he had killed.

After verifying that there was no one else in the car and that the street was clear, Thabit focused his attention on Dawud. In his mind, he was still going over what he had seen. Then he said, "Dawud, I have seen men killed and I have had to do some killing myself, but I have never seen a man killed so swiftly....so efficiently, and with only bare hands. Where in Allah's name did you learn how to do that?"

From the expressions on both Dawud's and Afrah's faces, he imme-diately realized that this was not a subject for discussion, so Thabit added, "Well, it makes no difference...we are running out of time, and I am sure this son of a diseased donkey has friends that will come look-ing for him."

Thabit paused, looking back at the house, and then at the dead man in the front seat of the taxi. Coming to a decision, he said, "Let us put this bag of goat turds in the trunk, then we can put the luggage in front, and I will drive you to the airport."

Unceremoniously shoving the driver's body toward the passenger side, Thabit opened the car door and gestured for Dawud to give him a hand.

Wanting to help, Afrah went to the back of the taxi, and located the trunk latch. For once, she was glad she was a girl. She had no desire to touch the body of that...bad man. Fumbling with the latch, she soon figured out how it worked and released the trunk, letting it spring open. By then, Dawud and Thabit where standing next to her, with the body slung between them. As soon as the trunk was open, Afrah gasped and stepped back. There, staring at her, through open, dead eyes, was the mutilated body of a man, an older man, in his late sixties. His face was badly bruised, his nose and jaw had obviously been broken, and she could see his bloodied hands. All the fingers had been cut off, leaving only stumps. For a second, everyone just stared and then Thabit spoke, saying, "Shit...this must have been Captain Mustafa's friend."

Afrah turned away; she could no longer look, her stomach was beginning to churn, and she felt like she was going to be sick.

Now visibly angry, Thabit looked down at the man they were carrying and with disgust in his voice, said, "Dawud, let us get this dog's ass in the trunk."

Dawud tried not to look at the old man's body, as he and Thabit lifted the driver and roughly dumped him into the trunk. Thabit quickly went through the driver's pockets, and removed a cell phone and an official-looking document from the man's jacket. Unable to find anything else, he hastily arranged the heads, torsos, and limbs of both men so that the trunk lid would close, albeit with some effort.

Thabit went about inspecting the taxi's interior for anything that looked...wrong. There was always the chance that they would be stopped at a police checkpoint, and they did not want to be asked too many questions.

Thabit took the suitcases and expertly wedged them into the front passenger seat. A few minutes later, Thabit was turning the taxi east onto Wazir Akbar Khan Road. Dawud and Afrah were in the back seat, each staring out of their windows at the city that had been their home, a city that had now become too dangerous for them.

As they passed the Child Health Hospital, they veered right around the Massoud Monument, and headed north on Great Massoud Road, toward the Kabul International Airport.

Dawud remembered that Thabit had given him the document he

had taken from the man's jacket. Looking at it, he realized it was the Authorization they would need to get through the airport security checkpoint. He must have taken it from the old man.

Dawud cursed himself. Why had he not thought about the airport checkpoint? His father, a Lieutenant General in the ANA, had taken him through that very checkpoint at least four times, and it had always been a hassle.

The airport was only five minutes away when Thabit suddenly veered off the highway, through a potholed, gravel parking area, and into an opening in the side of an abandoned warehouse. As he was doing so, he explained that the car was feeling heavy and that the springs were nearly bottoming out. The sagging rear end would raise suspicions as to what was in the trunk. They had no choice, the bodies would have to be removed.

Dawud cringed as he thought of having to handle the dead men. He had already gotten blood on his shirt sleeve and he could still smell the faint, but distinct, scent of the man's urine on his hands.

As soon as the car came to a stop, Thabit jumped out, followed, albeit less enthusiastically, by Dawud. Without speaking, Thabit opened the trunk and the two of them reached in, grabbed a limb, and pulled. The bodies were limp; the indignity of death had caused them to release their bowels and bladders. The odor of blood, excrement, urine, and sweat caused Dawud to gag and he almost threw up. Thabit had done a good job of packing the two men in, and now it was taking a lot of effort to free them. Even so, it took them only a minute or two to dislodge and drag the bodies out of the trunk, and onto the oil-stained and litter-strewn concrete floor. Thabit grabbed a handful of old, oil-soaked rags and threw them into the trunk. They would cover up the odors in case someone wanted to get a closer look. Later, he would use the driver's cell phone to call Captain Mustafa and tell him about his friend, and where he could find his body. The other man meant nothing to him...well, not exactly nothing. One fewer Islamic fanatic was always something to thank Allah for.

Back on the highway, they soon spotted the airport security zone. Slowing, Thabit was required to turn into one of several narrow lanes, separated by heavy concrete blast barriers. The lanes led to reinforced guard houses manned by soldiers in full battle gear. Dawud and Afrah were both growing nervous, not just because of the security check, but because they were running out of time. They had less than four minutes before the helicopter was supposed to lift off. Fortunately, the line they were in was short, and they quickly reached the barrier. Thabit assumed a relaxed and confident posture. Then, looking directly at the guard, he presented him with the document. The guard took it and read it carefully. Looking back at Thabit, he studied his face for a long moment, and then looked over his shoulder at Dawud and Afrah. Another guard had stepped to the rear of the taxi and had opened the trunk. Verifying the trunk was empty, the guard closed it and gestured to the guard standing next to Thabit, who, in turn, handed Thabit back the document, ordered the barrier be lifted, and waved him through. Thabit accelerated, but kept his speed slow enough not to attract too much negative attention. The military would not hesitate in firing on a civilian vehicle, if they thought the driver was acting suspiciously. As they crossed through the entrance to the North Side Cantonment (the military section of the Kabul Airport), Dawud spotted a lone Afghanistan Air Force Mi-17 helicopter on the nearby helipad. Its turbines were coming to life and its rotor blades were slowly picking up speed. Thabit did not hesitate, and accelerated toward the helicopter, coming to a screeching stop along its left side, a few meters outside of the shadow of the rotating blades. In a matter of seconds, the suitcases were aboard, and Dawud and Afrah had climbed up the steps and were standing in the doorway. They had not had time to say good-bye to Thabit, whom they saw leaning up against the taxi, watching them. Waving, Afrah mouthed the words "thank you." Thabit smiled and waved back. As Dawud was shown to a seat, he thought about Thabit. He had been guarding them for several weeks, yet they had only spoken to him three or four times, and then only briefly. However, today, in less than an hour, they had gotten to know Thabit. Dawud was sure he was a good man, and would now miss having him around.

Thabit would stay until the helicopter had lifted off and was out of sight. Actually he would stare at the empty sky for a long time after the helicopter had disappeared, still wondering about Dawud, wondering how this mild mannered...university student had so efficiently managed to kill a man.

Dawud and Afrah were directed to sit in fold-down seats that faced another row of seats across the aisle from them. They were told to buckle up and were then handed headsets with attached mics. With the headsets in place, the engine noises were dramatically muffled and they could hear the crew speaking to each other. A moment later, the helicopter started to shake as if the thing was going to come apart, but gradually it lifted off, climbed slightly, dipped its nose, and accelerated forward and up. Several minutes into the flight, the pilot's voice could be heard, advising them that the flight time would be about two hours and that this was a routine supply run to the Taleqan Air Field, which was northeast of Taleqan. Dawud and Afrah were to disembark at Taleqan Air Field. There was a pause and then the pilot's voice again could be heard saying, "There is a growing insurgency presence in the Taleqan area, and it is not unusual for them to shoot at this helicopter. This should not be a problem, since the bottom of this craft is armored."

Dawud and Afrah looked at each other. The pilot's words were meant to reassure, but when they had first boarded, they had both noticed light streaming through numerous small, round puncture holes on both sides of the helicopter. Now, as they studied the craft more closely, they saw several patches, presumably covering old battle wounds. Apparently, hits to this helicopter were not limited to its armored bottom. Furthermore, the crew was wearing thick flak vests and they were sitting on others, in an apparent attempt to protect their...posteriors. Dawud and Afrah had not been offered flak vests, and they suspected the ones the crew were sitting on were spares, meant for passengers such as them. Nonetheless, they were along for the ride, and there was not much they could do about it.

The flight was loud and bumpy, but in many ways, exhilarating. This was Dawud's and Afrah's first helicopter ride, and both spent much of their time twisted in their seats and crooking their necks so they could see out of the small windows behind them. Almost exactly two hours later, Dawud could feel the helicopter begin to descend. A moment after that, he heard a "ping," then another, and another. The pilot's voice came over the headset, saying, "What you are hearing is small arms fire hitting the fuselage. We should be in a more friendly sector in just a minute."

The pilot was right – a couple of minutes later, the craft's landing gear touched down on the concrete helipad and settled. Springing into action, one crewman opened the side door while another man took their headsets and gestured that they unbuckle and disembark. Dawud and Afrah did as instructed, and soon were standing on solid ground. Several seconds later, one of the crewmen handed them their luggage and pointed in the direction of a wide strip of open ground that was bordered, in the distance, by a perimeter road and a tall security fence. They were to make their way to the perimeter road and wait there until someone came to pick them up.

Luggage in hand, Dawud and Afrah trudged off in the direction he had pointed. It did not take long for them to appreciate Captain Mustafa's limit of "one suitcase each." As it was, their suitcases were heavy and cumbersome, making what should have been an easy stroll, into a slog. As they left the noise and activity behind, it became easier to focus on where they were. Looking around, Dawud saw that it was evening and that they were on a large military airfield, that seemed little used. The airfield was located in a broad valley, between two rugged, snow-covered mountain ranges. To the west, he could see distant street lights and a number of low, mud-brick, and cinderblock structures that must have marked the outskirts of Taleqan.

It was getting dark quickly, and with the darkness would come the cold, and tonight, the cold would be accompanied by a piercing wind that came down from the mountains. When they finally reached the road, the darkness had closed in around them. Turning their backs to the wind, Dawud and Afrah sat on their suitcases, wrapped their arms around themselves and stared into the night, as a sense of homesickness and isolation washed over them. Several minutes later, they heard the turbines winding up and the heavy thumping of helicopter blades, as the helicopter lifted off on its return flight to Kabul. Afraid of being targeted, the crew was operating in complete darkness. Dawud and Afrah could not see the helicopter, so they just listened. Part of them longed to be on board, wishing they could return to Kabul. It did not take long for the thumping sound to fade and soon there was nothing but silence, darkness, and the cold wind. Dawud and Afrah did not speak. They were now completely immersed in the darkness and isolation. There was no moon, but there were stars and they filled the sky with the kind of mystical light that can be seen only in the mountains. It was beautiful, but it was a cold and indifferent beauty. As he stared upward, Dawud began to feel his body begin to chill and knew they could not just sit there indefinitely. It was then when Afrah said, "Dawud, I hear something...I think it's a car."

A moment later, Dawud also heard it, and as he strained to see, the vague outline of a vehicle appeared. It drove without headlights and speeded directly toward them. As it got closer, they saw it was a pickup truck. The truck came to an abrupt stop a few meters from where they stood, and they could see it was an old, beat-up Toyota with a cracked front windshield. The driver was in deep shadows and for a long moment, no one made a move. Then, they saw the driver's arm extend out of the window and gesture for them to get in the back of the truck. Doing as instructed, Dawud and Afrah picked up their suitcases and walked to the rear of the truck, then hoisted their suitcases in, and climbed in themselves. The truck's bed was covered with trash, dirt, and an assortment of worn-out and broken hand tools, shovels, and a tattered canvas tarp. The man stuck his head partially out of his side window and ordered them to lie down, and to cover themselves and their suitcases with the tarp. While Dawud and Afrah were trying to comply, the man placed the truck in gear and took off, spraying a cloud of dirt and gravel in his wake. Trying to hang on to the tarp and still stay lodged in the bed of the truck, was all Dawud and Afrah could do. After a few minutes, the ride improved, as the truck turned onto a paved road. Twenty minutes later, the truck came to an abrupt stop, and they heard the driver open his door and get out. The tarp was pulled back, and they were able to see the face of the driver. He looked between 40 and 45 years old, and had a serious-looking, weather-beaten face. He looked at the two of them for a moment, and then quietly said, "You can call me Thauban. I do not have much time, so listen, and do exactly as I say.

A bus will be stopping here in about fifteen minutes. A man and a woman will be getting off. They have told the driver that they need to use the toilet, but instead, they will walk around to the back of the toilet buildings, where you will be waiting for them. You shall immediately switch clothing with these two people. The man will have an envelope in his jacket pocket. The envelope will contain two bus ticket receipts that show your journey began in Charikar, you changed buses in Pol-e-Khomn and Kunduz, and your final destination is Farkhar. When you have changed clothing, you are to get onto the bus. I too, will be boarding the bus at this stop and will have your luggage with me. I will be escorting you to Farkhar, but you are to act as if I am a total stranger. Do not talk to me, do not look at me.

Farkhar is the end of the line so everyone will be getting off. I will collect the suitcases and then I will walk to the far north corner of the bus terminal, where I will put the suitcases down and walk away. Wait a few seconds and then walk over, pick up your suitcases and continue to your destination.

There is one more thing. The bus is poorly lit but to ensure you are not recognized, you are to act reclusive. Pretend that you are tired from a long trip. Keep your faces covered as much as possible, avoid eye contact, and avoid speaking with the other passengers. If you do this well, you will resemble the people you are replacing, and, in time, the other passengers will not remember any of the differences. As you near Farkhar, you must become a little more social. The man can show his face, ask another man for directions to the mosque, and ask if there is any work in Farkhar. The woman can ask another woman for directions to the bazaar, or maybe, ask what fresh fruit is available this time of year. Neither of you is to speak much. Your Kabul accents and your education will give you away. Keep responses simple. If you are asked, give only your given names, you are brother and sister, you have come from Charikar, and you are staying at your uncle's house. Say nothing more about yourselves, but remember, it is important that the other passengers remember that you had ridden with them. Farkhar is a small town, and people will wonder where you have come from and how you got here. If you had come by car, they would wonder if you are somehow important, and why someone important would choose to stay in this poor little town. But if you come by bus, you are ordinary – almost everybody arrives by bus. Most people will not bother to think much about you.

That is all I have to say. You must now go...go hide yourselves behind the toilet buildings."

Dawud and Afrah jumped down from the truck and walked quickly toward the two squat mud-brick structures that Thauban had pointed to. The nearest one was the men's toilet and as they approached the rear of this building, the odor drove away any doubt that this structure housed a toilet pit. The women's toilet was only a few meters away, and Dawud kept his eyes on Afrah as she made her way to the back of that building. Neither of them could see the road from their positions, so they would have to just wait for what would take place next.

It was not long before Dawud first heard the distant groan of the bus' diesel engine. A few seconds later, the engine could be heard slowing, and then there was the sound of crunching gravel as the bus turned off of the pavement and rolled to a stop. For several seconds, he heard only the rough idle of the engine, and then he heard the mechanical clunk of the bus' door being opened. Less than a minute later, the shadowy figure of a man came around the corner of Dawud's building. At nearly the same moment, Dawud saw the silhouette of a woman who had come around the corner of Afrah's building. The man made eye contact with Dawud, nodded slightly, and without speaking, began to remove his clothing. Dawud followed suit and assumed Afrah was going through a similar exercise a few meters away.

In less than two minutes, Dawud had stripped and had donned the other man's clothing. His outfit now consisted of a worn, long-sleeve shirt, with sweat stains beneath each armpit; a dark green wool jacket that smelt vaguely of diesel fuel and also showed signs of wear, including frayed cuffs and threadbare elbows; and a pair of pants that were too big around the waist, but had been recently washed and in reasonably good condition. Dawud wished he could say that about the socks. He would much rather have buried them than worn them, but that was not an option. Next, there were the tennis shoes, a pair of cheap, high-tops, which were a little tight, heavily worn, but still serviceable. On his head, he wore a wool pakol (hat) that had an oily stain extending around the headband. And finally, there was the faded, black and white shemagh (scarf). Dawud was careful to arrange the shemagh, as he wrapped it around his neck. He knew the shemagh was a key part of his disguise, but wearing it in a way that suggested you were trying to hide your face would immediately draw attention. The insurgents often made this mistake, and people had learned to become wary of someone who avoided eye contact, and whose face was too concealed.

Just when Dawud thought he was set to go, the man stepped in front of him. He was comfortable in Dawud's clothing and they fit him well. Dawud fought to suppress a pang of envy, yet he did have to admit, Thabit's clothing had transformed this man into someone of means, someone who did not have to toil for a living.

The man looked hard at every detail of Dawud's...ensemble. Pulling on this, tugging on that, until he finally seemed satisfied. Then he began to study Dawud's face. This gave Dawud his first opportunity to get a good look at the man. He was two or three years older than Dawud, and had the same color hair and similar facial features, but his skin seemed a little darker, and his hair was longer and visibly oilier. As the man studied different sections of Dawud's face, Dawud could see his expression change, becoming more serious, almost worried. He then took his hands and vigorously ran his fingers through his own hair. After a few seconds, he stopped, examined his hands, and then proceeded to rub an oily residue onto Dawud's face, and the back of his hands. To Dawud, it smelt like a mixture of sweat and used engine oil. He had difficulty suppressing the urge to grimace, and while he was being...oiled, he recalled a conversation he had once had with Captain Mustafa. Captain Mustafa was explaining what witnesses tended to remember and what they forgot. He had said people would automatically formed an opinion of you the moment they saw you. It was a complex process that was inborn and found in all human beings. They register how you are different from them, and from those whom they are familiar and comfortable with. Obviously, people with physical features or behavioral characteristics that evoke a sense of fear or distrust, are usually remembered. But there are many other memory triggers that are often unique to a particular region, religion, social class, or even a specific individual. Although Dawud could not recall everything Captain Mustafa had said, he did remember one more thing. If you do not want to be remembered, you must look, think, act, and speak like everyone else, but that is more easily said than done.

This knowledge is useful to the police. When witnesses tended not to remember a person, it could still tell them a great deal about that person.

Dawud knew that many of the bus passengers would be simple, poor people, whose homes often did not even have electricity, and their water came from a community well. These people toiled hard for a meager living. A bath and freshly laundered clothes were often a real luxury.

It was quite apparent that this man was trying to transform him into one of these people, and was doing a remarkably good job at it. But Dawud also knew that he would have to be very careful. Appearances would get him just so far. The wrong gesture, and a poorly chosen word, could draw attention, and soon his appearance, his behavior, and the way he interacted would be scrutinized more closely. Dawud knew he would not pass such scrutiny.

Afrah's experience was similar. The burqa, which Afrah hated, was swapped out for another burqa, which she hated equally as much, but this one was clearly made of a cheaper fabric and was frayed in places, not to mention that it needed to be washed. Since the cuffs of her pants, her shoes, and her socks were visible below the hem of the burqa, all had to be swapped. At least she could keep her own shirt, which was actually her mother's shirt. Before she had left their home, she had wanted to take something that would remind her of her mother. The shirt was her mother's favorite, and had been given to her mother, as a gift, by Afrah's father. Wearing it had made her feel safer, almost as if her mother was somewhere nearby.

Once all of the details had been attended to, the man hurriedly explained that they had been sitting at the rear of the bus, but Dawud and Afrah should try to sit near the front where the people were not as familiar with them. With that said, this mysterious couple turned, and without another word, quickly walked in the direction of Thauban's truck. Watching them disappear into the darkness, Dawud turned to his sister and gestured that they too must go. As Dawud came around the corner, he saw people holding tickets as they boarded an old, beat-up-looking bus. Suddenly, he remembered about the envelope with the ticket receipts. Frantically, he searched his jacket pockets, but there was nothing there. By now Afrah had joined him and could see the anguish in his expression.

Now worried, Afrah said, "Dawud, what is wrong?" Dawud replied, "The envelope...I forgot to ask about the envelope." The importance of this struck Afrah immediately, and she replied, "The pockets, have you checked all of the pockets?" Dawud answered, "Yes, yes...I checked every one of them, they are empty."

Afrah was silent for a moment as she studied Dawud's jacket more closely. Then she spoke.

"Dawud, your jacket, I have seen this kind of jacket before. It has an inside pocket."

A glimmer of hope appeared in Dawud's eyes, as he unzipped the jacket and quickly felt for an inside pocket. A second later, his face flushed with relief as he produced a wrinkled, white envelope, inside of which were the two bus ticket receipts.

He had been careless. If he had continued his fumbling around, they would have missed the bus.

Afrah could see the embarrassment and frustration in Dawud's face and immediately felt sorry for her brother. Dawud was really smart, but was always so hard on himself. Reaching over, Afrah reassuringly squeezed his arm.

A second later, they were walking toward the bus, Afrah a couple of steps behind her brother, as tradition prescribed. The bus driver, a gruff, tired-looking man, gave their receipts a cursory glance and nodded. They were among the last to board and took the first two empty seats they could find. Thauban, who had boarded last, made his way to the back of the bus. When Dawud saw him pass, he looked away.

The doors closed and Dawud saw that the bus was nearly full. The passengers were mostly ethnic Tajiks and included two boys a few years younger than Afrah. They were street peddlers and immediately began trying to hawk their merchandise. This did not go unnoticed, and the driver barked out a stern warning that caused the boys to grudgingly return to their seats. The other passengers were a mixture of farmers, orchard workers, laborers, and a couple of men who looked like they worked on machinery. Dawud could see that his appearance had been designed to blend most closely with these men.

The bus also held more than a dozen women, and at least that many young children. About half the women wore the traditional blue burqa, while the rest covered their heads with loosely draped shawls, or hijabs.

Although the individual garments varied, there was still a uniformity in what these people wore. These were people of modest means and some were clearly poorer than others. This contrasted with Kabul, where bus passengers were usually a mix of the relatively well-off and the poor. If he and his sister had worn the clothes they wore in Kabul, they would have been stared at, whispered about, and...Remembered.

The night had become cold, so to keep the bus warm, the windows had been closed, causing the air to be heavy, rife with the smell of sweat, goats, garlic, diesel oil, and soiled diapers.

A moment later, the bus' engine rumbled to life and the bus lurched forward. They were on their way and the passengers were quickly settling in. Many tried to sleep, while others just blankly stared out at the darkness. Dawud and Afrah weren't sleepy but they let their heads slump forward as they pretended to nod off. This would give them some quiet time, and it was less likely that anyone would try to start up a conversation. Dawud was awakened by Afrah gently elbowing him. He had fallen asleep and as he raised his head, he saw that the passengers were beginning to stir. Everyone seemed to be busy. Some were putting away belongings and retying bundles, while others were coaxing sweaters and coats onto their young children. The sound of voices came from all around him, and it became clear that they were approaching Farkhar. It was now time for him and Afrah to make their presence known. Dawud loosened his shemagh so his face was more visible, turned to his right, and began speaking to the man sitting across the aisle. Afrah reached over and touched the shoulder of the lady in front of her. When the lady looked back at her, Afrah apologized for disturbing her, and told her that she wanted to compliment her on how well behaved her two young girls had been. Five minutes later, the bus pulled to a stop next to a solitary lamp post that dimly lit a plain, cinderblock building that must have been Farkhar's bus terminal.

As the driver shut down the engine, Dawud checked his watch and saw that it was 9:16 PM. It had been less than seven hours since they had left Kabul, and yet it seemed much longer. He was still talking to the man across from him when he glanced out the far side window. There, in the shadows, he caught a glimpse of several figures. As he watched, two more figures joined them and Dawud could see that these men were armed with Kalashnikovs and RPG launchers. From the looks of them, they were probably IMU (Islamic Movement of Uzbekistan) fighters. They wore turbans and their faces were covered by scarves. Dawud knew that there had been a resurgence of IMU activity, and that they were closely allied with both the Taliban and al-Qaeda. All three groups shared similar fundamentalist views and wished to see a strict version of Sharia Law imposed. However, the IMU was known to fund their jihad through organized criminal activity, particularly opium trafficking.

Afrah had noticed similar activity through her window, and had quickly scanned the terminal area for any sign of police or soldiers, but saw none. By then, the other passengers had begun noticing the armed men emerging from the shadows, and the jovial chatter was replaced by a low, nervous murmur. Women busily adjusted their burqas, while others tucked loose strands of hair beneath their shawls and then wrapped them snugly around their heads and faces. Hesitantly, people began to stand and merge into the aisle, and then shuffle toward the open door. Dawud and Afrah had also stood and had worked their way into the line, while attempting to appear as inconspicuous as possible.

Dawud had lost sight of the armed men and as soon as he had stepped down from the bus, he glanced around, hoping he could spot them and maybe avoid walking straight toward them. Failing to do so, he gripped his sister's arm, and drew her off to the side. They needed a plan, they needed some way to get out of there. Just then, one of the passengers, a small but rough-looking man with dark eyes and a dark, stringy beard, abruptly pushed past Dawud, as he headed toward the shadowy area at the right of the terminal building. As Dawud watched, three IMU fighters stepped into view. One of them, a large, rotund man, wearing a light-colored turban and a scarf that covered most of his face, watched as the smaller man approached. When they stood face to face the two men exchanged greetings and began to talk. Then the smaller man turned and pointed in Dawud's direction, or rather just past Dawud, toward the door of the bus. When Dawud turned to look, he saw the last of the passengers exiting and one of them was Thauban. Thauban seemed tense and immediately spotted the man pointing at him. Dawud could see his eyes dart around, and could imagine he was looking for a way to escape. A moment later, over a dozen IMU fighters stepped from the shadows and began spreading out as they moved in Thauban's direction. They were going to try and capture Thauban, and were attempting to box him in. Dawud tried to think of something he could do, some way he could help. His eyes were drawn to the roof of the bus. People were still in the process of removing several large bundles, and had inadvertently pushed a crate of live chickens precariously near the edge of the roof rack. The only thing keeping the crate from falling was a bunched-up length of rope, wedged beneath one corner. The loose end of this rope dangled down the side of the bus, giving Dawud an idea. Without hesitating, Dawud stepped toward the rope, turned his back to it, and carefully reached behind him until he had the rope in his hand. He then tugged and could feel the crate shift, but nothing more. Again, he tugged, and this time the tangle of rope came free and fell. A second later, Dawud was again standing next to his sister, hoping that something would now happen. He would not have to wait long before he heard a woman scream. Both Dawud and Afrah turned toward the bus and looked up to see the crate totter one last time, and then plunge downward. Chickens squawked, feathers flew, children screamed, and people scrambled for safety. Dawud and another man rushed to help, and somehow managed to slow the cage's descent enough to prevent it from bursting open.

The diversion had worked. It had created enough chaos to momentarily distract the IMU fighters, and give Thauban enough time to slip around the front of the bus and disappear into the darkness. Realizing their prey had vanished, the IMU fighters scrambled toward where they had last seen the man. The big man followed suit, though his movements were slower and far more laborious. When it became clear that no one knew where Thauban had gone, the big man became furious and began screaming curses. When one of his men inadvertently crossed in front of him, he awkwardly kicked at him, almost losing his balance and falling. Eventually, the tirade subsided and the big man regained enough control to start issuing more, rational orders. A few minutes later, the band of IMU fighters had broken up into two groups, and had set out in search of Thauban.

Dawud and Afrah had joined a group of passengers who had retreated to the far side of the bus terminal, well away from the fracas. When it became clear that the IMU fighters had gone, the passengers made their way back to the bus and returned to the business at hand. Several of the men climbed up onto the roof and resumed lowering baggage and crates to the men below. The baggage and crates were loosely stacked into piles, which were continually being restacked and restacked again as a groups of men and women sifted through the piles, searching for what belonged to them. Although a few vehicles had appeared, most of the passengers just hefted their belongings onto their shoulders, and with their children in tow, walked off in the direction of their homes.

As the number of people thinned, Dawud and Afrah began paying more attention to their suitcases, which had been placed on the ground next to two, large cardboard boxes. Thauban would not be there to retrieve them and technically, they had no claim to them. Still, they weren't about to abandon the suitcases, since they contained pictures and letters that could be linked to them. As the minutes ticked by, only a handful of the passengers remained. They seemed to be waiting for rides or for someone to come and help carry their bundles. Still, neither Dawud nor Afrah approached their suitcases, and only when they heard the bus' engine rumble to life, did they feel some relief. It was the bus driver's job to watch the baggage. Although the driver had chosen not to leave the bus, he had left the door open and had a clear view of the two boxes and the suitcases. He was the one person who would have seen Thauban with the suitcases, and might take notice if anyone else tried to claim them. The sound of crunching gravel made them turn, and they watched as the bus rolled out onto the road and then turned west, back toward Taleqan. When its tail lights finally disappeared, Dawud and Afrah walked over to their suitcases, picked them up and nonchalantly walked toward the side of the bus terminal. There, in the shadows, Dawud stopped and looked back; no one had seemed to notice.

CHAPTER SIXTEEN

Arrival

Captain Mustafa had provided them a hand-drawn map and had explained that Farkhar was laid out along the Khanabad River, and that Mawlawi Ahmed Abdel's house was at the north end of town, east of the river. As Dawud began studying the map, he quickly realized that you needed to identify certain key landmarks in order to use it. That would be next to impossible. There was no moon, the sky had become overcast, and it was so dark, he couldn't see the other side of the street. After staring at it for several more minutes, he remembered how good Afrah was with maps, and handed it to her.

Afrah was a "'map person"; she loved maps and all the new and exciting places they represented. It did not take long for her to see that someone had spent a considerable amount of time drawing this one. It showed the river, in some detail. It also showed clever little sketches of a bridge, a mosque, a marketplace, and several other notable structures...but not the bus terminal. Looking up, she studied the cinderblock building. She could faintly smell the mortar and saw that the cinderblocks were clean and new-looking. Apparently, this building had not been here when whoever drew the map had last visited Farkhar.

Unfortunately, Dawud was right. To be able to use the map, you had to be able to see the landmarks. Discouraged, she carefully folded the map and handed it back to Dawud. They would need to ask someone for directions, but it was now past 10:00 PM and it would not be safe, to knock on a stranger's door. Afghans were particularly sensitive about being disturbed at night, and would be as likely to shoot you as greet you.

They could head out into the darkness, and hopefully find the river. Then they could follow the river north, but how far should they go before turning east? And then how far east should they go? No, it was much more likely they would just get lost, wander around for hours, and then have to spend the night on the river bank. It would be better if they waited here until it was light. As they both resigned themselves to this fact, Dawud noticed movement out of the corner of his eye. Looking in that direction, he saw a woman approaching. She was clad in a burqa and had two young girls following behind. Stopping in front of Afrah, she asked, "Do you need some help?" Dawud remembered the woman and the two girls from the bus. They had sat directly in front of them, and Afrah had been speaking to the woman just before they arrived. Afrah immediately stood and eagerly replied, saying, "Allah be praised. Yes, yes, thank you. It is so kind of you to ask. We are strangers to Farkhar and do not know the way to our uncle's house. We have a map that gives us directions, but I am afraid it is not much use to us."

The woman studied Afrah and glanced, only momentarily, at Dawud, before she said, "I cannot read maps, but maybe you could tell me your uncle's name? I have lived in Farkhar all my life, and I know everyone that lives here." Afrah noticed hesitation and even a hint of suspicion in the woman's voice, and realized that, as far as she knew, Dawud and she were vagabonds, a pair of homeless drifters, the kind of people who were known to steal and illegally occupy vacant homes.

Afrah replied, "He is our uncle by marriage, and he has never lived here so I do not think you will know his name. The house was left to him by a relative, and had been occupied by his sister, a woman with the family name Abdel. Unfortunately, we do not know much about her, except that she died several years ago, and that she had lived to be quite old. Our uncle has been kind enough to let us stay in the house." The lady, somewhat coolly, replied, "I am sorry, but here in Farkhar, that family name Abdel is very common. Perhaps if you told me your uncle's full name, I would recognize it?"

Afrah knew she was giving out too much information, but this was a small town and people were naturally suspicious of strangers. She did not want to lie and besides, she was a terrible liar, so she decided to tell the truth, at least mostly the truth. Looking at the woman, she said, "My uncle is Mawlawi Ahmed Abdel. We were told that he has notified the lady next door that we are coming. She is the one that will give us access to the house...I assure you it is all very proper."

At hearing the name Mawlawi Ahmed Abdel, the woman seemed to relax and she looked at Afrah with renewed interest as she said, "Yes, the name Mawlawi Ahmed Abdel is familiar to me. He was Hasti's brother and Hasti spoke of him with great admiration and respect. She was a good Muslim, a good woman, but as you have said, she was very old and she suffered from arthritis in her hands and knees. We are all aware that Mawlawi Ahmed Abdel had been very generous with his sister. She had told us that he had wanted her to come live with him, but she refused. This was her home and this is where she wanted to die."

The woman became silent for a moment, as though thinking, then she said, "I believe we can help you, but I must speak with my husband first. Please, will you wait here."

The woman, with the two small girls gripping the fabric of her burqa, turned and quickly walked toward the distant shape of a man loading two cardboard boxes into the back of a pickup truck. Several minutes later, the woman and a man, presumably her husband, returned. The man was in his thirties and looked tired and dirty. He studied Dawud and Afrah for a long moment, grunted a barely intelligible greeting, and then gestured for them to follow him.

A few minutes later, the cardboard boxes, their two suitcases, Dawud, Afrah, and the two young girls were crammed into the back of an old pickup truck, on their way to Hasti's house. The man drove cautiously, with the truck's headlights off. The woman had said that the band of insurgents they had seen at the bus terminal might still be in town, and her husband did not want to run into them.

The two young girls watched them intently and burst out in giggles when Afrah pretended that she was going to tickle them. Five minutes later, they pulled to a stop in front of a low, mud-brick structure. This was Hasti's house. To Dawud, it looked sturdy enough, but like most mud-brick dwellings, it was a little squat. The doorway was only about a meter and a half high and would require everyone, except maybe children, to bend down in order to enter. Dawud looked up and down the street, and he saw that Hasti's house looked very much like the other houses. He also noticed that the street was unpaved and that there were no power poles. No power poles meant there was no electricity.

The front yard was enclosed by a plastered mud-brick wall that stood about a meter high. The walls on the sides of the property were closer to two meters high. From what he could see, the people living in this neighborhood were not wealthy, but the houses looked reasonably well-maintained and there was no litter that he could see.

Dawud and Afrah hopped down from the truck bed and retrieved their suitcases. Dawud thanked the man, who grumbled something back at him, and drove off. He could see the two little girls enthusiasti-cally waving at them, waves Dawud and Afrah both gladly returned.

In the window, next door, Dawud caught a glimpse of a candle be-ing lit, and a moment later, the door opened and out stepped a stooped, emaciated, old lady, wearing a hijab and with a thread-bare blanket wrapped around her shoulders. She had been told that a young man and a young woman, a brother and sister, would be arriving by bus, and that she was to wait for them so that she could let them into the house. The old lady had been waiting for them in the dark, not wanting to waste a candle. Using a knurly old stick as a cane, she hob-bled the distance over to where Dawud and Afrah were standing. Her breath labored, she studied them with dark, sunken eyes. Then, turn-ing to Afrah, she said, "You are Mawlawi Ahmed Abdel's niece." She said this more as a fact than a question. And before Afrah could re-spond, she continued, "I am the 'old lady,' and that is what you will call me, and that is what everyone else calls me. I am the caretaker, the one who keeps Mawlawi Ahmed Abdel's house clean and the rats out. For this, I am paid only 600 afghanis (~10.50 US Dollars) a month. It is too little money for all the work that I must do. It is a big house, an old house, and there is something that is always breaking." She further ex-plained that she had been the caretaker for over four years, ever since Hasti had died. She went on to tell them that this spring she had to buy a piece of corrugated metal to repair the roof, and that yesterday, the wind had blown in so much dust that it had taken her all day to clean it out. But what seemed to most upset her was having to wait "until the middle of the night" for them to show up.

Afrah studied the old woman as she spoke. Although her words and the tone of her voice came across as hard and cantankerous, Afrah's attention was drawn to the woman's eyes. Even in the dark, Afrah could see the deep sadness and hardship this woman had experienced. Yet, there was a gentleness there too, a gentleness that completely contradicted this caricature standing before them. Immediately Afrah knew that the complaining and crankiness were an act, one this old woman had certainly refined, but nevertheless, an act.

Afrah could see that the old woman had white hair and that it was long and straight. Her face was deeply furrowed, but her features were fine, and hinted at the beauty she had once been. Now her back was bent, her fingers were knurled, and her movements were awkward and painful. It was plain to see that she was malnourished and was nothing but skin and bone. Nevertheless, she held her head with a kind of grace and dignity that defied her age, and even more so, her condition. Afrah wondered who this woman really was. What had her life been like?

It was not long before the intensity of the old woman's ire dissipated, her voice quieted and they heard her say, "I am an honest woman, and I have had to work hard all of my life. But now, I am too old and have rheumatism in my hands. I will not be able to find work...Who would pay me?"

It was clear to both Dawud and Afrah that this woman had been surviving off of a meager 600 AFN a month, and that their presence meant she would likely lose that income.

Afrah cleared her throat and then said, "Madame, I have no doubt that you are an excellent worker, and Mawlawi Ahmed Abdel is very fortunate to have you."

On hearing Afrah say Mawlawi Ahmed Abdel's name, the old woman became visibly troubled. Looking up at the two of them, she said, "Please, I ask you, do not tell Mawlawi of my complaining...and my rudeness. I know that he has paid me what he can afford, and it is more than others get. He has never once questioned my work, even though he knows that some days I am too tired to sweep out his house and rid it of those spider webs. He never asks any questions and he has always paid me promptly.

I am an old lady, and do not like what being old has done to me. Sometimes I worry, and sometimes I get very mad, and I forget to be grateful to those that have helped me."

Afrah reached for the old woman's hand and held it, saying, "Madame, I promise that I...and my brother (giving Dawud a quick glance) will convey only our highest regard for the work you have done......In fact, I am so convinced that you are an excellent worker, that I would be foolish not to find a way to use your services. Perhaps you would be willing to help me settle in. I am afraid I am a city girl, and I need to learn much about living in the country. Of course, I will pay you a fair wage...and, if you are tired or are not feeling well, you may rest for as long as you need."

The old woman's eyes glistened with tears. She did not say anything for several seconds, then, in a strained voice said, "Child, why are you trying to be so...so kind to me? People have told me that I am not a very pleasant person and I have no reason to doubt them." Though the old woman had been touched by Afrah's offer, she was also confused, and there was more than a little suspicion in her voice. Afrah knew that this old woman could be exasperating and that she intentionally provoked people. But Afrah did not mind this bristly exterior, for she saw something special...no, something....precious. Replying, Afrah said, "Madame, my offer is sincere. I do need your assistance and would be grateful for whatever help you could offer me." The old woman looked down at her knurly hands for a long moment, then, without raising her head, said, "You do not know me and yet you make me this offer." Pausing again, she then continued, "Child, I cannot accept money for helping my neighbor, for doing something that is my duty as a Muslim. Allah has always provided for my needs and I trust in His will."

Without support from family, poor women, particularly old women, had a very difficult time surviving. Afrah knew that without her help, this old woman would not make it through the winter. She would speak to Dawud and they would come up with something.

Dawud had quietly stepped away from the two women. It was common for more conservative Muslim women to avert their eyes and not speak, while in the presence of a man, particularly a man who was a stranger to them. He knew his sister certainly did not subscribe to this belief, but in deference to the older woman, he gave them some space. Still, Dawud was curious, so he remained close enough to hear much of the conversation. It immediately became clear that the old woman's situation was desperate, but what had most caught his attention was his sister. He had thought of her only as a young girl, barely 16 years old, yet she was interacting with this old woman, with the grace and dignity he would have expected from his mother. Afrah was growing up and he was suddenly very impressed by the person she was becoming.

When the old lady had finished saying what she had to say, she removed a heavy brass key from her pocket. The key had a cord tied to it, with the other end tied to a safety pin she had attached to her dress. It was obvious she took her caretaker job very seriously. Without saying a word, she stepped past Dawud, hobbled up to Hasti's front door, unlocked the antique brass padlock, and opened it. She then stepped in front of Afrah and explained that there were several candles and matches on a table, to the right of the door. Having nothing left to say, she reached out and touched Afrah's arm, then turned, and hobbled away toward her house.

Afrah entered first, followed closely by Dawud. It was pitch black inside the house, and the place smelled earthy and had the faint aroma of herbs and spices. It took several seconds to locate the stubby candles and the matches. Lighting two of the candles, Afrah handed one to Dawud and they began to explore the house. In the dancing shadows, they were able to see that there were three separate, sparsely furnished rooms. It did not surprise them to find the place clean, which was no easy feat, since the floor was made of packed clay and sections of plaster were missing, exposing the crumbly mud-bricks below. After a quick check, Dawud was grateful that there was no evidence of water damage, suggesting that the old lady had managed to maintain the roof. Water damage, from rain or melting snow, caused havoc to mud-brick structures and could make a building uninhabitable in only a season or two.

Though clean, the walls had not been painted in decades and were a dingy brown in color. Two of the rooms were small, each only large enough for a narrow bed, and a paint-chipped, wooden bureau. The third room, the main room of the house, was larger but still only about four meters on a side. It was used for food preparation, eating, bathing, entertaining, and pretty much everything else. This room was furnished with a sturdy wooden table and three less-sturdy-looking chairs, plus an old wooden cabinet. Hasti must have used the top of the cabinet to cut and prepare her food, as evidenced by the deep grooves in the surface.

It was Dawud who spotted it first – the ancient, ornate, cast iron stove. This was a real surprise and was something that was completely out of place. Stoves like this were found in the kitchens of the elegant, old mansions in Kabul, not in austere, mud-brick structures like this one. They had been told there was a stove, but they had expected a simple, rusty metal box on some sort of pedestal. They would not have complained, since most of these houses had only crude fireplaces, or simple fire pits, for their cooking and heat. Drawn to the stove, both Dawud and Afrah carefully ran their fingers over the ornate, nickel-plated fittings, and marveled at the artistic detail in the castings. Touching the metal soon reminded them of how cold it was, and they immediately set out to find some firewood. But after several minutes of searching the house and the yard, they had found nothing they could use for fuel. So, unless they wanted to burn the furniture, they would not have a fire that night. While searching for firewood, they had also noticed there were no dishes, utensils, pots and pans, or any of the countless other things they would need to make this a home. Dawud and Afrah both knew they were lucky to have a roof over their heads, and they knew it would fix up nicely, but, at that moment, they felt the coldness, the darkness, and distant strangeness of the place. As they stared silently at the cold stove, they heard a knock on the door. Worried that the IMU, or some other variety of jihadist, had tracked them down, Dawud told Afrah to go and stand by the back door. If someone tried to force their way in, she was to make a run for it. When Afrah was in position, Dawud stood to the side, just in case someone started shooting through the door. Then, clearing his throat, he barked in the most irritated and authoritarian voice he could muster, "Who is there?"

He was immediately relieved to hear the voice of the old woman, who replied, "It is me, your neighbor from next door. I have something for your sister; now open the door before I drop it."

Dawud was glad to hear that it was the woman's voice, but at the same time, felt as if he were being scolded. And it was a feeling he somehow knew he was going to have to get used to. Opening the door, he saw the old lady, precariously supporting a plain aluminum tray that held a small metal plate of steaming hot rice, a few pieces of dried fruit, and a chipped, porcelain tea pot that was emitting a cloud of hot, fragrant steam. Next to the tea pot was one ceramic tea cup. Squinting up at him, the old woman said, "This is for the young lady...I do not know about you yet."

Before Dawud could reply, Afrah nudged him aside and greeted the old lady. Afrah saw a look of surprise that was instantly replaced by concern. Tears formed in the old lady's eyes, as she looked into Afrah's face. It was then that Afrah remembered she had removed the head covering of her burqa, and now the old woman could see her...scars.

Tears running down her face, the old lady said, "Child, I have seen this once before, it is the work of the Taliban. – 'May every last one of them be deprived of Allah's blessing'."

Afrah had worn her scars proudly, using them to constantly remind herself of what those mindless, religious fanatics had done to her and to her mother. She would not forgive them and one day they would pay. However, now, as she looked into the old woman's eyes and saw her tears, Afrah could not speak. Her eyes, too, filled with tears that soon began to flow down her cheeks. Embarrassed, and disgusted with her display of self-pity, she lowered her head and turned away. For a moment, the old lady did not say anything, and then she painfully hobbled over to Afrah and said, "Now Child, I have embarrassed you, and for that I am sorry. It is that I have seen so much in my life, many good things, that is for certain. But I have seen far too many bad things. In my old age, I am becoming more and more worried that too many bad things are being done in the name of Allah. I know that I am a simple woman; I do not read, I do not write, yet, I know, in my heart, that this is very, very wrong."

The old lady paused for a moment as she thought. She was not good at words, and for far too long, she had found it easier to be rude and offensive than to offer comfort. Then in a quiet voice, she said, "Forgive me, I know that I should not be speaking of such things, but Child, when I first saw you, you frightened me. It is not that I feared you would harm me...no, it was that I knew you were not like the others and that I....." Catching herself, the old woman paused. She would not say what had truly frightened her. It would serve no purpose and she could not change it. Sighing, the old woman continued, "Yes, it is true that you have been...marked, but it has become clear to me that you bear this mark for all of us, and it makes you more beautiful than you will ever imagine.

You see, I have always had a sense for such things, but until now it had meant little to me. It was like knowing that beneath a leaf was a green pebble. This was a clever trick but I soon tired of green pebbles."

Glancing at Dawud, with her now-familiar distrust and contempt, she said, "The rice and tea, they are getting cold. Here, you take this, your sister must now eat."

With that said, the old woman handed the tray to Dawud, turned, and hobbled out, back into the darkness.

Dawud and Afrah both knew this...peculiar old woman was desperately poor and seriously malnourished. She could not afford to give away her food. Dawud and Afrah could not ever remember being hungry, not really hungry. How could they take food from someone who had so little to spare? Not knowing what to say, both Dawud and Afrah stared at the open door for several long seconds. They wanted to call out to her and insist that she eat the food, every morsel, but they knew they could not. Somewhere deep inside Dawud's mind, he could hear his mother's voice reciting a proverb she had so carefully taught him.

"To return a gift given from the heart is to break the heart of the giver."

As young children, he and Afrah had been taught this simple proverb, but not until now, had they understood how...how complicated
adherence could be. Dawud placed the tray on the table and then
closed the door.

They both stared at the tray of food; neither of them had an appetite, not now, yet they knew that not eating would, in its own way, be
disrespectful. Of course Afrah insisted that they share, and they ate
without speaking, without tasting. Afrah would be sure to return the
tray, the dish, and the tea pot and cup, the very next morning. She
would be sure to thank the old lady profusely, she would acknowledge
her kindness and generosity, and then she would compliment her on
the food, and how it was exactly what they had desired.

Exhausted, all they now wanted to do was sleep. Dawud had discovered one, threadbare, wool blanket beneath one of the lumpy
mattresses. It smelt musty, and moths had eaten holes in several places. Thinking it might help to shake it, Dawud took the blanket out back
of the house, and repeatedly shook it and swatted it until he thought it
might come apart. By the time he came back into the house, Afrah had
lit two more of the stubby candles and had organized the sparse fur-
nishings. She had chosen her bedroom, the one with the small window
that looked to the southeast. Dawud insisted she take the blanket and
as he stepped away, he smiled to himself. It was the first time he had
seen his sister so...full of life, in a very long time.

Before retiring to her room, Afrah turned and said, "Dawud, I think
we will like this place."

That night, both Dawud and Afrah prayed that Allah would protect
their father, and that he would show mercy to the old woman next
door.

CHAPTER SEVENTEEN

Settling-in

Time passed quickly, the days were full and soon Dawud and Afrah had made the small mud-brick house comfortable, and stocked with all the basic necessities. It was vital that they draw as little attention to themselves as possible, yet their very presence was a curiosity. For Afrah, anonymity was made easy by the burqa she wore whenever she left the house. Dawud, on the other hand, drew stares whenever he appeared in public. Those living in Farkhar weren't altogether unaccustomed to seeing strangers. There were the usual refugees and before the fighting had increased, the Farkhar District had been a sightseeing destination. Nevertheless, there was something about Dawud that made him stand out. He credited it to being from the "big city," or maybe it was because his father had been a General and he had unknowingly picked up some of his traits. When he asked Afrah why people seemed to notice him, she just shrugged, then smiled and quipped, "It's because they must know you are related to me."

It was not long before the questions started: "What is your name? Where do you come from? Why are you here in Farkhar?" were top of the list. Not answering was not an option and would have immediately raised suspicion. Instead, Dawud and Afrah concocted a story that would explain who they were and why they were here. First, they agreed that they would use the surname Ullah. Afrah had read somewhere that Ullah was one of the most common surnames in Afghanistan, so it would be very difficult for someone to verify. Next, they claimed that they had left Kabul because their home and their father's tapestry business had been destroyed, in fighting between the army and the jihadists. Dawud and Afrah had chosen to use the tapestry business, because of what their father had told them about their real grandfather, and the fact that they actually knew quite a bit about tapestries. It had been one of their father's interests and he had passed it on to them. They would continue their story by saying the loss of their father's business had caused their family to suffer a financial hardship, and their father and mother had been forced to move into a very small apartment. Uncle, Mawlawi Ahmed Abdel, their father's sister's husband, had seen how difficult their living conditions had become, and offered Dawud and Afrah his vacant house in Farkhar. They would stay there while their mother and father worked on rebuilding their business. An effort that would take many months, maybe a year or even more.

Dawud and Afrah would repeat this story dozens of times, and when questioned further, they would feign discomfort at having to further discuss their unfortunate circumstances.

There was little doubt that the old lady knew that Dawud and Afrah had secrets, but she never asked questions. Instead, she took Afrah beneath her wing and taught her the oddities of the town's marketplace. Afrah was introduced to a number of the vendors, some of whom were notorious smugglers. Since the fighting had increased, the smugglers were the town's only reliable source of rice, tea, and cooking oil. These men and their string of donkeys traveled cross-country, mostly at night. They knew the land and they knew how to avoid the insurgents, the militias, and the ANA. They also knew what was going on in the neighboring villages – who got married, who gave birth, and who died. Because of this, they served as a type of news service.

As time passed, Afrah learned which of the merchants were the friendliest and most trustworthy. She learned how to choose the best cuts of meat, the freshest vegetables, the freshest bread, and the best cheese. Afrah would always buy a little more than she and Dawud needed and then insist that the old woman take the extra, so it would not spoil or go to waste. The old lady would gently scold Afrah for not better managing her budget, but in the end, she would take the extra food.

They had been there only a week when Afrah discovered that the old woman loved to cook, and the one thing she loved even more was to teach Afrah how to cook. Soon, the elegant, old cast iron stove was being used to cook something from early morning to late evening. It took some experimenting, but soon the old lady and Afrah were preparing meals that were the envy of the neighborhood. Afrah was not as inexperienced as she had let on. Her mother had taught her how to cook, and she had become quite proficient at it. But here, in this isolated, little town, there was a limited selection of ingredients, and even fewer spices and seasonings. In many ways, Afrah had to relearn how to cook, and using a wood stove made it an even bigger challenge.

Cooking turned out to have some unexpected advantages. The old woman would always taste the fruit to be sure it was ripe. She would taste the vegetables to be sure they were properly seasoned, and she would be sure to taste the meat to be sure it was tender. This meant she was eating more and Afrah had to do less coaxing. On days when the two of them cooked larger meals, it was easy for Afrah to persuade the old woman to eat with them, and to take home some of the lefto-vers. These efforts were paying off, and the old woman was steadily gaining weight, she had more color in her complexion, and her energy level had increased. This later improvement was problematic for Dawud, since the old woman was constantly finding things for him to do, and then would supervise his every move.

To get some time to himself, Dawud had gladly taken on the re-sponsibility of purchasing firewood. He would do this scientifically. He would identify the available wood varieties, and then determine which ones burned the hottest and lasted the longest. Then he would decide the most economic mix of firewoods. After querying several neighbors and a couple of older men whom he had met at the mosque, Dawud determined that a mixture of about 20 percent dry brush and 80 percent seasoned pistachio limbs was optimal. Firewood was sold in bundles of various sizes. The larger bundles where intended to be car-ried on the back of a donkey, while the smallest bundles could be carried by a woman or child. As one might expect, the ratio of fast-burning brush, to larger diameter, slow-burning pistachio limbs, varied between sellers. Every three or four days, he would have to go to the marketplace, find a suitable mix, and then haggle over the price. This was becoming a monotonous and tedious exercise, one that he had be-gun to dread.

It then occurred to him that if he bought directly from one of the nearby suppliers, say, a pistachio orchard that routinely trimmed their trees, he could save some money and get a superior mix. Soon, word got out that the newcomer was going "direct," and bypassing the old-time wood sellers. The next time Dawud showed up at the pistachio orchard, nearly a dozen wood sellers were waiting for him. They didn't say anything; their looks and the meter-long pistachio limbs they car-ried, said all he needed to know. For the next couple of weeks, Dawud was forced to pay the asking price, since none of the wood sellers would haggle with him, and others refused to sell him wood at any price.

With winter coming, the need for firewood increased and Dawud was having to purchase a bundle once every two or three days. This was when Dawud decided he would buy in bulk. If he bought three or four weeks' worth of firewood at one time, he would have more latitude to specify the mix and to negotiate a better price. He could not carry three weeks' worth of firewood, so he would have to purchase a used wheelbarrow. Dawud calculated that the wheelbarrow could pay for itself in just two months and then he would start showing some real savings. The next morning, he purchased a sturdy wheelbarrow from a nearby neighbor, and shuffled off to the marketplace. There, he found a wood seller with a decent mix of wood, and as he had expected, he was able to purchase six bundles for about the price of five. This meant he had saved 16 percent. Dawud was pretty pleased with himself as he loaded the bundles onto his wheelbarrow, but his confidence began to dissipate when he found that six bundles was far more than his wheelbarrow could handle. The wood seller he had bought the wood from, had cleared out his inventory, and had packed up and gone home. Dawud would not dare to entrust any of his wood with the other wood sellers, most of whom he recognized as members of the gang that had driven him away from the pistachio orchard. Having no other choice, Dawud balanced the last two bundles precariously atop the four others, and set out for home. By the time he had made it halfway, the wheelbarrow had toppled three times, each time dumping the entire load onto the road. When the bundles fell, some of the more brittle branches broke into pieces that were too small to bother picking up. Tired of restacking his bundles and realizing that he was losing wood each time the wheelbarrow toppled, he decided to come up with an alternate plan.

Carefully scanning the area, he found a spot where he could hide two of the bundles, while he hurried home with the other four bundles, unloaded them, and hurried back. It took only about 15 minutes to make the round trip, but when he returned, he found an old man sitting on top of one of his bundles. Breathing heavily from running, Dawud politely asked the man to stand. He explained that the two bundles of firewood were his, and that he needed to load them onto his wheelbarrow. The old man did not move and just stared at Dawud. When Dawud stepped closer, the old man reached for the heavy stick that lay against his leg. From the looks of him, he had every intention of striking Dawud if he came any closer. By then several people had gathered around and were watching, with some interest. A young boy, maybe 10 or 11, stepped up to Dawud and informed him that the old man was Adib, and that the firewood was on his property. Dawud was familiar enough with property rights to know that property owners often felt they had rights to everything and anything that was on their property. It was becoming clear that he might lose both of these bundles of firewood if he didn't think fast. A few minutes later, everyone had gone about their business and Dawud was wheeling one bundle of firewood home. He had agreed to pay the old man one bundle as rent, for temporarily storing the firewood on his property.

That evening, Dawud was unusually quiet and when Afrah asked him what was wrong, he explained to her what had happened. Afrah knew about the pistachio orchard incident and now, when she heard about his latest misfortune, she became silent. For a moment, Dawud thought she might be angry with him, but then he noticed the expression on her face and her body shaking. A second later, Afrah could not hold it in anymore and she burst out into laughter. But it did not stop there. To Dawud's dismay, his sister got to her feet and while laughing so hard that tears streamed down her face, she sprinted next door to share the story with the old woman. It was not long before Dawud could hear both his sister and the old woman roaring with laughter. Dawud brooded for several more minutes, and then, even though he fought it, a smile appeared at the corners of his mouth.

Now, whenever Dawud went to purchase firewood, children would follow him, and a small crowd of adults would gather around to see what he was going to do next. Even some of the old-time wood sellers would close shop, and come over to watch. Seeing that he was quickly becoming a kind of odd-ball celebrity, Dawud decided to suppress any new ideas he might come up with, at least for now. He settled in to a routine of purchasing four bundles of the best mix available. This bored the spectators, and he was soon left alone.

Winter came quickly and the nights became long and cold. Dawud and Afrah had set aside some money, and Dawud purchased a simple but sturdy metal stove for the old woman. Until then, she had been using her small, inefficient fireplace to try and keep warm. As expected, the old woman protested, but Afrah managed to smooth over her ruffled feathers by convincing her that the stove was not very expensive, and it was the very least they could do, in return for all the help that she had given Afrah. Soon, the heavy snows arrived and it became apparent that the old woman was not using the stove. She had no money for firewood, and it had become impossible for her to go out and gather even the most meager amount of twigs and branches. Afrah insisted she spend much of the day at their house, where the cast iron stove radiated a pleasant warmth all day and night. Dawud and Afrah were always sure to have enough firewood to spare some, and Dawud would slip out each evening, and build a small fire in the old woman's new stove. It would take nearly half an hour before the ice in the tea kettle would melt, and another half hour before the air temperature would rise above freezing.

The winter seemed like it would never end and by the time spring had arrived, both Dawud and Afrah were sick and tired of the cramped space, the constant bone-chilling cold, the gloomy days, and the endless nights. It was also apparent that they had only enough money to last a few more months. The long winter had given Dawud time to think, and he realized how isolated they had become. They had been in Farkhar for over seven months and neither their father nor Captain Mustafa had contacted them. In fact, they had almost no news from Kabul, and had no idea what was happening anywhere else in the world. As far as they knew, Kabul could have fallen to the Taliban and the Taliban could be marching north.

Dawud and Afrah had been regular attendees at a local mosque, and Dawud remembered that the Mullah owned a battery-powered radio. Dawud also knew that the Mullah regularly visited with the Malik (headman), and that the Malik had electricity and satellite television. Dawud avoided politicians of every kind, mostly because he did not trust them. If, for just a second, the Malik suspected he and his sister were wanted by the Taliban, Dawud was sure they would be thought of as some kind of bargaining chip. Something to be traded away at just the right time. No, interacting with a politician was out of the question, but hanging out at the mosque might be a good place to catch up on the news. The Mullah had wanted Dawud to translate a poem from Arabic to Dari, and when Dawud had agreed, the Mullah had asked him to teach an Arabic class. Dawud had refused, worrying that it would draw too much attention to him. But now, he was having second thoughts. He and his sister were no longer a novelty, and people had begun to accept their presence as natural. Anyway, teaching had some benefits. He wouldn't be paid, but the students often provided gifts, based on what they could afford. He had seen students give chickens, vegetables, even a pair of sandals.

The next Saturday, Dawud spoke to the Mullah and a week later, Dawud was conducting his first class in basic Arabic.

Ten scared, wide-eyed boys, stared up at him from two rows of wooden benches. After a few awkward moments, Dawud did some adjusting of his material, and soon there were smiles and even occasional laughter. At the end of class, an hour and a half later, everyone was busy practicing their new Arabic words.

Dawud worked hard to make the class fun and interesting, and soon there were five more students, and his desk was soon stacked with eggs, apples, cheese, and pistachio nuts – lots of pistachio nuts. A few weeks into the class, the father of one of his students approached him. His name was Vafa, and after a brief discussion about how well his son was doing, he offered Dawud a job. Vafa was an intelligent, energetic man, in his late thirties. He had inherited his father's pistachio processing business, and now wanted to expand it. The man was literate, but like many Afghan men, he had received a religious education, which usually meant he had been taught to read and write at a local mosque, and the experience had been focused more on religious instruction than general education. Now, he was in need of more practical skills like accounting and inventory control. Vafa's son had told him that Dawud had been a university student, had studied mathematics, and wanted to be an engineer. Vafa's math skills were, at best rudimentary, and he saw Dawud as the answer to his prayers. Unfortunately, the man could not pay very much, and Dawud would have to accept a good part of his salary in pistachio nuts. Dawud liked the man, and he liked pistachio nuts, so he accepted the job. It turned out that the money wouldn't be enough to cover even their most basic living expenses. However, sacks of pistachio nuts were beginning to pile up in a corner of their house. These were far too many pistachio nuts for him, his sister, and the old woman to eat, and they would spoil if kept too long. As their financial problems grew, Dawud began bartering pistachio nuts, first for firewood, and then for eggs, cheese, and vegetables. Still, they had plenty of pistachio nuts, so Dawud bartered away five sacks of pistachio nuts for two, skinny goats. Supplementing the goats' diets with stale pistachio nuts, they soon began gaining weight and the doe began producing some of the richest milk they had ever tasted.

Within a couple of months, Vafa's business had increased enough to give Dawud a raise, but by then their system of bartering, and the gifts Dawud was receiving for teaching Arabic, were providing them a relatively comfortably lifestyle. So every month, Afrah would take the money Dawud had earned and she would tuck it away.

Each Saturday afternoon, after his Arabic class, Dawud would spend some time talking to the Mullah and listening to his radio. There was never any mention of his father or Captain Mustafa, but it seemed Kabul was becoming more violent. Taliban student rioters had caused a temporary closure of the university, demanding an end to both co-educational classrooms and the teaching of non-Islamic subjects.

Spring and summer were passing quickly, and Dawud began to dread thinking about all that needed to be done before the cold winds and snow once again descended upon them. Still, it was late summer and both Dawud and Afrah were determined to enjoy it. However, as the days passed, Dawud began feeling that the squat, little mud-brick house they had called home for more than a year, was not really their home. It seemed to be more like a way-point to some unknown destination.

On one late summer evening, Dawud was washing up and sensed something was off. Afrah, who would always engage him in cheerful conversation, had said almost nothing to him that entire afternoon. Something was bothering his little sister, and as he dried off, he studied her. She was nestled into one of her over-stuffed pillows and was looking at the stove, or at least in its direction. Her eyes were focused on something, something that was far away, and there was just a hint sadness in her eyes. Walking over to her, Dawud sat down on a cushion and asked, "Afrah, is something wrong? Are you not feeling well?"

When she realized Dawud was speaking to her, Afrah replied, "I am fine, Dawud. Do not worry...I...I am just feeling a little bit sorry for myself. Sometimes, I get foolish thoughts, but they will pass." Although he usually neglected to tell her, his sister meant the world to him. She was now only 17, yet this girl, this young woman had managed to set up a comfortable home that anyone would be proud of. She had cared for the old woman next door, ensuring that she was fed, kept warm, and most importantly, made to feel important. She had managed their money carefully, and they had everything that they needed. He felt fortunate that she was with him, and he was now concerned by the sadness in her eyes, and in her voice. Reaching over and touching her shoulder, Dawud said, "Please, Sister, talk to me, tell me what is bothering you, maybe there is something I can do?"

After a long pause, she looked up at him and he could see that her eyes were red; she had been crying. Suddenly worried, he asked, "Have I done something wrong?" Afrah gave her brother a smile, although there was little joy in the smile, and then she said, "No, Dawud, you have not done anything wrong...at least not recently. I was just thinking about school... Do you think I will ever be able to go back to school? I know I will never marry. I will not have children. Honestly, what man would take me as a wife? There are so many pretty girls to choose from. I know this to be true. I can see it each time I look into a mirror, and I can see it each time I pass a group of girls that are my age. Their faces are not scarred. This is a fact and I have accepted it. I do not feel bad anymore...really, I do not. But I would like to go back to school...someday. I know I cannot go back now. I've been saving some of the money you have given me. It is not much but it might help...a little bit."

Dawud's heart sank and his eyes stung as tears began to form. Over the past months he had hardly noticed his sister's scars. But now that he looked at her, he could see that there was still a little ruddiness and some discoloration. It was much better than it had been, and it did not take away from his sister's beauty. She had long, shiny auburn hair, and her features were fine, almost delicate. Her eyes where large, soft green in color, kind, and fiercely intelligent. And then there was that smile; Afrah had the ability to light up a room with her smile. It was hard to explain, but in some strange way, the...marks had made her even more beautiful. He remembered what the old woman had said about how the marks had made her look even more beautiful, and he understood what she was saying. His little sister did not know these things about herself...how could she?

Dawud took a breath and said, "Afrah, I know that I am just your brother and you may not think I understand these things, but please listen to me. You have become a beautiful woman. The mark does not diminish that beauty." Dawud paused for a moment, as he looked at his sister, and then continued, "Afrah, you...you have been splashed with acid and your mother has been murdered. These crimes were committed by those who could not tolerate the thought of educated women, nor could they tolerate a woman who would dare to stand against them. Yet, you have not cowered; you have not submitted to their will. Instead, you have become stronger. When you smile, it is as if the sun is shining, but it is not the smile of a young girl, but the knowing smile of a woman, a beautiful woman.

And now, my Sister, as far as men and marriage are concerned, I am afraid you will not have a problem attracting men. On the contrary, I am more afraid that you will have more suitors than you care for...It may sound strange to you, but in my mind I can see there is a man out there, he is waiting for you. I cannot make out his features but he is strong and he is tall, and I believe you will think him to be handsome. But, more importantly, I know that he is a good man and he is a brave man. He will care for you Afrah, he will care for you more than he cares for anything in this world. This is what I know with absolute certainty.

Now, as far as school is concerned, I promise you that I will do everything I can to get you back into school. Allah willing, one day you will graduate from a great university, and I will have the honor of being there."

Afrah had carefully listened to every word her brother had said, and it had brought tears to her eyes. He was bossy and he always forgot to pick up after himself, but he loved her, and he really tried to take care of her. Sometimes, he knew things...things she couldn't explain. Maybe he knew this too, but it didn't matter. He had made her feel better, and that was enough.

Taking a moment, Afrah wiped her tears away, and then she looked at her brother and said, "Thank you, Dawud...You are kind to me and I am very glad that I am your sister." Dawud was relieved and said, "Now you must smile for me. This house has become cold, and it needs you to smile for it." Afrah hated smiling on command, but she could not help herself, and she did as he asked. On seeing his sister's smile, Dawud sighed and said, "Ahh-h-h yes...the house is warm again."

CHAPTER EIGHTEEN

Stranger

On a Monday afternoon, in mid-September, Dawud was cleaning up a trowel he had used to patch cracks in the stucco of the side wall, when he noticed a tall, lean-looking man, with scruffy, sandy-colored hair and beard, walking directly toward their house. As he got closer, Dawud got a better look at him, and saw that he was young, not much older than he was. His skin was deeply tanned and his clothing was worn and dirty. He had the appearance of a man who had been living out of doors. At first Dawud thought he might be one of the local herders, but there was something about him, an air of self-assuredness that wasn't generally associated with herders. Dawud immediately tensed. He had seen this...cockiness before. A couple of years ago, he had noticed three men pass him in the hallway of the Engineering Building. He had noticed them because they carried themselves with that same self-assuredness. Later, he would learn that they were the al-Qaeda cadre and that they had been trying to recruit one of his classmates.

As the man stepped through the gate, he locked eyes on Dawud and walked directly toward him. Stopping in front of Dawud, he paused, studying him for a moment, and then asked, "Is your name Dawud Hawadi?"

Dawud saw the man watching him, ready to judge his response. Taken aback by the man's directness, and what he might represent, Dawud had waited a fraction of a second too long before he replied, "No...no you have come to the wrong house. My name is Dawud Ullah. Now would you please leave. I have a great deal of work to do." The man did not move, instead his eyes went to Dawud's right hand, the one that was holding the trowel. Seeming satisfied, he smiled and said, "It seems that we have a little disagreement here. You see, I have been told that Dawud Hawadi lives at this house. I have also been given the description of Dawud Hawadi...and you certainly match that description. And finally, I was told to positively identify Dawud Hawadi by the scar on the back of his right hand." Looking down at Dawud's hand, he continued, "And Allah be praised, there it is." Dawud wanted to yell to Afrah to run, he wanted to strike the man with his trowel, and then join his sister in a sprint for their lives. But Dawud did none of these things. Rather, he found himself looking into the man's face. There was something dangerous about this man, yet Dawud found himself liking him. There was nothing in this man's eyes that caused Dawud to think he meant him any harm. As Dawud was pondering his situation, the man spoke, saying, "Well my friend, are you Dawud Hawadi or not?" Not knowing quite what to say, Dawud replied, "What is it you want with Dawud Hawadi?" The man replied, "I have a letter for Dawud Hawadi, from a...police officer in Kabul. Perhaps you could tell me the name of this police officer?" Dawud's heart raced; could it be that Captain Mustafa had finally written? Hesitating for a moment, Dawud then replied, "There are many police officers in Kabul." As if anticipating this answer, the man said, "Ah yes, but there is only one that is a close friend to Morad Hawadi." If this man knew his father's name, he would likely know about Captain Mustafa, so Dawud decided to take chance, and replied, "Are referring to Captain Mustafa?" The man smiled, and said, "Bingo" – a word Dawud did not understand. The man then reached into his vest pocket, withdrew a sealed, green envelope, and handed it to Dawud. He then turned, and walked away, without saying another word.

Afrah had been standing next to the window, listening, and as soon as the man left, she ran to the front door, opened it, and rushed to Dawud's side. For a moment, they both just stared at the green envelope, and then Afrah nudged her brother and gestured toward the door. Several seconds later, they were both standing beside the cast iron stove and Dawud was ripping open the envelope. Carefully, he removed a single, type-written page that read:

Dear friends:

I apologize for taking so long to write, but these days, communicating is a challenge, and until recently, I have not had any news about our mutual friend, the Doctor. However, now I do have something to report. It has come to my attention that the Doctor has finally identified four individuals who suffered from a particularly destructive mental disorder. As you are aware, the Doctor has been searching for one of these individuals for quite some time. The man was known to be especially ill and his behavior has caused harm to others. The Doctor has been generous enough to treat all four of these individuals, and I am glad to report that they are completely cured.

Note that the Doctor continues to search for other individuals that suf-fer from this mental disorder, and is now focusing on those that are known to be transmitting this terrible affliction. I expect to hear of more cures in the near future.

Unfortunately I must report that earlier this month, several of these mentally ill individuals visited the Doctor's office, in hopes that he would cure them of their torment. Not finding the Doctor present, they became distraught and a fire erupted. Regretfully, the Doctor's office was com-pletely destroyed.

Please be advised that the number of individuals inflicted with this mental disorder is rapidly growing, and it will soon be a serious epidemic. I have heard of major outbreaks in Kunduz Province, and there are a grow-ing number of cases in the northern and eastern districts of Takhr Province. Takhr Province is particularly vulnerable, since the existing men-tal health staff will not be able to control the outbreak. If you know of anyone who is living in this area, I suggest you advise them to take appro-priate precautions.

Due to my situation, I will not be able to offer you the kind of assistance I have provided in the past, but I have contacted a friend of mine, a Spe-cialist in curing this particular mental disorder. He has offered to help. Be advised that he is a foreigner and has access to some very potent antidotes. I suggest that you be careful. The Specialist is committed to curing as many of these mentally disturbed individuals as possible. However, with the affliction growing so rapidly, there are substantial risks involved.

I will close now, but rest assured that I will contact you if there is more news about our good friend, the Doctor.

May Allah bestow his blessing upon you.

Assalaam alaikum

M

Captain Mustafa appeared to be concerned about secure communi-cation and was attempting to obscure the meaning of his words. He was undoubtedly one of the best intelligence officers in the Afghan National Police; however, Captain Mustafa did not excel at creative writing. Nevertheless, the letter endeared the Captain to Dawud and Afrah, and would have amused them if the subject had not been so...serious. Through his rather transparent metaphors, he had com-municated that their father was still alive and that he had killed four jihadists, one of them the man who had murdered their mother. The fact that their father had actually accomplished this, was hard for Dawud and Afrah to believe. They knew that many years ago, Morad Hawadi had been a ferocious warrior, but to them, their father had always been thoughtful and gentle, and exceedingly slow to anger. Besides, he was a graying, 61-year-old man who needed glasses to read, and who had chronic bursitis in his right shoulder. Now this elderly Arabic paladin was on a quest to hunt down those who had instigated the attacks on Afrah and their mother.

The letter had also reported that the Taliban had gone to their home, looking for their father. Failing to find him, they had set the house on fire. This saddened both Dawud and Afrah, but not nearly as much as they might once have thought. Over the past year, they had learned to become less attached to things.

Next, Captain Mustafa had told them that the Islamists were gaining strength in Takhr Province, and that the Government forces were too weak to stop them. Farkhar was located in Takhr Province, which meant Farkhar may soon be overrun.

Dawud and Afrah had always known that Farkhar was only to be a temporary home, and that sooner or later they would have to move on. Actually, they had been surprised to have been able to spend 14 months in this quaint little town. They had made friends here and they had become part of the community.

The last part of the letter was more confusing, but after discussing it, they concluded Captain Mustafa had contacted someone who was a foreigner, someone he thought was particularly effective at fighting the Islamists. This foreigner had agreed to help, but neither Dawud nor Afrah had any idea who he was or how he would contact them. At first they thought the man who had delivered the letter was the foreigner, but he seemed too young to be a "specialist" and he didn't have that...look in his eyes. Captain Mustafa had the look, Pasha Jawid had had the look, and so had a number of other seasoned warriors their father had introduced them to.

After reading over the letter several more times, Dawud carefully reinserted the page back into the envelope, and reluctantly inserted it into the stove, where the fire immediately engulfed it. Dawud and Afrah watched, and a few seconds later, there was nothing but thin sheets of black ash that soon broke apart and drifted up the chimney.

There was no need to say anything; they both knew that they had to get ready to leave. In their minds, Farkhar was quickly becoming a place in their past and everything around them took on a differ-ent...hue.

Although some foreigner might help them, they couldn't count on it. They would have to assume they were on their own – a realization that immediately made their stomachs churn.

It took a moment before Dawud and Afrah could think clearly, but as the details of an escape began to form, it became increasingly evi-dent that they would need money, money for food, for shelter, for transportation, and for payoffs. Once they left Farkhar, they would be strangers and sooner or later, they would cross paths with someone, someone who would sense that they were fugitives and would see it as an opportunity to earn some money. They would need to be paid off, so that they would look the other way.

Having several small caches of money hidden around the house, it took them several minutes to retrieve what they had. Placing the mon-ey on the table, they began to count. It didn't take long and when they had finished, Dawud and Afrah were both noticeably disheartened. It was Afrah who spoke first, saying, "Dawud....we have only enough money to last us a few weeks, no more. Dawud knew this to be true. Although they had saved most of his meager salary, it had not been very much, and nowhere near enough to finance their escape. Still, their situation was not dire. Trying to appear reassured, Dawud said, "I think we'll be ok. There is still plenty of money in the bank. Tomorrow morning, I will take the bus to Taleqan. They have a bank there, and I will withdraw enough money for us to live on for a year." Afrah did not say anything, but she wasn't so sure. They had avoided withdraw-ing the money because the account might be monitored, and a transaction could lead to their location. Now, though, access to the money seemed more important than the risk of some bank employee revealing what branch it had been withdrawn from. The real reason Afrah had her doubts was that she did not think the money would be there. Over the past year, she had heard dozens of stories about how the Bank, or the Government, had managed to steal people's money. It had been over a year since their father had...disappeared and he was likely not in good standing with either the Taliban or the Government. By now, someone had surely figured out a way to get their hands on the money.

Dawud and Afrah spent the next few minutes dividing up what little money they had. Dawud insisted that Afrah take most of it. If they were separated, it would be far more important that she have the money. They both understood that a woman traveling alone drew attention, and was often targeted. Having a little money meant she could pay for someone to escort her, or she could bribe her way out of a difficult situation. They each placed their portions of the money in their money belts and secured the belts around their waists. From now on, the money would have to be with them at all times. Next, Dawud retrieved the two, black nylon backpacks that he had only recently purchased. Although they were the best he could find, they were cheaply made, so he had paid to have them reinforced. Now, he was sure they were durable enough to survive a long trek. By late that evening, they had the backpacks stuffed with gear. It had been necessary to repack several times, in order to keep the weight down to something that could be handled. Tomorrow morning, before he left for Taleqan, they would stash the backpacks behind the small shed at the rear of the old woman's yard. That way, if someone was watching their house, they could stay out of sight by simply sneaking behind the old woman's property, reaching over the wall, and retrieving their packs.

It was a good plan, but something was bothering Afrah. In a somber voice, she said, "The old woman, what about her? What will she do when we are gone?" Dawud had also thought about the old woman, and replied, "We will leave her everything we have. The goats, the pistachio nuts, our food, our pots and pans...everything. When I get to the bank, I will arrange to have some money sent to her, enough so that she can eat, clothe herself, and keep warm."

That night, Afrah's mind buzzed with thoughts of what might happen and where they would go. Unable to sleep, she was up before dawn, preparing a breakfast and a lunch that Dawud could take with him.

That evening, Afrah was at the bus terminal, waiting for Dawud's bus. It reminded her of when they had first arrived in Farkhar, and how strange and...scary it had been. Now, the place was familiar to her. She knew the smells, the sounds, and she could easily find her way around, even at night.

Afrah was staring into the darkness when she spotted the bus' headlights, far off in the distance. A few minutes later, the bus rolled off the highway, onto the gravel, and came to an abrupt stop. Dawud was the eighth person to get off and it took her only a second to see the disappointment in his eyes. Dawud saw her immediately and struggled to appear positive. On the walk back to their house, Dawud told Afrah what had happened.

When he had arrived at the bank, he had noticed that there were many people standing in line. Everyone had seemed tense and irritable. As he had taken his place in line, he'd heard people say that the insurgents had occupied Nahrain, and that the Ali abad-Khanabad Road was closed because of the fighting. The bank was limiting withdrawals to no more than 60,000.00 AFN. That was only about a tenth of what they needed, but he had thought it would get them by for a few more months and he could withdraw more later. When he'd reached the teller's window, he had presented his bank book and his identification documents. The teller had studied them and then typed some information into the computer. A few minutes later, the teller had advised him that the Government had frozen Morad Hawadi's account, and that he would not be able to make any withdrawals. Dawud had demanded to speak to the bank manager, and after waiting for nearly two hours, he had gotten to talk to an old, tired-looking man who had told him, "The Government has declared Morad Hawadi dead and there are no known beneficiaries to the account. If you have a claim against the account, you will have to travel to Kabul and personally present your claim to the Bank regulators, a process that could take up to a year and cost about 200,000.00 afghani."

None of this surprised Afrah. She had heard similar stories from neighbors and people at the marketplace. Nonetheless, she could see that her brother was taking this very hard. He was worried, and she knew that he was worried about what would happen to her. Squaring her shoulders and smiling her very best smile, Afrah said, "Come on, Dawud, Allah has given us strong bodies and good brains, we'll figure something out."

The next morning, Dawud and Afrah decided to do a survey of one of the nearby canyons. They would have to leave soon and they needed to know the countryside better. Dressing in warm clothing that was durable and comfortable enough for a long trek, they set out before dawn. They would head northeast, toward a canyon that one of the smugglers had suggested would make a good escape route. If anyone inquired, they would tell them they were out gathering firewood, or collecting herbs and roots.

Afrah would always wear her burqa, whenever she went out in public. Even after living in Farkhar for over a year, very few people knew what she looked like. Although she had gotten used to the burqa, Afrah still hated it. It represented a capitulation to a belief she had come to despise. Whenever they were far enough away from town, Afrah would remove the burqa and stash it in a cloth shoulder bag that she would always carry with her. Beneath the burqa, she wore her hijab and a warm, long wool jacket. Beneath that was a light wool sweater, a simple cotton parshaan (overdress), and a pair of traditional wool trousers. More than half of Farkhar's young women did not wear burqas, and Afrah had carefully studied how these women dressed, and how they interacted with men and other women. She had been pleased that, generally speaking, these women dressed comfortably, and she now emulated their dress so that she would not look out-of-place. With warm undergarments, mittens, and heavy socks, Afrah could still move around easily and could spend all day outside, even in below-freezing weather.

The Khanabad River was about two kilometers to their west, and they were following a narrow trail that led into a steep canyon. Several hundred meters ahead of them, the canyon sharply veered to the left and disappeared. There was something foreboding about the place, causing Dawud and Afrah to walk cautiously, studying the steep cliffs on each side. There were hundreds of narrow recesses and cracks where someone could hide. Dawud had the uncomfortable feeling that they were being watched, and was about to suggest they turn around, when there, in the path ahead of them, was a man. He was tall, and he was wearing a brown pakol, and a ragged blanket draped over his shoulders. He seemed to have appeared out of nowhere and was now just standing there...waiting for them. Dawud's first inclination was to stop and turn back. They were in an isolated area, about five kilometers from Farkhar, and they had not seen another human being in well over an hour. Although the man was too far off to identify, Dawud noticed that there was something familiar about him. After a few more tentative steps, Dawud recognized him. He was the man who had delivered the letter from Captain Mustafa. The man gestured for them to come forward. Unsure of what to expect, Dawud instructed Afrah to stay back, but she would have no part of it, so the two of them cautiously approached the man. It was the man's rugged, youthful face and that peculiar confidence that again got Dawud's attention. Although he was even scruffier looking than he had remembered, the man still exhibited a kind of openness, albeit tinged with a heightened awareness of his surroundings. As Dawud and Afrah got closer, they could see the man's eyes continuously scan the canyon walls and brush, as if he were watching for something.

Quietly, almost in a whisper, the man said, "Dawud, what the hell are you doing here? This place is dangerous. You and Afrah must turn around...now!"

Seeing the puzzled looks on their faces, the man continued, "Look, there are maybe fifty or sixty Taliban fighters less than two kilometers up ahead, and they are heading this way. A scouting party will be here in only a few minutes. You have got to go back, and when you get to the river, stay as close to it as you can. Stay off the road."

Dawud could see the man was serious and there was a sense of urgency in his eyes. From behind him, Dawud heard his sister ask...in English, "Are you the foreigner?"

In large cities like Kabul, some of the old traditions have given way to more Western thinking, but here, in the remote country side, it was most unusual for an Afghan woman, particularly one accompanied by her brother, to directly address a strange man. What made this even more astonishing was that his sister was speaking English to him, and asked him if he was...the foreigner. To Dawud, the foreigner was kind of a secret, and he had always thought that the foreigner would introduce himself. Bewildered, Dawud turned and looked at his sister. She was staring directly at the man, and had that knowing expression on her face. It then occurred to Dawud that the man had addressed both of them, him and Afrah. He had actually looked directly at Afrah, not just a passing glance, but a real look. Just as women did not directly address male strangers, Afghan men did not acknowledge the presence of a woman, particularly when she was accompanied by a family member or her husband.

Dawud's mind immediately began to reprocess what he knew about this man.

He was tall, maybe 188 cm (6' 2"). This probably put him in the fifth percentile of Afghan men – unusual, but not that uncommon. Dawud was also tall, at 186 cm, and never particularly felt out of place.

His hair was thick and sandy-colored, and his eyes were a light blue. This probably meant that he came from eastern Afghanistan, the Nuristan region, where about a third of the population had light hair and light eyes.

His grooming, clothing, and hygiene suggested that he was a poor laborer or herder, yet he had the lean, athletic build, powerful arms and the thick neck of a man who was well-nourished, and who had done a significant amount of physical training.

He spoke fluent Dari but with a slight, almost imperceptible accent. People from the Nuristan Province mostly spoke Pashtu, so it was reasonable to think that he would speak Dari with an accent.

But the biggest disconnect was the man himself, the way he carried himself, the way he acted. He stood straight and he had the presence of a man who had a lot of confidence in himself. Generally, Afghan men seemed more guarded, more cautious in the way they presented themselves. And then there was that...directness. This was an American trait, a trait you learned as a young child, a trait you would not always be aware of, and one that might be difficult to conceal.

And finally, there was the fact that this was the man who had delivered Captain Mustafa's letter. Clearly, this man was connected to Captain Mustafa, and now he had just happened to show up, in this remote canyon, to warn them about the Taliban.

Once again, his sister had connected the dots before he had. He was either slow at this kind of thing, or she had this unique ability to assess a person at just a glance. She could tell if someone was lying, or if they were tired, angry, or scared. But what was really fascinating, was that his sister could generally tell if a person was...good. Dawud had long ago given up trying to keep secrets from her, and he should not have been surprised at her seeing through this man's facade.

Dawud could see the man was taken aback by Afrah's question. At first, he tried to look puzzled, as if he did not understand, but Afrah just kept staring at him with that knowing, unblinking expression. It took only a moment for the man to realize that he had been bettered, and another moment before a surprisingly big, friendly smile appeared. He looked away, as he tried to formulate a response, and then turned back to Afrah and, in perfect American English replied, "Dang, you're good. You got me, I'm a foreigner but I'm not the foreigner you are referring to. That guy is my boss. By the way, if you're interested, my name is Jake."

Switching back to Dari, he continued.

"Please Afrah, you do not have much time. Now you and your brother must get out of here...now."

Afrah again addressed the man directly, and in English, said, "Thank you...Jake...thank you for warning us. We shall do as you have asked."

Dawud was more than a little fascinated by this peculiar exchange. He had never before seen his sister speak so openly to a man, to a stranger. Afrah saw Dawud's bemused expression and nudged him hard, in the ribs, and then said, "Instead of standing there like some silly duck, let us go."

Without saying anything, Dawud turned, and he and Afrah moved quickly back down the trail. They had gone about a hundred meters when Dawud turned to see his sister looking back over her shoulder. She was looking for Jake, but he was gone. This was the first time his little sister had ever shown any interest in a man, and there was little doubt that Jake was also interested, although he had made a sincere effort not to show it. Shaking his head, Dawud sighed but said nothing, and when he looked back a second time, Afrah had returned her focus to the path in front of them.

The trail soon got wide enough for them to walk side by side, and after several minutes had passed, Dawud looked over at his sister, and, with an amused glint in his eyes, asked, "Sister, this...Jake, is he a good guy?"

It took some time for Afrah to answer, as she seemed to ponder the question, and then she said,

"Yes...yes, Dawud, he is a 'good guy,' a good and brave 'guy.' I also know that he is a terrible liar, and I like that about him."

Dawud thought about her answer for several minutes, and then he smiled to himself. As they turned a bend in the path, they picked up their pace. Twenty minutes later, they could hear the river. Per Jake's instructions, they followed the river, staying out of sight of the road. Seeing the outlying buildings of the town, Afrah stepped behind some large boulders, removed the burqa from her shoulder bag and slipped it on over her clothing.

It was early afternoon when they arrived back in Farkhar, and they immediately noticed an unusual number of cars and trucks. They were traveling north, out of town, and they were packed with people, animals, furniture, and every other sort of personal possession. Men without vehicles were pushing fully loaded carts and wheelbarrows, their wives and children trailing along behind. Still others were hurrying about the street, and some had gathered together and were engaged in animated discussions. Everyone looked worried, even scared. As Dawud passed a group of men, he recognized their baker. He was a pleasant, middle-aged man who was a widower. He had two teenage sons who worked in his shop, and attended Dawud's Arabic class. Dawud approached the man, and after a brief greeting, asked him what was going on. The man looked at Dawud with wide eyes, and exclaimed, "Khomri and Baghlam have fallen, the Quetta Shura, the Haqqani, the Hezbi Islami, and even al-Qaeda, they are all coming and will soon be in Farkhar. They have blocked off the road south, and it is just a matter of time before the road north will be closed. The police have not shown up for work, some police have been seen leaving town. There are no soldiers in Farkhar, no one is here to protect us. It is going to be very bad, Dawud...very bad."

Dawud thanked the man, and he and Afrah continued on their way. They had made it only a few steps when they both heard the faint but distinct sound of automatic gunfire and several loud, popping explosions coming from south of town. Dawud and Afrah picked up their pace; they both now knew it was time, time to leave Farkhar. They would pick up their packs, tell the old woman to take everything they had left behind, and say goodbye. They would then head for the far side of the river, and go north as quickly as they could.

"Afrah,...Afrah, Afrah." Dawud heard his sister's name being called, and strained to see where the sound was coming from. There, near the corner where the butcher shop stood, he spotted the old woman. She was about a hundred meters away, staggering awkwardly toward them. Dawud and Afrah rushed to her and reached her just as the old lady collapsed to the pavement. The side of her dress and her left pant leg were soaked with blood. One of her eyes was badly bruised and was swollen closed. There were dry blood and bruises around her mouth, and Afrah could see that one of her front teeth was missing. Cradling the old woman in her arms, she rocked her gently and said, "Allah have mercy. What...What has happened to you?"

The old lady reached out and took Afrah's hand, and desperately gripped it. Afrah could feel her hand was cold, she was trembling, and her grip was weak. Then, with a small, painfully wheezy voice, she pleaded, "Child, listen to me, you must not go to the house...The Taliban, they are waiting for you and Dawud...They broke your door and they went inside your house... I could hear them breaking things." Tears were now flowing down the old lady's face as she gasped for more air, then she continued, "They came to my house. They wanted to know about you...where you were, when you were coming back. I did not tell them anything and ...one of them hit me in the face. I...I spat at him..." This brought a faint smile of satisfaction to the old woman's face, and then she said, "Yes, yes Afrah, may Allah be my witness, I tell you, I spat at him...This made him very mad...he...he had very bad teeth, and his breath smelled like a dead goat. He said...you, you and Dawud... were heretics, and evildoers. They said that they were going to be behead you for your crimes against Islam...What foolishness. My...my sweet child...I know that neither of you is a heretic or evildoer."

The old lady's face had become pale, almost grey, and her features were distorted with pain as she gasped for air. Her voice growing weaker, she said, "Child, they searched my house, they found your backpacks. They said...I was helping heretics. They yelled at me...saying I was a heretic too. I told them I was a good Muslim...and you and Dawud were not heretics, you were good Muslims...but they did not believe me. The coward...the one that smelled like a dead goat...he got very mad...Two of them held my arms while he hit me. When he got tired, he took out a long, shiny knife and put the point in my chest...He slowly pushed the knife into my flesh, as they all watched and laughed. In the name of Allah, I believe this devil wanted to witness my life leave me. When he thought he had killed me, he pulled the knife out, wiped it on my dress and walked away...I...am much stronger than...that devil thought I was...I waited, I did not move for a long time, and when they were gone, I got up and I...I came to find you...to warn you. They are hiding in your house. They want you to think everything is normal, then they will grab you. Now...now you...and Dawud...you must run away...You must not let them catch you."

The old lady tried to gasp for air, as foamy blood oozed from her mouth. Beneath her, on the pavement, a deep red puddle of blood grew larger. She again weakly tried to gasp for air, but this time, she could not manage. After a moment she lay motionless, her struggle to breathe had stopped, and her eyes stared emptily at the sky. The baker had seen the old woman collapse and had come over to help. On hearing the old woman's words, he placed a hand on Dawud's shoulder and said, "You must go now, Dawud. I will take care of her."

Afrah softly wept, her arms tightly holding onto the old woman.

Dawud touched Afrah's shoulder and said, "Sister, there is nothing more we can do. I am so sorry, but we must leave her...we must go while we still have the chance." Afrah looked up at him, tears streaming down her face, and said, "Dawud, you go, I...I cannot leave her like this...I cannot." Dawud knew his sister, he knew the old lady had filled a hole in her heart that her mother's death had left. Now, losing both of them must be tearing her apart. At first, Dawud did not know how to respond. Then, in a low, serious voice, he said, "Afrah, in your heart, you know that I will not leave you...If you will not go, then I will stay with you, but Afrah, they will kill us, they will kill us both, and you are making it very easy for them."

It took Afrah a moment to fully register what her brother had said, and as she did, something happened to her, and Dawud could see...fire return to her eyes. She gently kissed the old woman's forehead, and carefully placed her down onto the pavement. Wiping away her tears, she rose to her feet, looked at Dawud, and said, "Yes...of course you are right. They will kill us, and the last thing I want is to make it easy for them. Their offenses grow by the minute and I have sworn to hold them accountable...Let us go."

CHAPTER NINETEEN

Escape

Dawud grabbed his sister's hand and the two of them bolted toward the river.

The gunfire coming from the road north of Farkhar had intensified, and they had not gotten far before they heard the sound of men shouting and women screaming. From nearby he heard a bust of automatic weapons fire. Dawud didn't know if the Taliban were in pursuit, all he knew was that they had to run. If they were caught, they were dead.

Seconds later they turned down a narrow alley and could see the river directly in front of them. If they could make it across, they might be able to slip into the heavy brush and disappear.

They hit the ice-cold water at a full sprint and immediately found themselves battling a swift current that seemed determined to sweep them away. Afrah was still wearing that cursed burqa and was struggling to pull it up out of the water when the rushing current caught the billowing fabric and she was suddenly wrenched off her feet.

Afrah's hand was yanked from Dawud's grip. Turning, he saw his sister rushing away from him, her arms and legs thrashing as she desperately tried to keep her head above water. She was being swept into a stretch of river that narrowed and led to roaring white rapids.

Afrah struggled to keep her legs out in front of her, hoping that they would cushion her collision with the enormous rocks that were in her path. A moment later she saw a boulder the size of a bus, and she was heading directly toward it. She twisted and turned, trying to free herself from the burqa but nothing worked, and she was tiring. Soon she wouldn't have any strength left and the current would drag her under.

The water in front of her suddenly dropped away and she was sure that she was going to be pulled down and then slammed into the massive boulder that was now less than a dozen meters away. As she felt herself begin to drop all she could do was close her eyes and hold her breath.

But instead of falling, Afrah was suddenly yanked up and in the next instant her face broke through the surface. Coughing as she tried to gulp in the fresh air, she saw Dawud standing over her...holding on to her. He seemed as big as a tree, planted in the river bed as solidly as any of the great rocks that surrounded them.

The next thing she remembered was being set down on the far river bank. Cold, exhausted, and soaked to the bone, she tried to stand, but her legs would not support her weight and she had to hold onto her brother.

Together, they began moving toward an opening in the brush. Afrah's strength was returning but the water-soaked burqa was pulling at her as if she was dragging the river with her.

A shot sounded behind them, and Dawud heard a bullet zip past. More shots rang out, and loose dirt and fragments of rock showered them. In front of them was a shallow recess in the riverbank and Dawud dove into it, pulling Afrah down with him. They landed with his body covering hers just as a hail of bullets smashed into the gravel. The brush was still ten meters away, but it might as well have been ten kilometers. They weren't going to make it.

The gunfire slowed, and Dawud could hear yelling. He was too far away to understand what they were saying, but he thought he heard the sound of men entering the water. He slowly raised his head to see at least a dozen Taliban on the far bank and another two in the river, nearly halfway across.

Dawud knew that once they got to his side it would be all over. He and Afrah would lose the little cover they had and the Taliban fighters could simply shoot them.

They had only two choices – stay there and accept their death, or make a run for it and pray that through some miracle they wouldn't be gunned down in the process. The second choice would at least mean they had tried, and maybe Afrah would have a chance. He would try to shield her with his body, and if he could stay upright long enough she might make it to the brush. Dawud reached down and squeezed Afrah's arm. He whispered, "Can you run?"

Afrah thought that just walking unaided would be a challenge, but she was not going to let her brother down. Taking a deep breath, she replied, "I bet I can run faster than you."

Hoping she was right, he whispered, "On three, we will get up and make a run for the brush. Do not stop, do not look back...just run."

He didn't think either of them would make it, but they were out of time. The two Taliban fighters were just emerging from the water. In a second they would be on the bank and in position to shoot.

"One, two, three." Dawud began to rise, and the instant he did the shooting began.

"STAY DOWN!" Dawud heard a voice yell at him from somewhere in the brush just in front of them.

Without pause Dawud threw himself back on top of Afrah, just as a round tore through the back collar of his jacket and another passed through his upper sleeve, so close to his skin that it burned him.

The instant he was down, a fusillade of gunfire erupted from the direction from which he had heard the voice. Whoever was shooting was so close that the report of his weapon was deafening, and he could feel the heat of the rounds pass over them as they hurtled toward their targets on the other side of the river.

The rapid fire continued for only a few more seconds, and then slowed to what seemed like carefully placed shots. The piercing pain in his ringing ears did not fade, and he realized that the muzzle blasts had damaged his hearing. The background roar of the river was gone; it was as if he was underwater.

The air was permeated with the acrid smell of gunpowder, fragmented rock, and hot metal. He could feel Afrah trying to move beneath him, and she was saying something, but Dawud could not make out the words. He was grateful that she was still alive, that they were both alive. Should he move? Was there a Taliban fighter waiting nearby, ready to finish them off?

He reflexively jerked when he felt a pull at his arm.

Looking up, he saw a man crouched beside them. It took a moment, but Dawud recognized him. It was Jake, the man they had last seen on the trail only a few hours ago.

Jake was pulling at him and yelling something that Dawud could only partially make out. After a moment he realized that Jake was asking, "Are you hit?...Is Afrah all right?"

Dawud loudly exclaimed, "I...I think I am all right, but I do not know about Afrah." Carefully, he rolled to his side and reached for his sister's shoulder.

He could feel her body trembling as she raised herself to her elbows and looked at Dawud with teary eyes. It took her a long moment before she could speak, and then, in a quiet, shaky voice, a voice that Dawud sensed more than heard, she said, "I...I thought they had shot you and it would have been all...my fault. I was so stupid. We should have left Farkhar when you first asked me, but I just sat there, feeling sorry for myself...I'm going to get us killed. I know I am."

Her eyes were full of tears, and she reached for her brother and hugged him tightly. Dawud held on to her and said, "It's my ears, I cannot hear you. Are you all right? Nod your head if you're all right."

Afrah choked back her sobs and nodded her head.

A deep, muffled voice came from somewhere behind Dawud. It was Jake, and he seemed to be yelling something. Dawud strained to listen, and he was able to make out the words, "Get up! We have got to get out of here!"

He saw that Jake was crouched down, warily scanning the far bank. Jake was wearing body armor and a vest with numerous pouches, most of them stuffed with extra magazines for the RPK light machinegun that he had held at his waist. Dawud quickly rose to his feet and helped Afrah to hers.

They could not help but look back to the other side of the river, toward Farkhar. They saw bodies everywhere. Several were lying in the blood-streaked water, the stain stretching for many meters down the river. Other bodies were splayed among the rocks. One man lay on his back, his right knee bent at an unnatural angle, his stomach ripped open, and his intestines strewn around him. The two men who had made it across the river lay on their backs only five meters away. One had no face and his chest had been riddled with bullets. The other had been nearly cut in half.

"MOVE!" Again, Jake's muted voice came through the ringing in Dawud's ears.

He knew Jake was right. They had stayed much too long. The Taliban would be back, and the next time they would be better prepared to fight.

As Afrah struggled to extricate herself from the wet, clinging burqa, Jake stepped over to her, pulling a folding knife from his pocket, and began to cut away the tangled fabric.

Then Jake froze. He stepped back and said, sounding awkward and apologetic, "I am sorry. I didn't think..."

Afrah interrupted him. "Jake, do not stop...please, we must hurry...remove this thing."

Jake looked cautiously over at Dawud. Dawud realized what Jake must have been thinking – that a man, a foreign infidel, who, uninvited, cut away a Muslim woman's burqa might very well have committed an unpardonable sin. This was not an issue, for he shared his sister's contempt for the garment and for what it meant. Without pause, he nodded his approval and a few seconds later, the burqa lay in a shredded heap and the three of them were hurrying into the brush.

Dawud was at the rear of their short column, and he was now armed with one of the dead Taliban's Kalashnikovs. Jake was up front, setting the pace though he frequently glanced back to check on Afrah. Dawud too frequently glanced behind him, but he was looking to see if any Taliban fighters were in pursuit.

Soon they emerged from the brush onto a narrow trail and turned north, away from Farkhar. Now they were able to move more quickly. Jake took up a pace that was only slightly slower than a run. Afrah and Dawud followed suit. The pace seemed natural to Jake and his gait was fluid and smooth. This was not the case for Afrah and Dawud, who both fought to keep up.

After half an hour the two of them were clearly struggling, but Jake kept pushing them. They had somehow managed to keep up the grueling pace for another fifteen minutes when Jake suddenly stopped, gestured at a fallen tree a few meters off the trail, and whispered, "Take cover!"

The words had just left his mouth when there was a sudden burst of gunfire, and bullets shredded the brush and kicked up dirt less than a meter away from them.

Jake dove to the side of the trail and began returning fire. Dawud and Afrah scrambled to the fallen tree. Afrah got there first and was lying flat as bullets tore through the air. Dawud got there a second later and assumed a prone position with his rifle at the ready. The brush around the fallen tree was dense, and they could see into it only a couple of meters. Jake was drawing most of the fire, but had nothing but brush to shield him.

The ringing in Dawud's ears was lessening, yet he had not heard the sickening thud of a bullet hitting a human body, but Afrah had, and immediately knew Jake had been hit. She didn't know exactly where he was but she wanted to go to him. He needed her, she knew he needed her. As she started to move toward Jake, Dawud grabbed her and held her in place. When she looked at him, she saw he was confused and realized he had not heard the terrible sound. With her mouth next to Dawud's ear, she said, "Jake has been hit." Dawud understood and replied, "You're going to get yourself killed." He paused for a second and then said, "I'll go, I think I can work my way around back of those shooters." Just as he finished speaking, Afrah heard a second round hit Jake and his firing stopped. Dawud still hadn't heard the second round impact, but he had felt his sister's body jerk and then saw the tears fill her eyes. He also noticed that Jake was no longer shooting back, and immediately realized he may be... dead. Squeezing Afrah's arm, he pleaded, "Promise me you will stay here. I'll go to Jake. I can do it but I can't do it if I'm worrying about you." Afrah looked up at her brother, and saw the concern and urgency in his expression, and then she looked away and nodded.

Dawud slowly crept forward, peering out from beneath a dry, scrawny bush, and he could see Jake lying on his back. His rifle lay on the ground, about a meter away, and Jake was trying to roll onto his side so he could reach for it. His left shoulder was blood-soaked and his left arm lay limply at his side. Shifting his body, Jake was finally in position to reach his rifle with his good arm, and had just gripped it when another round slammed into him, knocking him back. This time, Jake did not move. His eyes were closed but Dawud could see labored breathing and knew he was still alive. Rising to a crouch, Dawud was about to dash to Jake's aid, when he caught sight of movement to his left. Freezing, he waited, and a second later, one of the Taliban fighters emerged from the brush, only three meters from where Dawud stood. He was a small man, made to look even smaller as he moved forward in a crouch. He wore a sweat-stained turban and a dirty, threadbare jacket and pants. The man had dark, intense eyes, a shaggy, black beard, and a wild expression on his face. He carried a Kalashnikov, but must have run out of ammunition, since the magazine was missing. Dawud watched as he slowly withdrew the long, shiny knife he had sheathed at his waist. In two more steps, the Taliban fighter was standing nearly atop Jake, and with his back to Dawud. Seeing his opportunity, Dawud raised his rifle, aimed, and pulled the trigger. Nothing happened. He pulled the trigger again, and again, still nothing. The man hovered over Jake, his knife held as if he planned to cut Jake's throat. Having no time left, Dawud charged the man. Gripping the rifle firmly, he slammed the butt into the back of the man's head with such force that Dawud felt the man's skull collapse. The force of the blow had propelled the man, face first, into the dirt. Dawud immediately moved forward, positioning himself to strike a second blow, when he caught sight of another man. A second Taliban fighter stepped onto the trail, about thirty meters away. For just a moment, they made eye contact and then the man began to raise his rifle. In only a second or two, he would have Dawud in his sights. Instantly, Dawud bolted toward him, at a full sprint, and covered the ground with amazing speed but it would not be fast enough. He knew that all of their lives were at stake, and pushed even harder. As Dawud hurtled toward him, he could see the man squint as he lined him up. The shooter's finger entered the trigger guard and then he began to squeeze the trigger. At this distance, the man would not miss him; Dawud was dead, and he knew it. Ten meters, eight meters, five meters and Dawud heard the shot and waited for the bullet to impact. Instead, he saw the shooter's head snap back, a spray of red exploding from the back of his skull. At that same instant, Dawud saw the muzzle flash of the shooter's rifle. His aim had been thrown off just a fraction of a centimeter, but enough to cause the bullet to miss. Although Dawud had no time to react, he could actually see the bullet come at him, and he felt it pass near his right ear. The gunman's head snapped to the left and he was flung backwards onto the ground. Coming to a stop, Dawud found himself standing over the man. His left eye and the back half of his head were gone.

"Dawud, Dawud, are you all right?" Although his hearing had improved, there was still a loud ringing in his ears and his sister's voice seemed very distant. Confused, he turned and saw his sister standing next to where Jake lay. Afrah had Jake's Kalashnikov at her shoulder and there was a faint whiff of gray smoke rising from its barrel.

Only later would Afrah explain what had happened. When Dawud had charged and struck the first jihadist, Afrah had been only a few steps behind him. She explained that she was not about to just sit there when she knew Jake was hurt, and who knew what was going to happen to Dawud? When Dawud had charged at the second jihadist, she had seen that he was too far away and that Dawud would not reach him in time. So she had bent down, picked up Jake's rifle, and shouldered it. When she had tried to sight-in the jihadist, Dawud was in the way. Dawud was running straight at the man, and was completely blocking her view. Finally, a glimpse of the left side of the jihadist's face had appeared, just to the right of Dawud's neck. She had fired, and was instantly convinced she had killed her brother. It was several seconds before Afrah would open her eyes, and when she did, she was relieved to see Dawud standing over the jihadist, who was sprawled out on the ground.

Hitting that tiny portion of a man's face would have been a miraculous feat for even the most skilled marksman. Yet Afrah had made the shot, even though she had never fired a rifle before. Dawud would never understand where she had learned how to sight a target, how to breathe correctly, and how to apply steady, gentle pressure to the trigger. When Dawud had asked, Afrah would say, "You think that because I am a girl, I do not know anything about guns. I am not stupid. I watched you and father fire rifles many times. It did not seem particularly difficult to do."

Unsure of whether the danger was over, Dawud picked up the dead man's rifle, and this time, checked to see that it was functioning correctly. As he inserted a full magazine, he noticed that he could hear the distant roar of the river. Grateful his hearing was returning, he pushed the river sound to the back of his consciousness so he could focus on human sounds, anything that would reveal the presence of more fighters. Carefully, Dawud began moving through the thick brush, stopping every few steps to look and to listen. After searching for nearly fifteen minutes, he had found five bodies, five men Jake had managed to kill before he had been shot.

Stepping from the brush, Dawud headed back to where Jake lay and where his sister hovered over him, tending to his shoulder. As Dawud approached, he saw that Jake was unconscious and that his shoulder was a mess. The bullet had gone clear through, creating an ugly entry wound and a larger, even nastier, exit wound that exposed shredded muscle, splinters of bone, and there was blood, lots of blood. Afrah had made a bandage from strips of her overdress, and was trying to wrap his shoulder, but the bandage quickly became soaked. Desperate, Afrah began applying pressure to the wound. The warm blood oozed from between her fingers, but she kept pressing and after a few minutes, the bleeding slowed. As Afrah began to tire, Dawud stepped in, and as he pressed against the shoulder wound, he felt its unnatural malleability. Jake's shoulder bone had been shattered and no longer provided it any structure.

Afrah had been so busy tending to Jake's shoulder, she had forgotten that he had been hit by several bullets. As this memory returned, she was suddenly afraid that she had missed spotting the other wounds, wounds that might even be more serious than his shoulder. Immediately Afrah began to examine Jake's other arm, and then both of his legs. To examine his torso, she needed to open his bulky ammunition vest and the body armor beneath it. Opening the ammo vest was relatively simple and she was able to push it aside, but when she began unzipping the front of Jake's body armor, she noticed two slugs embedded in the fabric. On opening the heavy, bullet-resistant vest, she was relieved not to see any blood, but as she undid Jake's shirt, she saw his chest was covered by a massive bruise and it was immediately evident that at least two of his ribs were broken. Afrah's heart sank. Jake needed to be in a hospital. He needed a skilled surgeon, antibiotics, pain medication....They had none of these things and they had no prospects of getting them.

Jake's complexion was pale and his shoulder wound continued to seep blood. It was becoming clear that if they didn't do something soon, very soon, Jake was going to bleed to death.

Having been unconscious for nearly twenty minutes, Jake's eyes slowly opened and at first he seemed unable to comprehend where he was or what was happening. Struggling to pull himself up, he felt someone holding onto him. He had no strength to fight, and the effort had caused a white-hot pain to explode in his left shoulder, leaving him nauseated and on the verge of blacking out. After a moment, the worst of the pain passed and he turned his head to look at who was holding him down. After blinking several times, his eyes became wide and he could not help but stare. There, hovering over him, was the face of an angel. The pain and the nausea seemed to go away as he lay staring up at this...this heavenly creature. "Jake...Jake you're going to be all right, I'm going to take care of you." The angel was speaking to him and her voice sounded worried, but at the same time it was familiar and had pleasant sound. It took a few seconds before he recognized that it was Afrah's voice, and that Afrah was the...angel. His eyes glistening with tears and his brow beaded with sweat, he attempted a weak smile, and then tried to clear his throat. The movement caused him to grimace, as the pain, in its full glory, returned. Closing his eyes, he lay motionless, letting the crest pass. Then, in a weak, hoarse voice, he said, "You...you're so damn beautiful." The words drained him of his strength and it took several long seconds before he could again speak. With his eyes only partially open and speaking in a near whisper, Jake asked, "Afrah...am I dead?" Afrah held him more closely to her as she said, "No Jake, you're not dead...I'm not going to let you die." Jake again tried to smile and then said, "I...I guess angels can do that? But if it doesn't...work out, it's...OK. I got to meet a real...angel." Jake's head tilted to the side and he became silent. Thinking he might be dead, Dawud clumsily felt Jake's neck for a pulse, and was relieved when he finally found the right spot, and felt Jake's heart still beating.

When Dawud looked at Afrah, he saw the desperation and anguish in her eyes. Reaching out, he touched her hand and said, "It is in Allah's hands. We will do everything we can, and as long as there is breath in his body, we will not leave him...even if I have to carry him in my arms." Afrah did not say anything and Dawud wondered whether his words had brought her any comfort.

Looking up, Dawud saw that it was already afternoon. His eyes were drawn to the trail north and he immediately sensed something, something that made him clench his jaw and tighten his hands into fists. He didn't know what was causing this reaction but he sensed there was something out there. Dawud hated the feeling; it was as if he should...understand. It was important for him to understand, but that didn't matter. All he had was a...feeling.

Uneasy, Dawud turned to Afrah and said, "You know that we cannot stay here much longer. We are going to have to move Jake, even if the bleeding does not stop." Dawud pressed harder against the bandage, but the blood just kept oozing from between his fingers.

Her heart breaking, Afrah watched as Jake's life slowly seeped from his body. Then suddenly, she turned to Dawud and said, "Cauterizing, yes that is the word, cauterizing, you once told me that in ancient times, people cauterized a wound with a hot iron and this stopped the bleeding. Do you know how to do this?" Dawud replied, "I remember reading something about cauterizing a wound, but it was a long time ago and I have never done it, or even seen it done." Her voice now determined and even hopeful, Afrah said, "Dawud, you are going to have to try...Jake is dying...we have got to do something." Dawud understood how desperate the situation had become and tried to recall what he had read, but all he remembered was that the high temperature of a red hot iron seared a wound and caused the blood to coagulate...stopping the bleeding. There was something else he remembered. Cauterizing a wound could cause a lot of tissue damage and it increased the risk of a serious infection. Without antibiotics, such an infection would likely kill Jake. Nonetheless, stopping the bleeding was the immediate priority; they would have to deal with an infection later. Taking a deep breath, he hesitantly replied, "Alright...I will give it a try."

Afrah readied Jake by removing the blood-soaked bandage and cleaning the wound, as best she could. Meanwhile, Dawud built a fire and began heating the tip of a knife, the knife he had taken from the body of the man who had tried to cut Jake's throat. When the blade finally glowed a dull red, he went to work, and soon the sight and smell of burning flesh was turning his stomach. It took nearly 20 minutes to do the job, mostly because Dawud had to reheat the knife tip five separate times. Finally, when he had finished, he closely studied the wound until he was reasonably sure the bleeding had completely stopped.

Even though Jake was no longer bleeding, they knew that moving him was dangerous, and the trek was going to be anything but smooth. However, staying would surely be suicide. It would only be a matter of time before more Taliban showed up, and they would not take kindly to the rather substantial body count the three of them had left in their wake. Yes, it was definitely time for them to go.

Afrah worked quickly to re-bandage Jake's shoulder, then she moved among the dead fighters, gathering spare ammunition, blankets, and food. Meanwhile, Dawud set to work constructing a simple litter. He used dead tree limbs, strapped together with strips of cloth and belts. It was decided that Afrah would wear Jake's ammo vest and carry Jake's Kalashnikov, as well as their water and the food that she had gathered. Dawud would carry one of the Kalashnikovs he had taken from a dead jihadist, and he would pull the litter, with Jake strapped to it. Constructing a litter and padding it with blankets had taken longer than he had expected, but that had been only half the challenge. Moving Jake onto the litter, and figuring out how to strap him into it, became a challenge in its own right. By the time everyone was ready, there was less than an hour of daylight left.

Scanning the surrounding hillsides, Dawud spotted a distant rock outcropping. It was maybe one or one and a half kilometers northwest of them and up a rather steep incline. It looked much like all the other rock outcroppings, but Dawud thought this one might offer them some concealment, and it had a good overview of the trail and the river. The problem was going to be getting there. The litter was heavy, even when it was empty, but with Jake strapped to it, it was going to take every bit of his strength to pull the thing. Forcing himself to focus on their destination, Dawud hoisted up one end of the litter and began dragging it. Afrah's job wasn't going to be much easier. The fully packed ammo vest, a loaded Kalashnikov, a half a dozen full water bottles, and the sack of supplies weighed almost as much as she did.

With Afrah in the lead and Dawud trailing, they had made it only 50 meters, when Dawud suddenly froze. Afrah sensed he had stopped, and turned to see her brother lowering the litter. Dawud gestured to Afrah to stay as he unslung his Kalashnikov and cautiously moved toward a shallow ravine about a dozen meters down the slope.

Dawud was having that...strange feeling again, but now it seemed that thousands of fragments of information were converging. It was like Kabul, when he had encountered the taxi driver and had instantly known so much about the man. This time, Dawud knew that just past the edge of this ravine, he would find a slightly wounded man. His name was Commander Muhammad Haider. He and his six bodyguards were on their way to Farkhar, where he planned on taking command of over two hundred Taliban fighters. His journey had been interrupted when his party had encountered Jake, and he was not aware that there were others with Jake. Jake had come up on them so fast that he and his men only had time to scramble for cover and start shooting.

Knowing this was strange, but what was even stranger was that Dawud knew everything about Commander Haider. He was an intelligent man and a good strategist, but he was not a brave man. He loved pilav, a dish of steamed rice, mixed with lentils, raisins, carrots and lamb. Commander Haider fashioned himself as an expert on the Qur'an and the hadith (the teachings, deeds, and sayings of the Prophet, may peace be upon him) and took pleasure in manipulating their words in ways that gained him power and wealth. He was also a pedophile and murderer. Commander Haider sexually molested young boys and when he was finished with them, he strangled them using a red, silk cord he carried with him in the right front pocket of his jacket. If this man were allowed to live, he would continue to prey on young boys, and would ultimately molest and kill two of them whose names are Nabil and Kaliq. Dawud didn't know why, but these two boys were important and Commander Haider must not be given the opportunity to harm them...or anyone else.

Now able to look into the ravine, Dawud saw the man, less than three meters away. He had his back to Dawud and was crouched down, holding a Kalashnikov as he peered over the far side. Dawud knew that when the shooting started, a bullet had grazed Commander Haider's right thigh. Having a low pain threshold and no interest in participating in a real firefight, he had scrambled away, trying to find a place to hide. He had soon come across the ravine and had been hiding there ever since. As Dawud studied Commander Haider, he could smell the man's fear, but even more pronounced, Dawud could smell the stink of evil. Then, in an instant, Dawud was on the man. Commander Haider did not have time to react before Dawud cut his throat and nearly decapitated the man. Dawud did not remember slinging his rifle, or pulling the knife from its sheath, but Dawud did remember hearing the young boys crying for their mothers and begging to be spared.

When it was over, Dawud looked down at the body and wondered how he had done this.

Later, when he returned to where he had left Jake and Afrah, he found his sister tending to the wounded man, trying to get him to drink some water. His mind still spinning with the image of what he had done...he did not speak. Afrah had seen him approaching, and she had seen the blood on the front of his jacket and his sleeves. At first she thought that it might be Dawud's blood, but she soon saw that he was not injured. Afrah also saw that...look in her brother's eyes and immediately knew that she should not ask.

Looking around, Dawud saw that it would be dark soon. The past few nights had been near freezing and they would have to figure out how to keep Jake warm. Dawud was about to pick up the litter when he noticed the two deep ruts it was leaving behind. A blind man could follow those ruts and they would lead directly to them. Dawud broke off a branch from a nearby bush, and used it to erase the ruts all the way back to where they had started. He would have to repeat this process dozens of times before they felt no one could track them.

The trek was nothing less than torturous. The muscles in Dawud's thighs burned, his lower back ached, but they kept moving. As the grade got steeper, all he could do was take two or three arduous steps, then rest for several seconds, and then move forward again. After countless rest breaks, one near catastrophic tumble, and numerous close calls, they made it. It must have been 10 or maybe 11 and the night air was cold and still. For the last five hours, they had doggedly traversed several smaller hills, half a dozen ravines, and countless dense thickets of thorny brush. But now the dark silhouette of the rock outcropping was towering formidably above them. Carefully placing Jake down, Dawud collapsed, his clothes wet with sweat and his muscles burning, he could do nothing but sit there and try to breathe. It took several minutes before Dawud had recovered enough to stand and to stiffly shuffle toward the rock formation. He needed to find a place to hunker down, a place where they could build a fire that could not be seen from the valley below. As he made his way to the back of the rock formation, he spotted a fracture that was about half a meter wide, and seemed to cleave the rear third of the formation from its front. Dawud entered the gap and feeling his way, followed it until he felt a recess in the rock sidewall. Retrieving his disposable lighter, he thumbed the wheel, and ignited a small flame. The flame threw little light but there was enough to illuminate an opening into a cavern. On closer inspection, he could see it was barely tall enough to stand in and about three meters on a side. The dirt floor was strewn with debris that included some dry leaves and small twigs, which Dawud quickly gathered into a pile and lit. As the fire took hold, the flames threw off enough light to see the cave more clearly, and immediately he noticed the disordered stack of twigs and dry grass that must have once served as a nest for some small animal.

By the time Dawud reappeared, Afrah had undone the straps that had held Jake to the litter, and was again trying to get him to drink some water. After Dawud had described what he had found, Afrah gathered her things and set out to prepare a place for Jake. Meanwhile, Dawud tried to figure out a way to transport Jake without causing him too much harm. Placing his arms beneath Jake, he slowly lifted him but almost immediately set him back down. He was heavy but that wasn't the real problem. With Dawud carrying Jake, they were too wide to make it through the narrow passageway. His injuries precluded a shoulder carry, so Dawud would have to improvise. Wrapping Jake in a blanket, he carried him to the gap opening. From there, he half carried and half dragged him to the cave. This last two meters took some time since Jake was a big man, and Dawud had to be careful not to bang him up too badly as he maneuvered around several tight turns.

Afrah was waiting, and helped Dawud place Jake on the bed of blankets she had laid out. The fire was now burning more intensely since Afrah had dismantled the abandoned nest and had fed the fire with a sizable armful of dry twigs. It would not last long, but already the cave had become comfortably warm. Afrah tended to Jake, while Dawud went out to retrieve the rest of their supplies and gather more firewood.

When Dawud emerged from the narrow passageway, he began

walking out into the darkness. When he was satisfied he was far enough away, he turned and looked back at the rock formation, and not seeing any firelight, he hiked to another location, and again studied the rock formation for any hint of light. Dawud repeated this exercise until he was convinced that no one, up or down the valley, would be able to see the light of their fire. This was only a partial relief, since the smell of wood smoke now hung heavy in the air, and would certainly draw attention to them. They were high above the trail and Dawud hoped that if they kept the fire small and hot, it would not produce much smoke, and with a little luck, it would be drawn uphill and dispersed.

Jake felt cold so Afrah had covered him with another blanket, but now he had begun to shiver. Removing her jacket, she placed it over Jake, and in doing so, saw that Jake's bandage now showed new traces of blood mixed with a yellowy fluid. He became semi-conscious, and began speaking about angels, but none of it made any sense. Afrah did her best to get him to swallow some warm water. Then Jake suddenly developed a fever. She tried to cool him by removing the blanket and placing cool, wet rags on his forehead. Fifteen or maybe twenty minutes later, his breathing became very weak, and his body started turning cold and clammy. This worried her more than the fever, since he was not shivering anymore, but was just turning cold...slipping away. Nearly desperate, she used the heat of the fire to warm one of the wool blankets, and then wrapped Jake in it as tightly as she dared. While it cooled, she heated its replacement, repeating the process over and over again. It was after 1:00 AM when she noticed his breathing was a tiny bit stronger and his skin was less ashen. Exhausted, she fueled the fire and lay down next to Jake. Afrah placed her arms around the man and held him tightly against her, and then she began to sing to him. She sang in English, in a quiet and gentle voice. She mostly knew children's songs, songs that her mother had used to teach her English. Afrah was sure English, American English, was Jake's native language, and it might bring him comfort to hear words he was familiar with.

Dawud was standing guard, perched on a ledge that was about two meters from the narrow gap that led down to the cave opening. He was wearing Jake's ammunition vest and now regretting not taking his body armor, but it had seemed too heavy at the time.

With a fully loaded Kalashnikov resting on his lap, he studied the valley below. A sliver of moon illuminated the barren slopes, in a pale white light that would make it more difficult for anyone to approach undetected. The terrain behind him quickly ascended to a vertical cliff that even a mountain goat would have trouble traversing. Deciding that the only practical approaches were from somewhere below him, or maybe from one of his sides, he focused his attention to those areas. At around 2:00 AM Dawud found himself getting drowsy, so he stepped away from his perch and climbed down into the gap. Peering inside the cave, he saw that Afrah was lying next to Jake, holding him against her and singing to him. Jake looked a little better, or at least he didn't look as if he were about to take his last breath. Satisfied, he returned to his perch and resumed his sentry duties. The night air was cold, making his fingers and toes numb. He could also feel the coldness in the stone ledge penetrate the seat of his trousers, and regretted not picking up a blanket when he had last looked in on his sister.

It was about 3:00 AM when a faint, distant sound caught Dawud's attention. It was coming from somewhere below him and to the north. As he scanned the area, he first saw nothing but just the same dimly lit, shadowy landscape that he had been staring at for hours. Still, the sounds were becoming noticeably louder, and after straining his eyes, he began to notice shadowy movements about half a kilometer to the north. As he focused on the area, he began to see the dark silhouettes of men, armed men, who were on the trail that passed about seventy-five meters below him. It was the same trail on which they had encountered Commander Haider and his men. As best he could tell, there were more than a hundred fighters and they formed a snake-like column that disappeared into the darkness. As the lead element approached and crossed beneath where Dawud was perched, he could see that some of the men carried RPG launchers, while others bristled with spare RPGs. Dawud suddenly remembered the fire. If the smoke drifted down toward the Taliban, they would immediately detect it, and someone would be sent out to locate the source. Dawud slowly slipped away, and silently made his way to the part of the gap that was directly over the cave opening. There, he leaned over and whispered, "Afrah, put out the fire, Taliban."

Returning to his perch, he quietly watched the column pass below. The lead element was nearing the place where the bodies lay, and Dawud suddenly regretted not dragging the bodies off the trail and far into the brush. Seeing their dead comrades would certainly cause alarm, and sure enough, the moment they stumbled over the first body, Dawud could see a ripple move through the column as it came to a stop. Dark silhouettes began scrambling to each side of the trail, immediately taking up defensive positions. Dawud had focused his attention on the front of the column, hoping they wouldn't send out patrols. That was when he heard the muffled sound of nearby footsteps. They were coming from his right and sounded close, much too close. Silently, he cursed himself for paying so much attention to the head of the column at the cost of ignoring his right flank. Turning his head slowly, hoping the motion would not reveal him, he caught sight of dark figures silhouetted against the night sky. They were only five or six meters to his right and a little below his position. Although he was not sure, he thought he saw two or three more dark silhouetted figures a short distance behind the first two. They were traveling parallel to the column, and moving directly toward the rock outcropping. There was no way to tell if this was just a small patrol, or the lead element of another column. Cautiously raising his rifle, he pointed it toward the closest figure, but he did not dare pull the trigger, knowing the shot would reverberate across the valley, and would be certain to draw everyone to him. Given his circumstances, his only hope was that these men would just pass by, and not see him. As he watched, he couldn't help but notice how quietly these men moved, and how they blended into the background. One of them was now close enough that if Dawud had leaned forward he could have reached out and touched him. Holding his breath, he could hear his heart pounding and hoped the sound would not give him away. Dawud was watching one figure, then a second figure slowly pass, when a hand shot out from behind him, and grabbed him around his nose and mouth, yanking his head back...then Dawud glimpsed the blade of a knife moving up toward his neck. He managed to block the man's wrist, stopping the blade only a few millimeters from his throat. The man's other hand was still pulling back on his head when Dawud instinctively stopped resisting, and instead drove his head and upper body backward, slamming the back of his head into his attacker's face. The impact had caught the man off-guard and he was knocked back, giving Dawud a fraction of a second to push the knife arm away and swing his Kalashnikov toward his assailant. As he did this, he felt the cold steel of what he was sure was the muzzle of a pistol, press against the back of his head.

"Don't move, don't make a sound," a low voice growled, just barely loud enough for Dawud to hear. Dawud did not move. The voice then ordered him to slowly lower his rifle, place it on the rock ledge beside him, and then put his hands on the top of his head. Complying, Dawud cautiously turned his head toward the man with the pistol. What he saw momentarily confused him. The man with the pistol must have been standing in a shadow, because only a black pistol with some kind of cylinder attached to the barrel was visible. The rest of his body was so deeply in shadow that even his outline was not visible. As Dawud placed his hands on his head, he watched as the man emerged into the moonlight. He was completely covered in black and he appeared to have weird, protruding eyes. Several seconds passed before he realized that the protruding eyes were night vision goggles. Dawud's mind raced, trying to make better sense of what was happening. Several other men, also clad in black and wearing night vision goggles, slipped silently from the surrounding darkness, and positioned themselves on each side of Dawud. He could now see their rifles; they were not the familiar Kalashnikovs, but suppressed, M4 carbines.

Seeing their stealth, the night vision goggles, and now the M4s with the tube-like noise suppressors attached to their muzzles, Dawud was certain these men were not Taliban or even ANA Special Forces – these were Westerners, probably Americans. Sure of this, Dawud decided to take a chance. Using his sister's tactic, he spoke in English, and in a quiet voice he said, "You are Americans. Do you know who Jake is?"

There was little doubt that Dawud's words had caught their attention, and for a long moment no one spoke. Then, Dawud heard the low voice ask in American English, "What do you know about Jake?" Dawud could only see the man's black silhouette, but even so, he could see that he was a tall, lean man. He stood motionless, the protruding lenses of the night vision goggles boring into Dawud. Looking back at him, Dawud replied, "Jake was helping us but we ran into some trouble."

The words had barely left his mouth when he heard a thud, and then one of the Americans fell to the ground. From the darkness, a female voice barked, "No one move. You will let my brother go, and I will not kill you." The situation had suddenly taken a different turn, and Dawud could not help but be amused at how his little sister had again come to his rescue. Somehow, she had knocked one man down and was now facing off at least another five heavily armed American soldiers. Yet her voice was strong and confident, and Dawud was quite sure his little sister was not bluffing, but he was also sure she would not act rashly. As he lowered his arms, he noticed that no one had replied to his sister's demands. Apparently, these men were not accustomed to being taken by surprise, and even less accustomed to backing down. The standoff lasted for only a couple of seconds before the tall man, speaking in Pashtu, said, "And what is your name?" Afrah barked back, "It is none of your business. Now are you going to let my brother go, or do I start shooting?" The man replied, this time in American English, saying, "Afrah Hawadi, Captain Mustafa has said many kind things about you. My name is Harris, I believe Captain Mustafa refers to me as the 'foreigner.'

Now please let us all put down our guns before someone gets hurt. And we'd best not forget that there are well over a hundred Taliban fighters less than half a kilometer from here, and I don't think we want to invite them to our little party." Harris paused as he removed his night vision goggles, then he continued, "Seriously, you must tell me about Jake. Do you know where he is?"

Both Dawud and Afrah were taken aback by the turn of events. They had little doubt that he was the "foreigner." It made sense, yet turning themselves over to some covert American military unit was not exactly what they had expected. Afrah was still pointing her rifle at the man, when he slowly holstered his pistol and then stowed his night vision goggles in the canvas bag attached to his belt.

Waiting for the young woman to digest what he had told her, Harris couldn't help but be impressed by this rather unusual brother and sister duo. There was obviously more to them than he had originally thought. As these thoughts passed through his mind, Afrah stepped from the shadows, and stood directly in front of the tall man. She studied him as if she was trying to make up her mind, and then, in a more conciliatory tone, said, "I will take you to Jake...he is badly hurt. Do you have a doctor?" Harris turned to one of the other men and said, "Doc, go with this young lady." One of the black-clad figures stepped forward, and a moment later, he and Afrah had disappeared into the darkness.

The man Afrah had knocked to the ground grunted some very explicit curses, as he first got to his knees, and then shakily rose to his feet. Dawud saw that the man was holding a knife, and realized that he was the same man who had tried to cut his throat. Dawud smiled and shook his head.

CHAPTER TWENTY

Deal

Doc tended to Jake and did what he could, while the Americans assembled a clever, prefabricated stretcher. Jake was strapped into the stretcher, and two of the Americans hefted him up and began making their way back.

It took nearly five hours to reach the remote, mountainous base camp. During the arduous trek, Dawud curiously watched as each man, including Harris, took his turn at carrying Jake. Now, as Dawud and Harris sat at a rickety table in a small, crumbling mud-brick building, Dawud asked Harris why the men had been so eager to carry Jake's stretcher. Harris replied, "We're a small unit and we spend months, sometimes years living in close quarters, in hostile and isolated places. Over time, we become like brothers, and Jake is one of our brothers...one of the best of us. He's smart, easygoing and one hell of a warrior." Harris paused for a moment and then continued, "Jake has helped carry more than his share of stretchers, and he has held the hands of a lot of good men, as they took their last breath. Every man in this unit owes Jake in some big way, and this is our small way of thanking him. Dawud understood, for that had been the reason he had dragged Jake to that rock outcropping. He too had wanted to say...thank you.

Both Dawud and Harris were silent for a while. Dawud had finished off two bottles of water, and was now working on devouring his third energy bar, something called "Soldier Fuel."

Their mud-brick building was one of four similar structures that were located at the edge of a desolate, narrow valley, over 20 kilometers from Fakhar. The snow-covered peaks of the Hindu Kush Mountains glistened in the early morning sunlight. Dawud had thought it a magnificent sight, but it was also cold and threatening. The four buildings were all that remained of a small settlement that had long ago been abandoned. Jake was in one of the nearby structures, being attended to by Doc, the unit's medic. Next to him was the now notorious Afrah Hawadi. Afrah watched everything Doc did and peppered him with endless questions.

When she had first seen Doc, she had been reluctant to let Doc touch Jake. It was as if she had been keeping Jake alive solely through her willpower and didn't trust anyone else with the task.

Back at the cave, Doc was wearing his night vision goggles and was immediately able to spot Jake. Actually, that shouldn't have been possible, since the cave had absolutely no ambient light. His version of night vision goggles utilized the latest Gen 3 image intensifier tubes, and were useless in caves. Yet, there was Jake, faintly glowing as if he were charged with some kind of undulating energy. As Doc stared, the entire cave suddenly lit up and he realized Afrah had started a fire. As the fire caught, Doc removed his night vision goggles and again stared at the man lying on the cave floor. He wasn't glowing, at least not as he could see, but as Doc approached, the hair on his neck, head, and arms stood straight up as if he had entered some kind of powerful magnetic field. Turning to Afrah, he saw she was looking at him with a mixture of wariness, concern, and anguish in her young eyes. Doc had been a Special Ops medic for over six years and had seen a lot of strange things, but this topped everything. The moment he had looked into Afrah's eyes, he knew that he needed her permission to touch Jake. And when he had asked, she seemed to consider the request, and then, barely perceptibly, nodded. In that same instant, the...energy field was gone.

As Jake's head slowly cleared he heard voices. As he opened his eyes, he saw Doc and next to him, he saw the angel...no, no that beautiful young woman was Afrah, or at least that was what his mind was trying to tell him. His mouth felt sticky and his tongue felt thick and heavy. He wanted to speak but he couldn't form the words. Doc's voice registered and he heard him say, "Jake, you're going to be all right. We're gonna medevac you to a field hospital tonight." Although this information was of some interest to Jake, at this moment, all he wanted to do was to look at Afrah.

Jake's wounds were serious, and according to Doc, he should not be alive. A bullet had severed the subclavian artery and he should have bled-out long ago. Jake needed to be in a hospital's intensive care ward and he needed to be there now. Even so, the best Harris had been able to do was to arrange for a medevac, HH-60M Pave Hawk helicopter to pick him up at around 2200 hours. Jake would be flown north to Uzbekistan where he would be treated at an Army medical evacuation hospital. Army surgeons had already been alerted and would be standing by to provide the initial treatment. Then Jake would be prepped for evacuation to a military hospital in Europe.

Now was the hard part, the wait. Harris used the time to debrief Dawud. Although this was a structured exercise, he kept the atmosphere informal, allowing Dawud to explain his interpretation of events, in his own way. Dawud told him everything, leaving out only his rather unexplainable insights and premonitions he had had about Commander Haider. He did mention that he had killed a fighter whom he thought might have been an important man...possibly a Commander. Harris was interested in this man and jotted down the rather detailed description Dawud provided, including the red silk cord that had been in his jacket pocket. When the debriefing was over, Harris offered Dawud a cup of tea, and the two men spoke casually about living in Farkhar and Kabul. It was while they were speaking about Kabul University that Harris sat up straight and said, "Dawud, there are some decisions we are going to have to make, but first I'd like to thank you again for saving Jake's life. We're all pretty impressed with what you and Afrah did. The question now is, what do I do with the two of you? As I see it, I can escort you to another village, where you can hang out until the Taliban come visiting, or...you can come and work for me."

Dawud stopped chewing on the last piece of his energy bar, looked up at Harris, and said, "What would I do?" Harris replied, "Look Dawud, I'm fairly sure you're smart enough to know that I'm here to make life for the Taliban, al-Qaeda, and all of the other Islamist groups as uncomfortable as I possibly can." Harris paused for a moment and then continued, "I'd like you to help me. You have certain talents, certain skills I may be able to use. Son, I need someone to get inside their organization, and I think you just might be that guy. Putting it more simply, I want you to be an operative...a spy. Make no mistake, my young friend, it's dangerous, damn dangerous work...You will be dealing with some serious people, some real nut-cases, and there's a fair chance you could be discovered."

Harris again paused, this time he seemed to be trying to decide whether he should say more. Then he said, "Dawud, you should know that this...war has not been going well. The 'good guys,' people like your father and Captain Mustafa, are being cut down, one at a time. I do not know what has happened to your father but four days ago, Captain Mustafa was shot in the back. I am told he is alive but he will never walk again." On hearing this news, Dawud's heart sank and he wished that somehow they could be there to help the man. For as long as he could remember Captain Mustafa had always been there watching out for them. No one had been watching out for Captain Mustafa and now there would be no one there to take care of him.

Harris continued, "This does not mean the fight is over and the Taliban have won. Even with these setbacks, there are many good men and women working very hard to keep a lid on things, to keep the Taliban and al-Qaeda destabilized. But we need more help, we need good...smart people on the inside, people like you. So what do you say, Dawud, do you think you have the heart and the stomach to be a....spy? If it's not your cup of tea, just say no, and I'll do my best to get you and your sister set up in some other town, and then I'll be on my way."

Dawud understood what Harris wanted him to do, and he had to admit that he was tired of running. He wanted to fight back; he wanted his life to make a difference. He had also not forgotten about that...Thalj Shayton character and knew that one day he would come looking for him.

Actually, becoming a spy was one of the best ways he could think of to make himself disappear and yet allow him to strike back at his enemies. Dawud raised his head, looked Harris directly in the eyes, and said, "What about my sister? What would happen to Afrah?" Harris had anticipated this question and was ready. Replying, he said, "I understand you and your sister are close, and I think we can work something out. First we would find a way to fake her death. Then Afrah would be given a new identity, one that would include all the necessary identification documents and even a passport. I would see that she is given some money and relocated to a city where the Taliban are still weak. I will also see that she has a safe place to live and a job with an organization that is friendly to us. A place where we have people that will look out for her."

Dawud immediately replied, "That is not good enough. There is no place in Afghanistan that is safe from the Taliban and they are quick to learn the names of those who have supported the foreigners. These are the people that are first to die. No Harris, I want Afrah to be safe, I want you to send her to America...I want you to make it so that she can live in America as long as she wants. I also want you to send her my salary so she can have money to spend and a good place to live. And one more thing Harris, I want you to get her into a good university.

If you do these things... I will agree to work for you."

Harris sat there quietly digesting Dawud's demands. He was not surprised at Dawud's straightforwardness. In Afghanistan, everything was subject to negotiation, and Harris had come to appreciate that these negotiations offered a unique insight into a negotiator's personality. Dawud was a bright kid, and there was something special about him, but he had made demands that Harris would never be able to meet. Still, he hated to lose this kid. The money was not a problem but gaining entry into the United States, and then securing a "green card," housing, and admission into a good university was something his bosses would never agree to.

Nonetheless, Harris would not forget that Dawud and Afrah had saved Jake's life. It was then that Harris got an idea. Clearing his throat, he said, "What you have asked for would normally be impossible, but what you...and your sister did for Jake, may have changed things. You see, Jake's father is an important man. He is a United States Senator. When he hears of what you did, I think he will try to help.... Let me make a few calls and then we'll talk again."

Knowing the conversation was over, Dawud scooped up the last energy bar, and left Harris to make his calls. As Dawud stepped outside, it suddenly occurred to him what he had done. If, somehow, Harris accepted his terms, he would be sending his little sister to America, without even discussing it with her. She was going to kill him. What had he been thinking? Nevertheless Dawud also understood, deep down inside, that this was a once-in-a-lifetime opportunity. Afrah would have a chance to live in a safe country, to get an education, to have the opportunity to be anything she wanted. Dawud knew he had done the right thing, but he was not so sure Afrah would agree.

It was nearly noon before Dawud was summoned back to the small mud-brick building. On seeing the young man enter, Harris said, "It's going to be a while before they get back with me, so just hang in there."

Harris was trying, Dawud could see it in the man's expression. As he stepped back outside, he wondered whether he should talk to Afrah, but decided not to. If his terms were rejected, there was no need for her to know, and if they were accepted, he would have plenty of time to tell her.

It was late afternoon when Dawud was again summoned. Harris

was talking on his satellite phone, when he looked up and saw Dawud enter. With just a hint of a smile, he spoke into the phone, saying, "Sir, he just walked in. I'll hand him the phone."

Gesturing for Dawud to come forward, Harris handed him the phone and said,

"Dawud, Senator Pawlak would like to speak with you...Senator Pawlak is Jake's father."

Dawud suddenly felt uncomfortable and wasn't sure what he was supposed to say. He took the phone from Harris, and after a second or two answered, in his best English, "Hello, Sir." At first there was no reply, but, in the background, Dawud could hear the sound of a woman quietly sobbing, and then a man's voice, choked with emotion, said, "Mister...Mister Hawadi, we understand that our son Jake has been seriously wounded and the fact that he is alive is because of what you and your sister have done for him. I would like you to know how grateful we are. We owe you a great debt....Please sir, would you be kind enough to speak to my wife? She is standing here and very much wishes to speak to you." Before Dawud could reply, he heard the trembling voice of a woman say, "Thank you, Mr. Hawadi...we are so grateful for what you and your sister did for our Jake. He...he is our only child...and you have made it possible for him to come home to us. God bless you, Mr. Hawadi." Before Dawud could respond, the woman handed the phone back to her husband, who said, "Mr. Hawadi, I can think of no words to adequately express the depth of our gratitude." Dawud interrupted, saying, "Sir, I am afraid you misunderstand what happened. It is my sister and I that owe our lives to Jake. He has been seriously wounded...because of us...because he was trying to save our lives. What we did was a small thing and does not compare to what Jake did for us.... It is we that are grateful and it is we that must offer you an apology, for we are the reason your son has been shot."

The line was silent for a long moment, then Dawud thought he could hear Senator Pawlak draw a deep breath, and then he said, "Mr. Dawud, you are still a young man and someday, God willing, you will have a child, and then you will understand how precious such a gift can be, and how much a parent hopes and prays that their child will grow to be a good man, to have courage to do the right thing, even when it is hard...even when it is dangerous. What you have told me about our son, makes us very proud of him. Nevertheless, Jake would not be alive if it were not for you and your sister. I cannot tell you how great a loss that would have been. Do you not see, Mr. Hawadi, what our son did, does not in any way diminish what you and your sister did?

Now sir, Mr. Bartnik...I believe you know him as Harris, has explained your situation to me, and I have made a few calls. It appears that your father, General Morad Hawadi, is well-known and well-respected by a number of my county's highest-ranking intelligence officials. When they heard that General Hawadi's son and daughter had been responsible for saving the life of Lieutenant Jake Pawlak, United States Army, Special Forces Command, the wheels were set in motion. Apparently, there are certain legal provisions that permit your sister to enter the United States and gain permanent residence. Your sister is to be issued a 'special circumstances' visa on her arrival at the U.S. Embassy in Tashkent, Uzbekistan. Ms. Hawadi will then be eligible to begin the process of acquiring a permanent visa." Senator Pawlak paused for a moment and then said, "Mr. Hawadi, there's one more thing. My wife and I have discussed this, and we would consider it a great favor if your sister would come and stay with us. Mr. Bartnik has told us some things about her, about what had happened to her and to your mother. It would be a privilege to have this young woman in our home, and we promise we would take good care of her."

Dawud had not expected this, and did not know what to say. Every day, since they had left Kabul, he had been afraid for his sister. He was responsible for her safety, for her wellbeing, yet he could not ensure any of these. Still, could he send her to a strange land, and to a stranger's home? Senator Pawlak seemed decent enough, for someone that was a politician, and Dawud had immediately taken a liking to Mrs. Pawlak, but what finally convinced him was Jake. Jake had an easy way about him, yet he was confident and had the courage of two tigers. But mostly, Jake...smiled easily and in a way that was disarmingly sincere and warm. Surely the parents of such a fine man had to be good people. What he would decide had implications that were far greater than he could imagine. Dawud said, "Sir...Your offer is very generous and I will speak with my sister. If she agrees, then I too will agree." The reply was immediate. "Thank God. That is all we can ask for. Mr. Hawadi, my wife and I will anxiously await your reply, but I am afraid that my wife has already gone off to prepare a room for your sister. Thank you again, young man, thank you so very much...for everything. Goodbye."

It had been nearly an hour since Dawud had spoken to Senator Pawlak. Dawud had taken Afrah aside and presented her with an edited version of the events of that afternoon. At first Afrah did not speak; she simply looked at him with a mixture of shock, hurt, and disbelief. Then in a voice that broke, she said, "Are you sending me away? Have I done something wrong?"

Her response had pierced Dawud's heart and it completely demolished any remaining threads of composure that he had been clinging to. His little sister must think he was a monster, someone who could turn his back on her. For as long as he could remember, Afrah had never asked for anything, except to be around him. She now believed he was banishing her, sending her away. Tears filled Dawud's eyes and his voice would not come. Then, finally, in a quiet, halting voice, he said, "You are my sister, but more than that, you are a gift, a precious gift that I have been given. I am truly honored to be your brother. To think of you going away makes me feel sick...sadder than I will ever be able to express. But sister, Afghanistan is much too dangerous of a place for you. The Taliban have thrown acid on you, they have killed our mother, they are hunting our father, and they are hunting us. Yesterday, we survived, mostly because of Jake, but what about tomorrow, and the day after? There will not always be someone there to rescue us, and next time, Allah will not be so generous. Your safety is my responsibility, my duty...no, my privilege, and I am afraid I cannot keep you safe here. Please sister, this is your chance. Please go to America, become someone important. I will try to follow and in two or maybe three years, we can again be together, and you can show me where you live, where you go to school....you can introduce me to your American girl friends."

Afrah's heart was breaking, but as she always did, she carefully listened to what her brother had to say, and when he finished, she said, "This is not fair; this place is dangerous for you too. What will happen to you? I have shown you that I am a good shot, I will be able to protect myself, and I can protect you too. Anyway, you do not know how to wash your clothing, and you eat very badly."

Dawud was greatly relieved that the tone had changed, and she no longer thought he was abandoning her. He explained that Harris had very important work for him to do. However, Dawud was careful not tell her exactly what that work consisted of. He assured her that he would be safe, he would learn how to do his laundry, and he would make a point of eating better. They held hands for a long time, both already feeling the desperate loneliness that they knew was soon to come. After he promised over and over again that he would follow her to America, she agreed to go.

Dawud returned to the small mud-brick building. When Harris saw him enter, he immediately reached for his satellite phone, dialed, and then handed it to Dawud. Dawud took the phone, put it to his ear, and listened. After only one ring, Dawud heard Senator Pawlak's voice answer.

"Hello."

Before Dawud could respond, Mrs. Pawlak came on the line. Her voice was animated with excitement and apprehension.

"Mr. Dawud, has your sister agreed to come stay with us? Please Mr. Dawud, please say she will."

From her voice, Dawud could tell she was a cultured woman, with a kind and energetic voice. Although Jake was different from his mother, he was also a great deal like her and now Dawud could clearly sense the similarity. Dawud answered Mrs. Pawlak's question, in a voice that was at once heavy with loss and worry, yet somehow pleased and excited for his sister.

"Yes, Mrs. Pawlak, my sister has agreed."

Mrs. Pawlak could not immediately reply, and Dawud could hear her softly weeping through the phone. It took her several seconds before she regained her composure and could again speak, wanting to know if there was anything Afrah immediately needed. What was her favorite food? Did she have any allergies? Did she like dogs? Apparently the Pawlaks were taking care of Jake's dog while he was in the service. But mostly she had been worried that even though she and her husband were cramming, they knew far too little about Afghanistan and even less about the Islamic religion; they were afraid that somehow they might say something, or do something that might hurt or offend Afrah. Dawud was warmed by this woman's concern and assured her that Afrah was a strong, healthy, intelligent young woman, and was quite capable of adapting, and, yes, she loved dogs. She would do just fine.

Later, as Afrah and Dawud waited for the medevac helicopter that would take both her and Jake away, they found themselves enveloped in a kind of melancholy and a dread of the separation that they knew would profoundly change who they were. They would soon be making their ways, separated by oceans and continents, and each would have experiences that they could never again truly share. In some ways the time seemed to pass painfully slowly, yet they both feared the passing of each minute. Dawud and Afrah spent as much time together as they could, but Afrah still needed to help Doc out with Jake, and then Harris had taken her aside and had spent nearly an hour and a half with her, debriefing her on what had occurred the previous day. He documented everything and then asked her dozens of questions about her parents, their lives in Kabul, and the time they had spent in Farkhar. When Harris had finished asking questions, he had sent her back to Jake and sent word for Dawud to come see him. When Dawud arrived, he was photographed, fingerprinted, and blood samples were taken. Finished with these chores, Harris asked Dawud for his jacket. When Dawud asked why, he was told the man whose throat he had cut might be someone of interest, and they hoped to confirm his identity by performing a DNA test on the now-dry blood on the jacket sleeves. Harris managed to find Dawud a suitable replacement jacket and sent him out as he prepared the package that would be sent to Langley.

It was getting late, and Afrah dropped in on Jake to see if she could help Doc prepare him for transit. As she entered the small mud-brick structure, she was glad to see that Jake was fully awake. Sitting down beside him, she asked how he was doing, and soon the two of them were engaged in an easy and comfortable conversation. She updated him on what was happening and told him that she would be traveling with him. This pleased him and he asked how she had arranged that. Afrah hesitated for a moment and then she told Jake about the "deal" Dawud had worked out with Harris. Jake did not know exactly what her brother had signed up to do, but for Harris to arrange Afrah's entry into the United States, meant he had something big in mind for Dawud...something that was probably going to get the kid killed. Harris was a good man, but first and foremost, Harris was a dedicated intelligence officer, and his job was to establish and then maintain a network of operatives who could feed him useful information. Yet, if Dawud had not made this deal, Harris would have done his best to set him and his sister up in some little town, and then he would be forced to cut them loose. As every Taliban commander in the northern region was hunting them, they wouldn't have much of a chance. Simply put, Dawud had bought his sister a chance for a real life, but he was afraid Dawud had paid a dear price. Jake respected this young man, and hoped that if he had been in Dawud's position, he would have been both smart enough and brave enough to have done the same thing.

Afrah was asking Jake if he knew how long it would be before Dawud could come and visit her, when they both heard it. It was far off in the distance but they both knew the sound of an approaching helicopter. Afrah immediately stiffened and her eyes filled with tears. She stood up, excused herself, and ran from the structure. When outside, she frantically searched for her brother, and after a few seconds, saw him standing next to one of the fuel drums. The muffled thump of helicopter blades was growing louder, and Afrah immediately felt panic wash over her. Running to her brother's side she reached out to him and took his hand. The helicopter was a black mass emerging from a sky that was only slightly less black. Then, in only a matter of seconds, the helicopter touched down, throwing up a cloud of dust. Dawud and Afrah stood side by side, when Afrah reached out for her brother and wrapped her arms around him. She held him tightly, and she could feel his large, powerful arms grip her. Several men wearing dark flight suits and night vision goggles exited the helicopter, turned, and reached back into the dark opening to retrieve a stretcher. A moment later, they were jogging over to the small mud-brick structure where Jake and Doc were waiting. After only several seconds inside, the door opened and the two men, carrying Jake, exited and headed toward the helicopter.

It took a moment for Jake to spot where Dawud and Afrah were standing. When he did, he told the stretcher bearers to go over to them. Dawud and Jake looked at each other for a long moment, and Jake held out his hand and said, "Thanks, buddy. I owe you big-time." Dawud took his hand and shook it, as he replied, "No Jake, it is you that repeatedly saved our lives and we were strangers to you. What we did was nothing compared to that. You are a good man and it is we that owe you...big-time. May Allah protect you and may he be there to help you recover quickly."

Jake gestured for Dawud to come closer. Reaching up he gripped his shoulder, and whispered, "Dawud, your sister will be fine. My parents are good people, and I know Afrah will be well cared for." Jake paused a moment and then continued, "I don't know what good I'll be, but I'll be watching out for her too." Jake's eyes darkened and his expression became serious as he looked at Dawud for another long moment, and then said, "I think I know what Harris has in mind for you. I know you have the guts but it's a dirty, nasty business... Don't do anything stupid...God be with you, my friend."

As they parted, Jake looked over at Afrah and said, "There's something about your brother, and I know that you see it too...He's going to be OK." He saw she knew what he meant, but he also saw the heartache and the worry in her face, and he could not help but feel that something very special was about to be torn apart.

Dawud watched the crewmen carry Jake to the helicopter and heft him up into the doorway. Just then he felt someone touch his shoulder. Turning, he saw Harris, who said, "Son, it's time for Afrah to go. I spoke to the crew, and they know to watch out for her. It's about an hour's flight to the Uzbekistan border, and then another fifteen minutes to the airfield. A female Army officer will be waiting for Afrah when she touches down, and she will accompany Afrah to the American Embassy in Tashkent, where people will be waiting, and will give Afrah the necessary travel documents and a visa to enter the United States. The female officer will then accompany her to the military airfield at Tashkent, and see that she gets on board the C-141 transport to Ramstein Air Base in Germany. At Ramstein, Afrah will board another military transport that will take her to Andrews Air Force Base in Maryland. She'll be well taken care of. There are going to be some special-ops people traveling with her, and the word is out that Afrah is one of their own. Senator Pawlak and his wife will meet Afrah when she clears customs at Andrews."

Afrah had been listening and was the first to speak, saying, "What is going to happen to Jake?" Harris replied, "Jake is a pretty tough guy but his shoulder is a real mess. He's going to need a lot of highly specialized care and a lot of time to recover. When the chopper lands at the Uzbekistan airfield, he will be transported to the nearby CSH (Combat Support Hospital). A team of top-notch physicians will take over his care and when he's stable enough, they'll fly him to Ramstein, where an ambulance will take him to the LRMC (Landstuhl Regional Medical Center). It's a good hospital and they've got a lot of experience in putting warriors back together."

Everything was now moving quickly, and their time together was coming to a close. Dawud embraced his sister and pulled her close to him. Afrah put her arms around her brother and pressed against him until she could hear his heart beating. Would she ever see him again? Would he keep his promise and come to America? She hoped he would. Every cell in her body was already beginning to miss him and she desperately wanted to believe she would see him again...yet Afrah knew that would not happen, and she was as certain of this as she was of her own name. Now she realized that she had always known this day was coming, she had known it for as long as she could remember. It took every bit of her strength not to break down when Dawud slowly released her and then stepped back. She could see that his eyes glistened with tears as he raised his hand and placed it against his heart and said, "May Allah watch over you, my sister, As-salaam alaikum (Peace be upon you)."

Afrah responded by slowly placing her hand over her heart and replying, "May Allah also watch over you, my brother. Waalaikum assalaam (and peace be upon you)."

A helicopter crew member had been anxiously standing by and now approached saying, "It's time to go, Miss."

Afrah could hear the big turbines begin to speed up as she was led to the helicopter's open door. The turbulence from the spinning blades whipped up the dust, and tore at her clothing and hajib. As she was helped through the open doorway, she looked back at her brother. Through the whirling dust, she could see Dawud was standing there, looking toward her. Everyone else had retreated back from the storm of swirling sand but Dawud stood there as if he were made of a column of stone.

As she looked at her brother, suddenly the world turned a brilliant white and became absolutely silent...and then Afrah was instantly inundated with sounds – the roar of fire, explosions, and the thunderous rumble of collapsing buildings. Through the billowing smoke and the flames, she saw the girl, the one with those familiar green eyes. She was running toward her, her hair was wild and her face was streaked with soot and dirt, her clothes were tattered, and around her waist she wore that strange golden belt. At seeing the girl, Afrah's heart swelled with pride, yet Afrah was frightened, she didn't know why but something terrible was going to happen.

"Miss, are you all right?" The voice was that of a man and it was coming from somewhere far away. Her heart was pounding and a cold perspiration covered her entire body. The sounds of fire and the explosions were gone, replaced by the helicopter's turbines cranking up and the odd smell of ozone and scorched wool. Squatting next to her was a crewman, the same man who had escorted her to the helicopter.

His expression was a mixture of concern and...confusion. Afrah then realized she was lying on the floor of the helicopter, and everyone was looking at her with expressions that she was having difficulty interpreting. Rising to her feet, she looked at the crewman apologetically and said, "I am so sorry, I...I."

Afrah scrambled to come up with some explanation that he and the others might accept. She could see Jake struggling to release himself from the straps, as the flight medic attempted to restrain him.

Thinking quickly, Afrah said, "I have not...eaten for a long while, I think, maybe I am very hungry, and...and I fainted?" She knew she did not sound convincing. The statement sounded more like a question than an explanation; nonetheless, it did the job. The crew wanted to get airborne, and they accepted her explanation, although those who had witnessed the incident had serious reservations and even concerns for their safety.

In addition to her and Jake, there were five crew members on board, including a flight medic. To them, this tiny, remote outpost was smack-dab in the middle of "Indian territory" and as dangerous has hell. The longer they hung around, the more attention they would draw and that wouldn't be good for them or the men they were leaving behind.

As the door slid closed, Afrah tried, unsuccessfully, to catch one last glimpse of her brother. In her mind, she could picture him squinting through the swirling cloud of dust and sand, trying to see into the dark interior of the helicopter. Afrah hoped that he had not seen her collapse, for it would have served no purpose and it would cause him to worry.

Experiencing these...spells was not altogether new to her, although this one had been particularly loud and vivid, not to mention terrifying. In the past, the visions had usually been pleasant or at least interesting...but not this time. Having actually collapsed was also something new and something she hoped wouldn't happen again. The girl with those green eyes had visited her before, but she had been younger and had not worn that odd, gold belt. Afrah had no idea what these...visions meant, but like now, they had left her sad and anxious.

Seconds later, the helicopter lifted off, climbed, and then veered northwest to the Uzbekistan border.

Jake's stretcher was less than a meter away and he had not taken his eyes off of her since they had boarded the helicopter. He had seen her turn toward her brother. Her body had become rigid and the crewman reach for her, to steady her. He had seen the blue arcs of electricity leap from Afrah and strike the crewman, knocking him off his feet. At that same instant he had heard the turbines stall, and then the flight instruments flickered and go black. For a second or two he could not see Afrah. Actually it was so dark he wouldn't have been able to see his hand if he had put it directly in front of his face. The next thing he knew, the turbines had again begun revving up and the flight instruments had come back to life. Jake watched the crewman get up and hesitantly approach Afrah, who had also been knocked down. Cautiously the man reached out, relaxing only after he was not shocked when he touched Afrah's arm. It took him only a moment to help the young woman to her feet; though embarrassed by what had happened, Afrah did not seem injured.

The second Jake had laid eyes on this young woman, he had seen that she was stunningly beautiful, and at that same instant, he knew she was...different. It was as if she were able to see through him, causing Jake to begin rethinking his career choice. Until then, he had thought he was a good undercover operative, better than most. Yet Afrah had found his well-practiced portrayal of an Afghan herder to be little more than amusing. Yet, she had not been condescending.

Then there was that shooting incident. Although he had been hurting and was nearly unconscious, he had seen what had happened. Afrah had run over to him, picked up his rifle, shouldered it, and after a fraction of a second, fired. The shot was impossible. There was no way she could have hit that man without having the bullet pass directly through Dawud's head.

Yet most bewildering was what had happened to him after the shooting. He was dying, in fact, he could swear that he had died, and even now he was having difficulty coming to grips with the fact that he was still alive. Although he did not understand, he believed that Afrah had literally fought the "grim reaper" for his life.

Jake felt strongly drawn to this young woman, but at the same time, she scared the hell out of him.

Training

Five days had passed since Dawud had been recruited by CIA, Paramilitary Operations Officer Harris Bartnik, and now the senior intelligence officer was having reservations. It wasn't that Dawud didn't have what it took to make an excellent undercover operative. No, the problem was that Harris couldn't figure out who Dawud really was.

The morning after Jake and Afrah had left, Dawud began a strict training regimen that was designed to teach him the skills needed to function and survive as an undercover operative. At first, Harris was pleased at how quickly Dawud was picking up the information, but now, after five days, Harris was beginning to think Dawud was just a little...different. Sometimes Harris felt the young man could look inside of his head, and then there was the way that he...learned new material. It didn't seem that Dawud was learning anything, but rather he was retrieving knowledge that he had learned at some point in his past.

Playing on a hunch, Harris had given the young man two, recently developed tests for operatives in the National Clandestine Services of the CIA. The first test was the EAAT or Espionage Aptitude Assessment Test, and the second was the OPAT or Operative Psychological Assessment Test. Dawud "aced" the EAAT, but scored all over the map on the OPAT. The computer program scoring the OPAT designated the results as, "Unable to Assess", a designation that suggested either two or more subjects had taken the test, or the subject had been trained to "game" the test. Harris knew Dawud had taken the test alone and was reasonably sure he had not "gamed" it. Rather, Harris believed Dawud was not like everybody else. This had caused Harris to wonder whether placing Dawud among a bunch of al-Qaeda sociopathic megalomaniacs was such a good idea.

Spy training, as Dawud called it, began at dawn and ended at 2200 hours. The purpose of the training was to teach espionage, sabotage, and surveillance techniques, as well as basic survival skills, which included weapons training, escape and evasion, and hand-to-hand combat. The training would last three weeks and Dawud was determined to do well, and soon found himself loving every minute of it.

By the end of the first week, he had mastered skills that had eluded many of Harris' more senior operatives. As the third week rolled to an end, Harris and the other members of the team were finding it difficult to keep him challenged.

As the training wound down, it was time for Dawud to be tested in a real-world situation. He would accompany a team of operators to the outskirts of Sikham, a modest-size village of about six hundred inhabitants. Sikham was about eight clicks southeast of their base camp, and aerial photographs had shown it to have about two hundred structures clustered around the intersection of two, deeply rutted dirt roads. Most of the structures were constructed of mud-bricks, but there were also a few cinder-block structures, some of which were the homes of Sikham's more wealthy residents, while others appeared to be main street commercial buildings. Regular flyovers had shown no unusual activity and no one had ever reported anything suspicious. This made Sikham an ideal training site, a place that would represent only minimal risk, but a "real world" place where Dawud could practice the skills he had been taught.

After being briefed on what they knew about the village, Dawud was issued a miniature digital camera, disguised as an inexpensive ballpoint pen. A tiny, wireless earbud was inserted deep into his ear canal, and a small wireless transmitter/receiver and mic were sewn into the lapel of the heavy coat he was to wear. In addition to voice communications, the camera interfaced with the transmitter, allowing digital images to be automatically transmitted, in real time. Due to its small size, the transmitter only had a range of about one kilometer. Two of Harris' men, designated Hawkeye 1, would be positioned on a jagged rise about half a kilometer west of the village. Hawkeye 1 was equipped with a more powerful transmitter and would be in contact with Harris, whose call-name was Badger. After some debate, Dawud was assigned the call-name Crow. The call-name was given to Dawud by the radio operator, whom everyone called Nebraska. Nebraska had heard Harris refer to Dawud as a "smart ass" whenever Dawud would beat him at some exercise. Well, it happened that Nebraska once had a pet crow whom he had frequently called "smart ass." Since "management" would never approve "'smart ass," everyone agreed that Dawud would be "Crow."

Hawkeye 1's overwatch position allowed them to communicate with Crow, and to observe much of what happened on the two intersecting dirt roads. It also offered them a view of the approaches to the village. If something looked wrong, they could alert Dawud, and then they could provide cover fire while directing him to the best escape route.

Dawud was assigned the identity of a dead man, whose name was Afig Hafeez. Harris explained that Afig was a 19-year-old Pashtun man who had died in a U.S. Combat Support Hospital. He had been severely wounded in an airstrike, but before he died, he had told interrogators that he had been raised on the outskirts of Kabul and most recently had been living as a homeless refugee in the Char-Qala slum. About a year ago, Afig had been recruited by al-Qaeda. He, his mother Haliah, his younger sister Leeda, and six others, most of whom were known to be al-Qaeda fighters, had died in the airstrike. Afig's father, Omeid Hafeez, had been a religious teacher and had been working for the Taliban when he was killed by the accidental detonation of an IED. Afig had completed the equivalent of a secondary education, in religious studies. He had hoped to travel to the Pakistan tribal regions of Waziristan, to learn how to become a bomb maker, and then he had planned to return to Kabul and avenge the death of his father.

Harris had handpicked this alias since the man's death had been recent, and the CIA had been fortunate enough to have compiled an extensive dossier on him. Afig Hafeez had no other living relatives and his two closest friends had died in the airstrike. Dawud and Afig both had a younger sister and they shared a number of physical characteristics. Both were about the same age, both were tall and lean, and both had been raised and educated in Kabul. Of course, no one except the CIA knew that Afig Hafeez was dead.

Dawud was dressed as an itinerant peddler and was given a large, worn-looking bag, stuffed with used children's clothing. There was always a high demand for used children's clothing and Harris had been sure to throw in a number of garments with popular Western European and U.S. labels, which were thought to be of better quality, and sold far more quickly than those made in Afghanistan or Pakistan. The women of Sikham would be excited to see what this new peddler had to offer, and would be far more interested in his goods than in him.

Dawud's assignment was straightforward. Using his cover, he was to find out who the village Malik was, and how resistant he and the residents of Sikham were to the Taliban. Since Dawud would be in Sikham only a few hours, the goals were aggressive, but the exercise was meant to assess Dawud's ability to clandestinely acquire useful information. There was no pass or fail but if Dawud was as good as Harris thought he was, he would have his assignment completed before noon, and be having tea with one of the town elders, before he was back on the road.

They had left the base camp at about 3:30 AM and had been trekking through shin-deep snow for two hours. The sky had turned a leaden grey and there was a bitter cold wind blowing off the snow-covered slopes of the nearby Hindu Kush Mountains. Dawud shivered as the frigid cold air found its way through the patoo, heavy wool blanket, and his quilted jacket. Looking up, he saw a line of dark, menacing clouds moving toward him, promising more snow and more of the cold bleakness. Dawud and the two men of Hawkeye 1 parted ways about two kilometers from Sikham. Dawud would travel the remaining distance alone. Trekking through a white, frozen countryside, the only sounds he heard were the distant howl of the wind, and the crunch of the dry snow beneath his feet. As he got closer to Sikham, the quiet desolation was interrupted by the sound of a far-off barking dog. Since Afrah had left, Dawud had felt alone, and now, as he was making his way through this bleak landscape, he felt as if all of mankind had ceased to exist.

Dawud had received only one brief communication from his sister. She had told him that she had arrived safely, and that she was doing fine. She liked her new home, and asked about him and how he was doing. By now, Dawud was quite familiar with the work that Harris did, and knew that everything about Harris and his operation was Top Secret. Everyone on the team understood that personal communications were filtered through sensors at Langley. He knew his sister, he knew she would have written him many pages, but he had received only four, awkward sentences. Remembering those four sentences made his heart ache, and he had to stop for a moment and try to clear his mind. He needed to focus on his mission, and on his new identity.

Looking around, Dawud could see the first signs of human habitation that designated the outer edge of Sikham. The snow-blanketed mounds had long since lost their shape and he couldn't tell if they had once been dwellings or animal sheds. The smell of wood smoke reached his nostrils and he could see the thin wisps of grayish white smoke rising from several dwellings about a hundred meters ahead. The inhabitants of Sikham were now rising and building their morning fires. Dawud swung his bag over his shoulder and resumed his trek toward the crossroads and the center of Sikham. The structures he now passed appeared to be in better condition and a few were even constructed from cinderblock, and boasted high security walls. The village did not have electricity, or at least Dawud could not see any power poles. In the windows, he could see the light from candles and kerosene lamps, neither having much success penetrating the gloomy grayness of the outside. This changed as Dawud approached the crossroad. There he saw a sturdy looking cinderblock building, whose professionally printed sign identified it as the bakery. Bakers are known to rise early and this baker was no exception. What was unusual was that this baker must have had a generator, and from the number of lights that were illuminated, it was a big one. The hum of the generator's engine soon became clearly audible, and bright light streamed from several of the bakery windows as well as from windows in the fort-like structure adjacent to the bakery. Dawud saw that the two buildings shared the generator, and that they both were probably owned by the same person. The situation was curious, since a large generator, and the fuel to operate it, were relatively expensive. Although bakers had an important position in every village Dawud had ever been to, they were not known to be particularly well-off.

It was still early, and Dawud didn't expect to see anyone out in the street for at least another half hour, so he decided to find a place to hunker down and use the time to watch and see if anything interesting happened. Looking around, he spotted an opening to a narrow passageway that led back between two nearby buildings. It was only a few steps away and the soot-dusted snow had not been disturbed. Confident that no one was using the passageway, he glanced up and then down the road. Seeing no one, Dawud moved into the opening and disappeared into the shadows. The high walls on each side provided some much-appreciated protection from the wind, and standing even a meter back from the opening, he could still clearly see the bakery and most of the adjacent building. Pulling the wool blanket up over his head, he settled in and watched. The sky, still heavily overcast, was only marginally brighter and it began to snow. Just as Dawud was trying to nestle farther into the bag of children's clothing, he noticed five men exiting the building next to the bakery. Two of the men quickly stepped out ahead of the others, and began to carefully scan each side of the road. As their eyes turned toward the passageway, Dawud drew farther back into the shadows. When the men were satisfied that they were alone, they gestured to the others, and a moment later, four of the men assumed a box formation around a central figure, and began walking toward the bakery. All of the men were huge, including the man at the center of the formation. The men surrounding him looked as if you could break a sturdy tree limb across their heads and they would hardly notice. The man in the center was slightly taller than the others, and had the broad shoulders and the trim physique of an athlete. He wore a fur cap and had a black and white shemagh (scarf) that covered part of his face. Dawud could see that the man was pale and wore gold, wire-rim glasses, the kind worn by some of the professors at Kabul University. Although he strained to see more detail, the bodyguards were blocking his view.

Still, it was obvious that the man in the center was someone very important. Even the way he carried himself suggested that he was used to exerting authority. In contrast, his four bodyguards had primitive features and looked more like muscle-bound street thugs. As they got closer, Dawud noted the scars on the face of one of the bodyguards. These could be al-Qaeda or Taliban, albeit rougher and considerably larger looking specimens than any Dawud had previously encountered. Each man had a wool blanket draped over his shoulders. The blankets hung low and bulged in a way that suggested they were being used to conceal something. This was confirmed when Dawud caught a glimpse of a Kalashnikov protruding from beneath one of them. Although the men were still quite a distance off, Dawud reached into his pocket, removed the ballpoint pen/camera, and began taking pictures. He focused on the center man and then noticed the white beard and white eyebrows. This caused Dawud to pause for a second. As the men got closer, Dawud resumed taking pictures, although his hands were noticeably trembling. It was as if he was looking at a mythical character...who had assumed life-like characteristics.

Was this Thalj Shayton, the...thing his father had warned him about? The thing that had hunted his family for untold generations? Dawud almost forgot that he was still taking pictures, pictures that would be automatically transmitted to Hawkeye 1.

As the men got closer, Dawud could hear fragments of their conversation. They were speaking Arabic, and he was able to hear one of the bodyguards addressing the white-bearded man as Dr. Dicos. Dawud suddenly realized that the path the men were taking would lead them directly past where he was hiding. In only a few seconds they would be able to look down the passageway and see him. Looking around, he saw that there was nowhere to hide. The passageway was walled in on both sides and ended at a heavy, wooden door that was padlocked. Dawud cursed at himself. He had violated one of the most basic surveillance rules... "Always leave yourself an escape route."

He had made a mistake, and now he had no way of getting out of there unseen. With maybe two or three seconds before they would see him, Dawud placed the ballpoint pen back into his pocket, slung the bag of clothing over his shoulder, and stepped out into the road, emerging only about five paces in front of the men. Trying to appear calm, Dawud walked toward the intersection, hoping that he would pass as just one of the locals, or better yet, a traveling peddler who had sought shelter while waiting for the marketplace to open. Allah willing, they would think his appearance was just a coincidence. Then he heard several nearly simultaneous "clicks" of Kalashnikov fire select switches being moved to the "Fire" position, and immediately sensed rifle muzzles being pointed at him. He could try to run but they were much too close. In the next second he heard a deep, gravelly voice shout out, "Stop!"

Dawud stopped and slowly turned to see two of the bodyguards aiming their rifles directly at him. The other two men had their Kalashnikovs at the ready, scanning the road and nearby buildings, as they hurried the white-bearded man, the man they had called Dr. Dicos, toward the bakery. Dawud slowly dropped his bag and raised his hands. The two bodyguards had spread out and were about three meters away when one of the men shouted at Dawud, demanding to know what his name was, and what he was doing there. Dawud turned slowly and looked directly at him, replying, "Sir...my...my name is Afig Hafeez...I am just a poor peddler...I sell children's clothing...here, here in my bag...I can show you...You can see that I am telling the truth. Today is market day and if Allah is willing...I will make a little money and I will be able to buy some food."

The men's dark eyes bored into Afig, studying his every expression, his every move. They watched him for what seemed like a very long time. Harris had told him that al-Qaeda, the Taliban, and even NATO

soldiers used this technique because people would become very uncomfortable with the silence, and imagine all sorts of things that can
cause them to panic and begin saying things they shouldn't have. Finally, one of the men ordered Afig to keep his hands high above his head,
turn away from him, and drop to his knees. As Afig complied, he worried that he had not been convincing enough, and these men were
going to execute him. Risking a quick glance, Afig got a glimpse of the
burly bodyguard who had been growling the orders. He was the one
with the scarred face and was now squatting down next to Afig's bag of
clothing, cautiously feeling the contents. The other man had moved to
Afig's right side and had shouldered his rifle, aiming it squarely at
Afig's head. After a few seconds, Afig could hear the bag being opened
and the contents being dumped onto the snow. He could hear garments being tossed around and then he was ordered to stand up,
spread his feet wide, and keep his hands in the air. When Afig had
complied, he felt the man's hands patting him down. He knew that if
the bodyguard found his earbud, mic, or transmitter/receiver, he was
dead. It took only a few seconds before the man found his cheap-
looking ballpoint pen. The bodyguard clicked it once, examined it
briefly, and discarded it. After a few more stressful moments, the man
seemed satisfied that Afig's story was checking out. They had not
found anything suspicious – no weapons, no explosives. Finally Afig
was ordered to pick up his stuff and move on. The second bodyguard
lowered his rifle, and growled, "Allah has had mercy upon you today.
Now leave, before we change our minds."

Afig cautiously turned, to see the two men were already walking
toward the bakery. Dr. Dicos was standing there, back lit by the light
streaming through the window. The man seemed to be staring at him.
Afig turned away and began to pick up the garments that had been
strewed about. As he completed this task, he searched for and eventually found the ballpoint pen, which he returned to his pocket. When he
looked back, Dr. Dicos was gone, and the two men who had confronted him were now standing guard on each side of the bakery door. They
were alert as they scanned the road and nearby buildings, but showed
little interest in Afig, only occasionally turning their eyes in his direction. Afig slung the bag over his shoulder, and began walking toward
the marketplace.

Soup

Afig had made it to the intersection of the roads, when he heard four clicks emitting from his earbud. It was the signal to "report status." Hawkeye 1 had probably not seen the confrontation but they should have received the images. It had not occurred to Afig to transmit the two-click distress signal until now. As the situation worked out, Afig realized that asking to be rescued would have caused more problems than it would have solved. It was becoming clear to Afig what being an undercover asset really meant.

Trying to be inconspicuous, he reached for his collar, located the seam in which the transmitter button had been concealed, casually traced it where he could feel the button, and pressed three times, to indicate he was OK. He wanted to know if Hawkeye 1 had received the images, but he was still in sight of the bodyguards, and now there were more than a dozen people moving about, some only a few steps away.

In an area just east of the crossroad, a few vendors were setting up their karachis, the wooden wheelbarrow carts on which they displayed their goods, while other vendors occupied their simple stalls that were nothing more than wooden plank tables set between four poles. The poles supported a roof of corrugated metal that provided some shelter from the falling snow.

It was now time for Afig Hafeez to become Afig the vendor, the seller of used, children's clothing. Harris had tried to convince him that "the product was good enough to sell itself," and there was little doubt that the garments were going to be in demand. However, Afig was quite sure they would not "sell themselves." He had been to hundreds, maybe thousands of open markets and had seen the way a crowd reacted to popular products, and it did nothing to put him at ease.

Wandering among the stalls, he searched for a place where he could set up shop. While doing so, his thoughts went back to the events of that morning. He had been in Sikham for only an hour when he had crossed paths with Dr. Dicos...or was that man really Thalj

Shayton? If he had been Thalj Shayton, why had he not done something? Afig had been completely at his mercy. Whatever the encounter had meant, Afig was certain that he had not seen the last of that man.

After wandering around for several more minutes, Afig spotted a vacant, rundown stall, out at the far edge of the marketplace. The corrugated metal roof was gone and the table sagged under nearly half a meter of snow. It was not ideal but it was better than spreading his goods out on the frozen ground and the stand did offer a good view of the bakery.

Afig saw a nearby vendor preparing his stall, and made his way over to the man. He was in his late fifties and had a tired, weather-beaten face. Bundled in several layers of heavy clothing, the man had just finished clearing snow from his table and was now unpacking an assortment of aluminum pots and pans. Afig approached and stopped about a meter from the man, who did not bother looking up and seemed intent on ignoring his presence. After standing there for a few seconds, Afig cleared his throat and said, "Assalaam alaikum." Irritated at being disturbed, the man gave an audible sigh and looked up at Afig. After giving him a brief inspection, the man replied, "Waalaikum assalaam."

Afig could not tell whether the man was naturally a jackass or whether he was having a bad day. Not caring either way, Afig asked, "Sir, do you know who I must speak to for permission to use that stall?" The vendor had turned away from Afig and was now arranging his pots and pans. Unsure whether the man had heard him, Afig was about to repeat his question when the man said, "What are you selling?" Afig gestured to his sack and said, "I sell children's clothing; all of it is good quality, mostly American and European."

The vendor seemed to relax once he knew Afig was not in the pot and pan business. He stopped what he was doing and was quiet for a moment as he gave the situation some thought, then he said, "The stand belonged to Mohammad Abasin. Mohammad died last summer. But his daughter has a small child, a girl, maybe two years old. Since Mohammad died, the family does not have much money. You see it is a cold winter, and the little girl has outgrown her old sweater."

Afig knew what the man was asking for. Setting his bag down, Afig shuffled through it and then produced an almost new, girl's red sweater, size three, which he handed the old man and said, "I am sorry to hear that Mohammad is dead. Perhaps now his granddaughter will be a little warmer this winter." The man examined the sweater, and then smiled as he replied, "Mohammad was a generous man. I do not think he would mind if you used his stand...for today."

Although he was not sure what authority the vendor had, Afig decided that he had just negotiated one day's use of a broken-down stall, for the price of one, nearly new girl's sweater. Afig thanked the man and bade him goodbye. As he set up shop in his new "place of business," no one seemed to notice or care. In about 15 minutes, the children's clothing was attractively displayed and he was open for business. Almost immediately, women gathered around and then began to ask, "How much for the sweater? What do you want for this shirt? How much for those pants?" Setting a price was not difficult since he only had four basic prices –, one for shirts, one for sweaters, one for pants and dresses, and one for the big ticket item, jackets. There was one exception to his basic pricing, a boy's, size Small, nearly new, blue Nike jacket. Afig had set a high price for it, since he knew it would draw people to his stall and he did not want to sell it until he had depleted his inventory.

The problem that soon emerged was not his pricing; the problem was the haggling. Everyone always assumed the asking price was only the starting price. The selling price was always something less. Negotiating with two and sometimes as many as five customers at the same time was exhausting, and made watching the bakery a real challenge.

Afig had been open for business for about an hour and a half when he noticed a gaunt, young boy, about three or four years old. He had confidently pushed his way to the front of the small crowd and was staring at the blue, Nike jacket. The boy's face was dirty and he had messy, light brown hair, but what was most noticeable was that sweet, innocent smile, and those big, curious and slightly mischievous, bright green eyes. The eyes, in particular, had a way of making you...almost not notice that he was terribly thin and was shabbily dressed in a threadbare sweater that was at least one size too small for him. His pants were in no better shape; both knees were worn completely through, showing skin beneath. On his feet, the little boy wore an old pair of tennis shoes whose toes had been cut out so he could wear them long after he had outgrown them. Afig had little doubt that the boy was hungry and cold, but still that blue jacket had drawn him. A murmur rippled through the crowd and Afig looked to see a tall, straight-backed man approach. He wore a worried expression on his face and was frantically looking around, as he worked his way through the small crowd. On seeing the small boy, he headed directly to him, bent down and wrapped the child in an old blanket, and then, carefully picked him up and held him close. The boy's big, bright eyes never left the jacket, and it was not long before the man noticed. Afig could almost see him deflate slightly, yet he pulled himself together and asked, "How much for the jacket?" Afig knew that this man did not have enough money to buy a handful of rice, let alone the prize item on display. Yet he had still asked, partially to placate the boy, but also as an act of ...defiance. He was probably in his early thirties and had a strong, deep voice. Afig thought he might have been handsome, if it had not been for the long scar on the left side of his face and his dirty, tattered clothing. The scar ran from his forehead down into his scruffy, dark beard, bisecting the outside corner of his left eye. From Afig's position, he could not see if the man's eye had been damaged, and it would not have surprised him if it had. Two women standing nearby chuckled in amusement that was clearly laced with disdain. They too had been eying the fancy blue jacket, but when they had found out how much it cost, they had decided that they could not afford it. Now they stood there and glared as this wretched man inquired about it. Afig could see how much this irritated them and then realized the man was doing it on purpose. Everyone became quiet as they waited to see what Afig would do. Feeling uneasy, Afig sensed that there was more happening here than he was aware of. As he studied the man more closely, Afig saw that his good eye was alert and intelligent, and that he carried himself with a kind of dignity that did not fit his situation.

Afig knew what the crowd expected him to do, but he was not about to turn this man away. Harris had once said "A person who felt unjustly treated was more likely to speak openly to a sympathetic stranger, than to his neighbor." Afig did not know this man's story but he was fairly certain that there were real or perceived injustices involved. Realizing that he was taking too long to respond, Afig said, "On a day like this, my father would tell me 'Allah has blessed us with snow and a cold wind, so we can better enjoy hot soup.' Well, it is snowing and we have a cold wind, but, regrettably, I have no hot soup. Yet, as always, Allah provides. If I am not mistaken, there is a lady, maybe five stalls from here, who is selling hot soup from a large pot." Looking at the tall man, he continued, "I ask you, Sir, if I gave you some money, would you be kind enough to purchase a nice, large bowl of hot soup for me? Of course, I will pay you for your trouble." Many of the women gasped in shock.

At first, the man's face registered surprise, which quickly transformed into confusion mixed with suspicion. Murmurs rose from the crowd, and Afig noticed some of his customers were looking at the man, and then at him with growing disapproval. The man had clearly noticed their response but had chosen to ignore them, as he replied, "Twenty afghanis for the soup, and twenty-five afghanis for my time." Twenty-five afghanis to walk a few dozen meters, over to the soup lady, seemed a bit high, since twenty-five afghanis would buy a kilo of potatoes or about the same amount of onions. Knowing this, Afig realized that twenty-five afghanis would keep the man and his boy alive for another week or maybe two. Not hesitating, Afig replied, "You have a deal, my friend." Afig's response brought more and louder murmurs from the crowd, and Afig sensed they were on the verge of open rebellion. Thinking quickly, Afig added, "For the rest of you, I will be offering my most generous fifty percent discount on the next five sales, but you must act immediately, and, please, only one item per customer."

As he was making this offer, Afig slipped the blue Nike jacket off of the table, and placed it out of sight. As soon as his offer registered, the women surged forward and began pushing and shoving to gain access to the garments on display. Stepping back, Afig tactfully counted out and then handed the man forty-five afghanis. The man took the money and hesitated as he seemed to study Afig, then he turned and disappeared in the crowd.

When two girl's dresses and a boy's pair of trousers sold for the promised 50 percent discount, everyone forgot about the man, the soup, and even the blue jacket. The high demand for children's clothing, particularly heavier winter items, made it a good morning for sales and Afig's stock had been reduced by nearly half. Realizing the tall man had not yet returned, he looked over toward the soup lady, but did not see him. Another 20 minutes would pass before Afig spotted the two of them approaching from the opposite direction. The tall man was carrying the small boy in one arm, and a metal container in his free hand. It was nearly time for noon prayer and the crowd had thinned down. Currently having no customers, Afig hurriedly stuffed his remaining stock, as well as the blue Nike jacket, into the bag, slung the bag over his shoulder, and headed toward a storage shed that was about a dozen meters west of his stall. He was in plain view of the man and gestured for him to follow. Afig had chosen the shed because he wanted more privacy, an out-of-the-way place where the man might feel more comfortable talking. The distance wasn't far but he was forced to traverse a meter-high snow berm, and several minutes passed before Afig reached the shed. There, he noticed the crude, branch lattice door was wired shut, but Afig could see through the gaps in the lattice, and confirmed that the shed was empty. The man had followed and soon reached Afig. Pleased to see the man, Afig said, "Allah be praised, the soup has arrived." Gesturing toward the woman, he continued, "Did you not buy it from the soup lady?" Afig wanted to get to know this man, and was curious as to what his explanation might be. The man's expression suggested both a tired seriousness and a hint of irritation. Looking directly at Afig, he replied, "Here, in Sikham, one must provide his own container when he buys soup. Since you did not provide me a container, and I did not see that you had a container, it was necessary for me to retrieve one from my house. It is also widely known that that old woman waters down her soup, so that one is buying little more than a few vegetables in some hot water. Knowing this, I went to the home of a neighbor, an old woman who is known to make a most excellent Shorwa (red meat soup). During the winter months, Sikham's more wealthy families pay her to make Shorwa to serve at special events. Fortunately, she had some Shorwa left over from a Shab-e-shashjust (evening-of-the-sixth), when a Mullah blesses a newborn. The old woman was happy to take the twenty afghanis and she provided you with a generous portion." The man paused for a moment, but before Afig could respond, he continued, "Though it is not my business, I have noticed that you have been nearly 'giving away' your stock of children's clothing, and why is it that you are always watching the bakery? I do not know who you are or what you are doing here, but I do not believe you are a vendor.

Nonetheless, I have agreed to bring you hot soup and I have now done so. When you have finished, leave my container at the stall, and I will be by later to pick it up."

Afig was stunned by the man's words. He had been reasonably satisfied with his theatrical skills, yet this wretched, half-starved man had been able to see right through him. Scrambling to recover, Afig put on his most serious expression, looked directly at the man, and said, "I have come from Kabul and I am not yet familiar with your ways. In

Kabul, soup vendors provide a simple, paper or plastic container, and I thought it would be the same here.

And yes, you are right, I am not a very good vendor. Actually...I am a terrible vendor, I charge too little and I do not like to haggle. Uncle Abdel says I will not last the winter and I have little reason to doubt him.

And then there is the bakery. You see, I have a weakness for bakeries, or rather I have a weakness for cookies, pastries, and sweet breads. The bakery is in plain view, and I must admit that I have given too much thought to the Khajoor (deep fried cookies), Cream Rolls, and Gosh-e-Feel (elephant ear pastries) that might be in there, waiting for me."

Afig was reasonably satisfied with his response and thought that it made enough sense to deflect further suspicion. The only problem was, the man's expression suggested he did not believe him. Again, Harris' words came to him, "When you have done something to cause suspicion, provide a brief and reasonable explanation, then let it go – saying too much makes you sound more guilty than saying too little." So Afig did just that, he "let it go" and changed the subject, saying, "That soup smells delicious..." But before he could say anything else, the man handed him the pot and said, "I will be by later to pick up my pot." Then he turned and began walking away. So far, the questioning had not gone well, and the only thing that Afig had discovered was that he had a lot of work to do, on his skills as an undercover operative.

As Afig watched the man leave, he saw the small boy looking at him from over the man's shoulder, except he wasn't looking at him, he was looking at the pot of soup. For now, the business of spying would have to wait. Clearing his throat, Afig called out, "Sir, sir, this soup, it is for you...for you and your son. It...was always meant for the two of you. Now please, take it, it will warm the boy much faster than a blanket." The man stopped and then turned to stare at Afig for what seemed like a long time, and then he said, "I must get my son out of this cold. The place where we live is nearby. If you come with me, maybe all three of us can...share the soup."

Afig nodded, slung his bag over his shoulder, and the three of them set out toward a cluster of small, squat structures about two hundred meters west of the marketplace. They walked single file, following a narrow foot path through snow that was nearly to Afig's knees. After about 10 minutes, they arrived at a small, mud-brick structure that had once clearly been an animal shed. The man put the boy down, and without saying anything, opened the door and let the boy inside. He then bent down, and stepped through the low entryway. Afig followed and found himself in a candle-lit, low-ceiling room whose dirt floor was covered with a piece of threadbare carpet. The room's meager furnishing consisted of a straw mattress, a quilt and a blanket, and several straw-stuffed burlap bags that served as pillows. These pillows surrounded a small, low wooden table, on which were three lit candles. Though the place was clean, it still smelled strongly of the animals that had been its previous occupants. There was one small window that was no larger in height or width than a soccer ball. It let in some light, but it was the candles that provided a majority of the light and served as the room's meager source of heat. Though the room was warmer than outside, Afig could still see his breath fog.

Afig was the first to speak, saying, "It is good to be out of that wind and I thank you for your hospitality." The man had been standing there, staring at the walls, seeming to wish he had the power to change them. On hearing Afig's voice, he turned and said, "I live in nothing more than an animal shed, but...as you say, it is out of the wind. Now let me take that soup." Afig handed the pot to him and watched as he felt the side of the pot. Shaking his head grimly, he said, "It is still warm, but it is no longer hot. I am sorry but I do not have fuel to heat it." Afig replied, "It is not a problem, warm soup is also very good." To the man's right was a low shelf made from a wooden box tipped on its side. On it was a meager assortment of utensils, two metal cups, and two metal bowls. Selecting the two cups and a metal bowl, he poured the soup into them and carefully handed Afig the bowl, which contained the largest portion. He then handed his son one of the metal cups, which was about three quarters full of soup. The pot had not been that large and though he could not see into the man's cup, Afig knew he had kept very little for himself. Once the soup had been passed out, the man said, "I have not had company for over two years and I am afraid I have forgotten my manners. My name is Mitra Bashar and this," gesturing toward the small boy, "is my young son Omaid."

Afig was glad the man had become more relaxed, and replied, "I am pleased to meet you, Mitra Bashar, and you too Omaid. My name is Afig Hafeez." The man's posture eased as he gestured for Afig to sit on one of the straw pillows. There would be room enough for just the three of them, and as Afig sat, Mitra and Omaid followed.

The boy's eyes studied Afig curiously, seemingly intrigued at having a visitor; however, his eyes were soon drawn to the cup of soup his father had given him. Seeing this, his father said, "It is all right Omaid, you can go ahead and eat." The little boy cautiously raised the cup to his lips, and took a small, hesitant sip. From the expression on his face, it was as if the soup sickened him, and for a second Afig thought he would vomit. Seeing this caused a lump to form in Afig's throat as he realized that the child had reached that stage of starvation where some people no longer desired food. Taking in the boy's sunken eyes, grey complexion, and small, gaunt body, Afig knew that Omaid could not survive long.

Mitra moved to his son's side and Afig could see the man's eyes tear-up as he gently encouraged the boy to eat more, and with his father's help, the child managed to put down the partial cup of soup. Several times, the boy had gagged and Afig was afraid he would throw up the desperately needed nutrition. When they were finished, Omaid appeared exhausted and began to shiver as he laid his head against his father's chest. Mitra covered the boy with the quilt, and then wrapped his arms around the boy and held him tightly.

Afig had no appetite and instead of eating his soup, he poured his portion back into the pot. When Mitra finally looked up and their eyes met, Afig saw in his expression the absence of pretense, and the presence of a sadness and a worry that was...almost desperate. Before the man could speak, Afig said, "I will leave my portion of the soup for you and the boy."

Mitra was taken aback by Afig's gesture and felt a rage sweep over him. However, the rage was not directed at Afig; it was directed at himself, at his inability to take care of the people he loved. No...this young man was just trying to help, but Mitra Bashar might be beyond help. Mitra and son were dead, they had died over two years ago and now their physical presence...their miserable bodies were being ravaged by starvation, and they both would soon be as cold as the wind that blew outside their door. Tears welled up in his eyes, his back straightened, and his fists clenched in an attempt to contain his rage, but then it drained away and an unnatural calmness took its place. It was as if he had...surrendered but he didn't know to what. Was he finally accepting their inevitable death? No...he didn't think so, but then what?

Mitra looked over at where Afig sat and saw the young man studying him. Neither man spoke for several long seconds, and then Mitra said, "You are an unusual man, Afig Hafeez. I do not know what to make of you." The little boy had fallen asleep in the man's arms, but Afig could hear a raspy sound in his breathing. Starvation rarely was the cause of death. No, starvation decimated a person's immune system, and infection or disease would likely kill that person before starvation did.

The man's expression became more serious, as he continued, "What are you doing here? Everything about you is ...wrong." Afig thought about how to answer and then he looked at the man, and replied, "Mitra, you are correct, I am not who I have claimed to be, but I cannot tell you who I really am, except that my presence here in your home might cause trouble for you. I do not wish harm to come to you or Omaid, so I will leave if you want me to."

Mitra straightened up, and his tone became more direct, when he replied, "You have given me little information, but that may be fair, since you do not know who I am or the trouble that you may be in."

Afig looked at the man quizzically, but before he could speak, Mitra said, "Of course, you do not understand. Well, I see that it is necessary that I tell you my story." Mitra looked past Afig and began, "My wife died...no that is not correct, my wife was savagely murdered...two years ago last fall." Mitra was silent for a long moment before he continued, "I had to travel to Fayzabad, to pick up a load of animal feed. You see, I was a merchant and I made a good living selling animal feed, seed, and...fertilizer. That evening, when I returned home, my wife was dead and Omaid, who was not yet two years old, was being cared for by a neighbor lady, who told me what happened."

Mitra Bashar paused as tears welled up in his eyes, and he could not speak. It took a long time before Mitra again had control of himself and continued: "Jahandar Hawass, first son of Forood Hawass, the town's baker and Sikham's Malik, had been attracted to my wife for many years, but she had never liked the man, and when she chose to marry me, Jahandar became very angry. Unhappy that he could not stop the marriage, and later, even more unhappy that she had borne me a child, he left Sikham. Jahandar was gone for several months and we heard that he had joined a nearby group of Taliban fighters, but even the Taliban did not want that miserable snake. Forood Hawass had to pay the Taliban a great deal of money so that they would not kill his son, but instead return him to Sikham. On the very day I was in Fayzabad, the

Taliban brought him to Forood's house, untied his hands and legs, and left him there like a piece of garbage. Humiliated and angry, Jahandar went straight to my home. He wanted to see Nahal, my wife, but she refused to speak to him, and locked the door. This made him even more angry, and he went away, but returned with a large sledgehammer, the kind used to break rocks with. Jahandar beat on the door until it had broken into pieces. Everybody knew what was happening, but they feared Forood Hawass and turned away. Everyone except the neighbor lady. She is a brave woman, and she and Nahal had been close friends. When Jahandar got inside of my house, he beat and raped my wife, and then he beat her to death with the sledgehammer. My neighbor lady had heard Nahal screaming, and she...she alone came to help. She brought a heavy metal pipe, and when she saw what that man was doing, she hit him with it, she hit him many times. It was too late to save Nahal, but she did save Omaid. I am certain he would have killed the boy next. Jahandar, now hurt and bleeding, became scared of what he had done, and ran away.

When I heard what had happened, I went to find Jahandar Hawass. He was hiding at his brother's house, a place where he would always go when he had done something wrong. When they saw me, they yelled for me to go away. They said that my wife was nothing but a whore and Jahandar was doing his righteous duty, as a Muslim, to kill her. As Allah is my witness, I swear I am not a violent man, but Afig, I killed that haramzadeh (bastard) and his "swine" brother, I killed them with my bare hands. They both had knives and I was cut many times, but I did not feel any pain. It was over quickly, before Forood Hawass knew what was happening and before he could send out his thugs to stop me. Later that day, I was arrested and I was taken to Forood's office. He wanted me executed on the spot, and would have done it himself, if it had not been for the other elders, who insisted that there be a trial. My neighbor lady was called to testify and when she was finished describing what she had seen, none of the elders dared convict me of murdering Jahandar Hawass. But Forood Hawass was not finished with me. He convinced the elders that I had provoked his second son into a fight and was responsible for his death. In the end, the council found that I owed Forood restitution – blood-money. Though everyone knew that I was justified in killing both men, they again chose to look the other way as Forood took all of my money, my house, my truck, and my business. But that was not the end of it.

Forood began spreading the word that I had been in Fayzabad to see another woman, and that Nahal had had extramarital relationships with at least two other men. Of course everything was a lie, but that did not matter. It was not long before many of the people had forgotten what really happened, and began to believe Nahal deserved what had happened to her, and that I had gotten away with murdering two righteous men. Still, Forood was not satisfied. Last year, he let it be known that he would severely punish anyone that gave me a job, offered me food, or took me into their home. Forood wants me and my Omaid dead, he wants us to die slowly and very painfully.

I would have taken Omaid and left Sikham a long time ago, but Forood has made it clear to me that if I left, very bad things would happen to my neighbor lady and her children. He has not forgotten that it was her testimony that showed the village what a vicious animal his son really had been.

Afig, this woman saved Omaid's life and my life. I have sworn to do whatever I can, to keep Forood from hurting her."

Mitra paused for a moment, as his eyes were drawn to the pot of soup, then continued, "The soup...I was not completely honest about the soup lady. It is true that the woman waters down her soup, but even if I had wanted to buy soup from her, I could not. She would not sell soup to a murderer and adulterer."

Afig did not know what to say. His heart went out to Mitra and his little boy as he wondered how it was that life could be so hard on some people. The silence continued as his eyes went from Mitra to the little boy. Omaid had been quietly listening, and Afig could see the tears in the small boy's eyes. Until now, Afig hadn't noticed that the boy never spoke, and realized how much his world must have been shattered by the vicious act of one violent man. When Afig looked up at Mitra, he saw the man was lost in thought, the hardness had returned to his face, and he stared blankly at the wall opposite him. The candles cast dark, jerking shadows across him and his son, giving the effect that they were on the verge of flickering out of existence.

Clearing his throat, Afig said, "Mitra there are now many things I do not like about Sikham, but I am in need of information. Would you be kind enough to answer some questions for me? I must apologize in advance, for I do not wish to be offensive, but my time is short and my questions will need to be direct."

The sound of Afig's voice startled Mitra and he jerked as if being awakened from a deep trance. It took him a second or two to focus in on what Afig had said, and when he did, he replied, "Yes, yes go ahead, you may ask whatever you like."

Afig had been out of radio contact with Hawkeye 1 for too long. He had 20 minutes or maybe half an hour before someone might come looking for him. It had also been over an hour since he had last watched the bakery, and didn't know where the Dr. Dicos character might have gone.

Inhaling deeply, Afig began, "Who owns the bakery and the house next to it?" Mitra replied, "As I have said, Forood Hawass is the village baker, he is the one that owns the bakery building and the one next to it. Though the man is rich he says he loves to bake and he tells people that it is his true calling."

Afig said, "You say Forood Hawass is rich; where does he get his money?"

Mitra replied, "I can tell you, it is not from his bakery. No, Forood Hawass has other ways to make money. He is the 'top man' in Sikham, the Malik and a member of the Shura (the Elders' Council). Of course, there is the usual baksheesh, and nothing gets done in Sikham without his palm being greased. But that is not where he makes his 'real' money. Forood Hawass is a man of opportunity. When he took my business, he soon realized that it could make him wealthy. There is little money in seed or animal feed, but fertilizer, that is where the opportunity lies. You see Afig, it is well known that the Taliban receive their money from opium and donations from foreigners, but what is less well known is how the Taliban acquire their explosives. Explosives for bombs, or what the Westerners call 'improvised explosive devices.' These bombs kill and maim far more of their enemies than their bullets do. Well, it turns out that many of the Taliban bombs are made from ammonium nitrate, a very common fertilizer and a product I have sold for many years.

Back in 2010, Karzai banned the sale and use of ammonium nitrate, but it can easily be acquired in Pakistan. I still know people in the fertilizer business and they have told me that every two months, Forood travels to Pakistan, where he purchases several tons of bulk ammonium nitrate and, on another day, he purchases an equal amount of ammonium sulfate.

Back in Afghanistan, the Government is eager to have farmers use non-explosive fertilizers like ammonium sulfate so they have encouraged its importation. Forood knows this so I have heard he packages the ammonium nitrate in sacks labeled as ammonium sulfate, and the ammonium sulfate in sacks labeled ammonium nitrate. He then sells the ammonium sulfate to the Pakistani farm cooperatives near Peshawar. Jamil, my cousin is a member of one of these cooperatives and he has told me that Forood sells them what he calls 'accidently mislabeled' sacks of ammonium sulfate at a big discount. The price is good so they say nothing.

Forood then transports the ammonium nitrate fertilizer to Afghanistan. He has been seen at the border with two truckloads of fertilizer in sacks marked ammonium sulfate. Since he is now a legitimate fertilizer distributor and his cargo is clearly labeled as ammonium sulfate fertilizer, the customs people simply ask to see papers showing that he had actually purchased the ammonium sulfate. Once this is established and the customary baksheesh offered, he is waved through.

Now Forood is free to transport his cargo anywhere he wishes. He can even request a military escort in areas where bandits are active. I do not know exactly where the Taliban take possession of the ammonium nitrate, but I do know that when the trucks arrive in Sikham, they are empty and the next day it is customary for Forood Hawass to celebrate with a party for his friends.

There is one more thing. Forood's...special business relationship with the Taliban is why the Taliban stay away from Sikham. Sikham is a small, unimportant village and as long as it is free of Taliban, the Government leaves it alone."

Although everything Mitra said would have to be verified, Afig was inclined to believe the man. This was valuable information, far more valuable than he had expected. His time was short and he was anxious to tell Harris what he had learned, but there was still one more thing Afig needed to know about. Taking a moment to construct his question, Afig asked, "There is a man in your village, a man who is protected by four, large bodyguards. He is in his mid-forties, tall, powerfully built, and has a white beard and gold, wire-rimmed spectacles. Do you know who this man is and what is he doing here?"

Afig could immediately see that this question had disturbed Mitra Bashar, and even in the dim light of the candles, Afig could see a mixture of surprise and a trace of fear in the man's face.

For a long time Mitra Bashar did not reply, and Afig was afraid his cooperation had ended. Then Mitra cleared his throat and in a very quiet and deliberate tone of voice, said, "This is not a question you should be asking. The man you describe, he...he does not exist."

Afig replied, "No Mitra, he does exist, I have seen him with my own eyes, I even know his name, but I need to know more." Mitra Bashar had become clearly uncomfortable with this subject, and when he replied, his voice was deadly serious. "This man you speak of, his name is not to be mentioned in this house. Even Forood Hawass fears him. If you are smart, you will forget you saw him and will not ask any more questions about him." Afig replied, "I cannot do that. This man is of great interest to me." Mitra Bashar was silent for a moment and then said, "Then you are a fool. This man is no ordinary man. I hear many whispers, but most of what I hear does not make any sense." Afig replied, "Please, tell me what you have heard." Mitra Bashar looked at Afig with a trace of annoyance which slowly turned to resignation, and said, "He was first seen three days ago, but the old men say he had been here before, many, many years ago. They say he comes to Sikham only when the weather is very cold, and one of the old men, who claims to have seen him four different times, says the man was not alive since he never once has seen his breath fog the air." Afig said, "Mitra, listen to me, it is very important that I learn as much as I can about this man. Is there anything that would help me understand who he is, and what he is doing here?" Mitra was silent, as he thought. Then, after short moment, he looked up and said, "I do not know if it is connected, but people had said there is a young woman with this...man. She is a prisoner or maybe she is his slave, but whatever she is, she is treated poorly." Mitra Bashar paused for a long moment, before continuing, "There is still more. I have heard a rumor, just this morning, that says the man goes to the bakery early every morning but does little except to...sit there. He has taken over Forood's office and sits in his big leather chair...waiting. I did not know what to make of this, but now..." Mitra Bashar paused and studied Afig closely before he continued, "Now you are here...another mysterious stranger."

Mitra Bashar and Afig were both silent. Both understood the implication.

It was getting late and time for Afig to leave. He had much to report to Harris, and he still wanted another look at that bakery. Standing, Afig turned toward Mitra, and saw that his son was now awake and was watching him. Mitra also rose, and the two men looked at each other. Afig could see that the man was concerned about him. This man, who had suffered so much, and who was near starvation...was concerned about him. Touched but embarrassed by the sentiment, Afig looked away.

There was little doubt that if this man and his little boy were to survive the winter, they were going to need whatever help Afig could offer. After thanking Mitra Bashar for his hospitality, Afig stepped to the door, opened it, and stepped outside. Mitra Bashar and Omaid followed close behind. As the two men stood, face to face, Afig handed him his bag of used clothing, into which he had slipped just over 30,000 afghanis, all the money he had made that day and the 12,000 afghanis he had brought with him. It would be enough to feed them and keep them warm through the winter, and maybe through the spring. But come summer, Forood would again be grinding his heel into Mitra's back. Regretting that he had so little to give, Afig said, "This is not much, but I want you and Omaid to have it. I now have no more use for it." Then, before Mitra could react, Afig continued, "I have enjoyed your company, and the information you have provided will be very useful. .....Mitra Bashar, I am very sorry about what happened to your wife, and what Forood is doing to you and Omaid."

Mitra did not reply and was initially reluctant to accept the bag, but that reluctance crumbled when he looked down at his son. The little boy was clinging to his pant leg with his small, thin hand. The sight of the child's emaciated body tore at his heart. Taking the bag, he put his hand on Afig's shoulder and said, "Thank you, my friend, we will make good use of these." Mitra paused for a moment and then continued, "Be careful. I know that you can hear him calling, but do not be in such a hurry to fly into the flame.

Assalaam alaikum." Afig did not know how to reply, so he just said, "Waalaikum assalaam."

Afig turned and walked away but after eight or nine steps, something made him stop, and he turned to look back at the sad little structure. There, he caught a glimpse of Omaid looking back at him, through the partially opened door. Though he was in shadows, Afig could clearly see the boy's green eyes focused on him. Afig immediately turned away, for what he then saw was not the child but rather the dirty, blood-spattered face of a man in his early twenties. Those innocent green eyes were gone and in their place were eyes hard as steel, and burning with anger and hatred. Omaid Bashar would survive, grow up, and one day he would become a...killer, no he would become a murderer. Afig did not want to know this. He wanted to believe in the...hope and the promise that was every child's birthright. As he continued walking, the snowfall had become lighter. It was mid-afternoon and though it seemed impossible, the sky had become even darker.

CHAPTER TWENTY THREE

Shed

A chill passed through Afig as he pulled his blanket up over his shoulders and head. He had almost forgotten how miserably cold it was. Even so, he had work to do and needed to find someplace from which he could contact Hawkeye 1, a place where he would not be disturbed. As he made his way back toward the bakery, his eyes scanned both sides of the path but saw nothing suitable. Then, after traveling nearly halfway back to the bakery, he spotted a small shed near the rear of a vacant plot of land. Packed snow formed a narrow pathway that led to the shed but there were no recent footprints. Carefully, Afig looked around to see if anyone was watching. Seeing no one, he turned onto the path and hurriedly made his way to the shed. As he got closer, he saw that the mud-bricks were crumbling and if repairs weren't made soon, the structure would not last another season. After one last look around, Afig stepped up to the narrow door, carefully pushed it open, and peered inside. His eyes strained to see into the darkness, but soon he was able to make out a pile of straw, and what looked like a row of mud-bricks stacked against one of the side walls. A section of the back wall had collapsed, opening a gap almost half a meter wide and over a meter high. A heavy, oilcloth tarpaulin had been loosely draped over the breach, and swung back and forth as it was buffeted by the wind. Afig was hesitant to enter and stood in front of the doorway, listening. Several minutes passed, but all Afig heard was the flapping tarpaulin and the howling wind. Crouching so his head would clear the low entryway, Afig entered the shed, stopping just inside as he waited for his eyes to adjust. Soon he was able to see more clearly, and quickly established that the straw pile and mud-bricks were the only things occupying the shed. Satisfied, Afig leaned back against the wall, and prepared himself to transmit. He thought of the Hawkeye 1 team, which was only about four hundred meters east of him. They had been hunkered down on that windswept rise for almost six hours. Afig cringed at the thought and could not help but admire the toughness of these men. The shed was in line-of-sight of the rise and he was reasonably sure that Hawkeye 1 had a clear view of it.

It was time to make radio contact. Although Afig had practiced the procedure, this would be his first real-world voice transmission and he felt a little nervous. Clearing his throat, he pressed the transmit button and said, "Hawkeye 1...Hawkeye 1 – this is...Crow - over." Hawkeye 1 responded immediately, "Crow – Stand by, Badger wants to talk to you – over." Afig responded, "Roger, Hawkeye 1. Crow standing by." Afig waited nearly two minutes before his earbud crackled and a voice said, "Crow – This is Badger, are you receiving – over." Afig replied, "Badger...you are coming in loud and clear – over." Badger responded, saying, "Crow – This is no longer a training exercise, I repeat, this is no longer a training exercise. Subject in transmitted images is of very high interest. I need subject's current location – over." Afig was a little surprised at the direction and urgency of the transmission, as he replied, "Badger – Surveillance ceased approximately two hours ago. Subject's last location was at the bakery, the cinderblock building on the southwest corner of the intersection. – over." There was no reply for several seconds and then Badger said, "Crow – Try to confirm subject is still at that location. If possible 'tag' subject, – over." Afig knew that "tag" meant attaching a tracking device onto the subject, or to someone who was always close to the subject. If this was not possible, he was to attach the tracking device to something the subject carried with him or the vehicle the subject traveled in. Afig replied, "Badger – Understand...will confirm location of subject and tag...Badger, I have additional information – over." Badger replied, "Go ahead Crow – over."

Afig took several minutes to convey what Mitra Bashar had told him. When the transmission finally ended, Afig had his assignment. To tag Dr. Dicos he would first have to disassemble the pen/camera and remove the tiny locating beacon inside. A drone or low-orbit satellite would pick up the beacon's signal, and lock in on it. Once tagged, Dr. Dicos would not be able to evade detection, and could be easily followed or targeted for an air strike. The beacon was really small and he did not want to lose it, so he decided to leave it in the pen until he had a better plan.

The bakery was not far from the shed and if he got started now, he would have a couple of hours to get the job done. As he began to move toward the opening, he caught movement at the corner of his left eye. Looking in that direction, he at first saw nothing, but then a clump of straw slid from a pile. Thinking the straw had been disturbed by a small animal, maybe a mouse, Afig hesitantly took a step forward, intent on examining the straw pile more closely. The wind howled outside and a dusting of snow drifted down through cracks in the roof. Seeing no more movement, Afig decided that whatever had dislodged the straw was probably gone, and he was about to turn away when the straw pile...exploded.

Something, a dark figure leaped up and charged at him. It took a moment before Afig realized it was a man but by then the man had knocked him to the ground and was trying to straddle him. It was then that Afig noticed the man held a large chunk of brick above his head, and was about to drive it down into Afig's face. Recognizing his predicament, Afig raised his left arm to block the blow, and with his right arm delivered a powerful punch to the man's side – just below his ribcage. The force of the blow caused the man to buckle and expel a gush of air. Simultaneously, Afig bucked and the man was dislodged from his position and thrown to the side. Springing to his feet, Afig tried to remember his hand-to-hand combat training, and attempted to stomp his adversary while he had the advantage. But it was no use, the man sprang to his feet, crouched, and charged at him.

As the man came at him, Afig waited until the last fraction of a second, and then lunged out of the way and shot a right jab to the man's throat while planting a powerful left hook on the side of the man's head. This combination immediately took the fight out of the man and he stumbled backward, trying to stay on his feet. Afig knew he should move in to finish him off, but had no more fancy moves. Harris had taught him the jab and the hook but he had not had time to learn anything else.

It took a second or two, but the man recovered, although he now seemed much less interested in direct engagement. Mumbling curses that Afig did not quite understand, the man's eyes darted around the small space, and then he crouched as he moved to Afig's left. But instead of charging, he reached down behind a row of mud-bricks, and snatched up a meter-long piece of rusted iron rebar. Up until then, Afig felt he had a fighting chance, but this changed everything. The space was small but if he managed to get a good swing, the iron bar would surely shatter bones, and he would soon be dead. As the man raised the iron rod, Afig lunged at him, knocking him backward and causing him to trip over a row of mud-bricks. Both Afig and the man slammed into the side wall and came to rest in a heap, with the man on the bottom and the iron rod still firmly in his hand. Afig grabbed for the iron bar as the man scrambled to get away. Afig could not believe the man's resilience as they both again stood facing each other, but this time they were both gripping the iron bar. The first one to let go would probably end up dead. They shuffled in a circle for a few seconds, each trying to gain an advantage, then both men noticed the large amount of snow drifting down from the ceiling. Just as they looked up for the source, a large section of the shed's roof collapsed, knocking both men down and burying them in debris. As Afig scrambled to free himself from the tangle of rotted wood poles, lattice, and sheets of shattered clay and ice, he saw his opponent was already free and rising. This was not good, since he was still pinned under several of the larger wood poles.

The man was just standing there, staring at him with a mixture of both rage and fear. That was when Afig noticed that he was clutching his right arm, which swung limply at his side. Neither man had the iron rod, which must now have lain buried somewhere beneath the debris. Shoving aside the last of the larger poles, Afig began to pull himself up. Seeing that Afig had not been injured, the man's eyes darted to the breach in the wall and before Afig had gotten completely free, the man had pushed the tarpaulin aside and slipped through the opening. Though Afig could no longer see the man, he could hear him yelling for help. Afig could tell the man was heading toward the crossroad and knew he was in trouble. Making his way to the entryway, Afig could now see the man was already 30 meters away, too far to run down in a foot race. All he could think to do was to press his transmitter button twice – indicating he was in trouble. As Afig exited what remained of the shed, he thought he heard a faint...thud and saw the man stop. Then there was a second thud, and the man's knees buckled and he fell forward, onto his face. Afig knew what had happened; Hawkeye 1 had taken the man down. For a moment, Afig just stared, knowing that he had, in effect, ordered this man's execution. But now was not the time for him to think about it. He had to act and he had to act quickly. Pressing the transmit button, Afig said, "Hawkeye 1, I'll drag him behind the shed. I don't think anyone will find him there for at least a day or two." Hawkeye 1 did not immediately reply and Afig realized that they too were dealing with killing the man. Then Afig's earbud crackled and Hawkeye 1 said, "Roger that, Crow."

Looking around, he saw no one; the road was empty, and there were only a few inhabited dwellings in the area, and they were nearly a hundred meters away. As Afig approached the body, he began to notice details he had not seen before. The sweat-stained turban, the matted hair and beard, the ruddy skin, and the tear on the right shoulder of his jacket. The man was about 30 years old and had likely been an unemployed laborer or maybe a Taliban deserter. There was no way to know. All Afig knew was that the man had had the misfortune of selecting this shed and bedding down in this straw pile. Afig did not want to look at his face. Instead, he grabbed his feet and immediately smelled the familiar odor of warm urine that he had now come to associate with death. He dragged the body behind the shed and searched his pockets. Finding nothing of interest, he quickly covered the body with debris and mud-bricks. He then covered this with snow, trying hard to blend the burial mound into the surrounding landscape. As he backed away from the scene, he kicked at the trail of blood that stained the snow a bright red. When he was finished, only white was showing. From the way the snow was being blown around, it would not be long before all traces of what had happened would be gone. Looking around one last time, he reached for the collar of his coat and clicked the transmitter button three times to indicate he was OK and everything was a GO.

Although Afig did not know it, his little training exercise was now a high-priority operation that had the attention of none other than the CIA's Director of the National Clandestine Services. To protect the operation, a four-man "mop-up" team would slip into Sikham, retrieve the body, and sanitize the site. The body would then be transported to some faraway location, stripped of anything that might identify it, and then buried in an unmarked grave. Even if it was someday discovered, the death would quickly be dismissed. Every day dozens and sometimes hundreds of people were killed in blood feuds, land squabbles, and the ongoing insurgency.

Captured

As Afig set out toward the bakery, it began to snow, lightly at first, but by the time he was in sight of the cinderblock building, the snow had begun to fall heavily. Approaching the intersection, he could see that the marketplace had closed and everyone was gone. With the bakery directly across from him, he realized that he did not have a plan. He couldn't exactly walk into the place and ask if Dr. Dicos was there. Unsure of how to proceed, he decided to spend some time looking around. Bracing himself against the blowing snow, he cinched the blanket with one hand and used the other hand to retrieve his "ballpoint pen." Approaching the building, he turned right and made his way to the entry door, taking pictures as he passed. He didn't think the picture would have any use but there was no one around, so it was a low-risk effort, and it would show Hawkeye 1 and Harris that he was doing something. When he reached the corner, Afig stopped and cautiously peered around, hoping to see that the bodyguard was still posted by the side door. If he was, it meant that Dr. Dicos was likely inside. As the door came into view, Afig immediately saw that there was no guard. This should not have been a big surprise, since the weather was miserable and the bodyguard may have sought shelter. But it could also mean Dr. Dicos was gone. As he tried to decide what to do next, he thought he heard what sounded like a woman screaming. Looking in the direction of the sound, Afig was able to make out two large men dragging a woman who was kicking and flailing about. As they got closer, Afig recognized the men as two of Dr. Dicos' bodyguards, and they were heading toward the bakery's side door. Not wanting to be seen, Afig pulled back around the corner and waited a few seconds before looking out again. There, he saw the bakery side door open and a third man step out. This man was brandishing a Kalashnikov, and Afig recognized him as another one of Dr. Dicos' bodyguards. A few seconds later, the two men had dragged the woman up to the third man and had yanked her to her feet. Though the woman wore a full burqa and Afig could not see her face, her voice and the intensity of her struggle suggested that she was young and obviously quite fit. The woman stood there for a moment and then suddenly lunged at the third man. He was easily twice her size but the ferocity of her assault drove him backward, forcing him to shield his face from the onslaught. The attack lasted only a second before the two other men grabbed her and pulled her away. The third man, now embarrassed by his response and enraged by the woman's audacity, approached her, and without warning, drove the butt of his Kalashnikov into her abdomen. All three men laughed as the woman doubled over, went to her knees, and vomited. To her credit, she did not let out a cry but the fight had been knocked out of her, and she offered little resistance as they dragged her into the bakery. The man with the Kalashnikov stayed behind and took a moment to do a quick scan of the area. When he was satisfied, he followed the other two men, closing the door behind him.

This had all happened in a matter of two or three minutes, and Afig was now quite sure he had found the woman Mitra had described. While cursing himself for not having found a way to help her, Afig quickly came up with a plan. Admittedly, it was not much of a plan but it went something like this: Although the baker was a loathsome character, the bakery operated as a legitimate business. All morning, he had seen people going in empty-handed and coming out with bundles. What if he walked into the bakery and pretended to be a customer? He could look around, maybe, take a few pictures, and he might even catch a glimpse of Dr. Dicos, which would be "positive confirmation" that the man was still there. And then there was the woman. He might get to see that woman again, and this time, he would find a way to help her. As he thought about it, Afig realized that his plan was really...bad. Inside the bakery, he would likely encounter Forood Hawass, Sikham's Malik, a merciless tyrant, and a man who made his fortune selling explosives to Islamic extremists. Also there were at least three, and more likely four, huge Neanderthals in there, any one of which was capable of ripping his head off. And finally there was the infamous Dr. Dicos, a giant of a man in his own right, whom the CIA seemed to think was a very bad person, capable of...who knows what. Was this really the best he could come up with???

Ten, eleven, twelve, Afig counted the paces to the front entrance. The closer he got, the worse his plan sounded. By the time Afig had hold of the door handle, he had thought of a dozen ways this plan could get him killed, yet, he did not hesitate. Afig turned the handle and pushed the door open; now if he could only manage to stay alive.

It took Afig a second to adjust to the brightness. The room was all white – the ceiling, the floor, the walls, everything. The next thing that hit him was that he was the only customer. This made sense, considering the weather outside, but somehow, he'd imagined there would be at least one or two other customers. It would have made it possible to blend in, but now he stood out like a cockroach on a white tablecloth. At least the shop was warm and as the aroma of fresh bread and pastries registered, he realized how hungry he was. A couple of meters in front of him were two large, expensive-looking, chrome and glass display cabinets filled with an assortment of breads, cookies, and pastries. To the left of these cabinets was a glass counter, on top of which sat a modern cash register. The man behind the cash register wore a spotless white apron, a neatly pressed white shirt, and matching white pants. He was in his mid-sixties, overweight, and he wore glasses with thick black frames that were in contrast to everything else in the shop. When he looked up at Afig, Afig immediately knew he was looking at Forood Hawass. The man had attempted a smile but the best he had managed was a sneer, and it was his eyes that gave him away. There was no feeling, or warmth in them. It was as if you were looking at the eyes of a store mannequin.

As the baker sized Afig up, the sneer disappeared and was replaced by what best could be described as a scowl. Afig knew that he must look like some shiftless vagabond who had no money and had likely come into the bakery to get out of the cold. Actually, that was the look he and Harris had strived for, and he really had no money. He had given everything he had to Mitra, so it would not be long before the baker figured out he was not going to buy anything, and would have him tossed out.

With the ballpoint pen concealed in his hand, Afig stepped toward the display cabinets and began to examine the pastries. The baker watched him for a moment, and then looked down at the ledger he had sitting open in front of him. Seeing his opportunity, Afig took the man's picture. He did it as secretly as he could and was nearly positive the baker had not seen him. Since there was no one else to photograph, and the bakery looked pretty much like...a bakery, albeit an extraordinarily white and rather prosperous one, he decided to return the pen to his coat pocket. As he was doing so, the door in the back wall opened and a man entered. Afig immediately recognized him as the bodyguard who had searched him. He was the one bodyguard who was not present when they had brought the woman in, so now it was confirmed that all four bodyguards were here. Inside the shop, the man now looked even larger and more powerfully built than he had remembered. The bright lights revealed the ruddiness of his complexion and the coarseness of his hair and beard, as well as his unusually blunt and primitive features. The bodyguard paid no attention to Afig, and instead walked directly over to the baker, who was suddenly quite uncomfortable. The bodyguard's expression was impassive but Afig sensed that he did not think much of the baker. He could not hear what was being said, but whatever it was, it had gotten the baker's attention, because his head turned sharply toward Afig. His eyes wide, he stared at him as if he was looking at some...exotic creature. Sensing it was time to leave, Afig turned toward the door, only to find another one of the bodyguards blocking his way. He was the huge, scar-faced man who had searched him earlier that day, and he was also the man who had struck the woman with the butt of his rifle. The Kalashnikov was slung over his shoulder and he had his massive arms crossed over his barrel chest. Afig had no idea how the man had gotten behind him and when he turned back toward the baker, he saw that the man was again attempting to smile, and as before, had managed only a sneer. Afig and the baker stared at each other for a moment, and then the baker said, "Welcome to my humble establishment, my name is Forood Hawass, and now please, would you like something, some pastry, and perhaps some hot tea? You are my guest and you may have whatever you like."

Afig felt the hairs stand up on the back of his neck. This was as Mitra had said, they were waiting...waiting for him. These pleasantries were just a facade, but at least they had not tried to kill him...not yet. So he decided to play along. Taking a deep breath, he replied, "Ah, everything looks so delicious, but no, no thank you. I am sorry but I must be going." Afig turned toward the door, and as expected, the bodyguard had not moved. He was standing like some kind of giant bear, then slowly he uncrossed his arms and un-slung the Kalashnikov, never once taking his eyes off of Afig. Afig quickly scanned the room, looking for a way out. That was when he noticed the slot in the door was open, and he could see a pair of eyes staring out at him. These were no ordinary eyes and Afig immediately knew these eyes belonged to Dr. Dicos. He was being observed...no he was being tested, much as a rat is tested to determine how he would react to certain stimuli. Realizing that he was the....rat, he decided to make their lives a bit more interesting. In one swift motion, he charged toward Forood Hawass and dove over the counter, slamming into the man before he had realized what was happening. Forood was knocked backward, colliding with the bodyguard, who was thrown off balance and knocked against the back wall. The glass counter shattered and then the display cabinets tipped and fell over, shattering the glass and scattering pastries and cookies everywhere. Even before the glass fragments had settled, Afig was on his feet and prepared to charge at the scar-faced bodyguard. He was massive and smiled as he registered what Afig had in mind. He eased his Kalashnikov to the floor, and then stood, rolled his shoulders and gestured for Afig to make his move. Afig was now sure that they did not intend to kill him, but he suspected they didn't have any qualms about beating him to a pulp. His only hope had been to create enough havoc that somehow an opening would appear, and he could escape. But if he tried to fight this man, he would be facing some serious pain. Afig was exploring his options when the deafening blast of a gunshot caused his heart to momentarily stop. As he jerked around, he saw Forood Hawass standing no more than two paces from him, a pistol in his right hand, aimed directly at Afig's head. The expression on his face was frozen in rage, as his arm slowly dropped to his side, and the pistol fell to the floor. He stood there for a long moment before his knees buckled and his body crumpled to the floor. He was sprawled face down, and Afig could now see blood seeping from a small, round hole in the back of his pressed, white shirt. Looking up, he saw the other bodyguard. He was holstering the pistol he had used to shoot Forood Hawass. Scrambling to put the pieces together, Afig realized Forood Hawass was going to shoot him, but instead, the bodyguard had shot him first. Though Afig had no idea why, these people were intent on keeping him alive.

Still thinking that if he could get by that mass of muscle blocking his exit, he might have a chance, Afig steeled himself for what he would have to do next; but as he started to turn toward the man, two huge arms enveloped him and locked him in an iron bear hug. The room instantly went dark and Afig saw the face of a young man...he had Asian features and wore a camouflage uniform. His name was...Lance Corporal Norman Tanaka. The mountain of a man who now had hold of Afig was going to kill Lance Corporal Tanaka in three weeks, two days, two hours and seven minutes. Afig knew the exact moment Norman Tanaka would die and knew that he must not allow this to happen. As Afig struggled to take air into his lungs, he saw the other bodyguard was approaching. He was holding something in his right hand and before Afig could react, he slammed the object against Afig's thigh. Afig could feel the sting of the needle and the rush of something cold enter his muscle. Kicking out, his foot struck the man in the face, causing him to fly backward and slam into one of the overturned display cabinets, the injector still in his hand. Afig didn't know what he had been injected with but didn't think he had gotten a full dose. Nevertheless, he could feel something happening to him and knew he did not have much time. In a desperate effort to free himself, he first pulled himself forward, causing the man holding him to brace himself and pull back against him...and then Afig suddenly reversed his direction, and exploded back with all the strength he had.

The man was caught off balance and struggled to stay on his feet as he stumbled backward. Still gripping Afig, the two of them smashed through the bakery's front door and tumbled into the snow. The bodyguard landed on his back with Afig on top of him. His grip had held but the struggle had given Afig a brief opportunity to reach into his pocket and retrieve the ballpoint pen. Squirming to gain position, Afig drove the ballpoint pen into the man's groin. The bodyguard screamed and tightened his grip but Afig was already plunging the ballpoint pen in a second time, this time much deeper. The bodyguard screamed again, howling curses at Afig, but he still did not let go. Afig yanked the ballpoint pen free, and again drove it into the same wound. Blood was gushing from the bodyguard's groin. An artery had been severed and the loss of blood quickly weakened the man, and Afig was able to free himself. The bodyguard still fought to get hold of him but Afig pushed himself away from the man, got to his feet, and began to run. He thought he could hear shouting coming from the bakery but his world was shutting down, and he wasn't sure what he was hearing. Run, he had to run, but soon it was all he could do to just stay on his feet. Now staggering as if drunk, he found his way to an open gate in one of the nearby walled houses. He couldn't remember how he got there, but he stumbled through the opening and collapsed to his knees. He struggled to clear his mind when he noticed his blood-soaked sleeve and hand. He was still holding the ballpoint pen and awkwardly proceeded to unscrew the top, removed the small capsule-like beacon, and swallowed it. For a moment he stared at the pieces of the pen he was holding, and then he flung them as far away as he could. He could hear sounds again, people yelling and boots grinding against the frozen ground. He didn't have much time but all he wanted to do was close his eyes. The earbud, yes, yes the earbud and what else, the coat, no...the collar of the coat, yes, that was it. He had to get rid of the earbud, and then the transmitter sewn into the collar of his coat. His vision was blurred and he had lost much of his coordination, yet he was able to remove the earbud and toss it away. Then, with what little strength he had left, Afig ripped open the seam of his collar and pulled out the transmitter, looked at it for just a moment, then awkwardly pressed the transmission button. He spoke slowly and his words were slurred, "Dicos at baa...bakery...Swallowed beacon... Don't have.....time...they're coming."

He released the button just as he heard voices. Someone was talking in his earbud...no, he'd thrown that away. The voices were close, just on the other side of the wall. He was beginning not to care anymore, but still, with the last bit of strength, he threw the transmitter and mic into a nearby snow drift.

Seconds later, three armed men came rushing through the gate. Afig was leaning up against the wall, head slumped forward, unconscious.

Watching

Harris and three other men, garbed in snow camouflage, were trudging through thigh-deep snow as they ascended a steep slope toward the ridge line. On the far side, the Taliban had set up a winter camp and they were amassing supplies for a spring offensive. The Americans were nearly 10 clicks east of Sikham, and less than 50 meters from the ridge, when Harris' wireless earpiece buzzed. The incoming transmission put their objective on hold. Too exposed, Harris signaled his men to move to a cluster of twisted pines, about 20 meters off to their side. The pines would both conceal them and give them a more defendable position. Once everyone was in place, Harris leaned back against the trunk of one of the ancient pines, and retrieved his sat/com radio. While still breathing heavily, he pressed the button and spoke quietly into the tiny boom mic, "Hawkeye 1, this is Badger, go ahead."

During the subsequent transmission, Harris would be relayed a set of images that he viewed on the small tablet PC. The images showed a large man wearing wire-rimmed spectacles. He was in his mid-forties and had pure, white hair and a white beard. Four rough-looking men were positioned around him and looked like bodyguards. After viewing the images for several seconds, he decided to forward them to his supervisor at Langley.

Harris would spend the next two hours hunkered down in nearly a meter of snow. By the time all the transmissions ended, he was part of "Operation Frostbite." Operation Frostbite was classified Top Secret, and was assigned two objectives. First: Neutralize the threat presented by the Zulfiqar Project. And second: Apprehend or terminate the man known as Dr. Dicos (a.k.a. Ayn al-Hasud, and Thalj Shayton). Langley didn't have a lot of information about the Zulfiqar Project, except that it had a biological element and that its objective was the destruction of Western civilization. Islamists were known to make grandiose threats, but so far, they had not had the talent nor the resources to execute. Yet, there was always a possibility that some lethal organism had fallen into their hands. Harris knew well that these were not nice people, and they were just crazy enough to want to cause a worldwide pandemic or some other apocalyptic event.

Neither had Langley provided much information about Dr. Dicos, except that he was believed to be wealthy, unusually intelligent, and the mastermind behind the Zulfiqar Project. The Agency knew that Dr. Dicos was providing material support to violent extremist groups, and that he had been doing so since the early nineteen hundreds. This would make him well over a hundred years old, so it was believed that there were multiple people portraying themselves as Dr. Dicos. Although American and European intelligence agencies had been hunting the man for decades, only now did they have "actionable" intelligence. Harris was told that the current Dr. Dicos was linked to at least 8 of the most violent extremist Islamic organizations in the Middle East and Asia. He was thought to have a close relationship with the leadership of the Taliban, al-Qaeda, and the Islamic State of Iraq and the Levant (Islamic State).

Until Harris had transmitted the images taken by the asset now known as Crow, there had been only one other photograph of Dr. Dicos, and it was believed to have been taken around 1966. When facial recognition software had matched the recent images of Dr. Dicos to the earlier photograph, it had created quite a bit of head-scratching. Both images showed the same Dr. Dicos. The man had not aged, not even the slightest.

While the Agency knew very little about the Zulfiqar Project, they knew enough to be concerned. There had been numerous, unconfirmed, reports suggesting the Zulfiqar Project was a weapon so powerful that it would ensure an Islamist victory over the West. As such, the Agency had classified the project as a potential WMD (weapon of mass destruction) and Dr. Dicos had been elevated to the top of the top three most wanted persons list. DTRA (Defense Threat Reduction Agency), DOD (Department of Defense), and the DHS (Department of Homeland Security), as well as a dozen other alpha character agencies, had immediately become involved. There had even been a high-level scientific investigator named Dr. Gregory T, assigned to Operation Frostbite. He was to be Harris' POC (point of contact) for all scientific issues.

Harris would be given whatever support he needed, including satellite surveillance, drones, and two Delta Force assault teams as well as combat air support. A surveillance satellite was already being redeployed and would be overhead in less than two hours. Two high-altitude UAVs (unmanned aerial vehicles) were moving into position before his conversation was over.

With their current mission scrubbed, Harris and his team headed back to base camp, arriving early afternoon. The base camp was in a high mountain valley that was about four kilometers from Hawkeye 1's position, and about that same distance from the center of Sikham. It would serve as Operation Frostbite's TOC (Tactical Operations Center). Agency techies and Delta Force operators were expected to be inserted that night.

Harris had been back for less than 15 minutes when Crow had made radio contact with Hawkeye 1, who had relayed the transmission to him. He had conveyed the Agencies' interest in the white-bearded man, and had learned that Crow had actually heard the man being addressed as Dr. Dicos, the most recent known alias of the man the Agency was hunting. Harris had been reluctant to immerse Afig deeper into the operation, but he had his orders and instructed Crow to confirm the location of Dr. Dicos, and then "tag" him if possible. Afig was good but way too new for this kind of assignment, and Harris worried that he had just gotten the kid killed. Before ending the transmission, Crow had conveyed some interesting and useful information about a man named Forood Hawass, Sikham's baker.

Harris was completing his report on the transmission when his earbud buzzed. Again it was Hawkeye 1, and as he listened to the transmission, his stomach sank. Hawkeye 1 had "put down" a man who had been hiding in the shed during Crow's previous transmission. The body had been concealed but the scene would have to be "mopped up," which meant sending in a team.

Harris cursed to himself. He had been in the business long enough to know that an operation could quickly be unraveled by events that seemed unrelated, and now hoped that this wasn't such an event.

About 20 minutes later, Harris again heard his earbud buzz. Switching to Speaker, he listened as Hawkeye 1 relayed what was happening. Crow had entered the Sikham bakery at 1440 hours, and then at 1448 hours, Crow and a large, unidentified man were observed crashing through the bakery door and scuffling in the snow outside. Crow had managed to disengage, leaving the other man bleeding heavily. Crow ran about 50 meters and then began to stagger. Hawkeye 1 couldn't tell if he was injured or drugged. They lost sight of Crow at 1454 hours but observed three other men exiting the bakery, in pursuit of Crow. At 1456 hours, Hawkeye 1 received the following transmission, "Dicos at baa...baakery...I swallowed beacon....Don't have.....time...they're coming." End transmission.

The transmissions had drawn in every member of Harris' team, and now half a dozen men hovered near the radio. They all knew Dawud, they knew what Dawud and his sister had done for Jake, and they had grown to like the kid.

These men were not amateurs, and even the least experienced of them had been on dozens of missions. Harris and a couple of the other men had been on hundreds, but none had ever gotten so...so fucked up, so quickly. They had all been specially selected and then trained to be "shadows," to go in, do what they had to do, and leave without anyone knowing that they had ever been there. Dawud, on the other hand, had turned out to be more like a tornado than a shadow. Now everyone wondered if the kid would survive long enough to see another sunrise.

A few minutes later, Nebraska tapped Harris on the shoulder. He was carrying a tablet PC, which he gestured to as he said, "We're patched in, we've got an aerial." Harris could see a fuzzy, aerial view of the bakery and assumed the fuzziness was a result of the snow. The screen showed the blinking red light that designated the location of the beacon, directly over the bakery. As Harris studied the images, he noticed activity in the yard next door. Three black SUVs were pulling out from under some kind of netting. They drove out through a gateway and turned directly toward the bakery. At that same moment, Harris' earbud buzzed. Switching the speaker on, Harris said, "Go ahead Hawkeye 1 – Over." Hawkeye 1 immediately replied, "Badger, I've got three black, G-Class Mercedes pulling up in front of the bakery." Harris answered, "Roger that, Hawkeye 1, we've got them on aerial but I want your eyes locked on that bakery. I want to know who gets in or out of those vehicles." Hawkeye 1 replied, "Roger that, Badger. Will lock eyes on bakery and advise. - Over"

Activity at the base camp had come to a crawl. Everyone gathered around the radio and waited. Minutes passed before the radio crackled to life, "Badger, I've got activity at the front door. Two armed males, they're each escorting a subject. One subject is a female, she's blindfolded and wearing a full burqa. Can't see her hands but it looks like she's bound. The other subject is ...it's Crow. He's blindfolded and his hands are cuffed... He doesn't look good, he's mostly being dragged. The female is being put into the back seat of the first vehicle. Crow is being put in the back seat of the middle one." The radio was quiet for a moment and then Hawkeye 1 continued, "Two more men are exiting the bakery. Can't say for sure but the one with the fur hat looks like our target. The other man looks like a bodyguard. They're getting into the last vehicle.

Doors closed...they're moving."

There were quiet murmurs emanating from the men who'd gathered around. Dawud was a prisoner, but at least he was alive. The radio crackled back to life, "They're heading south. I'm going to lose them in about five seconds...That's it. They're out of my line of sight." Harris replied, "Roger that, Hawkeye 1, we've got them on aerial. Good job. Stick around until you're relieved by Hawkeye 2. I don't know where the drivers came from, we've still got at least one bodyguard to account for, and I need to do a follow-up on the baker, name Forood Hawass."

Later that afternoon, a member of the Hawkeye 2 team would visit Mitra Bashar. He would introduce himself as a friend of Afig Hafeez and explain that Afig had been abducted by a mysterious, white-bearded man. He would then ask Mitra for his assistance in determining what had happened at the bakery.

Mitra listened but he had not been surprised that Afig had gone to the bakery, or that he had "crossed swords" with the white-bearded man. From what he knew, the white-bearded man represented some kind of malevolent force, far more dangerous than even Forood Hawass. In contrast, Afig represented something else. Certainly there was good in the young man, but there was something else, something that had made Mitra feel...uncomfortable. Mitra was just now coming to realize that he actually feared that Afig would not think him to be... good enough. In Mitra's mind, it was inevitable that Afig Hafeez and the man with the white beard would be drawn to each other. He did not explain any of this to the man, for he himself could not yet grasp what had happened. However, Mitra did not hesitate in offering his help and it was not long before Mitra was on his way to the bakery. Even as the snow fell, a large crowd had gathered and in the confusion it was not difficult for him to get inside, nor did he have any problems using the small sleeve camera to take pictures of the two bodies lying in pools of blood. Later, on returning to the shed, Mitra would give the man back his camera and describe the scene inside the bakery.

The two high-altitude UAVs were doggedly tracking the three-car convoy, transmitting real-time images to both Langley and Harris. As the vehicles moved farther south, Langley had to decide whether to take Dr. Dicos out or track him to his destination. The decision was made to track him in hopes that he would lead them to the Zulfiqar Project, or at least lead them to others involved in it. Harris quickly organized his men into two teams. The first team, designated "Beagle 1," consisted of four men plus Harris. At 1920 hours, a UH-60 Black Hawk helicopter arrived with the first contingency of Delta Force operators. At 1930 hours, Beagle 1 and two of the Delta Force operators boarded the Black Hawk and lifted off. After an aerial refueling, and directional updates from the UAVs, the chopper took off after the caravan. An hour and a half later Beagle 1 was within 10 clicks of the three SUVs. To avoid being detected, the pilot took a course parallel to the caravan and about five clicks off to their east.

The second team, designated "Beagle 2," would man the TOC and prepare for the onslaught of personnel and equipment.

At about 2305 hours, images captured by one of the UAVs showed two technicals emerging from beneath some nearby tree cover. One of the technicals pulled out in front of the convoy, while the other one pulled in behind it. The SUVs had not slowed and it was apparent that the technicals were providing an armed escort.

Thirty minutes later, the five-vehicle caravan pulled onto a dirt access road, and then stopped next to a building that an Agency aerial map identified as the *Sewakla District Hospital (Abandoned)*. They were in Maidan Wardak Province, an insurgency stronghold that was three hundred and twenty-two kilometers from Sikham. Thermal imagery established that at least five people entered the hospital building; however, the silhouette of a sixth person was observed passing in front of one of the vehicle's headlights, but no thermal image was registered. The blip from Crow's locating beacon identified him as the third person to go inside.

With fuel low, and the Black Hawk flight crew near exhaustion, the order was given to return to the Sikham TOC. The weather had cleared, and two of the Agency's most technologically advanced UAVs were circling overhead, so Langley was comfortable that no one could enter or leave the hospital area without being observed and tracked.

Meanwhile, a plan was being put together to have a six-man team, including Harris, dropped off in the mountains bordering the Sewakla valley. The team would then make its way to a location about four kilometers from Sewakla, where they would set up a new TOC.

Injection

As Afig lay strapped to the table, he thought of Afrah and his father. It had been just over two months since he had last seen his sister, and well over a year since he had seen his father. Would they find out what happened to him? Would he want them to? He knew spying meant you lived a lie, you lied about who you were, what you were doing, who your parents were, what you believed in...you lied about everything. He understood this but he had not been prepared for the loneliness. If these people were going to kill him, he would die as Afig Hafeez, a man quite different from Dawud Hawadi and a man who had already been dead for almost two years. Harris knew he was here, and of course, Harris knew who he was, but when these people were finished with him, would he still be Dawud Hawadi?

Afig wondered what the average spy's life expectancy was – was it a month, a year, or was it only a few days? He was not sure how long he had been here – two weeks, possibly more. If he did not survive, he was sure Harris would write his sister a letter, but he could not say much about the circumstances of his death, but rather his words would be chosen carefully and designed to evoke pride and express sympathy. Afig had seen these letters before; his father had written many of them and after a while, they had begun to sound much alike. To Harris and to his father, this was a war, and death was what happened in war. Afig worried about Afrah, worried that she would not understand and this made his heart ache. He wished he could somehow spare her.

"Assalaam alaikum" (Peace be upon you). Dr. Dicos' voice startled Afig and brought him back to that room, to that cold, steel table. Dr. Dicos was greeting the assemblage with his usual expression of indifference. However, the response he received was anything but indifferent. An excited chorus of voices simultaneously replied.

"Waalaikum assalaam" (And peace also upon you).

Dr. Dicos was standing in the opening, between the two rooms. He was wearing a white laboratory coat and carrying a silver metal briefcase. His cold blue eyes methodically scanned the room, stopping at each person, seemingly having the ability to examine their inner thoughts. When he came to Afig, he paused for much longer than he had for the others, but Afig could not read Dr. Dicos' face, and did not know what the pause meant. No one approached Dr. Dicos. It was as if they almost worshiped the man, but at the same time they feared him, feared getting too close to him.

Dr. Dicos began to speak, and his voice was powerful and oddly commanding, but in some strange way, lacked emotion. He reminded Afig of an actor who was delivering his lines with great skill, but an actor who had no interest in the character he was playing. Yet, everyone looked at him with the kind of reverence reserved for a "holy man."

Continuing, Dr. Dicos said, "Today is a great and wonderful day, a day when the end to this long and bloody struggle is at hand. You, my brothers and sisters, you shall be witnesses to an event that will change the world." Dr. Dicos paused to let these words sink in. Then he continued. "Each one of you has been specially chosen to serve this great cause, and now I ask you to have faith, to be diligent, and to be resolute, for today, together we shall rise up from our knees and we shall join in the greatest and the final jihad."

The men and women yelled out in chorus.

"Allahu Akbar! Allahu Akbar! Allahu Akbar!"

When the room quieted, Dr. Dicos continued.

"The infidels and the Zionists are a vulgar indignity and a provocation to the Prophet, peace be upon him, and to Allah, the one true god. Because we are a religion of peace and because we are slow to anger, they have thought us to be weak and have worked to humiliate us. They have taken our wealth, enslaved us, slaughtered our women and our children, and have left us with nothing.

And brothers and sisters, let us not forget the blasphemers, the hypocrites, and the apostates that live among us. They work tirelessly to denigrate and demoralize the faithful, for they wish to make us truly poor. They have but one goal and that is for us to question our faith and to have doubt in our resolve.

Fear not, for beginning today, we shall once and for all grind all of those filthy vermin beneath the heels of our boots.

Now friends, let us begin."

Dr. Dicos opened a metal briefcase, and removed two vials containing a green liquid that seemed to undulate, almost as if it were alive.

"This, my brothers and sisters, is the great **Zulfiqar!**"

The room broke out into joyous shouts.

"**Allahu Akbar! Allahu Akbar! Allahu Akbar!**"

When everyone had calmed, Dr. Dicos proceeded.

"In these rooms are four men and four women, and each has been selected to receive Zulfiqar into their blood. Zulfiqar shall then examine each of these individuals, and in the end, his judgment alone shall determine who is worthy to receive him. As already told to you by Mullah Hafiz Jallah, Zulfiqar will reward those he chooses, with many blessings, the greatest of which shall be a child, which shall be known to all the world as The Listener. The Listener shall know Zulfiqar as it knows its hand. The enemies of the true faith shall fall before The Listener as if they are dry leaves, and The Listener shall step on these leaves and crush them as if they were nothing.

My brothers and sisters, it is time to rejoice – the time of a final victory is near.

Praise be to Allah – let us begin!"

Again the room broke into a chorus of exuberant yells of, "**Allahu Akbar! Allahu Akbar! Allahu Akbar!**"

Dr. Dicos reverently distributed one vial to a male medical technician, and a second vial, of a slightly different shade of green, to a female medical technician. With the aid of an assistant, the seal of each vial was pierced with the sharp needle of a syringe, and then carefully, the barrel of the syringe was filled. At Dr. Dicos' command, a prescribed dose of the undulating serum was injected into each patient's IV injection port. Dr. Dicos' speech was still bouncing around in Afig's mind as he stared at the green serum traveling down the IV tube, into the needle in his arm. At first, it felt pleasantly warm, then his feet and hands started to tingle, and he began to feel dizzy, the room was spinning and he felt nauseated. A technician managed to position an emesis basin just below his chin, as Afig threw up the entire contents of his stomach. His blood pressure alarm sounded and he almost instantly began to profusely sweat. He was burning hot, then suddenly, he became freezing cold, and then hot again. Now only semiconscious, he heard a voice speak to him. It was Dr. Dicos, "Do not worry, brother, you are merely having a slight anaphylactic reaction to the serum, and we will soon have it under control."

Dr. Dicos could be heard instructing the medical technician to inject an array of different medications into his IV. It took a few long seconds, but Afig's symptoms began to settle down.

Afig was startled back to consciousness by the deafening crash of a falling metal tray, accompanied by multiple alarm buzzers. As he turned his head, he saw Aaban and Barr. Their eyes bulged, a foamy substance sprayed from their mouths, and they violently twisted and jerked in gruesome convulsions. A number of medical technicians were scrambling to tighten the men's wrist and leg restraints, while others were clearing their air passages and injecting various medications into their IV lines. Dr. Dicos was standing nearby, studying the men's reactions. Several minutes went by before he subtly shook his head. On seeing this, the medical technicians stepped back from the two men, and after a few more seconds of thrashing, they quieted and then lay completely still. No effort was made to revive the men and after a couple of minutes, the IVs and sensors were removed, and a sheet was drawn over their faces.

Afig felt little sorrow for these men. He had known them for only a brief period of time, and they had made it perfectly clear that they subscribed to an extremist and violent interpretation of Islam. They were true fanatics and had but one goal, which was to die as martyrs. On another day, Afig was sure he would be facing these men in combat, and he would kill them or they would kill him. He knew almost nothing about the women, and hoped they had not been so completely indoctrinated.

Although Afig was quickly feeling better, it still made him uncomfortable seeing the sheet-covered bodies. He knew that but for the mercy of Allah, that could have been him. Looking to his left, he saw Sahla, the third man. He was moving his head and hands. It looked like he had made it, but he did not look right. His face had a twisted expression and he was mumbling something Afig could not understand.

Looking toward the doorway, Afig raised his head so he could see better. Through the opening, he could see the four women in the next room. They were all stirring, so they had survived.

Bodies

Blade had just settled into a little niche on top of a small knoll that offered a decent view of the back of the Sewakla District Hospital compound. Harris had worried that the back of the building wasn't getting enough attention, so for the next eight hours he would be residing in this little cubbyhole, freezing his balls off and glassing the Sewakla District Hospital, home of Dr. Dicos and his prisoner Crow. Blade had done one sweep of the building, and was about to do it a second time when movement caught his attention. Four men were exiting a door carrying stretchers on which were two bodies, each completely wrapped in a white sheet. At the same time, a white pickup truck pulled up next to the men, and the bodies were unceremoniously dumped into the back. Two other men brought out a thick stack of woven grass mats, and proceeded to cover the bodies with them. A minute or two later, the pickup drove away. Blade immediately relayed what he had seen to Harris, who contacted Langley and was connected to the Drone Command at Holloman Air Force Base in New Mexico. After a moment, Harris heard a woman's voice say, "Badger, go ahead." Harris replied, saying, "Base, did you get a good aerial view of the two bodies dumped into the back of that white pickup?"

The woman's voice that answered was young, one of the new breed of cool, highly skilled, "Bot" warriors. Her name was Major Lora Baczewski, and she supervised the two High Altitude Long Endurance (HALE) drone pilots that flew Buzzard 1 and Buzzard 2, the two drones circling above the Sewakla District Hospital. Major Baczewski and the pilots were part of Operation Frostbite and she knew Harris (Badger), from previous operations.

"We're on it, Badger, both Buzzards are in position. We've got good imagery, the playback shows both bodies are wrapped in white sheets, no visible markings. From their size and shape, I'd guess they're males, both somewhere between 5′ 9″, and 5′ 11″, trim physiques and average weight. The bodies are pretty limber, so I think they're fresh. I can see four containers in the back of the truck. They look like gas cans... They stacked a bunch of grass mats on top of the bodies. I counted over a dozen.

Badger, They've left the compound and turned east. They'll be passing about three clicks from your position just about...now."

Harris wondered where they were going since the Sewakla Mosque was in the opposite direction. Normally, bodies are taken to the mosque, prepped and then buried. Replying, he said, "Keep on them, Base, I need to know where they're going."

Major Baczewski replied, "Roger that, Badger."

About five minutes passed before Harris' earbud crackled again. On it he heard Major Baczewski's voice say, "Badger, the truck has turned off-road, about five clicks from you. They seem to be heading toward a ravine, about half a click from the road."

Harris waited, and then he heard the Major say, "They've stopped by the ravine. They're removing the grass mats, stacking them in two piles, side by side...now they're placing the bodies on the mats...One of the men retrieved blankets from the cab. He's placing them over the bodies. The other guy is pouring something, probably gas onto blankets. It's a funeral pyre, they're going to burn the bodies, Yep, they're lighting them up. ...The bodies are burning. It looks like the men are going to stick around for a while. They've got all four gas cans out of the truck and they're only on the second can." Harris replied, "Roger that, Base. Let me know when they leave."

Nearly an hour had passed before Major Baczewski contacted Harris to inform him that the men had returned to their truck, and were heading back toward the hospital. A few minutes later, Housyar and Harris were on their way. Trekking cross country, it took nearly an hour to reach the still-smoldering remains. The air was heavy with the smell of burnt flesh and the faint odor of some kind of chemical, probably the accelerant. Taking shallow breaths, Harris began the gruesome task of taking photographs and collecting teeth and pieces of bone for DNA analysis. Attempting to collect samples of soft tissue was useless since the bodies were was so badly charred that was once flesh disintegrated when touched.

From the remains, it was difficult to determine much about either man. There was no way to confirm that Dawud was not one of them.

Bagging the last sample, Harris stepped back and studied the scene. It was obvious that someone had made a concerted effort to destroy evidence. They had done so even though Islam strictly forbids cremation. Bodies were to be treated with respect and preferably buried within hours of death. Playing on a hunch, Harris quickly collected a second set of samples. The first set would go to Langley, while the second set would go directly to Dr. T.

Three days passed before Harris received a message that Dr. T needed to talk to him. After several awkward communication glitches, Dr. T was patched through on an ultra-secure line, and Harris heard a man's voice say, "Mr. Bartnik, please forgive the dramatics but are you alone?"

Dr. T's voice immediately came across as friendly and unassuming. He was definitely not a young man, but Harris couldn't be sure whether he was in his late fifties or his late seventies. Harris looked around and saw no one was within earshot, and replied, "Yes sir, go ahead."

Dr. T then said, "First, let me say that I am personally quite impressed with what you have accomplished and on the excellent work of your operative...Crow. Believe me when I say this country owes you it's appreciation and respect.

I am also aware that you are concerned about Crow so let me get to the point. Our DNA analysis has confirmed that none of the samples belonged to Crow. Unfortunately, this does not mean he is still alive, but I believe we can now dare to hope so.

Harris was relieved to hear the news. Interrupting Dr. T, he said, "Sir, knowing that Crow was not one of those two bodies is a great relief to me, however, I would like to make something perfectly clear. It is Crow and Crow alone that has gotten us this far. My role was to simply place Crow in Sikham thinking it was a safe, field training site. It was Crow that came across Dr. Dicos and recognized him as a possible 'person of interest.' It was Crow who took the initiative to photograph him. It was Crow who discovered that Dr. Dicos and the local baker were collaborating and that the baker had been supplying the Taliban with tons of material from which they made IEDs (improvised explosive devices). And then it was Crow who, while drugged and being pursued, had the wherewithal to swallow the locating beacon. The beacon that has allowed us to track him to the Sewakla District Hospital and what appears to be Dr. Dicos' laboratory. And let us not forget that it is Crow that is being held prisoner and that his surviving this situation is highly unlikely."

Dr. T did not immediately reply and for a moment Harris thought they had been disconnected. Then Harris heard the man say, "Yes, I think I understand, and I thank you for bringing this to my attention. For some reason your Agency has failed to pass these details on to me. Of course you are absolutely right about Crow. He has demonstrated uncommon initiative and extraordinary courage. Clearly, he is the one who deserves the lion's share of the credit.

Now, Mr. Bartnik, there is another subject I need to discuss with you. It concerns the samples you sent me." Harris replied, "Sir, the bodies were severely burnt and there wasn't much left to work with." Dr. T responded, "I have no doubt that you provided the best samples available, however, the accelerant used to burn the bodies, was highly acidic and produced unusually high temperatures. Combined, they caused an aggressive denaturation of the nucleic acid and chromosomal DNA damage, or more succinctly, the acid and the heat destroyed most of the DNA. The fragments we did manage to salvage allow us to eliminate Crow as one of the bodies but it also revealed some very interesting aberrations.

Mr. Bartnik, I strongly suspect the DNA, of both subjects, has been dramatically altered and that these alterations were engineered.

Unfortunately, damaged DNA is extremely fragile and highly susceptible to contamination so what we have discovered cannot be considered indisputable. Still, I believe it suggests that Dr. Dicos is working on some kind of genetic experimentation, and I suspect we are not going to like what he comes up with.

Equally of interest is the matter of Crow's DNA. Your Agency had not been able to analysis Crow's blood because it had broken down prematurely. However, our laboratory has some of the latest equipment and some of the best clinical laboratory scientists in the world. They were able to extract sufficient DNA to eliminate Crow as one of the dead men and in doing so discovered that Crow too is an anomaly. You see, we humans have about three billion DNA base pairs; however, Crow seems to have at least five billion DNA base pairs. We have never seen anything like this, and cannot even begin to understand its implications."

Dr. T paused for a moment. His voice sounded worried and tired as he continued, "There are over seven billion people in the world. How is it that Dr. Dicos, a brilliant sociopath conducting genetic experiments on humans, is holding - as a prisoner, the most genetically unique individual I have ever come across?

To be honest, Mr. Bartnik, Dr. Dicos may have discovered a way to manipulate human genes that is many decades beyond anything our best research centers and universities can do. We cannot allow the…Zulfiqar Project to result in something so advanced that we would be helpless to defend ourselves."

Harris thought about what Dr. T had just said. He was not a geneticist, but he knew that our DNA makes us who we are. It was like a computer code that told our cells what to do. Changing this code would change who we are, and possibly *what* we are. Taking a deep breath, Harris said, "How much time do we have?"

Dr. T did not immediately respond, and Harris could almost sense him formulating his answer. Finally, Dr. T said, "As you might expect, that is a difficult question. I personally think that we should strike as quickly as possible. Yet there are others that believe if we strike too early, we may lose our chance at finding out more about the Zulfiqar Project. Are there other facilities? Are there…'hybrid' jihadists already walking among us? And one question that always causes pause, are any of the substances used in the Zulfiqar Project infectious or radioactive? Mr. Bartnik, these are only a few of the questions people have been asking. The truth is, we know almost nothing so the general consensus is to wait."

Harris did not immediately reply, in part because he was trying to process what Dr. T had said, and in part because it was his job to find answers to some of these questions. If Dr. T didn't know anything, it was because he hadn't provided him anything. Harris cleared his throat and said, "I understand and we'll do our best to find answers to some of those questions."

Dr. T ended the conversation by wishing Harris good luck and saying that he would pray for Crow's safe return. An "old school" gesture that Harris though was sincere, and he appreciated it.

Getting back to work, Harris saw that there were now at least 14 paramilitary operations officers, twice that many Delta Force operators, and 10 bio-hazmat people, with access to full Level A protective gear, already deployed at various locations around the Sewakla Hospital. Also, a fully equipped Ranger Regiment was prepositioned just across the border in Uzbekistan. This was the biggest operation Harris had ever participated in, and it was way too big. He knew that it was just a matter of time before one or more of the units were detected and everything would start falling apart.

Post-procedure

After he had been administered the Zulfiqar serum, Afig had remained strapped to the stainless steel table for over an hour. He was feeling much better; actually he was feeling...great. It was his hearing that he noticed first – it was getting more sensitive by the minute, and he could now hear the medical technicians breathing, fabric rustling, and the sound of metal instruments clanking against the metal trays. Afig could also hear the voices of the women, who were now excitedly chattering to each other, clearly relieved that they were still alive and apparently feeling fine.

When Dr. Dicos entered the room, Afig focused his attention on him. As he did so, he noticed Sahla was struggling against his restraints. His head was jerking back and forth, and his expression was that of a frightened and tortured animal. As Dr. Dicos approached him, Sahla grew angry and began to actually snap and snarl at him. Only after being administered a large dose of sedative did Sahla quiet down, but his eyes remained open, and Afig could still see his pupils dart back and forth.

Suddenly coldness engulfed him, then a voice said, "My brother, how do you feel?" Afig had dozed off, but he had sensed the coldness a second or two before the voice had startled him awake. Opening his eyes, he saw Dr. Dicos standing over him. As he tended to do, the man stared directly into Afig's eyes, searching them for something. Afig chose his words carefully. He did not want to reveal too much. Trying to look a little confused, he replied, "I am glad to be alive. What was that...serum you gave me?"

Dr. Dicos did not reply but appeared satisfied. His satisfaction had little to do with the substance of Afig's question, but rather with the fact that he still had the mental faculties to ask the question.

Afig suddenly realized that he could read Dr. Dicos' face. It was not as if he could read his mind, but he could get glimpses of what the man was feeling. Actually, Dr. Dicos didn't feel anything for Afig, or at least that was what Afig first thought. Then he caught a glimpse of something else. Dr. Dicos actually...hated him...and not just a little bit.

Afig slept the rest of that day and completely through the following night. It was not until the next morning that Afig was awakened by voices, loud footsteps, and smells...lots of smells. The smell of sweat, his own sweat and that of other people, but also there was the smell of eggs, toasted bread, cheese, soap, floor wax, disinfectants, and dozens of other smells – some he knew, and some he did not recognize. As he became more alert, he realized the voices he heard were coming from somewhere out in the hall, and were those of Dr. Dicos speaking to another man. Dr. Dicos was asking the other man if the testing room was ready. The other man replied "yes" and a moment later, Afig heard the bolt slide, and the door opened. Two men, armed with what looked like electric cattle prods, entered, and in a surprisingly polite tone of voice, requested that he rise and dress. They would be escorting him to the dining room for breakfast, and then he would begin a series of tests.

Afig complied, but while doing so he realized he could smell the sour odor of the men's sweat, and he could hear their hearts pounding; they were beating loudly and more rapidly than his own. To Afig's surprise, he realized that these men were afraid of him. Dressed in a loose shirt, baggy trousers, and sandals, Afig was led to what was obviously a dining room. On the way, he could hear whispered conversations, conversations about him. They were calling him "the one Zulfiqar had chosen," and the Chosen One. The Zulfiqar serum was obviously a very powerful drug, some kind of performance enhancer. Afig had heard of such drugs; some athletes used them to increase their strength and endurance. In this case, the Zulfiqar serum was improving his senses – his sense of hearing, smell, vision, and even his ability to sense a person's state of mind. These...sensory enhancements were interesting and would likely be useful.

Afig knew that he needed to conceal his new capabilities. If they found out about them, they might be able to block their effectiveness.

Over the next week, Afig and Sahla were subjected to a medical examination, physical strength tests, and endless batteries of cognitive tests. Though Afig could feel his strength and agility gradually improving, he managed to conceal these improvements from the technicians. He pretended to struggle with the eye test and in the end was able to convince them that he had only slightly above average vision. All these deceptions were made easier by Sahla. Although Sahla was showing extraordinary quickness and surprising physical strength, he was emotionally unstable, and subject to fits of rage. But what got Dr. Dicos' attention was his diminishing cognitive capabilities. Recently, Afig had heard the technicians discussing how Sahla had lost his ability to read even a simple sentence, and he was losing the ability to comprehend spoken language.

It had been a typical morning; Afig had just completed a battery of memory tests, while at the same time secretly listening to the three or four simultaneous conversations that were carried on at any given point in time. Recently, he had begun to hear conversations coming from beyond the steel doors, and was beginning to wonder just how much further his hearing would develop. Afig was also making it a point to study the gestures, the expressions, and the behaviors of the technicians, the guards, and even Dr. Dicos. He was watching for something that might give him an idea of what they were doing.

Since being administered the Zulfiqar serum, he had been kept in a secure area that resembled a prison or psychiatric ward. There were no windows, and only two exit doors, both of which were made of heavy steel plates. The doors faced each other across a wide corridor, and could only be opened from the far side. There were no handles, nor even a keyhole, on his side. One end of the corridor led to the staff's quarters, which Afig was not allowed to enter. The other end led to an open dining room, Dr. Dicos' office, and test rooms – each with heavy glass observation windows, a toilet and shower area, and their individual sleeping quarters. The entire area had been recently painted a glossy, pale yellow color. Fumes from the curing paint caused Afig's eyes to sting, and the glossiness gave the place a cold, institutional look.

There were always at least seven stern-looking, CMM (Crescent Moon Militia) guards on duty. He and Sahla were each assigned two guards; one guard was posted by each of the steel doors, and another guard was posted in front of the opening to Dr. Dicos' office. The guards did not carry firearms, but, instead they carried the long, electric cattle prods that they called "baton tasers." These batons were put to the test when Sahla went into one of his frequent fits of rage. He smashed equipment, and viciously struck one of the medical technicians, killing him instantly. It had taken at least five consecutive shocks from the cattle prods, to subdue the man. Afig could smell burnt skin, but even then, Sahla seemed only mildly dazed, and it was necessary to double handcuff his wrists and ankles before they could drag him away. After that outburst, Sahla was not seen again. It was rumored that he had gone completely mad, and had been confined to a cell in another part of the facility. Several days later, Merzad replaced one of Afig's CMM guards. Afig was told that Dr. Dicos was not pleased by Sahla's outburst, and thought it may have been triggered by the behavior of the CMM guards. Merzad was a familiar face to Afig and Dr. Dicos thought he may be more at ease with him.

Wedding

It was just after Maghrib (evening prayers), when Merzad came up to Afig and said:

"You are a lucky man, my friend. You are to be married. Mullah Hafiz is preparing the dining room for the ceremony, and now you must bathe and ready yourself. I will return for you at 9:00."

Afig did not reply. He had known something like this would happen. He had heard Dr. Dicos' speech and knew that this...this "experiment" was about using him and the other men as "breeding stock" in order to produce a child. What Afig had not given much thought to, was how they intended to do this. Everything had been so...so clinical, so sterile that he assumed the fertilization process would be the same. Now it appeared that Dr. Dicos intended to do things the old-fashioned way. This made Afig more than a little uncomfortable with this new development. Merzad saw the alarm on Afig's face and assumed it was a young groom's nervousness on his wedding night. Laughingly, he said, "Do not worry, the medical technicians have told me that you are already more virile than any ten of us ordinary men. You will not have any difficulty doing your duty."

Until that moment, Afig had discounted his increasingly strong, carnal urges as something all young men struggled with. But Merzad was right, he had been spending more of his time, thinking thoughts that could not be described as pure. Now, this too became a concern. Certainly there were many moral implications to him marrying, and one had to consider the woman. What would this marriage mean to her? Did he have the right to... deflower the woman when everything about him was a...lie? Surely her family...and probably everybody else would want him killed, if they knew the truth. Would the marriage even be valid? These and a dozen other questions flooded into his head; nevertheless, Afig was quite aware that if he wished to live, this is what he would have to do. It took only a moment for Afig to assess these concerns, review his options, and conclude that the situation was clearly regrettable, yet he had no choice but to proceed. The rapidity with which he arrived at this conclusion took Afig by surprise. A week ago, had he been confronted with this situation, he would have experienced considerable moral anguish, guilt, and indecision. He would probably have made the same decision, but it would have been an arduous process. This concerned him, and he began to wonder whether the Zulfiqar serum was in some way altering his character. Doing a quick mental review of his core beliefs, values, and allegiances, he concluded that they were intact, but he also realized his mental acuity had been enhanced. It was not that he was becoming some kind of genius, but rather he could think more clearly, and processed information more quickly.

Afig bathed, put on clean clothing, and then sat on his bed and thought about what he was becoming. At exactly 9:00, he heard the bolt slide, and Merzad entered, while the second guard, a nondescript man he knew little about, waited at the door. Afig was in no hurry, and walked slowly through the door, where the guards took their places and they made their way to the dining room. There, he stopped and peered inside. He could hear voices but he could not see anyone from where he stood. Taking a deep breath, Afig stepped through the opening and immediately saw a display of several lit, red candles. Two men sat at a rectangular table covered by a green cloth. One of the men was Mullah Hafiz, but Afig did not recognize the other man. Mullah Hafiz had been waiting for him, and when he saw him enter, he spoke, saying, "Please, Afig come stand in front of us." Afig hesitated for just an instant, while he decided how best to present himself. He then bowed his head in deference to Mullah Hafiz, and obediently did as instructed. When Afig was standing in front of the table, Mullah Hafiz looked up at him for a long moment, and then said, "Afig, my brother, the man sitting next to me is Fariad the madhun (marriage officer), who will preside over this auspicious occasion." Afig looked at the emaciated, middle-aged man with a tangled beard and greasy hair. His dark eyes were so deeply sunken that Afig could easily imagine he was suffering from some terminal disease. It did not take enhanced hearing to hear the wheezing in the man's chest, and he smelled strongly of stale cigarettes tinged with a trace of ammonia and sulfur.

Although the man seemed preoccupied with the document he was reading, Afig spoke, saying, "Assalaam alaikum." Afig's voice startled the man, and his eyes looked up. Seeing Afig standing there, his eyes brightened and he stared at him with great curiosity. Only after a long moment had passed did the man reply, "Waalaikum assalaam."

Satisfied that the introduction was complete, Mullah Hafiz stood up and gestured to two of the guards, who immediately turned and stepped from the room. Several minutes passed before the guards returned, escorting a solemn procession of eight, blue-burqa-clad women. Except for the lace-covered opening around the eyes, the burqas covered the women's entire head and body. The rather large number of women in attendance was initially confusing, but then Afig thought that his future wife might be accompanied by her mother, relatives, and even friends. This was not unheard of. Afig realized that he did not even know his bride's name. Actually, he didn't know anything about her. What if he did not like the way she looked? She might be too fat or maybe too skinny. What if she didn't like him and was determined to make his life miserable? Afig forced himself to stop thinking about these things. One of those women was going to be his wife, and that was that.

When the women had taken their places, Mullah Hafiz Jallah spoke, saying, "The brides are now to step forward." Three of the burqa-clad women stepped forward, forming a semicircle in front of Afig. A fourth woman was clearly reluctant to do so and was prodded into place by the woman behind her. As all four women stood there, facing Afig, he began to feel uncomfortable, and looked around for the other grooms, but no other men came forward. Mullah Hafiz noticed Afig's growing anxiety and said, "My brother, Islam permits a man to have four wives, so do not be concerned." Stunned, Afig thought that there must have been a mistake, and asked, "Forgive me, Mullah Hafiz, in my excitement, I am afraid I did not understand..." Before he could say more, a voice that Afig immediately recognized as that of Dr. Dicos said, "Afig, you, and you alone have been selected by Zulfiqar. It is you that will marry these four women, since they too have been selected by Zulfiqar, and now no other man may touch them. Now Mullah Hafiz, if you would please continue."

Afig's mind was spinning; he had come to grips with the idea of marrying one woman. It was a necessary thing, but to marry four women – how could it be that he would be marrying four women?

Realizing everyone was watching him, he collected himself and spoke the words he knew they were waiting to hear: "Forgive me, for this is such a privilege, such a great honor that for just a moment, I...I was overwhelmed." Dr. Dicos again spoke, saying, "Yes, yes of course you were. Mullah Hafiz, it is time for you to present the brides...now."

Mullah Hafiz, and everyone else in the room, could not help but feel Dr. Dicos' growing impatience. Straightening his back, in an attempt to assume his most dignified posture, Mullah Hafiz said, "Afig Hafeez, son of Omeid Hafeez, I would like to introduce you to Farrukh, daughter of Fila."

The woman to the far right of Afig stepped forward and bowed slightly, and then Mullah Hafiz continued.

"Afig Hafeez, son of Omeid Hafeez, I would like to introduce you to Shamail, daughter of Anoosheh."

Mullah Hafiz repeated the process for the next two women – Hasti, daughter of Huma, and Adelah, daughter of Ishtar. Afig agreeably nodded at each woman as she was presented. After the presentation portion of the ceremony was complete, Afig was told to make his proposal. Like most Afghan men his age, Afig had attended numerous weddings, and was familiar with the ritual. However, he had never witnessed a wedding that simultaneously married four women to one man, and he was now unsure of how to proceed. As tradition prescribed, he would not be able to address the women directly; instead he would have to address them through a relative. Since Afig was not aware that any of the women had relatives present, he chose to address his proposal to Mullah Hafiz Jallah, the acknowledged spiritual leader. Next, he had to determine which woman to propose to first. Not knowing their age or anything else about them, he decided to address the women in the same order Mullah Hafiz had. That decision led to his next problem: Would he remember all of their names? Perspiring, Afig took a deep breath and said, "Mullah Hafiz, would you please ask Farrukh, daughter of...Fila if she will be my bride?" Giving a satisfied nod, Mullah Hafiz turned to Farrukh and asked.

"Farrukh, daughter of Fila, do you agree to take Afig Hafeez as your husband?"

After a brief moment to signify contemplation, the woman who must have been Farrukh bowed her head, and quietly said,

"Yes, I accept."

The process was the same with Shamail and Hasti, but when it came time for Adelah to accept, she hesitated much longer than the others, and when she spoke, her voice was clear and strong, but Afig could hear her heart pounding and her rapid breathing. This woman was frightened and yet she was trying to hide it beneath pure determination. When Adelah finally spoke, she said, "Please, Mullah Hafiz Jallah...would you ask Afig Hafeez if he would describe himself as a good man, a kind man...and a just man?"

Everyone in the room gasped in shock. Afig could see anger instantly flash in Mullah Hafiz's face. He was surely thinking that this...woman had threatened to ruin his ceremony. She had the audacity to challenge the man who had been chosen by Zulfiqar. It was inconceivable that a woman could even imagine challenging the character of such a man. Afig knew this situation had suddenly become very dangerous for this woman. So, before anyone could react, Afig responded, "Please, Mullah Hafiz, tell this delightful woman that I certainly endeavor to be a good man, a kind man, and a just man. I hold these character traits absolutely necessary for a man to be a good husband. It is truly my hope that a woman, so thoughtful, would honor me by accepting my proposal of marriage."

Mullah Hafiz was now in a dilemma. If he chastised this woman, he would offend Afig, since Afig had now publicly expressed his desire to marry her. So, as Mullah Hafiz Jallah always did in difficult times, he looked at Dr. Dicos for guidance.

Dr. Dicos, displayed only a casual curiosity in what had just occurred, and after a brief moment, nodded his head, giving Mullah Hafiz Jallah permission to continue.

While this was occurring, the burqa-clad female escort who had accompanied Adelah into the room had positioned herself directly behind her. It was clear that a simple nod from Mullah Hafiz Jallah would have Adelah physically removed. Afig did not know what would happen to her, but he was sure it would not be good. There was something special about Adelah, and he knew he had to do everything he could to protect her.

Mullah Hafiz Jallah's face was still red, and his voice had risen an octave, when he addressed Adelah.

"Afig Hafeez states that he endeavors to be a good man, a kind man, and a just man, now, once more, I ask you, do you agree to take Afig Hafeez as your husband?"

Again Adelah hesitated, and Afig found himself stiffen in anticipation. Then, at the absolute last second, Adelah replied. Her voice was shaky, and it was now clear to all that she was frightened, but her tone still conveyed an undercurrent of rebellion as she said, "Yes, Mullah Hafiz, of course I must accept Afig Hafeez's...proposal."

Everyone in the room could hear the words she did not say – "because I have no choice." The anger in Mullah Hafiz Jallah's face had become almost intractable. Adelah's hesitation and her tone of voice had pushed him to the edge, so again, Afig took the initiative by saying:

"Praise be to Allah, for I am a very happy and fortunate man. My father once told me that women are like apples, often the best ones are at the top of the tree and hard to reach."

Although no one laughed, there could be felt a slight ease in the highly charged atmosphere. Afig was convinced that he needed to hurry this ceremony up. He did not want to give this woman the opportunity to further antagonize Mullah Hafiz Jallah. Next time, she would likely push him too far. Addressing Mullah Hafiz Jallah, Afig said, "Mullah Hafiz Jallah, I am embarrassed, but I have only the clothes on my back, and do not have anything suitable for the meher" (bride price). The meher is money or property that is given to the bride by the groom, or the groom's family. It must be described in the marriage contract and presented to the bride(s) during the official marriage ceremony. The first part of the meher is presented at the signing of the Nikah-Namah (marriage contract), and the second part is presented later and could even be given to the bride incrementally, throughout the marriage.

Afig felt the coldness and turned to see Dr. Dicos standing nearby. Afig glanced at the man, and for just an instant, their eyes locked. It was at that moment that Afig thought he saw the true Dr. Dicos, and what he saw terrified him. It was as if he had glimpsed into the force behind pestilence and utter chaos. No one thought these...these phenomena had consciousness, but they did, and more than that, they were deliberate and had purpose. One thing was clear – Dr. Dicos was not human. Then, just as quickly as the perceptions had come, they disappeared. Dr. Dicos had slammed down a mental barrier, blocking Afig from any further revelations. Standing before him was Dr. Dicos, the tall, imposing, powerfully built man with pure white hair and an equally white beard. Afig was a meter away from the man, and he could feel the air growing steadily colder.

Dr. Dicos reached into the pocket of his coarse, woolen vest, and removed a green velvet pouch, which he raised for everyone to see. When the murmurs of approval had subsided, he lowered the pouch, undid the cord, and removed eight glistening gold coins. Turning to Afig, he said, "Afig Hafeez, you are the only one to be chosen by

Zulfiqar. We, the humble servants of the one true faith, offer you these gold coins, so that you may have a suitable meher to present to your brides."

Reaching out, he placed the coins in Afig's hand, and then he firmly gripped Afig's shoulders, leaned over, and kissed him one time on each cheek.

The room seemed to become electrified and spontaneously burst into a loud chorus of,

Allahu Akbar! Allahu Akbar! Allahu Akbar!

Afig had involuntarily recoiled the moment Dr. Dicos touched him. The man was cold as ice, so cold that when Dr. Dicos had leaned toward him to kiss his cheek, Afig could see his breath fog. The kisses stung, and Afig was sure that if Dr. Dicos had maintained physical contact for even half a second longer, Afig would have suffered frostbite. Now he understood why no one ever touched Dr. Dicos, or for that matter, no one would stand within a meter of the man. It was then that Afig fully realized that Dr. Dicos did not care about Islam, and there would not be a "Great Jihad." No, this...man was perpetrating some kind of an elaborate hoax, and Afig was becoming increasingly uncomfortable with his part. He had imagined himself to be a minor character, someone lurking in the shadows, but it hadn't turned out that way. Afig now found himself to be a central character in a play that he did not understand and one that would almost certainly end very badly.

"Allah be praised." Mullah Hafiz Jallah's voice brought Afig back. The man had finished reading the Nikah-Namah (marriage contract), and was now addressing Afig.

"Afig Hafeez, son of Omeid Hafeez, do you agree?"

Afig had not been listening, and had no idea what had been stated in the Nikah-Namah. Hoping it had included only the standard text, he responded, repeating the required words three times,

"Qubul, qubul, qubul" (I agree, I agree, I agree).

After Afig had finished, each of the women was asked if they agreed. To Afig's relief, each, including Adelah, responded three times "qubul, qubul, qubul." The Nikah-Namah was signed by the groom, all four of the brides, and four witnesses. It took several minutes to distribute the meher, and then the women were escorted out of the dining room, and disappeared from sight.

CHAPTER THIRTY

Recollection

With the wedding ceremony over, Merzad and the other guard were preparing to escort the groom back to his quarters, when Dr. Dicos appeared and ordered them to bring him to his office. Afig's hands were immediately cuffed, causing him to wonder why the extra precaution.

After the cuffs had been inspected, he was led into the small office. The room was dark, the only light coming from the open door. As he had expected, the room was cold but unlike the rest of the facility, it was also drafty, and he could smell fresh outside air. The ceiling had been lowered and the far wall, the one that abutted the test room, was coated with a layer of ice crystals. The other three walls bordered corridors and had louvered openings at the bottom.

The guards had Afig stand next to a heavy iron ring that had been cemented into the floor. A chain was passed through the ring and around the chain of his handcuffs. Merzad then produced a heavy padlock and secured the ends of the chain together. After inspecting the chain and handcuffs one last time, the two men turned and stepped out of the room, closing the door behind them.

For a moment the room was completely dark, and then suddenly it was inundated with an intense, bluish white light. Afig was immediately forced to close his eyes but was still able to see the four burning spheres of the industrial size ceiling light fixtures, through his eyelids. A long time would pass before Afig's eyes had sufficiently adjusted for him to see the room. Still squinting, he could see a drab, grey-colored, institutional cabinet, desk, and chair. Except for a closed laptop computer, the desk was completely clear.

Dr. Dicos was standing next to the desk and the lights gave his normally white hair and beard a slight blue hue, giving him a cold, un-natural appearance.

Dr. Dicos' eyes studied Afig though the man still wore his usual aloof, almost disinterested expression. Afig had come to recognize this particular expression as one of only two expressions Dr. Dicos had in his entire inventory. With the other being an expression of dissatisfaction, Dr. Dicos was always either bored or irked.

After what seemed like a long silence, Dr. Dicos said, "My friend, I believe it is time for us to talk, to, as the Americans say, 'take our relationship to the next level.'"

Dr. Dicos paused, and then he slowly removed his gold, wire-rim spectacles. Nothing happened at first, but after a few seconds, Afig saw the man's small, round, black pupils, appear to grow. As the seconds ticked by, his pupils kept enlarging and soon Dr. Dicos' eyes had turned completely black, but not black in color. No, his eyes were deep, black...holes that seemed to be absorbing the light from the room. The ceiling fixtures dimmed and began to buzz loudly, as if they were trying to compensate for the load. Every muscle in Afig's body tightened, and he strained against the handcuffs, feeling their steel edges cut deeply into his wrists. Looking into those empty black caverns triggered something primal in Afig, something stronger and more savage than anything he had felt before. He was now certain that Dr. Dicos was Thalj Shayton, and that he was his enemy. Those two...openings in the man's head were causing tiny fragments of images, from his past, to flash through his mind. But these were not a past that he knew, but still a past that was familiar to him.

Seemingly satisfied with Afig's response, Dr. Dicos replaced his glasses, and his eyes instantly returned to the man's icy blue color. He waited for a moment as Afig struggled to recover, and then he said, "Your reaction should suggest that we are...let us say, acquainted. The form you now possess will make it difficult for you to comprehend, but do not be concerned, for in time, comprehension will come.

The purpose of my little...demonstration, was to make you more receptive to possibilities that you might otherwise disregard. You see, Afig, I am about to tell you a story...a story that you once would have considered the rantings of a madman."

Dr. Dicos paused for a moment, cleared his throat, and then continued, "Twelve thousand, two hundred and forty-three years ago, an entity...an ethereal entity, appeared on a grassy knoll that overlooked a distant river. Today that river has divided and has become two rivers, which are called the Euphrates and Tigris. This...entity could best be described as an incorporeal being, an ethereal manifestation of something whose presence may be sensed but in no way measured. This entity I shall now refer to as 'Dingir,' which is a name that first appeared on early Sumerian tablets, and referred to a guardian spirit that can occupy a physical form. Nonetheless, Dingir would soon encounter one particular creature, a young human female. The woman's name was Batya, and Dingir would communicate with her through her dreams and her thoughts. He would tell her many wondrous things, and she would listen and she would try to understand. Gradually Batya would not sleep, nor would she eat or drink. Her people soon began to worry about her, and they would bring her food and water. But the next morning, the food and water would still be there. Gradually, they became convinced that she had become possessed, and of course, she was. All day and all night, she would sit, cross-legged, on the top of that grassy knoll, staring east, at a distant mountain range. Sometimes, people would hear her speaking to someone, but they could not understand the words that she was using. Other times they could hear her laughing. When the sound of her laughter reached them, everyone would stop what they were doing, and they would turn their faces up toward the grassy knoll. No one could resist her laughter, for it had a sweetness to it and it lightened everyone's heart.

But there were also times when Batya could be heard weeping, a sound that carried across the gently rolling countryside as no other sound could. Everyone, even the hardest and strongest of the hunters, could feel the sadness engulf them. It would not be long before people would, one by one, lower their heads and weep with Batya. A full moon would come and go, so it became time for her people to move on. They begged her to come with them. Alone, she would surely starve or be eaten by the wolves that had, for many days now, stalked their camp. But Batya could not hear their pleas, and gradually, the people accepted that she would not be coming with them. With their stomachs empty, the seeds and the berries long gone, and the game hard to find, they decided that they must go. They would leave Batya behind.

Their journey would begin early the next morning, and they would head east, for that was the direction Batya was looking. Their hearts were heavy, and no one spoke, as each man, woman, and child filed past the spot where Batya sat. As they looked at her they saw that her eyes were wide with expectation, but she did not once take them off those distant mountains. It was when all of her people had passed, that they heard her call out what seemed to be a name, a name they had never heard before. A girl, maybe five or six years old, was afraid for

Batya and ran back to where she sat. She took Batya's hand and told her that she would not leave her. It was then that the young woman turned toward the little girl, and in a voice that was soft and gentle, said, "Do not be afraid, for this is the beginning." The little girl stayed with her a while longer, but Batya said no more.

To make the trek easier, the people would follow a stream that meandered eastward, but that afternoon, a group of them ascended a hill, where they would look back toward the distant grassy knoll. There, far in the distance, they could see the small figure of Batya still sitting there. As was their custom, they left before dawn the next morning and that afternoon, when they had crested a tall hill, they again looked back but this time they could no longer see Batya, for they had traveled too far.

Nearly a year would pass before these people would find their way back to that knoll. There, on the spot they had left Batya, they found a sturdy structure, one made of stones so heavy that even two strong men could not lift them. Having never before seen such a structure, they cautiously circled it several times, before someone found the courage to peer inside. There they saw Batya, who was sitting on a thickly woven mat, her shiny, chestnut-colored hair arranged in a single braid that hung halfway down her back. Her skin was clear and smooth, and her blue eyes were so bright that they seemed to shine. Batya wore a garment of a kind no one had ever seen before. It was made of a smooth, shiny material that was the color of the evening sky. In her arms, Batya was holding a small baby, a baby boy.... It is doubtful that you will believe me, but that baby boy was you."

Afig began to speak but Dr. Dicos interrupted him, saying, "I have much to tell you, so I expect you not to speak until I am finished. Continuing, he said, "Per design, you then and you now have no awareness of your origin, nor are you conscious of your purpose. In this way, your integration into the human species was complete and nearly undetectable.

Batya knew that her son and Dingir were one, and she also knew that your true nature and your purpose must never be revealed. Batya would have only one child, and so it would be for each descendent thereafter. She would be a devoted mother, yet she would find time to teach her people the things Dingir had taught her. From time to time, wandering bands of nomads would come across Batya's people, for that was what they were now called. These nomads marveled at the neat cluster of stone dwellings, the fields of wild wheat and barley, and the flocks of sheep grazing on the hills.

As you grew to manhood, others came to recognize you for your strength and for your courage. But those were not your only traits, for you were unique among men, but unique in a way that is difficult to describe. Let us say, other men would see a piece of fruit and eat it, but you would see an orchard, and plant it. Other men would see mud and pass it by, but you would see clay and the brick that it would become. But there was still more to you, for some thought you to be a kind and generous man, yet others thought you to be...violent and unpredictable. If provoked, whether it be by a bear or a band of marauders, you would not hesitate to engage them, and proceed to brutally slay all of those that were in your reach. Though this ferocity was well recognized, it was not the only reason you were thought to be dangerous and unpredictable. No my friend, you were feared because you killed even when you were not provoked. Batya understood why you were doing this, but she could not reveal the reason to others.

Many saw you as an amiable and clever man, but others thought you to be a....murderer, or mad. As time passed, you would have to leave Batya and her people. This would break Batya's heart for she loved you, yet she had always known the day and the hour you would leave, for this had been revealed to her by Dingir.

You would travel through the land both east and west. Wherever you stopped you would leave your mark and soon the peoples of the east and the west began to prosper. The changes you brought were not always well-received, for they were a threat to the old ways, to the way things had been done since time before memory. As in the past, when challenged, you did not hesitate to respond and each response became increasingly violent and lethal, for you now had followers and had taught them how to fight, and to use weapons that had never before been seen. But as before, you did not need to be provoked for you to kill. No my friend, you deliberately, albeit subconsciously, sought out certain individuals and then, without remorse, you took their lives.

Before I tell you more, I believe it would be useful if I gave you more   background. For two hundred thousand years, the human species had lived in relative harmony with nature. Though, it is true, they possessed a certain cleverness, human evolutionary progression had mostly stalled, and it seemed that these wretched creatures were destined to live out their existence as wandering scavengers. Then, some fifty thousand years ago, one of your kind visited this place and gifted the human species with language, religion, art, music, and even games. Still, these new human attributes did nothing to feed, shelter, and protect them, so their existence was no better than before. That all changed twelve thousand, two hundred and forty-three years ago, the day Dingir *'The Guardian'* arrived, for it was Dingir that brought these humans ingenuity, inventiveness, and most importantly, the irrepressible desire to subjugate nature. Soon was born what today is called the 'Neolithic Revolution.' Scattered bands of human scavengers would, almost overnight, be transformed into sedentary populations that grew crops and herded livestock. Soon there would be a surplus of food, which would lead to the inception of towns and cities. As the population grew, so grew the need to clear more forests, till more land, and divert more water for irrigation. Thousands of species were driven to complete extinction, while others were forced to retreat into the deepest forests. This... revolution was then followed by what is called the Bronze Age, and then by the Iron Age. Today, humans live in what they call the Space Age, but human population continues to grow, more forests disappear, and the land continues to be stripped of its nutrients. Fresh water grows more scarce and when it is found, it is often unfit to drink. Even the air is no longer safe to breathe as it has become thick with smoke and poisonous gases. This is Dingir's legacy, this is what he has brought down upon my domain.

Though it is true that you, the incarnation of Dingir, did not cause all of these things, it is equally true that these things could not have happened without you.

You may find my story entertaining, but it is doubtful that you believe what I am telling you. So let me give you an example, something that you might be able to identify with.

You see, some fifty-seven years ago, during the life cycle you now refer to as your grandfather, you lived in Saudi Arabia and worked as an agent in the Saudi Secret Police, the Mabahith..."

As Dr. Dicos spoke, Afig had grown increasingly uneasy but as the man had said, he did not believe him. But now, how could Dr. Dicos know about his grandfather and the Mabahith? Afig knew Dr. Dicos was trying to draw him into his...delusion...but still? Before he could give this any further thought, the sound of Dr. Dicos' voice drew him back.

"Most likely, you...your grandfather, joined the Mabahith because it offered you a number of advantages. The Mabahith had a vast and effective spy network that could quickly identify people that you might be looking for, and the Mabahith would protect you from anyone that might be looking for you. Also, you had access to documents, and a clandestine transportation network. And finally, you had the authority to kill, and few would ask questions.

With some research and a little baksheesh (bribery), I have been able to reconstruct your last assignment, which went something like this: You were tasked with performing surveillance on a husband and wife that both happened to be well-respected mathematicians. The couple had become peripherally involved with the underground movement that sought more equality for women. This was a particularly sensitive area, since women's rights in Saudi Arabia are defined by Islamic Law (Sharia) and tribal customs. The latter being the most oppressive. Therefore, proposals to give women more equality were not very popular, and were generally believed to be contrary to Islamic beliefs.

Your grandfather had been watching the couple for nearly a week, when his commander told him that the Commission for the Promotion of Virtue and the Prevention of Vice – Saudi Arabia's religious and morality police, or Mutaween, had warned him that their council had found the couple guilty of blasphemy, and they would be subjected to death. The commander had no interest in protecting the couple, nor did he have any desire to irritate the Mutaween, so he ordered your grandfather to 'stand down.'

However, your grandfather did not 'stand down.' Instead, he hid the couple, and began making arrangements for them to escape to England. Meanwhile, a separate organization of radicalized Islamic Clerics had become impatient with the Mutaween, and had decided to take the initiative. They tasked a team of three experienced assassins to find and kill the couple. It took a day or two but they eventually discovered where they were hiding, and the three men broke into the building. Your grandfather heard them, and in the battle that ensued, your grandfather killed all three of the assassins. That night, the couple departed for England.

Now here is where the story becomes more interesting. It seems the Mutaween did not appreciate the Islamic Clerics' interference, and saw it as a challenge to their authority. To show their disapproval, they encouraged your grandfather's commander to treat his disobedience with leniency, which he did. Unbeknownst to the Mutaween or the commander, one of the assassins was Abu Nussayr, son of Muhammad ibn Nussayr, a leader in one of the more militant branches of the Wahhabi sects, and the brother of one of the Clerics that had ordered the couple killed. You see, your grandfather had initially just wounded the young Abu Nussayr, and even though he did not represent an immediate threat, your grandfather had not hesitated shooting the man in the head. When Muhammad ibn Nussayr heard that a Mabahith agent had killed his son and he had not been severely punished, he assumed the Mabahith had conspired against him. Seeking revenge, he and a number of his followers attempted to assassinate a high-ranking Mabahith commander. The attempt failed, and ibn Nussayr, along with half a dozen of his closest lieutenants, were captured and executed. Worried that these religious zealots had become too brazen, the Mabahith would play a role in purging the group of their most extreme members and picking new leadership, men who turned out to be much less radicalized than their predecessors.

Now let us look more closely at the couple your grandfather rescued.

The husband and wife were Doctor Joseph Saif and Doctor Lana Saif. They eventually became full professors at a prestigious British university, and in 1978, they jointly published a paper that led to a breakthrough in the area of material science. This new material would dramatically alter spaceship design; however, its production produced a byproduct that was highly toxic and polluted the ground water near the production facility.

I could go on and tell you about the couple's three daughters, and how they attended university and became renowned scientists in their own right, but I don't think it is necessary.

Now you may be tempted to say that this was all...happenstance, and I might agree, if this had been just an isolated event, but that is not the case."

Dr. Dicos paused for a moment, as he mentally composed what he would say next. Then he said, "To me, it is plain to see that you have been systematically 'culling' the human herd, on one hand, and nurturing it on the other. You have killed those who interfere with your vision of human progression, and you have...fostered those who would advance that vision. In just over twelve thousand years, you have managed to transform a species, but in doing so you have destroyed their environment."

Studying Afig's expression, Dr. Dicos saw nothing but distrust and disbelief. Continuing, he said, "Still you doubt me, so I ask you to look back to the bakery in Sikham. There, two men died – Forood Hawass, the baker, and Abbas, one of my most loyal bodyguards. The baker was a very unpleasant man who was known to be a local tyrant, as well as a dealer in explosive... fertilizer. I witnessed your assault on the man and how, in just a blink of an eye, you demolished his prized bakery. I suspect you knew the man would react irrationally and that we had no intention of killing you. So I believe you had a part in forcing one of my men to kill Forood. Nonetheless, I am sure you would agree that Sikham and humanity are much better off without Forood Hawass.

Then there was my bodyguard, Abbas. By every account, Abbas was a sadistic and violent man, who had singlehandedly reduced the world population by at least fifty of its inhabitants. The man was nearly twice your size, powerful as an ox, and he was a professionally trained assassin. You should have been nothing to this man, yet you managed to kill him...with just a ballpoint pen.

Do you really think that an ordinary human could do such a thing, or would it be fair to say that even at your young age, you have already killed many times? In truth, I would not be surprised to learn that the bodies of those that you have killed... directly or indirectly...would fill this room to the ceiling."

Afig knew that he had not given much thought to the deaths that he had caused. It seemed that he had the ability to put these matters aside, an ability that he was now curious about. Dr. Dicos had been right about some things. He knew that the...visions he experienced had caused him to kill. It had also occurred to him, more than once, that he was possessed or maybe... insane. It seemed that he had two choices. He could accept that he was some kind of ethereal Guardian, tasked with culling the human species, or he was simply mad, and possibly some kind of homicidal maniac. Neither of these choices appealed to Afig, and he decided to reject both of them. He was not some kind of spirit and he was not insane. He was Dawud Hawadi, and he was going to try and figure everything else out as he went along.

Dr. Dicos continued, "All living creatures respond to stimuli such as hunger, cold, heat, and pain.

Then, you arrive, an entity that had never felt anything even as small as the sting of an insect, to say nothing of hunger, cold, or heat. An entity that had never experienced unsatisfied desire, loss, fear, or aging, and, most importantly, an entity that had never known death. These experiences had once deeply shaped the perceptions and the behaviors of those that live in this physical universe. You have proven to be truly dangerous because you are not able to understand that fear of a sudden and violent death is what heightens a human's appreciation of life, and what allows them to experience the beauty that surrounds them. To endure hunger is to savor the tastes of the most simple foods and to appreciate what is available. To suffer cold is to relish the warmth of a fire and revere even the most basic shelter. These experiences, and many more like them, are what it means to be a creature of nature. Yet you have striven to diminish these experiences, to make humans...separate from their environment. But humans are not like you, they are not some sort of ethereal entity that can simply exist. No, my friend, humans are physical beings, creatures little different from a rat or an ape. I tell you this: Humans are, and will always be, the subjects of nature and not the masters of it.

This is my domain and I am the one that is charged with restoring balance. I am the one that must set right the damage that you have done."

Dr. Dicos paused for a moment as he studied Afig's face. In his time, he had encountered a number of ethereal meddlers, but they had been minor entities and were disposed of easily. This was not the case with Dingir, for Dingir was every bit his equal. Nonetheless, Dingir's time had run out.

Dr. Dicos had been obligated to argue these points, and to try and educate Dingir. After all, he was his brother, and he took no joy in causing him distress. Yet, it was no surprise to Dr. Dicos that this...hybrid human standing before him was not susceptible to reasoning, for Dingir had always believed humankind was...special, possibly even divine. He tolerated their destructiveness much as a parent tolerated a misbehaving toddler. Yet, Dr. Dicos knew well that these "toddlers" were defective and predisposed to burning down the house, and the entire neighborhood.

In the end, it would not matter. Dingir was in his 500th and final reincarnation. His influence on mankind was now nearing an end, but there was still one last thing Dr. Dicos needed him to do. He would likely resist, but Dingir had a weakness. He was the "Guardian" and would not knowingly permit the suffering of innocents.

Dr. Dicos had now been silent for a long moment. He had finished his speech, and again studied Afig for any evidence that he had convinced him. Seeing only defiance, Dr. Dicos looked away and for a few seconds, neither man spoke. Then Afig cleared his throat and said, "Dr. Dicos, from what you have said and from what I have previously been told, I believe you are Thalj Shayton, the timeless and persistent creature that has been hunting those of my lineage for centuries. Yet, how is it that you have not...confronted one of my predecessors? If you had done so, at least your 'perception of reality' would have been passed down through the generations."

This upset Dr. Dicos, and it took him a moment to realize that he had become...angry, a human emotion he did not think he possessed. After a second or two, the disorienting experience passed and he was able to reply, "Unfortunately, your mental processes are only slightly superior to those of the wretched Sahla. However, it is encouraging to see that you have finally been able to associate me with the legendary character you know as Thalj Shayton. As for hunting those of your lineage, you again demonstrate your...simplicity. Though it is true that I have hunted, my prey is not of your lineage, for you have no lineage. You, Dingir, are constant, you have no ancestors, nor will you have any descendants. However, when you undergo a reincarnation, you do leave behind your previous physical form, much as a snake leaves behind his skin, when he sheds. This physical form is what I hunt, since it is still capable of mischief and must be disposed of." Dr. Dicos paused for a moment and then continued, "Has it never occurred to you as strange that so many of your ancestors have...disappeared, but their sole offspring always managed to survive? In truth, I have had you within my reach a thousand times, and never once have I touched you." Afig immediately replied, "Why?" Dr. Dicos looked away and then said, "It was necessary for you to...let us say, mature. Besides, the moment you had taken physical form, it was determined that you would reside here for 500 life cycles, after which you would depart, and humankind would be left without a 'Guardian.' This, my friend, is your 500th incarnation, but alas, I could not allow you to just leave. No, before you depart, there is something that you must do. In fact, I have had my people searching for you for seven years. I have had others prepare this facility, and still others have undergone special training to care for you. It has not been a simple process but I have had a great deal of human assistance. Despite all of their advancements, human-kind remains amazingly easy to manipulate. They respond particularly well to fear and greed, but what is most easily manipulated is their sense of self-righteousness. For it matters not how irrational a concept may be; all that matters is that it makes them feel morally and intellectually superior.

Today, it is radical Islam that offers me my pool of recruits, for it is they that shroud themselves in a self-righteousness that permits them to kill indiscriminately, and to ignore all conventional human law. They serve me well and all I have had to offer is a little money and the promise of an 'ultimate solution,' a 'Great Jihad' that would once and for all vanquish their enemies.

You have been well-concealed my friend, and it has taken my small army a considerate amount of effort to find you. Time and time again, I thought that I had you but Zulfiqar proved me to be wrong, for Zulfiqar alone can separate you from the others. You may have noticed that the Zulfiqar has caused some changes in you. At least for now, you are not quite the entity you once were. For one thing, you are temporarily unable to depart, or more precisely, you are unable to leave your physical form. To be sure, there are other changes but I do not wish to speak of them now."

Afig was trying to put the pieces together but there were still so many questions. Not sure where to begin, he said, "I assume that you are not an Islamist, nor will there be a 'Great Jihad,' so then what is it that you intend to do?" Dr. Dicos replied, "I am certainly not an Islamist and I have no intention of leading these humans to some kind of Islamic paradise. But a more interesting question is whether I am a jihadist. In a literal sense of the word, I must say that I am. Though you are curious about what I intend to do, I will say only this: You will father a child, and that child will permit me to restore order and balance."

Afig sensed his opportunity to question Dr. Dicos was coming to an end, and he still had many more questions. Speaking quickly, he said, "It is obvious that your temperature is much colder than that of a human. Why? And the women, who are they and how were they selected?" Dr. Dicos looked at him when he answered, "You may think of my temperature as an adaptive response to the place where I dwell. This, of course, will not answer your question, but it was not intended to.

Now for the women, they have been selected because they are excellent physical specimens and of prime child-bearing age. They have been injected with a female variation of the Zulfiqar serum, in order to weed out any latent mental or physical deficiencies, and to prepare their wombs to receive your semen.

It may be of interest for you to know that a team of physicians have certified that the women are virgins. They have been kept isolated to ensure that no other male has had access to them." Dr. Dicos paused for a moment and then continued, "It is now time for you to return to your quarters, where you have some...work to do..."

Though he didn't know what he planned to do, Afig knew Dr. Dicos was dangerous and he needed to stop him. The obvious answer was to refuse to...breed with the women. This would prevent them from getting pregnant, and that would remove a key element of Dr. Dicos' plan. It was a simple solution...too simple.

Almost as if he knew what he was thinking, Dr. Dicos continued, "I look forward to your success. The child that you will father will be an exceptional creature. Such a creature has never before walked the earth. Needless to say, I have anticipated that you may elect to resist me, so let me explain the...rules. Once you have impregnated one of the females, the other three will be given a substantial amount of money, a house and then released. Meanwhile, the pregnant female will be treated like a queen, given excellent medical care and every luxury she could desire.

However, if you are presented a female and it is then determined that you did not deposit your semen inside of her, I will assume that you are resisting me, or that the female I have selected is an inferior specimen. In either case, she will be given to Sahla and replaced with another, more suitable specimen. You may be interested to know that Sahla has grown to be larger and stronger than you remember. The guards refer to him as the 'beast,' for that is what he has become. Of course, he is completely deranged and extremely violent, but what might interest you most is that Sahla is in a state of perpetual arousal. There is little doubt that he will have his way with any female he is offered. The question is, will he dismember the female while he is raping her, or will he wait until afterward?

After three breeding sessions, if none of the females is pregnant, they shall all be offered to Sahla, and replacements brought in. There is a considerable supply of healthy, attractive, young women available, and I am sure that I can eventually find one that you will be able to impregnate."

Dr. Dicos was quiet for a moment, letting his words sink in. When he was satisfied Afig understood, he continued, "There is one more thing. It may have occurred to you that...Allah forbid, you could have an accident, you might be killed. If that happened, you would not be able to meet your breeding obligations, so the females would be of no use to me. As such, they would be given to Sahla, either individually or together. I have not yet made up my mind."

Dr. Dicos had not missed the flash in Afig's eyes, and instantly knew his message had been communicated. The meeting was over, and he turned to walk toward the door, when he stopped and turned back to Afig. Dr. Dicos' hard, cold eyes bored into him and when he spoke, his voice more closely resembled that of an animal than of a man. "We shall not speak again, but I offer you this final...admonition. The day will soon be upon us, when every word you have ever spoken will be unspoken. Every deed that you have done will be undone. Every grain of sand your foot has displaced will be returned to its original position. When this is finished, there will be no trace that you had ever existed.
"

Farrukh

Merzad un-cuffed Afig, and he and another guard returned him to his room. Afig and the men did not speak, and only after the other guard had stepped from the room did Merzad say, "I do not know what is troubling you, my friend, and I know it is not my business, but tonight is your wedding night. If it is possible, you must put aside your trouble and think only about the woman that you will soon be entertaining in your bed. Of course, I have not seen the faces of any of your wives, but I have heard rumors that say all four of them are beauties. Though it is not fitting that I tell you all that I have heard, I will say this: When Allah blesses a young man with a desirable wife, he may perform two, three and maybe even four or five times in one night. But it is said that your wives are so desirable that you will have no difficulty performing a dozen times or more. I personally do not think this is possible, but that is what I have heard." Merzad paused a moment and studied Afig. Seeing that the young man was in no mood to speak, he continued, "Well my friend, it is time for me to go and fetch one of your wives." Merzad turned and walked from the room. The door was closed behind him and then locked. Afig could hear Merzad's footsteps walking away.

If he had wanted to, he could have heard the heartbeat of the other guard standing outside his door, but Afig had no interest in the man's heartbeat, and chose to tune it out. With the room now quiet, he could not help but think of the conversation he had had with Dr. Dicos. Yet, the things Merzad had said, the rumors about his...wives, soon came to dominate his thoughts. It was not that he did not appreciate the seriousness of the situation, because he did. It was that he didn't know what he was supposed to do. Anyway, the women were now part of this. As he thought of this, he realized that he was soon going to be alone in a room with a woman who probably had every intention of having sex with him. It was not long before Afig found his eyes glued to the door and felt his heart pounding as he began to imagine what the woman might look like. What shape would her breasts be? Would she have a slim, hourglass figure? Would her buttocks be firm and round? These were not clean thoughts and he wondered whether Dr. Dicos may be right. At their most basic, were humans – at least human males – nothing more than...animals?

Nearly half an hour would pass before Afig heard the distant groan of the heavy, iron hinges that he had come to associate with one of the steel doors opening. This was followed by approaching footsteps, one set of which was Merzad's and the other two were lighter, presumably those of women. He listened as the steps got closer and finally stopped, just outside his door. A moment later, there was the sound of the bolt slide, and then the door opened. Merzad stepped in and Afig noticed that he had a smile on his face, the kind of smile one man gives another man, when the pleasures of a woman are to be experienced. Seeing this, Afig's stomach clenched, and he felt nauseated. The time for speculation and indecision was now past. This was not something that might happen tomorrow or in an hour; it was happening right now.

Taking a deep breath, he stared as the door began to slowly swing open, revealing two burqa-clad women. One of the women wore a blue burqa while the other one wore a white one. As customary, their heads were slightly tipped downward to avoid making eye contact. The woman in the blue burqa was more heavyset and stood a step behind the other woman, so Afig assumed that she was the matron. The closer woman, the one in the white burqa, was slightly taller than the other one, and the way the burqa draped over her shoulders, suggested her shoulders were square and that she had a slim physique. She must have sensed him studying her, because she raised her head to look at him, and for just a moment he was sure that their eyes had met. But then she lowered her head, in a way that suggested that she had been caught doing something wrong. A second later, the matron could be seen nudging the woman, prompting her to enter Afig's room. As she moved forward, the delicate, white fabric billowed around her, giving her a ghostly appearance – an affect that was further enhanced by the fact that he could not see her feet. This made it seem as if she floated into the room.

Merzad stood there, with a stupid grin on his face. He watched the two of them for a moment, and then turned and stepped out of the room, shutting the door behind him, and sliding the bolt closed.

Afig always said and did dumb things when he was nervous, so he quickly constructed a short speech, in which he would tell her that she had nothing to fear from him, he would not hurt her, and he would never force her to do anything. But should he explain to her that if she did not have sex with him, she would be...brutally killed? No, no that sounded like he was trying to coerce her into having sex with him. Afig was still working on his speech, when the woman suddenly stepped directly up to him and seductively began shedding her burqa. Beneath it, she was wearing only a sheer veil and a clingy, white night-dress that revealed her curvaceous form. Afig could not help noticing that she was shapely but slim, though she had an ample bosom. The nightdress clung to her in a way that revealed her long legs and any number of other tantalizing female details. She stood tall and straight, and there was a relaxed elegance to her posture. But what most drew Afig's attention were the curves of her hips, and her round, full breasts. As his eyes took in the woman, the speech he had composed, along with much of his cognitive function, just vaporized as the wom-an began to slowly unbutton her nightdress, stopping only after she had offered him a little more than just a glimpse of her naked breast. Afig knew he was staring, but he could not help it. Anyway, everything the woman had done, she had done to gain his...attention, and it had worked. Gradually, with much effort, he regained enough composure to draw his eyes upward, until he was looking at the woman's face. On-ly then did he remember that she still wore the sheer veil. The veil had the effect of drawing his attention to her eyes, which were large, deep, jet-black pools that brought to mind some wild, exotic animal. They were, at once, strangely seductive and foreboding.

Suddenly, Afig realized that he had forgotten the unveiling cere-mony. The unveiling of the bride's face is considered to be her gift to the groom. It represents the first time her face has been seen by a man, other than a family member. Afig took a deep breath, and slowly reached for the veil. It was then that his thoughts went to the woman he knew as Adelah. Could this be Adelah? He was not sure why it mat-tered, but he did not think Adelah could have those...those strange eyes... Could she?

Afig's hands were shaking by the time his fingers touched the veil. Awkwardly, he fumbled with it before the veil fell away, revealing the face of a young, 18-, or maybe 19-year-old woman. Her skin was clear, creamy smooth, and had a slight olive tint, which gave her a decidedly exotic look. The shape of her face was round, and her features were refined, and he thought she was quite pretty, maybe even beautiful. Next to her eyes, the girl's mouth caught his attention. It was small and her lips formed a natural pucker that was highlighted by full, moist lips. The girl's black hair was thick and shiny, and it fell, in wavy locks, all the way to the middle of her back.

Something drew Afig's attention back to the girl's eyes; they had suddenly become empty...actually, the girl's face was now expressionless, and her body had become rigid. It was as if he was looking at a mannequin. Studying her more closely, Afig realized that she did not see him, she did not seem to see anything. Only a moment ago, she had been watching him with those eyes, a teasing smile on her lips, and now, she was...well, gone. Afig could not help but think that this was, somehow, his fault. She must have been terrified at the prospect of having to...to be intimate with this strange man. As the seconds passed, his worries grew – she was not responding, she did not even blink. After what seemed too long of a time, he decided that he had to do something. Maybe speaking to her would help, but then he worried that the sound of a man's voice would make things even worse. Unable to think of anything else, Afig decided to take the chance. Quietly, he cleared his throat, and then, in as gentle a voice as he could muster, he asked:

"Miss, Miss, what is your name?"

Nothing, no response. At least his voice had not made things worse, so he decided to continue.

"My name is Afig...I will not hurt you...I promise."

Still nothing, but as the seconds passed, Afig watched in amazement as consciousness streamed back into those dark eyes. A moment later, she was looking up at him as if nothing had happened. The right side of her nightdress had slipped off of her shoulder, and had fallen low enough to completely reveal her right breast. Like most of the young men he knew, Afig had seen the illicit pictures of naked women that circulated through their ranks. He had also seen a few European and American films that showed brief glimpses of a woman's breast, but he had never seen a real one and so close up. Finding himself staring a little longer than he should have, he half-expected the girl to scold him, or at least, cover herself up, but she did neither. Instead, she slowly lowered her left shoulder, allowing the nightdress to fall away, revealing both of her breasts and gathering at her hips. Afig could hear the girl giggle as if his response was pleasing and amusing her.

In only seconds, this girl had gone from unresponsive to being a playful seductress. Afig was having some difficulty keeping up, but she quickly got his attention when she reached out and closed her hand around the engorged bulge at his groin. Afig instantly felt the heat of this girl's hand through the fabric of his trousers, and there was no doubt that she was aware of his arousal. Initially embarrassed, he thought that he should pull her hand away but found that he really didn't want to. From her expression, the girl was visibly pleased by the effect she was having on him, but then, without any warning, she abruptly pulled her hand away. Momentarily disoriented, Afig quickly regained his composure and looked at the woman as he tried to understand what was happening. She was staring at him, all traces of her sexy playfulness were gone and in its place was an expression of...revulsion. The young woman awkwardly crossed her arms over her chest in an attempt to cover her breasts, and Afig thought he saw her glance at her burqa. Not knowing what else to do, he just watched and after a few seconds, he saw resignation slowly wash over her, and then he heard her sigh and make an effort to speak. At first, the words didn't come, but when she tried a second time she managed to say, "Farrukh, her name is Farrukh."

Her voice seemed strange. It was not that she had a bad voice, it was that he had quickly become accustomed to her communicating through her facial expressions and gestures. And now to hear her speak, made her seem even more...different. She had been in complete control and had not needed to say a word.

Finally pulling himself together, he was about to reply when the woman continued, saying, "Please, you must forgive her, for being so...so shameless. She is a woman that has no modesty or inhibitions, and she exists only to experience carnal pleasure." The woman's eyes studied Afig for a moment and then continued, "I'm sorry but I find it impossible to understand how you can be so...fascinated by two female breasts."

Only moments ago this woman had quite deliberately and quite seductively bared her ...female breasts to him and had eagerly taken his...response to her, in her hand. And now she was addressing herself in the third person while describing herself as "shameless," and suggesting his fascination with those breasts was...incomprehensible. Did she actually want him to offer a rational answer? If she did, she would be disappointed because he did not have one. It was then that Afig realized he was being caught up in this woman's madness. This woman thought of herself as two different people, and the version that was currently present did not approve of the other version. Seeing that the young woman was waiting for him to respond, Afig said, "Farrukh, yes that is an...interesting name, but there is something I do not understand. This Farrukh person...where is she and...who is she?" The woman sighed impatiently and then answered, saying, "Afig, Farrukh is here when I am not, and you know very well who she is. She is the harlot that has most successfully seduced you."

Growing more perplexed, Afig decided to address this...odd situation, even more directly, in hope that he could make more sense of it. Suddenly feeling tired by the complexity his wedding night had taken on, he took a breath and said, "Madame, this woman...Farrukh, is this woman you?" The woman looked puzzled and then rolled her eyes in annoyance and replied, "Why is this so difficult for you to comprehend? It is true that we look alike, but when you see yourself in a mirror, do you think that reflection is you? Can you not appreciate that there is a difference? My reflection is Farrukh but she is not me and I am not her. Though I am reluctant to use such a word, I believe she is nothing but a...'whore.' Honestly Afig, your inability to distinguish between us is...disappointing.

Nevertheless, neither one of us is interested in you for your...intellect. Farrukh wishes only that you pleasure her, while I require your...semen to survive this horrible experience. To do so, I..."

The woman suddenly stopped speaking and a dark cloud seemed to pass over her. Her eyes became wide, her pupils were dilated, and Afig could see the veins at her temples begin to pulse. But then, as suddenly as it had started, the episode passed and there, standing before him was that playful, seductive young woman who had so mesmerized him. Though she did not speak, she managed to convey a hint of disappointment as she glanced down at the front of Afig's trousers and saw that the bulge was...gone.

Afig was still struggling to process what had transpired, when Farrukh stepped back from him just far enough so that he could see all of her. Smiling innocently, she placed her thumbs beneath the nightdress gathered at her hips and slowly pushed it down, letting it fall to her ankles. Feigning surprise and embarrassment, Farrukh first allowed Afig a long moment for his eyes to take her in before she made a mock effort to cover herself. While doing so, she slowly turned away from

Afig, exposing her back to him. Raising her arms above her head, she ran her long fingers through her silky black hair and began to sensually sway her hips. Afig soon found himself infatuated and could not take his eyes off of what he thought was the most incredible...backside he had ever seen. She was still swaying as she turned back toward him and began to lower her arms. Her fingers playfully brushed the tips of her breasts, and then lightly traced the flatness of her stomach until she had reached the creamy smooth skin of what Afig thought was her...most private part. As her fingers began to explore, Farrukh's eyes widened with anticipation. Soon her head tilted back, her eyes closed, and her face filled with an expression of dreamy ecstasy.

Though Afig felt troubled by the woman's sudden transformations, he found that he was not able to think clearly, or, more accurately, he was not able to think about anything except this sexy creature in front of him. There was no question that she was beautiful and of course it didn't hurt that she was naked, but there was more to it. Farrukh completely delighted in her sexuality and her femininity. Seduction was not something that she worked at, it was something that she was. Everything about this woman made you desire her. It was true that she did not possess a single gram of inhibition, nor was she in any way vulgar or obscene. Afig had never imagined there was such a woman, and he now very much wanted to touch her and have her touch him. He wanted to feel her pressed against him, and he wanted to be inside of her. Yet, at the same time, Afig wanted to run away from her as fast and as far as he could.

Farrukh reached out, and then gently guided Afig back toward his bed. A moment later, Afig found himself seated and there before him, less than a hand's width away were two of the most gorgeous breasts he had ever seen. There was no question what Farrukh wanted from him, for he was able to see the inside of her thighs glisten with her wetness. There was also no question that Afig wanted her, for he had managed an erection that was harder and more massive than he had ever thought possible.

Knowing that time was running out, Afig cleared his throat and tried to speak, but only muttered something unintelligible. Starting again, he began, "Farr...Farrukh, you do not have to do this, I...I mean I will not make you do this...I..." Afig did not have a chance to finish, for Farrukh's breasts pressed against his face as she pulled off his shirt. A few seconds later, his pants were gone, and she was pushing him onto his back. He could smell her perfume, and beneath that, the sweet musky scent of a sexually aroused woman. He could hear her heart beating, and her rapid breathing, as she straddled him and expertly guided him into her.

Several hours later, Afig lay on his back, exhausted. Farrukh was again positioning herself astride him even though he had already mated with her three times, ejaculating each time. As far as he could tell, Farrukh had experienced at least six orgasms. Each time he could feel her arch her back, open up to him, her body would spasm three, sometimes four times, and then wave after wave of pleasure washed over her. Afig had nothing left to give but that did not deter Farrukh as she positioned herself astride him. He felt her warm wetness as she pressed herself down onto him and began to gently move back and forth. It did not take long for Afig to once again respond. Several minutes later, Farrukh was on her back, her legs high in the air and Afig between them. She giggled with delight as he thrust into her again and again. Then, suddenly, she became quiet and her body became rigid. Worried that she was hurting, he got off of her, but Farrukh did not respond. Her body now felt as tight as a coiled spring and he again saw the darkness pass over her. Afig reached out and gently stroked her hair, as he softly spoke, "Farrukh...what's wrong? Can...can I do something?" There was no response, and Afig was about to try again, when Farrukh's eyes suddenly sprang open and focused on him. This was not Farrukh, for the creature glaring at him had every intention of tearing him to pieces. Her eyes were huge and her pupils fully dilated. Breathing rapidly, her nostrils flared and a moment later, her lips twitched, narrowed, and curled upward. Afig could see her glistening white canines and sensed she was about to strike. Instinctively he reached for her wrists and held her down just as Farrukh lunged toward him, growling and snapping as she did. He held her firmly in place and more than once thought that she might break his grip. The struggling lasted several long minutes before Farrukh gave in to exhaustion. It took several more minutes before the growling had completely stopped and she appeared to calm. Only then did Afig release her wrists. When she started to stir, Afig braced himself, but when he saw that smile, he knew that it was Farrukh.

This time, Afig felt no arousal, as the savagery that had possessed this beautiful young woman had been permanently seared into his mind.

He thought it had been a simple decision. Dr. Dicos had left him little choice, he would have to have sex with these women or they would be...killed. Though he had not told Dr. Dicos, Afig had added one condition, the decision to have sex or not to have sex would be left up to the women. Now, however, Afig wondered whether these women possessed the free will to make that decision. He was almost positive that Dr. Dicos and his dammed Zulfiqar serum had done this to Farrukh, but whatever had caused it, the woman should not be pregnant. Ashamed, Afig cursed himself for the part he had so willingly played in Dr. Dicos' scheme.

Looking at Farrukh, he could not help but wonder what she had once been like. Her personality was now badly fragmented but when she had been...whole, Farrukh must have been smart, fun, and of course, a stunningly beautiful young woman.

As he watched her, he could hear her heartbeat quicken and her breathing become more shallow as she began to seductively fondle her breasts. Twenty minutes ago, this would have aroused him, but now Afig felt only sadness and a tenderness for the beautiful young woman.

Farrukh sensed his impassivity and leaned toward him, intending to go down onto him but before she could do so, Afig took her by the shoulders and gently kissed her. He then held her close to him and whispered, "No more Farrukh. We have done enough...I'm so sorry." He knew that Farrukh desperately needed help but he had no idea what he could do for her.

Farrukh pressed herself against him and for a few seconds he just held her. Then the young woman pushed Afig away and drew her knees up to her chest, and wrapped her arms around them. Afig could hear her softly sobbing and then he saw her body tremble, a little at first, but soon her entire body shook and she began to weep. Moving next to her, he put his arms around her and spoke to her softly, saying, "Farrukh, it will be all right." Afig tried to believe that these words were true, but he knew they were a lie.

After a while, Farrukh became quiet, and Afig watched as she slowly transformed into the other version of this young woman. He could hear her heartbeat slow and he saw her looking at him with understanding and a sadness in her eyes. Then she cleared her throat and spoke, saying, "Afig, I have never understood nor have I ever approved of her behavior, but Farrukh is who she is. You do know that they will kill her?" Afig was strangely glad to be speaking to this young woman and though he didn't understand how, he thought...or maybe he just hoped that there was something she could do to help. As was Farrukh, this version was naked but she made no effort to cover herself. Afig appreciated this, for he too was naked and he was too tired to deal with all the...modesty issues. Looking at her, he replied, "I think you know that I have... successfully mated with Farrukh. This was as Dr. Dicos has demanded. He had told me that he would spare the women if I mated with them. Surely Farrukh will be spared...at least for now?" The young woman shook her head in disbelief and then said, "Are you that big of a fool? Do you not see that Farrukh is mad and when they realize this, they will dispose of her?" Afig knew this was true but the words still stung. Now curious, he asked, "How was it that Farrukh had been able to keep her...condition a secret?" The young woman looked away as she replied, "Before the serum, neither of us existed. It was Zulfiqar who gave birth to us. Until tonight, I have been the strong one, the one that has been present. But the moment Farrukh saw you, I lost control. Her desire is so strong that I have been relegated to the role of observer. Afig, do you not know that Farrukh...loves you and that she desires only to be close to you? When you...mate, you and she are one, and she is complete.

Now you have mated with her three times and each time you have done so, she has become stronger." Afig and the young woman were silent for a long time, and then she slipped off of the bed, and walked over to where her nightdress lay. Bending over, she picked it up, and proceeded to put it on. Afig could not watch her, for it saddened him to see how the nightdress slipped down over her and how it clung to that shapely form that he had become so familiar with. Next the young woman picked up her burqa, slipped into it, and then put on the head cover. Realizing she was going to leave, he called to her, saying, "I am sorry...But maybe, if you could keep her hidden for just a little while, I might be able to figure something out."

The young woman made no indication that she had heard him, but instead she stepped toward the door. When she reached it she stopped, and for a moment just stood there. Then, without turning toward him, she said, "I will try but I do not think it will work. You have given Farrukh...meaning and purpose. She now knows what it means to be alive, and I do not believe I can control that."

Without waiting for a response, the young woman raised her hand, and softly knocked on the door. A moment later, the door opened and

Merzad looked into the room, first seeing Farrukh, and then searching beyond her, until he saw Afig. It appeared that Afig needed to give his permission before Farrukh could leave. Reluctantly, Afig nodded and Merzad gestured back in recognition. He then retreated back through the door, closing it behind him. For a second, Afig wondered whether Merzad had misunderstood him, but then he heard Merzad's voice summoning one of the female matrons. Of course, Merzad, being a male, could not accompany the woman. For that, he would need a suitable female to act as chaperone.

Spy

The next morning, Merzad and another bodyguard, whose name was Muhammad, came to collect him. They would escort him to the dining room, where a breakfast of buttered nan (flat bread), boiled eggs, nuts and raisins, and tea awaited them. Afig looked and felt emotionally spent. He had not slept much, his mind continuously replaying those strange wonderful and awful hours he had spent with Farrukh.

Merzad was at the end of his twelve-hour shift, and looked nearly as tired as Afig.

The three men sat at the deeply scarred, wooden table splayed with platters of what was to be their breakfast. Merzad and Muhammad immediately began to devour the food, while Afig mostly pushed his around on his plate. This did not go unnoticed, and after several minutes, Merzad put down his fork and said, "I have instructed the chef to prepare you a special meal, but you are not eating. Did the woman not please you?"

Afig knew that even implying Farrukh had not pleased him, would put her in grave danger. So he donned what he hoped would pass as a satisfied expression, and answered.

"No, no, Farrukh was...fantastic. It is that we were very...busy last night. It is just that I am now a little tired." Merzad seemed to accept this answer, and after a short pause, said, "You have grown as big as a horse, and now, with your...night-time activity, you must eat."

Actually, Afig had noticed that his shoulders had become broader, and his muscles seemed bulkier. It had been difficult to confirm just how big he had become, since there were no mirrors in his part of the facility. He was sure his growth was directly related to the Zulfiqar serum and though he felt fine now, he could not help but wonder where this was heading.

"Twenty minutes." Afig looked up to see that Merzad was speaking to him. Having been distracted, he had not heard all of what Merzad had said, so he asked, "I'm sorry, what is happening in...twenty minutes?" Merzad smiled at him and said, "If you are this big of a mess after bedding one wife, I do not look forward to seeing what you will be like after you have bedded four of them.

I said, you have a medical scheduled in twenty minutes. Now quickly, finish up your food." Afig had come to like Merzad, at least as much as one can like his enemy. He had learned that Merzad had been a farmer and that he was embarrassed about being illiterate. One time, when he and Merzad had been eating a meal, Merzad told him that he would like to learn how to read, and Afig had agreed to teach him. They would have to be discreet, since learning to read would set Merzad aside from the other guards, and some would think that he was trying to be better than them.

Afig knew little about the other guard, only that his name was Muhammad, and that he was one of those full-fledged religious fanatics. A "fatal" character flaw, in Afig's opinion.

The cognitive and physical testing was now pretty much over, and Afig spent a lot of time in one of the old test rooms. It served as a quasi-reading room, and a holding cell. He would be handed a couple of dog-eared, religious books and left alone for an hour or so. This morning, he had been scheduled for a medical exam, but at the last minute, the technician assigned to perform the exam had taken ill. So, after breakfast, Afig had been escorted to the reading room. He didn't mind, since he had some thinking to do and the reading room, and his sleeping quarters, were the only places he was left alone. Well, he wasn't exactly left alone; a guard would stick his head in every five minutes, and there was a closed-circuit TV camera monitoring his every move. Still, it was an improvement over having some medical technician, who smelled of body odor and cigarette smoke, prodding and poking him. Afig also had another reason for liking this particular room – it abutted Dr. Dicos' office, and if he listened carefully, he could pretty much hear everything that was going on in there. The trick was not to give the person monitoring the camera images, any reason to get suspicious. He would follow a similar pattern each time, always being careful not to appear too interested in the shared wall.

The reading room had two, flimsy, straight-back wooden chairs, and a heavy, grey, metal table whose surface was marred by cigarette burns, and old coffee cup rings.

Afig was trying to decide which of the two chairs he would place his trust in, when he heard voices coming through the wall. He soon recognized one of the voices as that of the Staff Physician. The man had a habit of mumbling, but if Afig concentrated, he could usually understand most of what he said.

"...the hymen has been ruptured and there was a significant amount of seminal fluid present in the vagina. Of course it is too early to establish whether she is pregnant." Afig then heard another voice that he immediately recognized as that of Dr. Dicos, "That may well be but you failed to keep me abreast of her mental condition." The Staff Physician apologetically replied, "I am sorry, sir, but her previous episodes seemed to be minor...and only after her breeding did they become more pronounced. You see, we had great hopes for this particular female. Her hormone levels were much higher than the others, and tests showed her to be unusually responsive to sexual stimulation. Given Afig's age and his inexperience, we all felt she was the most suitable candidate for his first sexual encounter." Dr. Dicos immediately replied, saying, "Still, you have been warned about the side effects of the serum. If I had known that she was even marginally unstable, I would have found a healthier specimen. This female should have been given to Sahla. If Sahla were suitably muzzled and bound, the female might have survived a breeding session, and it would be most interesting to see their offspring." Dr. Dicos was silent for a moment, and then he continued, "I have only a week to complete these sessions so I do not have time to replace this woman. Watch her and report any changes to me."

Dr. Dicos' voice faded and was momentarily unintelligible. Afig had to wait several seconds before he heard the voices again. It was the Staff Physician speaking, "...completed preparation and she should be ready for breeding." Dr. Dicos replied, "Ah yes...Afig must once again perform. When he survived my 'black snake' experiment, I was sure Zulfiqar would choose him. My only concern is that I will not have him in my custody long enough. I want..."

The fragments of information were frustrating, but Afig was sure that Dr. Dicos thought he was not going to be there very long. Was someone coming for him...could he be talking about the Americans? Afig continued to listen, hoping he could glean a better picture of what was happening. A minute or two later, Afig heard the Staff Physician leave Dr. Dicos' office and someone else enter. At first, the words were mostly inaudible, but then Dr. Dicos could be heard saying, "...he has been asking questions, he wants to know what happened to his father." A male voice replied, and Afig recognized it as that of Merzad: "The

Imam was an obedient servant. It was unfortunate that he had to be sacrificed. Still, I am very confident that everyone believes the Imam disobeyed you, so there is no reason for his son to be suspicious. Even a Taliban commander should understand that disobeying Dr. Dicos would have severe consequences." Dr. Dicos replied, but his voice was muffled and several seconds would pass before Afig could understand what he was saying, "... I do not have time for this. I leave it to you to rid me of this problem.

Now Merzad, how is your relationship with Afig?" Merzad replied, "He is but a boy and suspects nothing. The staff has been instructed to interact as little as possible with him. I will be the only friendly face he sees, and I will be the only one that will talk to him. He has begun to trust me and has agreed to give me 'reading lessons.' Unfortunately, he still does not trust me enough to share his experience with the woman. It is his desire to protect her and this may... Still, I think he will come around..." Dr. Dicos' voice answered, saying, "Good...ready him. I have seen to it that the women understand what is expected of them and Afig understands what must........." Afig heard someone's footsteps in the corridor. Whoever it was, he was coming toward the reading room. Taking the open book in his hands, he casually stood, stretched, and then slowly walked toward the far side of the room. A moment later, the door opened, and Muhammad entered. Afig's reading time was over, and he was led off to the examination room, where two medical technicians were waiting.

Afig spent most of that morning mulling over the fragments of conversation he had heard. He knew that Farrukh would be examined and they had confirmed the presence of semen. But he worried that it would not be long before Farrukh's mental fragmentation would become too obvious. To Dr. Dicos, these women were nothing but...breeding stock and he would not hesitate in disposing of them.

As he thought of Farrukh, he also thought of Merzad. Merzad was a "plant." He was there to gain his confidence and then spy on him.

The Imam was yet another interesting topic. To Afig, it now seemed that Dr. Dicos ordered the Imam to have him beaten, and then, when Afig had not died, the Imam was executed. At first, Afig could not understand why. But then it came to him. The beating should have killed him, and if it had, Dr. Dicos would have taken credit for ordering the execution of an imposter. But when Afig survived, he had passed some kind of test, and Dr. Dicos was then anxious to see if he would survive the...Zulfiqar serum. However, Dr. Dicos now needed someone to blame for beating Afig. After all, how would it look if one minute, you are ordering a man beaten to death, and in the next minute, you are praising him as the Chosen One?

No doubt Merzad was a lying devil, but now that Afig knew what he was up to, he could be managed. Still, Afig could not hate Merzad. He was a spy, much as Afig was a spy. He had played his role well.

Shamail

Afig was mentally working through a number of questions he had not yet resolved. Could Dr. Dicos be killed? If he could be killed, would his underlings retaliate by killing the women? What would happen if Harris attacked the facility? Had Dr. Dicos given a "standing order" to kill all of them, before the facility could be captured? Was there a way to get to the women and protect them?

Afig had not forgotten Dr. Dicos' comment about only having a week to complete these sessions. He was also concerned that Afig would not be in his custody long enough. Was someone coming for him and Dr. Dicos knew it?

That evening, Afig was among those who had assembled to hear Mullah Hafiz Jallah conduct the evening prayer service. The service included the usual, long-winded sermon about the evils of the West and the horrors the "Great Satan" had inflicted on the humble, peace-loving Muslims. When the service ended, Merzad and Muhammad escorted Afig back to his room. Stopping at his door, Merzad leaned toward him and quietly said, "My friend, you have company."

Afig immediately knew what he meant, and this caused his stomach to clench. He prayed to Allah that this woman would be sane and that he would do nothing to cause her harm.

This time, he hoped he would be able to think more clearly. With Farrukh, his gonads had dictated most of what he had done; nevertheless, Farrukh had taught him many things, not the least of which was an appreciation for the power of sexual desire.

After hesitating for a second or two, Afig took a deep breath, opened the door, and entered the room.

Standing there, much as Farrukh had done, was a woman, wearing an identical veil and white nightdress. She was nearly as tall as Farrukh, but this woman had big hazel-colored eyes and long, straight, dark-brown hair highlighted with light brown streaks. The woman was staring at him with fear in her eyes that was so palpable that Afig thought she might scream and bolt for the door. To calm her, all he could think of doing was to smile. So he smiled. He knew it was a dumb-looking smile, and he hoped he did not look like he was snarling. With that...smile still plastered onto his face, he slowly walked toward her. Stopping about a meter away, he assumed his most relaxed posture, studied her for a second, and then asked, "Please, may I remove your veil?"

Although it did not seem possible, the woman became even more terrified by the request, or maybe it was just the sound of his voice. It took her a long moment to gather her courage, and then, in a small, quivering voice that was barely above a whisper, she replied.

"Yee...Yes...yes husband."

Slowly, Afig stepped forward, reached up, and gently removed the veil. As it fell away, he saw a pretty young woman, about the same age as Farrukh but otherwise nothing like Farrukh. Absent were those dark, haunted eyes, the seductive smile, and the ever-present, carnal hunger. In their place was only fear. He could hear her heart pounding, and though she was trying to be brave, her pale skin, wide eyes, forced smile, and quivering lower lip revealed an utterly terrified young girl. On seeing this, Afig was saddened. How could he be the cause of such fear in this woman? Why could she not see that it was as impossible for him to harm her, as it was for the sun to rise in the west? As he looked at her, he saw that her whole body had begun to tremble, and knew that he had better say something before the girl passed out. In a gentle, concerned voice, he said, "Please do not be afraid of me. I will not harm you. If...if you would like, I will get you a blanket so that you can cover yourself."

His words did not help, but rather, they seemed to make things worse. Now the girl was crying, and through the sobbing and the tears Afig could hear a small, frightened voice say, "Am I so....ugly that you wish to cover me?" On hearing these words, Afig realized that she may not only be afraid of him, but also she was afraid of being rejected by him. This astounded Afig, for he could not believe that someone as attractive as this young woman could ever fear being rejected by anyone, particularly someone like him. Seeing how miserable the girl was, he reached out to touch her cheek but as he did, the girl winced as if he had struck her. He had wanted to comfort her but now he could see that she was not used to this kind of tenderness, at least not from a man. Deciding this had gone far enough, Afig straightened and in a gentle but firm voice, said, "What is it about me that upsets you so much? Is my head too big, do I smell bad, or maybe it is my nose? I have been told that it is so large that it enters the room five minutes before I do. And there's one more thing, why can you not see how absolutely beautiful you are, and how much the sight of you pleases me?" He was not a comedian nor was he a poet, but his words were heartfelt and he hoped the young woman would listen.

It took several seconds for the sobbing to stop and then she raised her head and looked up at this...strange man. Afig could see that she was confused. Her eyes studied his face for a long moment, and then she looked down at her feet and said, "Your head is not too big, nor do you smell badly. And as far as your nose is concerned, you have greatly exaggerated. It entered the room no more than thirty seconds before you did." Afig was surprised at the girl's retort and could not help but break into laughter. He had thought her to be shyer, and had hoped, at most, to bring a smile to her face. Though the girl did not laugh with him, she smiled and it was a big and beautiful smile. As his laughter passed, he noticed that the young woman still seemed... uncomfortable. Of course this should not have been a surprise since Muslim girls are taught, at a very young age, to be modest and here she was standing, nearly naked, in front of a man whom she had seen only once before, and then only for a few minutes. Trying to put her at ease, Afig said, "Now then, will you tell me your name?"

Though no longer fearful, the young woman's voice still lacked confidence as she said, "I am Shamail. I am the daughter of Anoosheh." Again he had found himself holding his breath. Though Afig was almost positive that the young woman standing before him could not be Adelah, he was oddly relieved to have it confirmed.

"Is there something wrong?...Is it my name?" Shamail's voice brought him back and he saw her looking up at him with concern. Quickly collecting himself, he replied, "I am sorry. I sometimes can become distracted so you must be patient with me. Shamail is a very fine name and quite suitable for a young woman as beautiful as you are.

Now Shamail, if you will allow me, I have something that I must say." Shamail was again looking at him with concern as she replied, "What is it? What is it that you must say?" Afig continued, "I do find you attractive and, yes, desirable but you must know that I will never force myself upon you. Dr. Dicos has made it clear to me what he expects me to do and what the consequences will be if...." Before Afig could finish, Shamail interrupted, saying, "Husband, you are the Chosen One and I am but one of four women who will have the privilege of mating with you. One of us will bear you a child that will lead the faithful to a final victory over the infidels. Husband, it is not our eminent leader, Dr. Dicos, who requires this of you – it is all of Islam that requires it."

Hearing Shamail's response caused Afig's blood to run cold. Why hadn't it occurred to him that one or more of these women might actually believe Dr. Dicos? There was never going to be a "final jihad." Militant Islam was not going to rule the world. Yet, he saw no purpose in trying to change the woman's mind, and anyway, his truth would sound even more bizarre to her than some worldwide jihad.

Afig emphatically opposed forced religious conversion and to have this innocent young woman actually support it, was almost too much. This put him squarely at odds with Shamail, but as he calmed, he was reminded that his action or inaction would determine whether she would live or die. He knew that there were many reasons why conservative, strictly raised Muslim women might have certain predispositions to accept fanatical Islamic dogma. Nevertheless, many of these women were true fanatics, and deserved no more quarter than their male counterparts. Still, in other cases, these women were simply parroting the garbage they had been force-fed all of their lives. At their core, they were good and decent human beings who could never raise their hand to harm another. Afig sensed, or maybe he just hoped that Shamail might be one of these women.

She was very pretty, but pretty in a vulnerable and innocent way. The fear had gone, but now her eyes conveyed a growing uncertainty. Shamail had been waiting for a response, but seeing none coming, she said, "Forgive me for my foolishness but I had assumed that you were like other men, in that you were susceptible to powerful, carnal desires. I had expected that when you saw my near nakedness, you would take me, but instead, you hesitate, you appear to be pondering our situation. Only now am I beginning to understand that as the Chosen One you are not like other men. Perhaps your thoughts are so...immense that they cast a shadow over your carnal desires?

I admit that I have no experience, but I am willing to do anything to please you. You are only to ask."

Shamail paused for a moment, and Afig could see that her face was flushed, and then, to his surprise, she took his hand and led him to the bed. He did not resist when she knelt before him and untied the drawstring of his trousers, allowing them to fall to the floor. He was looking at her when he saw the surprise in her eyes. Her mouth agape, she stared in astonishment at what she saw before her. Obviously, she had never seen a man's genitals before, and the size of his must have caused her some...concern. It took a moment but the surprise was gradually replaced by puzzlement. She didn't know what she was supposed to do with this protruding organ. Finally, realizing that she had been staring, Shamail looked away. She was breathing rapidly and her face was red as she glanced back several times as if to reassure herself it was as she remembered it. Clearing her throat and in a breathy voice, she said, "I am so embarrassed, but I have not seen a man before...I mean I have not seen a man's...a man's...whatever it is you call it. I did not realize it would look so...so strange and it is much...bigger than I had imagined....I..am sorry, it is not right that I speak to you in this way."

Afig felt sorry for Shamail. The girl did not know what to do, and kept glancing at his growing erection as if it might somehow reach out and attack her. Gently touching the side of her head, Afig said, "Do not apologize, Shamail. It is perfectly natural and right that you would be curious, and maybe even a little concerned. To me, a woman's body is, without question, the most bewildering and confounding creation I have ever laid eyes upon. I have no doubt that, if your nightdress were to fall away, I too would stare, and I would likely stare harder and for much longer than you did. So why should you be any different?"

The way this man spoke confused Shamail. No man had ever suggested that anything she thought or felt was in any way comparable to the way that he thought or felt...It was the first time she felt that she could speak without being discounted or belittled. The feeling that she was someone, and that her thoughts and the words she spoke were, at least, a little bit important, began to take root in her imagination. But these thoughts also troubled Shamail. To entertain such things were contrary to how she had been raised, and she thought it might even be heresy. Was this man polluting her thinking? Should she be questioning this man's faith? She did not think so since he had been tested, and had been chosen by Zulfiqar. If she dared to be honest, she had taken in every word he had said, as if they had been made of the sweetest honey. The tenderness he showed her had caused her to feel a curious and not unpleasant stirring low in her stomach, and when she had seen his...manhood she was stunned at how imposing it was. Soon Shamail found herself thinking only of what it would feel like to have such a...monolith inside her.

Afig watched as Shamail's fears and insecurities slowly melted away, replaced by astonishment and...desire. Shamail wanted him but this desire was, at least in part, fed by the control she had. Though he could imagine himself swooping her up, removing her nightdress, and laying her on the bed, he did not. He felt sure that Shamail needed to do this in her own time and in her own way. This was not to say that he did not ache to make love to this pretty young woman, because he did. As these thoughts were passing through his mind, Shamail looked up at him and he could see that she had formed a plan. Standing, she reached down, grasped the hem of her nightdress, and slowly began to raise it up. She was unsure of what his response would be, and her eyes did not leave his as she lifted the nightdress to her knees, and then to her thighs. When proceeding any higher would reveal her genitals, Shamail froze. The idea suddenly terrified her, and all of her insecurities and inhibitions reemerged, screaming at her to stop. Her eyes pleaded with Afig to give her courage, for she really did want to rid herself of that nightdress. Shamail longed to be naked in front of this man, yet wishing such a thing had made her feel ....indecent.

Seeing the distress in the young woman's eyes, Afig leaned toward her and whispered, "Shamail, as I have watched you, I have wondered how is it possible that a woman can be so desirable. What is this power that you have? I have not been able to take my eyes off of you, but then how can a man who lives in the cold darkness not look at the sun and desire its warmth and light?"

Shamail's expression became puzzled. This man was so strange, and he talked...too much. She did not understand what he was saying and, right now, she had no interest in words. Still, Shamail could not help but smile, for the expression on Afig's face made her think of a shy, young boy, looking at a dessert he didn't know he already had permission to eat. But, what most struck her was the kindness in his eyes. A moment later the nightdress was off and Shamail leaped into Afig's arms, kissed him, and wrapped her arms and long, slender legs around him. It was not long before she was on her back and Afig was on top of her, exploring her body as she squirmed with delight.

Shamail now lay beside Afig, breathing heavily. This man had done things to her that had caused her to scream out in pleasure, a kind of pleasure she had never imagined possible. He had done this to her over and over again until she had only enough strength to breathe. She too had done everything she could to pleasure Afig, and she had succeeded, for he had left his seed deep inside of her and the sensation had been so...intensely erotic that she wanted him to do it again and again.

Shamail was at a loss to understand the effect this man had on her. As she thought about this, she studied Afig's face and saw that his eyes were open, and that he was looking at her. Studying him more closely, she saw a trace of a smile, a smile that Shamail now understood. Wanting not to miss her opportunity, she quickly mounted him. The part of her body that mated with his was now so sensitive that the feeling of him entering her made her shudder. It was not long before she felt that throbbing, pulsating feeling that quickened and intensified, finally spasming and erupting into an absolutely wonderful sensation that was immediately followed by waves of pleasure that washed over her again and again.

Shamail had lost count as to how many times Afig had made her feel this way, and could not imagine ever tiring of it. Again looking at Afig, she saw that he lay there, exhausted – his eyes were closed and she knew that she had...satisfied her man and this made her feel that the world was exactly as it should be.

Having fallen asleep, Shamail woke abruptly to find herself cuddled up against Afig, his arm wrapped around her and her head resting on his shoulder. She could smell the scent of his body, and felt the warmth of his skin and the hardness of his muscles. Reaching up, Shamail gently touched Afig's cheek and felt the coarseness of his beard and the strength of his jaw. She could not help but be amazed that this man was so big...so male, yet he was capable of such gentleness.

Wanting to be close to him, to melt into him, Shamail pressed herself up against Afig and he responded by pulling her more tightly against him, and soon they both fell into a deep sleep.

When Shamail awoke the second time, Afig was still asleep. His arm still held her against him, and she savored the sensation for a long moment. It was all about to end, for she had heard sounds in the corridor and sensed the dark cloud that was forming. In less than an hour they would come for her and she found herself already missing Afig. Tears filled her eyes, and Shamail began to quietly sob. Taking in a deep breath, and with it the last scent of her man, she gently lifted his arm and moved away from him. She quietly rose, picked up her night-dress, and slipped into it. She then stepped to where her white burqa hung and proceeded to put it on. Though she hated it, she knew their situation was impossible. Less than a hundred paces from where she stood, was a woman who had already been with her husband, and there were two other women waiting for their turn. Afig would make love to them, for if he did not, they would be killed. Dr. Dicos had told her this as he had explained that threatening her was a necessary "incentive," since the future of millions upon millions of faithful Muslims depended on the Chosen One conceiving a child. Because he did not know which one of them would become pregnant, he had said it was necessary that all of them be...bred.

Though the concept of being...bred was distasteful, Shamail had not questioned her role, for the world had never seemed very real to her, and she had been taught to obey without question. Now, however, her world suddenly seemed much more real and more than that, it seemed askew. Though Islam permitted it, and to have a contrary opinion would be blasphemy, Shamail was convinced that no man should have more than one wife. She thought it to be...unnatural and it conflicted with what she now understood to be love.

And then there was Dr. Dicos. There was something very wrong with that man. He was as cold as ice and spoke more like a machine than a man. Until she had come to know Afig, Shamail believed that men, particularly those who espoused great faith in Allah and advocated a strict interpretation of sharia law, were to be obeyed without question. Though Afig had been proclaimed to be the Chosen One, he had never once mentioned this, nor had he displayed any pretentiousness. In fact, Afig was a quiet, thoughtful young man whose most notable trait was his gentleness. Why was this, and why was the Chosen One held as a prisoner? She knew this to be true since there was no way to lock his door from the inside, but there was a huge, sliding, iron bolt on the outside. She had seen the door when they had let her in, and then she had heard the bolt slide closed after Afig had entered. These thoughts disturbed Shamail, for it meant she was part of something that she did not understand.

The knock at the door startled Afig, instantly waking him. Sitting up, he saw Shamail standing there, looking at him through the grill of that...absurd burqa. As he was about to rise and take her into his arms, the door swung open, and Merzad stuck his head inside. While giving

the room a quick once-over, he said, "They are here for the woman."
Shamail stepped toward the bed, and bent toward Afig, whispering,
"You are my husband, and I will long for you every day, and I will
dream of you every night, for as long as I shall live."

She then stood, turned, and walked toward Merzad. A moment later, the door closed, and Afig heard the bolt lock.

Pistol

"Take a deep breath...hold it...ok, now breathe." The balding, middle-aged technician, with yellowish teeth and stinking breath was subjecting Afig to a series of physiological exams that would take all morning. They had recently become interested in his growth; since he had been administered the Zulfiqar serum, he had grown nearly 8 cm in height and gained over 7 kilograms.

Having time on his hands, Afig thought of Farrukh, and hoped that this beautiful and amazing young woman would be safe, and that somehow her mind would be healed. And then there was sweet and innocent Shamail. Though they had been together only a few hours, Afig had grown quite fond of this pretty young woman, and wondered if she was all right and whether he would get to see her again.

It was near the end of the testing session when Dr. Dicos and two of his bodyguards, both carrying side arms, burst into the room. This was unusual, since Dr. Dicos almost never entered the test room, preferring instead to watch through the thick glass of the observation window. But what made this even stranger was the Kalashnikov slug over one of the bodyguard's shoulder. Up until now, the guards had been armed only with the taser batons. No firearms had been allowed beyond the steel doors.

Afig's hearing was now so good that he could listen to the individual heartbeats of everyone in the room. Dr. Dicos approached the senior medical technician, and gestured that he follow him to the farthest corner of the room. There, both men turned their backs to Afig, and Dr. Dicos, in a low whisper, said, "We have less time than I had thought. Prepare the last female for breeding, tonight. Tomorrow, immediately after Dhuhr (noon prayer), the females will be taken to the vehicles that will be waiting for them. We have no further use for Sahla, so he can be disposed of with the others."

The senior medical technician hesitated for a moment, and then replied, "Yes, yes your eminence. But I have not been able to confirm a pregnancy. Would it not be better to schedule a second breeding session?" Dr. Dicos, who was growing increasingly impatient, snapped back, "That is out of the question. After tonight, the breeding will be done. You are to examine the last of the females as soon as she leaves Afig's quarters. If she has been bred, she will be transported with the others. If she has not been bred, present her to Sahla before you initiate the cleansing procedure." Sounding particularly nervous, the senior medical technician took a deep breath, and then said, "Yes, of course, I will do as you say..." Pausing awkwardly, he then continued, "Forgive me, sir, but as your protocol requires, I must confirm that you have authorized the initiation of the... 'cleansing procedure' upon the departure of the last bred female." Dr. Dicos looked directly at the man and said, "That is correct. You, and the others, have been good and faithful servants. For this, you will be most blessed among martyrs, and granted Paradise."

With this said, Dr. Dicos turned, quickly glancing toward Afig, and then he and his bodyguards hurried out of the room. A few minutes later, Dr. Dicos, now carrying his metallic briefcase, could be seen leaving through one of the steel doors.

Afig felt himself tense as he replayed Dr. Dicos' words. The first thing that struck him was that Dr. Dicos referred to the woman who would be brought to him tonight, as the "last female." He had wed four women, so that meant one of his wives was unaccounted for. Was it Adelah? Had she pushed them too far? No, Adelah was fine, she had to be fine.

Dr. Dicos had also refused to allow a "second breeding session" and had made arrangements to have the women taken away. Something was putting pressure on the man and Afig sensed Harris might be somewhere nearby. But it was his last couple of statements that had Afig's attention. They were going to "initiate the cleansing procedure" and then he had said something to the affect that they, supposedly meaning the staff, "will be most blessed among martyrs, and granted Paradise." It took only a moment for Afig to surmise that the "cleansing procedure" and "martyrdom" were linked. Dr. Dicos had made no mention of him and since there would be no women left to breed, it would make sense for them to get rid of him...or did getting rid of him equate to the "cleansing procedure?"

To complicate things further, it looked like Dr. Dicos was on the run and Afig was running out of time. He wouldn't be able to wait for Harris to rescue him. Anyway, a successful rescue would be highly unlikely. The area where he and the women were being held, was heavily guarded and located deep in the bowels of the hospital. The Americans would have to fight their way in, and it would not be an easy fight, nor would it be a quick one.

A new sense of urgency swept over Afig as he realized that he had until noon tomorrow before the "cleansing procedure" was initiated. With this in mind, his eyes were drawn to the ceiling, or rather to a sprinkler head mounted in the ceiling above his head. He had noticed these before, but had thought them to be inoperable remnants of the hospital's original fire extinguishing system. However, as he looked more closely, he realized that it didn't look much like a sprinkler head. It looked more like some kind of nozzle and it was made from iron that had been discolored by heat. If Afig had to guess, he would say the thing was designed to spew fire, not water. There were dozens of these nozzles scattered throughout the entire area, which meant the place was designed to act as a...a giant incinerator, or in his case, a crematorium. The thick, steel doors would keep the heat in, and they would ensure that no one would get out. As gruesome as this sounded, it made sense. Not only would all the witnesses be eliminated, but all the blood samples, tissue samples, drugs, and documents would be destroyed. As Afig considered this, he sensed he was missing something, and then it came to him. In school, he had studied combustion, and remembered that the fire reaction required an oxidizer, which in most cases is the oxygen in the air. The vents that he had seen were too few and too small to provide an air supply large enough to support this big of a fire. Without an adequate air supply, the fire would soon slow and then extinguish itself. If this was going to be an effective incinerator, somewhere there had to be a large air supply duct.

Afig's thoughts were interrupted by noises coming from the corridor. Through the observation window he could see half a dozen armed guards entering through the steel doors. They took positions on each side of both doors, and the opening to Dr. Dicos' office. It was obvious that Dr. Dicos was not taking any chances, since the guards carried Kalashnikovs and plenty of spare magazines. The message was clear: Security had just been ramped up and no one was getting by those guards without their permission.

Afig would spend the rest of the day in the reading room. As word spread, the medical staff lost interest in the tests and most had retreated to their quarters. The armed guards were all business and wore solemn expressions, as they stared straight ahead, their lips moving as they silently recited prayers. When Afig had passed, he had noticed that the guards swung the muzzles of their rifles toward him, and their fingers entered the trigger guards. Since Sikham, Afig had believed these men did not actually intend to kill him, but that belief was now gone and in its place was a feeling that if he made a sudden move, he would be fired on by as many as six fully loaded assault rifles.

Afig scrambled to try to put together some kind of plan, but nothing seemed to have even a remote chance of succeeding. Several hours would pass before Merzad and Muhammad came for him. As they walked to the dining room, where the evening meal was being served, no one spoke. Afig was not in the mood to pretend to be friendly, and even Merzad didn't seem interested in conversation.

Muhammad wasn't hungry, and stood leaning against the door frame, while Afig and Merzad sat down at one of the dining room tables. Afig had hardly noticed the server, a nondescript man, who stood over him holding a circular tray covered with a dingy white cloth. On the tray were bowls of rice, vegetables, and some kind of meat. Afig was not hungry, but he automatically reached for one of the bowls, when he noticed the server's eyes look at him and then down at the tray. When the man repeated the movements a second time, Afig followed his eyes to where he saw the words, "gun under tray" written in grains of spilt salt. Afig turned toward Merzad, who was sitting across from him, and said, "Merzad, Muhammad looks depressed. Ask him to come and sit with us." Merzad gave a disgruntled sigh, and reluctantly turned to look at Muhammad and said, "Muhammad, quit sulking and come sit with Afig and me." Muhammad simply ignored him and gave no indication that he would come to their table. Merzad turned back toward Afig and just shrugged. By then Afig had retrieved the small pistol from beneath the tray, and had tucked it into his waistband, covering it with his shirt. When Afig and Merzad were again facing each other, Afig was savoring the aroma of a bowl of vegetables.

Everything had suddenly changed. Harris had somebody on the inside...but now what? Was an attack imminent?

Adelah

The meal, evening prayers, everything was a blur, and Afig suddenly found himself being led back to his room. Merzad was still in a somber mood and there was no smirk on his face when he told Afig that he had company.

As Afig entered his room, he once again saw a woman standing there. Her face was covered by a similar lacy, white veil, and she was wearing the obligatory, white, clingy nightdress. But this time, there was something very different about the woman. She stood tall, her back straight, and her shoulders square. Her hair was a lustrous chestnut color, and fell in graceful curls to her shoulders and down her back. Her eyes were a deep blue, the color of sapphires, and blazed with a fierce intensity that made it clear that she had no fear of him. Actually, she seemed to be daring him to approach. Afig immediately knew he was looking at Adelah, but with that realization came the sudden awareness that he had known her before. Though the veil covered her face, he knew what she would look like, he knew the scent of her body, he knew what made her laugh, and what made her cry. He knew a thousand things about her, but mostly he knew that he had loved this woman.

As Afig approached, he noticed the young woman tense, and her eyes narrowed, just slightly. His hands were shaking as he reached up and awkwardly began to remove her veil. Then, suddenly, he felt a sharp, searing pain. Looking down, he saw that Adelah was holding a knife, the blade driven deep into his left side. Reacting, Afig grabbed for her wrist, but she had anticipated his move, and deflected him. Meanwhile Adelah had withdrawn the blade, and thrust it forward a second time, this time intending to stab him in the stomach. Mid-thrust, the knife struck something hard that stopped it. Confused, Adelah pushed harder but the knife would go no farther. The slight delay had given Afig the chance to react, and he was able to grab her wrists, stopping her from thrusting the knife higher.

By then, Adelah's veil had completely fallen away, and the face that glared back at him was that of a beautiful woman...a woman who was determined to kill him. Adelah jerked her knee up, but Afig had sensed the shift of her body, and turned just enough to prevent her knee from striking his groin. His reaction had saved him from what might have been a punishing blow, but it had caused him to bend slightly toward her. Adelah slammed her forehead against his mouth and lower jaw, splitting open his lower lip, and loosening most of his front teeth. In the next two seconds, Adelah stomped down on the toes of his right foot, kicked him in his left knee, and bit his left forearm, ripping away a sizable chunk of his flesh. The woman was still going strong, when Afig finally had enough. Grasping both of her small wrists in his one massive hand, he used his other arm to grab the woman around the waist, slinging her over his hip, and carried her, kicking and squirming, to the bed. Still restraining her wrists, he leaned over her and pinned her down. She still held onto the knife, and tried to maneuver the blade so that it would cut into Afig's wrist. Seeing this, Afig tightened his grip, effectively immobilizing her hands. Still not beaten, she tried biting, kicking, bucking, and thrashing, but nothing worked against the man who was twice her size and as strong as an ox. Realizing this, Adelah became still, saving her strength, hoping that somehow, he would drop his guard.

Afig was leaning over her, blood from his split lip dripping down onto her white nightdress. Blood trickled down his arm, from the bite she had taken out of him, and more blood seeped from the wound in his side, staining the side of his shirt and trousers a deep red.

To Adelah's dismay, he hardly seemed to notice his wounds, and still seemed quite capable of breaking her in half, like a twig.

Seeing that she was calming, Afig eased up on his grip, but he would not be foolish enough to let her go, not yet. The wounds this woman had inflicted hurt, yet all he could think about was how beautiful she looked.

For several long seconds, his eyes took her in, and then he spoke, "Adelah, why are you fighting me? Do you not know me? Do you not know that I could never harm you?" Seeing that his words had meant nothing, Afig tried another tack, and said, "Do you not remember the wedding, surely you know that I tried to help you?" These words did have an effect, but not the one he had wanted. Adelah almost exploded with anger, spitting at him and flailing about, trying to free herself. After a few seconds, she again saw that her efforts were having no effect, so she stilled, and continued to glare up at him. Then in a hard, angry voice, she said, "Go to hell...you son of a donkey." Bristling with a new surge of rage, she continued, "You dimwitted ass. You expect me to be grateful to you for making me part of that bastard's scheme? You want me to bear you a child that would cause the slaughter of hundreds of millions of people?...I would rather be eaten by hyenas." Adelah's actions and words had made it quite clear that his presence had not awakened some long dormant memories of him, but that mattered little, for he was so struck by this young woman's courage and audacity that he could hardly speak. To her, he must have seemed like a giant. The circumference of his biceps was greater than that of her waist, yet she had attacked him with the ferocity of a tiger. Surely she knew that no matter how this had turned out, it would have meant her death, and quite possibly a horrible death.

Seeing this young woman's courage had humbled Afig, for here was a young woman who knew good from evil, and had not tried to rationalize or make excuses for the evil that she saw. In her place, would he have thought so clearly and have acted so bravely? He had his doubts.

As Afig stared down at Adelah, he was not sure what he should tell her. Then, slowly, an idea came to him. Taking a deep breath, he said, "If you promise to listen to me for just a few minutes, I will let you go." Adelah continued glaring at him and did not respond. Deciding to continue, Afig said, "OK...I am still going to let you up. In my waistband is a pistol. I do not think your knife can kill me, but maybe bullets will. So...if you still believe you need to kill me, take my gun and shoot me, shoot me in the head, and keep shooting until there are no bullets left."

Afig slowly let go of her wrists, and moved off of her. Standing near the edge of the bed, he lifted his torn, bloodied shirt, displaying the grip of a stainless steel pistol. Adelah now knew what had stopped her knife blade from slicing into his stomach, but what also got her attention was the stab wound, next to the pistol – it had stopped bleeding, and the gash had nearly closed.

Not trusting the man, Adelah rose hesitantly, and still gripping the knife, she assumed the fighting stance she had been taught as a young girl. Cautiously, she approached Afig and saw that he was watching her with great interest, but he showed no real concern. This was not what Adelah had expected, and it made her feel vulnerable. Thinking quickly, she ordered Afig to put his hands behind his head and lock his fingers together. As he did so, his shirt opened and Adelah could see his muscular chest, and immediately knew the short blade of her knife would have little effect on this man. Focusing on the pistol, Adelah took another step forward, reached for the grip, and yanked the pistol from Afig's trousers. The man had made no effort to stop her, and seemed to be just...waiting. Backing away, she expertly ejected the pistol's magazine, saw that it was full, and then reinserted it. Then she hesitantly placed the knife on the bed, gripped the pistol with two hands, aimed it directly at Afig's forehead, and then disengaged the safety.

Afig had watched her every move, and when he heard the click of the safety disengage, he began to have some doubts about his plan. Adelah's heartbeat increased, her breathing became shallower, and Afig watched as she crinkled her nose as if she had something unpleasant to do. Then he heard her whisper, in a voice barely audible, "May Allah have mercy upon me...I'm sorry...but I...I cannot let you live." Afig watched as she pressed the trigger and then heard the loud click.

Although Afig had not expected the pistol to fire, he still felt a wave of relief wash over him. The moment he had seen the pistol, he had recognized it as Harris' personal weapon, a 9mm, stainless, Kimber Solo. Harris was particularly finicky about safety, and would never have left a bullet in the chamber of a pistol that he knew would be passed around. Afig had watched Adelah to see if she would chamber a round. She did not. Although he had been "almost" positive that the pistol would not fire, "almost" left a lot of room for bad things to happen.

A surge of unexpected emotions flooded through Adelah, as she stared at the pistol. Then realizing that she was effectively without a weapon, she jerked her head up, half expecting to see the man closing in on her. But, he...he was just standing there. He had dropped his arms, but otherwise, he gave no indication that he would attack her.

Afig watched as panic filled Adelah's eyes. Actually, he was a bit shaken up since this was not happening the way he had planned. He had not expected her to press the trigger, and now he wondered if he had made a mistake. No, no, he trusted her...and he would prove it.

Clearing his throat, Afig said, "I think you need to chamber a round. I am pretty sure you'll get the thing to work, if you do that." Adelah's eyes returned to the pistol, and she stared at it, as if she did not know what it was. Then, almost instantly, her mind seemed to clear, and she aptly pulled the slide back, and released it, pulling it partially back a second time, just far enough to visually confirm a round had been chambered. Satisfied, she raised the pistol, and in that same two-handed grip, aimed it directly at Afig's face.

She wasn't supposed to do that. Afig's mind immediately filled with doubt, as his confidence vaporized. She had not hesitated chambering a round, and now he was staring down the muzzle of a loaded pistol, less than a meter away. Afig felt himself begin to sweat, and he wondered why he had taken such a risk. Did he want to die? Knowing it was too late to turn back, Afig found himself closing his eyes. His thoughts turned to the most merciful Allah, and he began to silently pray. Then, for just an instant, there was a clarity...an understanding that he was not alone, had never been alone. Initially, this revelation did not seem to be particularly profound, since he had heard the adage a thousand times. Then, as one moment led to another, Afig began to hear the voices, hundreds of voices. At first, they sounded very distant, barely audible, but then they became clearer, and he realized that these were not different voices, they were just one voice...a familiar voice, and it was reciting a list. As he listened, it became clear that the list contained words from many languages, some ancient and long ago dead, while others he knew. Afig immediately knew that this was a list of the names, names that the voice was called. To know the voice you needed to know all of its names, and to understand what each name meant in the time it was used. Strangely, Afig thought he knew the names and what each name meant.

Afig's eyes sprang open, and he realized that his eyes had been closed for only a fraction of a second. The pistol was still pointed at him, but now it was beginning to sway, slowly at first, but then more and more uncontrollably. As he looked into Adelah's eyes, he knew she would not shoot him. Gone was that stone-cold determination, that seething anger, and in its place was confusion, doubt, and a trace of something else...maybe regret. Adelah slowly lowered her arms and then she collapsed to her knees. Her body was shaking, and Afig could hear that she was quietly sobbing. Afig sat down on the floor beside her and waited. As her sobbing gradually quieted, he leaned toward her and asked, "Does this mean...I get to live?" The words caused Adelah to break down completely, and she wept, holding her face in her hands. He could see she was trying to speak, but the words were choked off by her tears, and it took many long seconds before he was able to understand them. "Why is it that I cannot shoot you? What is wrong with me? Am I so...so weak?"

Afig reached out and softly squeezed her hand, saying, "Believe me, Adelah, you are not weak, but you were wrong about me. I am not your enemy." Adelah fought to get hold of herself, and as her tears subsided, she slowly raised her head, looked at Afig, and said, "You say you are not my enemy. Then, how is it that you do Dr. Dicos' bidding? Are you just some mindless puppet, and if so, is not a puppet just the extension of the puppet master?"

Adelah paused, realizing that she had not given this man a chance to explain himself. Taking a deep breath, she said, "Who are you?...No, that is not right. You are not a man, so then, what are you?" To hear Adelah say these words extinguished all of his remaining doubts. Afig now knew that at least some part of him was...not human, though even that didn't sound right. Nevertheless, Adelah's words had caused him to better understand the presence he had felt. Being "not alone" was not referring to some abstract theological concept. He was literally not alone. Some mysterious force was there, all around him and inside of him. It could not act, but Afig could act on its behalf, and in fact, he had done so many times. Afig also realized Dr. Dicos was like him, but he was acting on behalf of something entirely different. He did not know how to explain it, but he sensed that these forces were at war, they had always been at war, and this war could never be won...nor lost.

Afig would begin slowly and hesitantly, but he would eventually tell Adelah everything...everything, from the time he had left Kabul, to the moment before she put down the pistol.

Adelah listened, but she also found herself focusing on the man's eyes. It was not long before she found herself fascinated by Afig and his story. When he had first entered the room, she was convinced that this man was evil. She would not have believed him if he had said the sky was blue. But then, everything had turned...upside down...or maybe right side up?

She had stabbed him and could still remember the feel of her blade cutting deep into his muscle. Even so, he had simply ignored the wound and an hour later, it had stopped bleeding and was almost closed. The bite on his forearm and his cut lip were also healing remarkably fast, and he seemed not even to be aware of them.

Clearly, there was something very unusual about this man. So unusual that she questioned whether she had remembered the events accurately. No matter if what he said was true, she was convinced that he had acted...irresponsibly. If he had made Farrukh or Shamail pregnant, what kind of horror would he have unleashed? As it turned out, Farrukh would never bear anyone a child, but there was still Shamail...sweet, innocent Shamail.

It was at that moment that Adelah began to understand why Afig had not stopped her from trying to kill him. He must have known that there was no bullet in the chamber, yet for just an instant, she had seen the surprised look in his eyes when she had actually pulled the trigger. Nonetheless, he had almost urged her to try again, and this time she had seen doubt and even a trace of fear in his eyes. Adelah was sure he knew that if she pulled that trigger a second time, the pistol would fire and he would...die. He was trying to prove something. He was trying to prove that she wouldn't kill him even if she believed he should be killed.

When Adelah had first heard Dr. Dicos explain his vision of fanatical Islamic madmen taking over the world, she became convinced that he and the one he called the Chosen One were evil, and had to be stopped. It had not taken her long to figure out that her only chance of stopping Dr. Dicos was to kill the Chosen One. If the Chosen One was dead, he could not breed and there would be no Listener. Unfortunately Farrukh and Shamail had been chosen to bed with Afig before she had gotten her chance. Still, only Shamail was at risk of pregnancy. Nonetheless, the Chosen One would not get another chance to mate with Shamail or anyone else. At least that was what she had thought when she plunged her knife into Afig. When stabbing him had not worked and when Afig had offered her his pistol, she had been caught off guard. Though she had not been quite so sure of herself, she had still pressed that trigger. When the gun had not fired, Adelah had been struck by a sudden and overwhelming feeling of horror and relief – horror at the fact that she had actually tried to kill this man, and relief that she had failed. There was absolutely no way that she was going to pull that trigger the second time.

Even now, Adelah did not really understand all that had happened, but it was suddenly more difficult to judge Afig for doing what he thought was...necessary to save Farrukh's and Shamail's lives. Wait! Was that what he was trying to do? Had he gone through that...crazy dangerous exercise because he wanted to have her understand???

Damn it, why did everything have to be so complicated?

Afig was not partnered with Dr. Dicos and he did not want to see a world ruled by a bunch of crazy Islamists. His enemy had been her enemy long before they had met; still, why did he have to have sex with those women?...What was wrong with her? She already knew the answer, so why couldn't she just let it go? Whether it made sense or not, Adelah had found not killing Afig to be a hard, heart-wrenching decision, so it seemed...unfair to think that in some way it was comparable to him – a man – saving the lives of two beautiful women by having sex with them.

The sound of his voice brought her back and she heard Afig say, "Adelah...there is one thing that I must be sure you understand. They will examine you when you leave my quarters. If it does not appear that you have mated with me, they...they, will kill you." Now, visibly distraught, he continued, "I do not tell you this to..." Before he could finish, Adelah interrupted, saying, "All of the women have been told that if we do not please you, and if we do not physically consummate our relationship, we will be displeasing not only Dr. Dicos but also Allah himself, and we will be put to death, or worse, we will be given to that beast, Sahla...Do not worry, we all understand what is expected of us." Afig had suspected as much, but he did not know how to reply. Adelah could see his discomfort and found herself feeling sorry for the man. She had listened to his voice for over an hour. She had looked into his eyes, and she had seen them light up when he spoke of his mother, his father, and his sister. She had also noticed how they lit up when he looked at her. Somewhere, along the way, Adelah had begun to...to like this young man.

It was Afig who spoke next, saying, "Adelah, I have told you about myself, and now I would like to know more about you. Who is this beautiful young woman who was so determined to kill me?" Adelah did not think of herself as beautiful or even pretty. It was not that she thought of herself as ugly, but rather it just was not that important to her. Yet, to hear this man call her beautiful had made her feel...strange...a good kind of strange, and she wondered if she could be beautiful. Her face flushing and feeling a little bit nervous, she took a deep breath, sat up straight, and began to speak, "I am Adelah, daughter of Ishtar..." Adelah hesitated for a brief moment and then said, "No, that is not exactly true, my sister and I were adopted by Bel and Ishtar Bazzi. This happened when we very young and we know nothing about our real parents, nor did we ever learn their names.

My sister, Mirah, and I were raised in Iraq, outside the town of Al-

Hillah. Our property lay next to the Hillah branch of the Euphrates River, where my sister and I spent many hours playing. We did not live far from the ruins of the ancient city of Babylon and I loved to spend my time searching for what I imagined to be valuable antiquities.

My adoptive father, Bel Bazzi was an important Ba'ath Party official, and when Saddam Hussein was removed, he was out of work, and forced to go into hiding. Gradually, we ran out of money, and Bel Bazzi became a very unhappy person. Two years ago, he walked out into the street and confronted a gang of Mahdi militia. After hurling insults at them, they promptly shot him to death. I think it was his own special way of killing himself.

Ishtar, my adoptive mother, had come from a wealthy family and she had a great deal of difficulty adjusting to the poverty that was now our lives. She refused to work, in part because she feared that someone would discover her Ba'ath Party connections, and in part because she thought work was below her. So it was up to Mirah and me to earn money. My sister worked at the bakery that was downstairs, from the room that we shared. I worked in a nearby marketplace, where I sold fresh vegetables. We did not earn much money, but the people we worked for were kind to us and we rarely went hungry.

It was at the marketplace that I met my friend Kinah. Her father was a wool merchant, and the family had recently come to Iraq from Afghanistan. Kinah had blue eyes that were nearly the same color as Mirah's and mine. Soon, all three of us became good friends. Kinah spoke very little Arabic and we spoke no Pashto. So it was decided that Mirah and I would learn Pashto while we would teach Kinah Arabic. As it turned out, Pashto became Mirah's and my secret language, and we spoke it when we did not want Ishtar to know what we were saying. Kinah's family had a small shop nearby, and they lived in an apartment behind the shop. Kinah, my sister, and I spent almost all of our free time there. Sometimes we would help dust the stacked bolts of wool fabric while listening to popular music. Other times Kinah's mother would teach us how to cook, and how to sew stylish clothing from pictures in magazines. We would laugh and talk until it was time for my sister and me to go home. We were all poor, but those were good days, days I will not forget.

Then, about three months ago, I was coming home from work when two men came up behind me and hit me with something. I was knocked to the ground and the next thing I knew, my hands were tied and a dirty sack was pulled over my head. The men that took me were AQI (al-Qaeda in Iraq), and they told me that Ishtar had sold me to them for one hundred and seventeen thousand Dinar (~$100 USD), plus a promise not to report her Ba'ath Party history to the Mahdi militia. Eventually, I was told that I would be sent to Syria as part of the 'Sexual Jihad Fatwa.' In other words, I was to become a legitimized whore whose religious duty it would be to...service the al-Qaeda and Islamic State fighters in Syria.

Eight of us women were being held, waiting to be transported across the border when a group of men and women came to our encampment. It was Dr. Dicos, a dozen of his bodyguards, and three female medical technicians. We were told that they were searching for an attractive young virgin. The AQI guards would be paid a great deal of money if one of their female captives qualified, so they lined us all up, and one by one, we were taken into a tent where the female medical technicians examined us. Three of the women were immediately disqualified, because they were determined not to be virgins. Another three of the women were disqualified because they had bad teeth, or medical conditions. That left two of us. The other woman, I do not remember her name, was much prettier than I was, but I was chosen because I knew Pashto. The next day, my hands were tied, with strips of soft cloth because they did not want the bindings to mark my skin. It seemed that I was to be kept presentable. This time, a clean, loosely woven sack was put over my head, and I was put in the back of a truck with two female guards. No one spoke to me and I was permitted to speak only when I needed water, food, or to relieve myself.

Three days later, I arrived in Al-Faw, where I was put onto a fishing boat and taken to Gwadar, Pakistan. In Gwadar, I was drugged, transferred to the back of another truck and driven north. I do not remember much, until I arrived in the village of Sikham, where I was held in the back room of a wealthy baker's house. I do not know how long I was in Sikham, or how I got to Sewakla. The next thing I remember is Shamail tending to my cuts and my bruised ribs, while I lay in my bed.

Farrukh, Hasti, and Shamail had arrived before me. Farrukh, Shamail, and I were not here by choice. Hasti was the only one that wanted to be here. From the beginning, Farrukh did not much like Hasti, and wanted little to do with her.

The four of us lived together, in one room. We spent our days doing physical exercises, taking child-bearing classes, and undergoing physical examinations. We were eventually told that we had been specially selected to be 'bred' to someone they called the Chosen One.

This is how we live...or, at least it was our life, until the day Dr. Dicos injected us with that damn Zulfiqar serum. The next day, Farrukh began acting strangely. We knew the serum had side effects, and if they became too severe, the woman would be taken away and 'disposed of.' Not wanting anything to happen to Farrukh, Shamail and I did our best to hide her strange behavior from the matrons. Then Hasti starting acting strangely, but her symptoms were not as bad as Farrukh's and she managed to appear reasonably normal. Neither Farrukh nor Hasti slept much, and sometimes when I would wake in the middle of the night, I would see the two of them glaring at each other. Over time, Shamail and I grew to fear both of them. When we sensed one of their episodes was coming on, we would avoid eye contact, speak only in whispers, and move slowly so as not to look threatening.

Farrukh had been the smart one, she had received an education, and she had been very kind and sweet to us. It broke our hearts to see the madness take her. The day she was told that she would be the first one to go to you, it seemed to lift her spirits and for a few hours we saw glimpses of the old Farrukh. But the morning she returned from your room, all traces of the Farrukh we knew, were gone. It was as if she was possessed by someone else.

On the evening after they had taken Shamail to you, I saw Farrukh begin to pace. When I spoke to her she did not respond, nor did she even acknowledge that I was present. When I got a look at her face, I saw that her eyes were open wide, her pupils were huge and as black as night, and she stared...unseeing. Honestly Afig, I was afraid she was going to go completely mad and attack the first person that came near her. That night, I could hardly sleep, wondering what I should do. Farrukh was going to hurt someone but if I warned the matrons, she would be taken away and she might even be given to Sahla. It was about three in the morning when I heard what sounded like a...growl. When I looked toward Hasti's bed, I saw Farrukh standing over her, holding a long, sharp stick. Before I could say anything, I heard Hasti scream and then I saw her writhe in pain, the end of the stick protruding from her chest. Farrukh had stabbed her with the sharp end of a broken broom handle, and Hasti was dead before anyone could reach her. Two matrons grabbed Farrukh and forced her to the floor. She did not resist, but just stared at Hasti's body and began to weep. As I watched, she became still and I could see that she had stopped breathing. It took several seconds before the matrons realized that Farrukh was also dead. There was blood and some kind of fluid seeping from her nose and ears. Afig...it looked as if her brain had...burst."

Adelah was silent for a long moment, as the scene replayed in her mind. Then, in a quiet and sad voice, she continued, "When Shamail returned, she too was...different, not mad, just...different. She seemed thoughtful and a little sad. When she learned about what had happened to Farrukh and Hasti, she began to weep. I tried to talk to her, but all she would say was that everything was wrong...and that they had lied to her. All that night, I could hear Shamail quietly praying but by morning, she had become silent. I did not think Shamail was losing her mind, but it seemed that she was trying to make sense of what was happening."

Plan

Adelah stopped, seeming to question whether she should say more. She was quiet for a long time as she stared at her hands, and the gun she was still holding. Then, she looked up at Afig and said, "There is more that I need to tell you but please, Afig, let me be right about you."

Before Afig could respond, Adelah continued, "My...my sister, Mirah, she is very smart and she has the courage of a lion. When Mirah saw AQI fighters go upstairs to our room, she followed them and she heard Ishtar...sell me. Mirah had been on her way to warn me, when she saw the two men take me.

Afig...my sister has somehow managed to follow me to this place." Adelah paused for a moment and then took a deep breath and continued, "I do not know how she did it, but my sister has found work here in the women's section of the hospital. She does housecleaning, and I see her nearly every day.

Three days ago, she told me that she had developed an escape plan. I did not want to tell Mirah that I had a plan of my own, and it did not include escape. I listened as Mirah explained her plan, and I saw how clever it was. I began to think that it might actually work and for a little while, I thought that I might go with my sister and forget about Dr. Dicos and this place. Yet, as the hours passed, I realized that I could not run away. Dr. Dicos was an evil man and capable of causing a great deal of death and misery. I believed then and I believe now that Allah has selected me to put a stop to his plan. When I explained to my sister that I planned to...kill you, she protested and pleaded with me. But where she is smart, I am stubborn, so in the end, she had no choice but to accept my decision. After some of my own pleading, I was able to persuade her to help me. This morning, my sister smuggled me the kitchen knife that I used to stab you with. When we were young girls, my sister and I befriended my father's bodyguard. The man taught us how to shoot, and how to fight with a knife. We were young and did not become experts, but we were eager students, and practiced for many hours."

Astonished by what he had heard, Afig replied, "Your sister is here, here in this...hospital, and she has figured out a way for you to escape? Adelah...you should have gone with her." Adelah replied, "At the time, I was convinced that I must kill you, for killing you would be saving many lives."

Afig could not help but smile. This was, of course, exactly the answer he should have expected from Adelah. Afig continued, saying, "Listen to me, Adelah, you must get away from this place. If your sister can still help, you must go with her." Adelah did not immediately respond. She had heard what he had said but suddenly found that escaping without...Afig was something she did not think she could do. This was completely insane since she had hit, kicked, bitten, stabbed, and even tried to shoot this man. And now she was having difficulty imagining not being with him? Finally, after several long seconds, she collected her thoughts, took a breath, and hesitantly replied, "Yes, of course my sister will help, and I think there is still time. She and Shamail are prepared to leave tomorrow morning."

Adelah's sister was going to take Shamail with her? Afig didn't know what to say. He had considered Shamail's safety his responsibility. To him, Adelah needed to get away from this place, and it seemed that she had a chance of doing just that. Once he thought she was safe, he had planned to get Shamail out. He didn't know how he would do it and it was probably going to get him killed, but he couldn't leave her. After a moment he responded by saying, "Adelah, I am sure your sister's plan is a good one, but will it not be complicated by both you and Shamail escaping at the same time? I think it would be better if I..." Before Afig finished, Adelah interrupted, saying, "Shamail has been a good friend to me and I will not leave her. Anyway, you should be thinking of your escape since it will be much more difficult than mine.....Afig, you do have a way to escape??" Afig immediately replied, "Yes, yes of course." He had responded too quickly and his words did not sound convincing, so he quickly added, "Now tell me about this plan your sister has come up with." Adelah suspiciously studied Afig for a second and then said, "I will tell you about Mirah's plan, but then I expect you to tell me about yours.

My sister has spent many days watching, listening, and getting to know a number of the guards and matrons. She has gone as far as befriending one of the female guards that is posted at the door of the women's section. The woman has told her that the night shift ends at

6:00 AM and before the two night shift guards can leave, they are required to have a short meeting with their day shift replacements. The meeting takes place in the nearby dining room and typically lasts only about six or seven minutes. During this meeting, a male 'temporary' guard stands in for the missing guards and is responsible for letting people in and out of our section. Interestingly, he does not have the clipboard that contains the 'visitors log'. The clipboard was passed to the day shift guards, who review it during their meeting. Sometime between 6:06 and 6:07, the meeting ends and the regular day shift guards take their positions and the 'temporary' guard leaves.

Mirah has discovered that during the seven minutes the 'temporary' guard is watching the door, he does not know who has already been allowed to enter, and thus who should be allowed to leave. Since we were given the Zulfiqar serum, we have been required to wear white burqas while all of the other women are made to wear blue burqas. So, as long as a woman has an identification badge, and is not wearing a white burqa, the 'temporary' guard has little interest in her.

For women, we have been treated well, almost as if we were... royalty. Everyone, including the male guards, has been ordered to be respectful. When the guards see the white burqas they see women that are fed well, women that are not required to work, and women that everyone is required to show deference to. It is difficult for them to imagine that these...privileged women would want to escape. Because of this, the emphasis of security has shifted from keeping us confined to keeping out those that might wish to harm us. Now, anyone who wants to enter must undergo a rigorous ordeal, but for those who want to leave, the process has become less intense.

But there is still more. The 'temporary' guard is always the same young man. Apparently it is not the kind of duty the more senior guards want. Anyway, being a young male, he has a natural interest in females. This young man has heard stories about Shamail and me. It has been said that we are beautiful and that we have voluptuous bodies. Now, thanks to my sister, the young guard has come to believe rumors that say the women in the white burqas wear nothing beneath them. They prefer to be naked and are described as having the faces of angels, and bodies so sensual that if an ordinary man were to look upon such a creature, he would be driven insane with sexual desire. Of course this young male guard knows that he should not think of such things, but when the women in the white burqas appear, he will not be able to think of anything else.

Tomorrow morning, my sister will come to work early. She will be afraid that I have attempted to kill you and that I am now dead. It is prearranged that at 5:45, she will be washing the corridor floor outside our room. If I have not returned, Shamail is to step into the corridor, nod toward my sister three times, and proceed to the toilet. Her three nods will mean that something has happened to me, and that she is prepared to go without me. However, if I am there, both of us will be leaving our room. When my sister sees me, she will know that I have changed my mind and that I will be going with them.

During the next few minutes, she will retrieve the identification badges, and the two blue burqas that she had hidden, in a nearby pantry. Shamail and I will be waiting for her in the toilet and when she arrives, it will take us only a minute or two to remove our white burqas, and put on the blue burqas and identification badges. When we are ready, we will step into the corridor while Mirah remains in the toilet. Shamail and I will pretend to be cleaning while watching the guards. When we see the two sets of guards leave for their meeting, Shamail will tap on the toilet door. Ten seconds later, my sister will step out, and casually walk up the corridor, until she can be clearly seen by the 'temporary' guard. She will be wearing my white burqa, and she will pretend as if she might be...just a little bit interested in the young man. Once I see that she has the guard's attention, I will gather up my cleaning supplies, and make my way to the guard, show him my badge, which happens to display a photograph of a tired, middle-aged woman, and Allah willing, I will be waved through. Five seconds later, Shamail will do the same thing.

Once Shamail and I are well past the guard station, my sister will return to the bathroom, change back into her blue burqa, and leave. She should have no difficulty passing through security since the guard has seen her badge many times. Mirah will catch up to us at the far end of the corridor, and then we will make our way out of the building. Between 6:10 and 6:12, we should be leaving the building, and once we are outside, we have only to travel a hundred meters down the access road and pass one final checkpoint. The men manning this checkpoint are foreigners, and they are hired to defend the compound from attack, and not to keep people from escaping."

Adelah went on to tell him how they expected to evade Dr. Dicos' men once they had escaped the compound. She told him about the stash of men's clothing and the supplies her sister had hidden. She told him about the map, onto which an old smuggler had carefully drawn the secret network of remote trails that led to Chagcharan, and beyond that, Herat.

Now that she had come to know Afig, she wondered if this part of the plan would be followed. Would Afig be coming with them, or should they go with him...and his American friends?

There was something that still bothered her. As her eyes took in this strange, handsome, young man, her thoughts went to Shamail. Shamail was her friend, and Adelah had been the one who had persuaded her to come with them. But Shamail had...slept with Afig, she might even be pregnant with his baby. It took Adelah several long seconds before she became truly aware of what she was feeling. It was...jealousy. Damn it, she was acting like some school girl. Adelah had never been jealous before and decided that this was, undoubtedly, the stupidest emotion she had ever felt. Knowing that it was completely unjustifiable and unquestionably irrational, made no difference...there it was. She was jealous, and she was jealous all the way down to her toes.

Shamail was really her friend...a good friend. She had only done what she had to do. She did not know Adelah would have...feelings for this man. Was that it? She had feelings for Afig? Maybe...no, she knew she liked this young man...she liked him very much. OK, she had feelings for him...and that would have been complicated enough. But it seemed that Shamail also had...feelings for Afig. Now how the heck was this all going to work out?

Afig had listened to Adelah's plan and had been impressed. It was far better than anything he could offer. Still, there were the Americans. Not knowing exactly what that meant, he said, "Adelah, your escape plan is good...no, it is a most excellent escape plan. Allah willing, tomorrow morning, you and Shamail will be free of this place." Afig paused for a moment, and then continued, "The Americans taught me that before you initiate a rescue attempt, you try and give hostages or prisoners what they called a 'heads-up,' a warning that a rescue attempt is at hand. A 'heads-up' gives the prisoner time to prepare for what is coming. Sometimes people need to find a place to hide so their captors can't easily find them and execute them as soon as the shooting starts, other times it is a good idea to find a safe place where they won't get hit by stray bullets. When the pistol was passed to me, I knew that it was my 'heads-up.' I can only guess when the Americans will attack, but I know that Harris has used a one-day warning period in the past. This means the Americans will make their move around 7:00 tomorrow morning...just as they serve breakfast.

Allah willing, you will have enough time to get away from here before the shooting starts. Once you are a safe distance from the compound, try to make contact with the Americans. It is likely that they will be watching you, so stop in an open place, remove your burqa, look upward, and raise your arms above your head, in the shape of a 'Y' and hold that position for a few minutes. They should recognize this signal as your wish to be rescued, and do not worry if at first you do not see anyone. They will be watching you from overlook positions, drones, and even a satellite. It may take them a little while before they realize you are signaling. When they come for you, raise your arms into the air and show them that your hands are empty. Make sure they can see you are not holding or wearing anything that could look like an explosive device. Tell them you are a 'friend,' and that it is important you be taken to Harris...Harris Bartnik.

To recognize Harris, look for a tall man, in his thirties or maybe early forties. He has light hair and blue eyes. He looks very much like the American soldiers you see in the movies. When you see Harris, tell him that you are a close friend of...Dawud Hawadi. Then tell him everything you can about this hospital, about the grounds, and about security. He will want to know where I am being kept, so tell him, but also describe what I now look like, and what I am wearing."

Afig paused for a second as he thought, then he continued, "Adelah, I know these men. They are hard men...fierce fighters, but they are good men. They may be able to stop Dr. Dicos, so do whatever you can to help them." Afig again paused, as he struggled for the words he wanted to use. After several seconds, he continued.

"If something happens and you cannot get to the Americans, try to make your way to the Sewakla mosque and I will meet you there. Give me no more than two hours and then you must go, you must disappear. If I am wrong about the Americans and if my escape is not successful, they will come looking for you."

Adelah had carefully listened to every word that Afig had said. She understood what she must do, and she would do exactly as he had instructed. Yet, it was what he had said at the end that had scared her. Though she knew that Afig had made many assumptions about the

Americans and she knew his escape would be difficult, Adelah wanted to believe that their plan would work and in just a few hours they all would be away from this place...together and safe. She did not want to even imagine herself waiting for him by the Sewakla mosque, to have him not appear.

They were silent for a long time. Both of their minds filled with thoughts of the coming morning. Yet, beneath the worry, they both felt a peculiar sense of resignation. It was as if everything they had ever done had led them to this place, and it would turn out exactly the way it was meant to be.

It was Adelah who spoke first, saying, "Afig, you have not yet told me how you plan to escape.

To me, it seems that it will be very difficult. When they brought me here, I remember passing so many guards. These men were not young boys, they were experienced fighters, and they are all armed with Kalashnikovs. Maybe it would be wise to wait for your Harris to come and get you." Afig replied, "Dr. Dicos does not like me and he will do his best to kill me as soon as the Americans attack. No, I think it is best that I not be here when the fighting starts. My escape plan is simple, and I will admit that my plan is not nearly as elegant as your sister's. I will begin my escape at 6:25 AM, which should give you, Shamail, and Mirah enough time to get away from the compound before the attack." Afig paused, and Adelah looked at him curiously and asked, "Yes, you will begin at 6:25 AM but how exactly are you going to escape?" Afig had not wanted to go into the details, mostly because they would not foster much confidence. Sighing in resignation, he said, I will break out of my room, make my way to Dr. Dicos' office, and escape through the air vent."

Adelah's eyes went wide in disbelief, and she could hardly speak. What Afig was proposing was not an escape plan...it was suicide. Horrified, her voice trembling, Adelah said, "That's it, you are going to 'break out of your room,' a room that has concrete walls and a very thick door that is bolted from the outside? Then you plan to 'make your way to Dr. Dicos' office,' through the two guards standing by your door and eight, ten, or who knows how many other ARMED GUARDS that stand between you and Dr. Dicos' office! And then you are going to 'escape through the air vent,' an air vent you have never seen, and cannot be sure even exists??? That is it...that is your plan?" Although Adelah had been a little more direct than he had expected, he was not too surprised by her reaction. She and her sister had been so meticulous in their planning, while his plan had the subtlety of a sledgehammer. Smiling a bit timidly, Afig replied, "I see that I have not dazzled you with my planning skills. Still, my plan is not as bad as you may think. Given the fact that a burqa is out of the question, and I now have nearly twice the girth and stand almost a head taller than even the largest guard, it is unrealistic to think that I can blend in, and somehow slip by unnoticed. Therefore, it has been necessary for me to use a more direct tack. After considering my options I have concluded that force...sudden, violent, relentless force may well be my best alternative." Seeing that he was not being particularly persuasive, he continued, "Since Dr. Dicos has given me that injection, I have grown in strength and have become as strong as two or maybe three ordinary men. Also, my body can absorb a tremendous amount of punishment and I heal very fast. Most of the guards had once been farmers, and have come to see me as some kind of docile beast...akin to a plow horse or ox." Still, there was doubt in Adelah's expression, and Afig knew that she did not understand what he was trying to tell her, so he said, "Apparently, I have not convinced you, so maybe, it will help if I give you a little demonstration."

Afig rose and walked over to the vertical metal column that was located near the center of the room. The column was one of the many steel columns that could be found throughout the basement level. They supported the weight of the two-story building, above them, and each looked to be at least as wide around as Adelah's waist.

Afig stood directly in front of the column, raised his elbow, cocked his shoulder back, and then swung his shoulder and elbow into the column. The impact produced a dull thud and the metal dented, and Adelah saw the four, large bolts, securing the base of the column to the concrete floor, snap off with a loud ping, and go shooting across the room.

It took only an instant for Afig to realize that he had struck the column too hard. It had been knocked out of place, and now concrete dust drifted down from the ceiling, where several long cracks were forming. He immediately went to work repositioning the column, and it took several long minutes before he was able to force it back into place.

Her mouth agape, Adelah could only stare. This man would never cease to astonish her. It was not possible for a man, even a large man like Afig, to do what he had just done, yet he had done it. Still having difficulty comprehending what she had seen, Adelah said, "Yes...yes I can see that you are very strong." Adelah paused as she tried to organize her thoughts, and then continued, "But they have Kalashnikovs and I do not think you are...bullet-proof." Afig replied, "I have come to discover many things about myself, but being bullet-proof is not one of them. It seems that I will have to travel the twenty meters from my room to Dr. Dicos' office using surprise, speed, and ferocity to minimize the wounds I might receive... Adelah, I am aware that this part of my plan has the most risk but I honestly do not know how else to do it." Adelah did not like this and could easily imagine ten or more Kalashnikovs blazing, bullet after bullet slamming into this man's body, and the thought terrified her, causing her stomach to churn. Even so, Adelah would make no further comments about his plan. She knew that she had nothing better to offer, and it would be mean and pointless to keep challenging him. Even worse, she was afraid she might undermine his confidence, and she knew that he needed to believe in himself for his plan to have any hope of success. No, all Adelah could do was to pray for Allah to watch over Afig and to keep him safe. She would repeat this prayer over and over again until this young man was again standing beside her.

Pregnant

A cold chill passed through Adelah. Hugging herself, she realized that she was still wearing the gauzy, white nightdress and that it was now tattered and stained with Afig's blood. When whole, the garment was so sheer that it was nearly transparent, but now the nightdress was so torn that it left her almost naked. More than once she had seen Afig looking at her, but she had made no effort to cover herself. Adelah liked this man's attention and had found herself strongly attracted to him. These were feelings she had never had for a man before, and with them had come worry, worry that she would not see him again, and worry that for them to have any chance of being together, she would need to make love to this man. It was not that she did not want to make love to him, for she could hardly think of anything else. Afig was a handsome, powerfully built man who had a way about him, a way of speaking to her, a way of treating her with a special kind of tenderness. Adelah had not known this kind of desire before, and it now seemed unimportant that Dr. Dicos had made it a condition for her to live.

Adelah found it strange that she had so quickly decided to kill this man, even when she knew it would mean her certain death. She had not shown even the slightest hesitation at driving that knife into him, yet here she was, sitting next to the one man in the whole world that she would welcome being ravished by, and she did not know what to do? Should she make the first move? After all she had done her best to kill him, and that cannot be the most seductive thing a woman can do. If she did make the first move, what did that mean? Was she supposed to say something or somehow throw herself at him? Before Adelah could give this more thought, Afig rose and then bent down and lifted her into his arms. She could hardly breathe as he carried her to his bed and gently laid her down. He then proceeded to carefully remove her nightdress. As he did so, Adelah's heart rate quickened and she thought of the two attendants who had so carefully prepped her for this night. They had told her not to resist, and to smile even though his touch may not feel good to her. They were wrong – Afig's touch not only felt good, it excited her to such a degree that she had become moist between her thighs. It was not permissible for the attendants, or for that matter for any woman to look upon another woman's intimate parts, so Adelah had been left alone to perform the obligatory task of removing what little body hair she had had. After she had done so, Adelah had spent a long time looking at herself in the full-length mirror. It had been the first time that she had seen herself completely naked and had noticed her full and round breasts, her narrow waist, her shapely rump and long legs, and her shaved genitals had made her feel...funny...a nice kind of funny. Lying there, Adelah was glad that she was a woman and she was thrilled by the effect she had on Afig.

He was a large man but his hands were gentle as they slowly explored the curves and recesses of her body. She made no effort to stop him when his hand reached her genitals, and he began to explore the moist and most sensitive part of her. It did not take him long to find where she ached to be touched, and not long after that before he softly began to stroke her, lightly and slowly at first and then more firmly and more rapidly. Adelah was being driven delirious by the sensation, and responded by arching her back and then pressing her pelvis upward, against his hand. Seconds later she cried out as she suddenly experienced a burst of pleasure so intense that she could hardly breathe. This would not be the only time Afig would bring her to such incredible heights of carnal pleasure, for he seemed to know exactly where to touch her, and how to touch her. Soon Adelah was pleading for him to enter her and as he did, her body shuddered with pleasure and anticipation, opening to him. He slowly pushed into her and began thrusting deeply as she moved with him in a sensual ballet. Afig's thrusts became harder and faster, enveloping her in a euphoria that grew more intense with each thrust until she could stand it no longer, and both she and Afig erupted in pure physical ecstasy.

They would make love for hours and during that time they thought only of each other. As Afig pulled her against him, Adelah felt certain that this was what paradise must be like.

Exhausted, they had fallen asleep in each other's arms and when Adelah awoke, Afig was looking at her as he carefully brushed the hair away from her face. When he saw that she was awake, he bent over and kissed her softly. A familiar and wonderful tingle swept through Adelah's body, and she gasped as air escaped her lungs. Then she inhaled, taking in the scent of this man, and she kissed him back with all the love and all the desire that she had.

Sometime later, Adelah lay nestled against Afig, his arms holding her tightly. She had not wanted to stop making love and only after Afig had given her his semen a third time, had her desire been mostly quenched. Still, Adelah knew that all it would take was Afig's touch and she would again yearn to feel him inside her. She had little doubt that Afig had awakened in her a voracious sexual appetite, but that was not the only reason she so enjoyed making love. Adelah had discovered that the intimacy she shared with Afig had somehow changed who she was. Though it seemed almost...silly to reduce it to such a simple term, she found herself in love. Her feeling for this strange man had caused her to see the world differently, to see it as only a woman could see it. She was sure Afig did not know he had done this to her, and she herself was not even sure what it meant. All she knew was that she was now different, and it was a much better difference. Her life had become...richer and much more complicated. Now, whether she liked it or not, her destiny was tied to this man.

As these thoughts passed through her mind, Adelah suddenly felt a strange sensation low in her stomach. At first she did not understand what she was feeling, but as the sensation intensified Adelah knew...she was pregnant. She was immediately overcome by a feeling of extraordinary euphoria, which was then followed by...terror. Having Afig's baby would be the most wonderful thing that could ever happen to her, but did it not also mean that she was going to give birth to the...Listener??? Some basic part of her silently screamed, NO! She and Afig were both decent, good people and their baby would be good too.

Adelah's eyes were closed, and she was so still that Afig had thought she might have fallen asleep. Careful not to disturb her, he reached beneath the corner of his mattress. Adelah felt him move and when she opened her eyes, she saw him holding a small pouch. Seeing that she was awake, Afig said, "These belong to you and Shamail. Inside are the four diamonds, the second part of your meher, and you may need them once you are away from this place." For a moment, Adelah did not understand what he was saying. Trying to focus, she saw the pouch, which brought back images of that horrible Dr. Dicos...and the wedding ceremony. It had been a time when all she could think about was killing Afig, and now...now it was she who would bring to fruition the very thing that she had wanted to stop.

Adelah thought of the baby growing inside her and she realized that she loved it. She and Afig had made this baby, and it was part of both of them.

Reaching for the pouch, Adelah took it from Afig. She wanted to tell him about the baby, she wanted to tell him they could use the diamonds to start their new life...as a family. But Adelah could not say these words, for it was not that simple. Afig's escape was going to be very difficult and he did not need to be worrying about the baby. It was then that she suddenly remembered Afig telling her what Dr. Dicos had said, – Afig had in him some kind of spiritual guardian that he called an...ethereal creature that supposedly made him more...durable than the average human being. But at the instant he conceived a child, the ethereal part of him would enter the child and Afig would become...mortal. Afig had many doubts about what Dr. Dicos had told him, and she had not given this particular detail much thought. But now she worried that Dr. Dicos was telling the truth, which meant Afig's chances of surviving his escape had just been sharply reduced. No, Adelah would not say anything about the pregnancy. Afig needed his mind to be clear, he needed to believe in himself, in his strength, and even in his...invulnerability.

Adelah was looking at the small pouch, but her mind was racing through all the possible things that could happen to them in the next few hours. Only when she heard Afig's voice did she force herself to focus on where she was and the man lying next to her.

Afig had been quiet as he studied the pistol, and then he said, "There is one more thing I would like you to have. It is the only possession I have that is not tainted by Dr. Dicos' touch. ...I want you to take this pistol." Adelah had last seen the pistol when she had placed it on the floor as Afig had lifted her into his arms. He must have picked it up at the same time he had picked her up. Afig continued, "Harris saw me admiring this pistol, and he told me that it had been given to him by his parents. He had just completed university and had been commissioned a young officer in the United States Marine Corps. They knew that he would soon be sent overseas and they knew that he would be in great danger. Though his parents were not wealthy, they had enough money to purchase it for him. It was a very good quality pistol, better than most, but they were still not satisfied, for they wanted to be absolutely sure that it would not fail him when he most needed it. After a long search, they were given the name of a man who was a highly respected gunsmith. He had a business in a place called Clifton, Texas. Clifton was far from where they lived and it took them nearly three days to drive there. The gunsmith had listened carefully to what Harris' parents wanted, and when they had finished he told them that he understood. For the next nineteen days, the gunsmith worked day and night and when he was finished, he had made what he believed was the smoothest operating, the most accurate, and the most reliable pistol he had ever produced.

On the day he was to deliver it, the gunsmith contacted Harris' parents and told them that his work was done, but he would like their permission to inscribe the words '*May God have his Angels watch over you*' onto the frame of the pistol.

Harris' parents would later learn that the gunsmith's son had been a soldier and that three years earlier, he had been killed in Iraq.

When I saw that it was Harris' pistol, I knew that he was out there, and that he was offering me his protection. As it turns out, Harris' pistol has already saved my life, although not exactly the way I would have expected.

Now, it is my turn to pass this pistol on to you. I pray that Allah will protect you, but if need be, you will now have the means to protect yourself."

Before he could go on, Adelah spoke out in protest, "No, no, I will not take your pistol. I will not leave you without a weapon. You are the one that will have to...to fight his way out of this place." Afig replied, "Adelah, more than anything, I want to be with you...to protect you. But it seems that we must make our escapes separately. You see, you must take this pistol...It is all that I have to give you, and it is the only protection that I can offer you.

Though it may seem strange, I believe this pistol has always been meant for you."

Adelah stared at him for a long time and thought, "How could this man keep doing such things? How could we have developed such a ...bond over such a short time?" From the look in his eyes, Adelah knew that he would not accept no for an answer, and she knew...down deep inside, that he was right. The first time she had held the pistol, it seemed as if it had been made for her. Fighting to hold back her tears, she replied, "I...I am very grateful for...for everything, and I will accept your pistol. But Afig you must hold me...you must tell me that...that you love me and that everything will be all right."

Afig held her, and he told her over and over again that he loved her with all of his heart.

Afig was still holding her, and whispering his love for her, when they heard a banging at the door, and then a voice yelled out, "They have come for the woman, you have five minutes."

Adelah's heart stopped beating and her stomach clenched. Next to her she could feel Afig's body tense, and she saw his eyes become dark. For a second Adelah thought that he would spring up and ram the door with the intent of killing everyone on the other side. Many seconds passed before Adelah could again breathe, and even longer before the darkness began to pass from Afig. As she looked at this man of hers, she could already see the hard, almost chiseled muscles of his body had softened – just slightly but enough for her to notice. This scared her and she began to think that if he was going to die, she wanted to die with him; but this thought passed quickly, for Adelah's mind went to the tiny life growing in her womb. She would not die, she would do whatever was necessary to save their baby.

Afig was holding her tightly, their eyes focused on the door, when Adelah began to slowly pull away. To do so tore her apart and the pain in her heart made her tears flow. She did not want Afig to see her cry so she turned away, stood, picked up her tattered nightdress, and put it on. She then put on her burqa while never letting Afig see her tears. Adelah quietly wept – she wept for him, she wept for their baby, she wept for the three of them. Knowing that she may not have the strength to leave him, Adelah prayed for courage. Holding the head covering in her hands, she willed the tears to stop and turned to look at him for a long moment, and then leaned over, and kissed him gently. As she pulled away, she felt Afig place the pistol into her hand. Reluctantly, she hid it beneath her burqa, and again looked at Afig. Their eyes met, and she saw in them something that she would never forget. Though his eyes were terribly sad, they were filled with more love and tenderness than she thought was possible for a human being to have. Adelah then knew, without a doubt, that Afig was not human. No, Afig was something far more magnificent, but even as she watched she could see the intensity in those eyes begin to fade. Adelah's heart broke into a thousand pieces, for a little at a time the man she loved was...disappearing before her eyes.

They both heard the sound of the bolt slide, and then they watched as the door slowly opened. Adelah slipped on her head covering, reached over and gently touched Afig's hand, and turned to walk away. At the door, she stopped, looked back at Afig, and through her tears she said, "It is time for me to go, my love." And then, in a whisper that she thought was too soft for anyone to hear, she prayed,

"Allah, you must give me strength, for you have let me love this man with all of my heart, and now I...I do not think I will be able to live without him."

Afig's hearing now seemed to be fluctuating, almost as if some part of it was failing. Still, he had heard what Adelah had said, he could hear her heart beating, and he could hear her softly weeping, as she passed through the door and out of his sight. A moment later, Afig was alone.

Breakout

Unable to take his eyes off of the wall clock, Afig paced back and forth. Adelah had been gone for less than an hour, yet it seemed ten times that long. Finally, the clock read 6:01 AM, and he knew that they would be making their move. It now required a great deal of effort, but if Afig concentrated he could still hear far better than before he had been given the Zulfiqar serum. So far, he had heard nothing but the usual muffled conversations, footsteps, and distant kitchen noises. At 6:06, Afig finally let out his breath. Everything sounded normal and the women should be making their way out of the building. All that they had left to do was to walk down the access road and get past that last checkpoint. Afig strained to listen and then at 6:10, he heard a sound that made his blood run cold. It was far off, but there was no mistaking it, it was gunfire. During his entire time at Sewakla Hospital he had not once heard a weapon discharge. Something had gone very wrong and as he listened, more gunfire erupted – this time from what sounded like dozens of weapons. Some of the gunfire was coming from nearby, and Afig wondered whether a team had breached the perimeter and were in the building.

There was little doubt that Adelah's plan had come apart and that a full-scale assault had begun. He had to do something and he had to do it now. Focusing on the heavy, wooden plank door, Afig took a deep breath, dropped his shoulder and rammed it as hard as he could. The impact did little but to crack a few of the wooden door planks, and knock him backward onto his rump. Momentarily dazed, his shoulder hurting like hell, Afig sat there and as his head cleared he began to re-alize that it was not only his hearing that was failing him; he was losing his strength, and probably his ability to absorb punishment. Before he could give this more thought, he heard someone slide the bolt open. Seeing his chance, Afig sprang to his feet, lowered his shoulder, and charged at the door a second time. With the door unbolted, the impact caused it to fly open, smashing into the person who had been standing on the other side. There was no doubt his strength had diminished but at the same time he was no weakling. The door hung there from only one hinge, and several of the wooden planks were now splintered.

Gunfire could be heard coming from the dining room, and not knowing what to expect, Afig cautiously looked up and then down the corridor, but saw only Muhammad, whose crumpled body lay in a heap next to the far wall. On the floor next to the man was a large-caliber revolver, the kind of thing you would use to put down an ox. To Afig, this suggested Muhammad might have come to kill him. Kneeling, he picked up the revolver and then rolled the man over so he could search him. Muhammad's head must have been struck by the door, because the side of his face and one of his eyes were badly injured, his nose was broken, and he was bleeding from both his nose and mouth. As he was checking the man's pockets, Muhammad began to move. He had never much liked Muhammad and didn't want this man giving him any trouble, so he grabbed the man by the hair, yanked his head up, and then slammed it down against the concrete floor. Continuing his search, Afig found five spare cartridges but nothing else of use. He had placed the spare cartridges into his pocket, and had begun to stand when he saw two guards rushing out of one of the nearby testing rooms. Both men had their Kalashnikovs shouldered and were focused on the gunfire coming from the other end of the corridor. Afig squeezed off a quick shot, and the large-caliber muzzle blast thundered through the corridor. The bullet had a devastating effect on one man's head, and before the other man could turn, Afig pressed the trigger a second time and again the muzzle blast reverberated. The bullet impacted the man in the middle of his chest, lifting him off his feet and slamming him into the wall behind him.

Knowing the capacity of the revolver was only five or six rounds, he released the cylinder, ejected the two spent casings, and replaced them with two fresh cartridges. With the revolver fully loaded, Afig began making his way down the corridor to where it turned toward the dining room. Outside, the gunfire was still raging but down here, in the basement, everything had become quiet. Had the Crescent Moon Militia (CMM) managed to repel the Americans? If he looked around the corner would he see gloating CMM fighters standing over the bodies of dead Americans?

Afig was at full alert and as he passed the two guards he had shot, he considered picking up one of the rifles, but there were a number of nooks and crannies that he might have to duck into, and the long gun might be too awkward. Just ahead of him the corridor turned to the left and led to the dining room, Dr. Dicos' office, and the two steel doors. There was a heavy bluish gray haze in the air, and the acrid smell of burnt gunpowder was strong. Afig could see dozens of pockmarks in the walls and just as he was about to take a quick glance around the corner, he heard footsteps shuffling his way. Crouching, he raised the revolver and a second later, a man, one of the hardcore CMM fighters, came stumbling into view. Like the others, he was armed with a Kalashnikov assault rifle, which hung across his chest. The man's shirt was soaked with blood and he was looking back over his shoulder, as if being pursued by some rabid demon. When he was less than two meters away, something made him turn toward Afig, and seeing the revolver pointed at his chest, he froze. Afig could see the surprise on the man's face, and he could see the painful realization in his eyes just as Afig pressed the trigger. There was another thunderous boom and the man was flung backward as the bullet smashed into him. Afig was staring at the grisly mess, when he heard a sound coming from somewhere behind him. Spinning around, he saw Muhammad, his face smeared with blood, one eye swollen closed, and his nose pushed unnaturally to one side. The man was kneeling by one of the dead guards, and aiming the guard's Kalashnikov in his direction. Afig dropped to the floor just as the crack of the rifle resounded through the corridor, and a bullet zipped by his head. On hitting the floor he rolled into position, hoping he would have enough time to aim the big revolver and fire before Muhammad sighted in on him. Another crack from Muhammad's rifle sounded and a bullet grazed Afig's forearm, while another one passed close enough to his neck to burn his skin. Muhammad's aim was off, his right eye was swollen closed and he kept shaking his head as if he was trying to clear his vision. Afig aimed and fired just as two more bullets slammed into the concrete wall beside him. As the haze and concrete dust cleared, Afig saw the blood-spattered wall behind Muhammad. His bullet had passed through his left eye and blown out the back of the man's head.

As Afig got to his feet, he felt his shoulder throbbing, his arm stung and was bleeding, his ears rang, and he felt as if he was going to throw up. As he was about to turn, he heard a voice say, "It...it seems that you are fairly hard to kill." Afig cursed himself for having not been more alert. He had gotten up slowly and he had his back toward the corner where trouble would most likely come from. Now somebody was behind him and close enough to hear his breathing. Yet the voice had not sounded threatening, nor had he ordered him to do anything like drop his revolver or put his hands up. Afig could hear that the man's breathing was labored, and then he heard him give a weak groan and exhale. A second later, there was the sound of a body falling to the floor and then...silence. Turning slowly, Afig saw a man lying motionless less than a meter away. Afig immediately recognized him as the kitchen worker who had passed him the pistol. He was badly wounded but Afig had been surprised too many times in the last few minutes, and wanted to be sure no one else was sneaking up on him. Cautiously approaching the corner, Afig chanced a quick glance around. What he saw startled him; there were at least a dozen bodies, and the floor was covered in pools of blood. Taking a second, longer look, he saw that bodies were those of CMM, Taliban, and lab technicians. Some bodies were stacked on top of one another while others lay behind overturned tables or across furniture. There was even a body jammed between the steel door and the frame, preventing it from closing. He could not see any American uniforms, which suggested that this...kitchen worker had been a one-man rescue team and had single-handedly caused all of this...mayhem. Turning his focus to the wounded man, Afig noticed he was not a large man, nor would you think of him as being muscular. If anything, he was a bit on the small side and...ordinary-looking.

Squatting beside the man, Afig ripped open his shirt and immediately saw two bullet wounds. One round had entered high on the right side of his chest and the other had passed through his left side, just above his hip. Next, he ripped open the man's bloody pant leg to find two more bullet wounds, one right next to the other. The bullets had passed through his left calf. Though he couldn't tell for sure, the leg wounds didn't look too bad but they were bleeding. The bullet hole in his upper chest looked the worst.

Afig had work to do but before he started, he took another quick look around the corner, and immediately saw that the body blocking the steel door was gone, and the door was closed. This was not good. Knowing there wouldn't be much time, Afig went to work ripping the man's shirt into strips, and rolling them into small, tight rolls that he inserted into the man's bullet holes. Packing the wounds was not a long-term solution, but he hoped it would slow the bleeding. Next he made bandages from the shirt, and quickly wrapped the wounds as best he could. Afig was grateful the man was unconscious, or Afig would not have been able to work so quickly.

As he readied the man to be moved, Afig caught a faint whiff of...gas. He had expected it when he had seen the steel door closed. A second later, he heard the buzzing of an igniter, and then flames roared from one of the ceiling jets at the other end of the corridor. At about the same instant, a large blast shook the building, knocking Afig off his feet. Scrambling, he managed to cover the wounded man with his body as chunks of plaster and concrete dropped from the ceiling. The blast had been from somewhere above him, and even with his...diminished hearing Afig could still hear the gun battle raging. Looking up, he saw that two more jets had ignited, and now the flames were less than five meters away. With the next jet directly above his head, Afig heaved the man over his shoulder and ran. He had managed to turn the corner just as the jet ignited and flames engulfed the spot where he had been standing. There was another blast and Afig was nearly thrown off balance. Running toward Dr. Dicos' office, his shoulder throbbed with pain as he maneuvered around bodies and toppled furniture. Reaching the door, Afig kicked it in as several more jets ignited only a couple of meters away. Entering, he quickly pushed the door closed, only to see the room go dark. The fire must have burnt through the wires and shorted the electrical system. As his eyes adjusted, there was enough firelight coming through the louvers and beneath the door, to let him see to get around. In the distance he heard the hammering sound of a heavy machinegun and the continuous chatter of small arms fire. Another blast shook the building, and the heavy machinegun went silent. Flames lapped at the edges of the door, and the temperature was rising rapidly.

Laying the wounded man on the desk, Afig quickly located the ceiling grill, climbed up onto the desk, and pulled the grill from its mount. Seeing something behind it, he began tearing away ceiling tile until he had made an opening large enough to see the one-meter diameter air duct. His heart sank as he saw the duct was sealed off by an iron grate. The iron grate must have been Dr. Dicos' way of ensuring no one would be leaving through the duct. Had he been at his peak strength, he could have ripped the thing from its base, but he was not at peak strength – in fact all kinds of strange things were happening to him. Feeling a sudden blast of searing hot air, he saw that the door had given way and flames were reaching into the room. Desperate, he grabbed the grate and pulled. Nothing happened so he pulled again, this time using every bit of his strength. There was some movement, though the grate itself remained securely attached. A short section of the duct had come loose, though, and with another tug, it and the grate came free and fell, slamming into a wooden cabinet and shattering it.

Looking into the duct, Afig saw rungs welded onto one side. Bending down, he grabbed the wounded man, and was reaching up for the first rung when he noticed the shattered cabinet and the stack of exposed files. Cursing, he put the wounded man down, jumped to the floor, and picked up a handful of files. Even in the firelight he could see that these were medical records. He did not recognize some of the names but he did see his name, Adelah's name, and Sahla's name on the tabs. Afig stuffed the files inside his shirt, leaped back onto the desk, and lifted the wounded man. Seconds later he was climbing up into the air duct which extended high above him through the two upper stories of the building. By the time he had climbed to the end the heat was nearly unbearable, and Afig could smell the fabric of their clothing begin to smolder. The end of the duct was closed off by a weather cap, which Afig struck with his uninjured forearm. The impact ripped the cap free and sent it flying through the air. A moment later Afig leaped from the duct, holding the wounded man tightly against him, as he awkwardly rolled onto the roof. His landing had been far from graceful and he worried that he may have caused the man further injury. Behind him, fire roared up through the duct, shooting ten meters into the sky. He carefully laid the man down and checked him for new injuries but found only a few additional cuts and bruises, along with singed hair, and some charred clothing. His leg had begun oozing blood and Afig was thinking about applying a tourniquet, when the man stirred.

As he fought to regain consciousness, he struggled against Afig, who held him firmly in place. Gradually the struggling stopped and the man relaxed, but then clutched Afig's arm as he stared at something over his shoulder. When Afig turned to look, he saw an American AH-64 Apache gunship closing quickly. It looked like a big, angry hornet coming in to sting them. The Apache came to hover close enough for Afig to make out the pilot's face, and saw that he was studying them. The wounded man released Afig and began to wave his arms. Realizing that they probably looked like CMM or Taliban fighters, Afig followed suit, throwing in an awkward smile, for good measure. These gestures had done nothing to change the serious expression on the pilot's face. Afig could see the man's expression harden, and he knew that the man was going to fire. As he dove on top of the wounded man, a burst of 30 mm cannon rounds seared a path not far above his body. Turning, Afig saw that a section of the roof, and the adjoining parapet, had been obliterated. The mangled bodies of at least four Crescent Moon Militia fighters had been flung into the air, and quickly disappeared over the side. Two more CMM fighters could be seen sprinting for the far parapet as the Apache repositioned itself, and again fired. Several of the rounds impacted the men as they leaped off of the roof, and then all Afig saw was a red mist. When Afig turned back, he saw the pilot was giving him the thumbs up, and then he pulled the Apache up, and banked away. Within minutes, grappling hooks were slung up over the parapet, and seconds later, a team of five American soldiers swung themselves up onto the roof, and began to spread out to form a defensive ring. Afig could see that these were serious men, and were eyeing him with both wariness and curiosity. Afig was sure that at least part of their mission was to rescue a young male asset whose call name was Crow. They had probably memorized his photograph, but in the many weeks during which he had been a captive, Afig had undergone a physical transformation. He had grown at least 8 cm (~3 inches) in height, and had gained over 7 kg (~15 lbs). Certain that this was not normal for captives, Afig could appreciate their curiosity.

One of the soldiers, a medic, was approaching, when Afig noticed an abrupt increase in heat being transmitted through the roof, and then, suddenly, the section he was squatting on shuddered and then sagged dangerously. Realizing that it was about to collapse, he waved away the soldier, scooped up the wounded man, and scrambled toward the nearby parapet. When he was reasonably sure this section of the roof was stable, he placed the wounded man down, and signaled the medic to approach. The medic immediately stripped away Afig's bandages and began to examine the man's wounds. Speaking through his tactical headset, the medic summoned two of the other soldiers and instructed them to jury-rig a sling. The men worked quickly while the medic administered a painkiller and applied field dressings. As the painkiller (something the medic called a Fentanyl lollipop) took effect, Afig could see the man's face was now less drawn, and his eyes were clearer and more alert. Disinterested in what the medic was doing, he looked at Afig for a moment and then said, "I am Colonel Singh. I know that you have been using the name Afig, but I am more familiar with your call name Crow, so if it is all right, I will call you Crow." Afig had no objections, so he nodded his consent. On seeing this, the man continued, "Crow...I was certain that I was a dead man. I thought it impossible to get out of that basement alive, yet...here I am. Thank you, friend...I owe you my life." Colonel Singh's expression became very serious as he continued, "Crow...this is not over. This is a very bad place and it wishes to see you dead...I can actually feel that there is something here reaching for you. I suggest you get down off this roof...get as far away from this place as you can." He paused for a moment and then his expression lightened, though Afig could still see the concern in his eyes. He said, "Anyway, Harris will probably have me shot if anything happens to you." Afig smiled, gripped the man's arm and he replied, "Colonel Singh, first, you owe me nothing. It is I that owe you. I have not forgotten that it was you that risked your life to pass me that pistol, and it was you, you alone who rid us of so many of those guards. This is what made our escape possible. You see, it is I who owe you my life." Pausing, Afig studied the man for a moment and then said, "There is something that I would like you to do. I have some documents I took from Dr. Dicos' office, and I need you to deliver them to Harris." Colonel Singh looked at him quizzically and asked, "Will you not be coming with us?" Afig hesitated for a moment and then replied, "No, not right away. There is something I must do first." Colonel Singh's expression was puzzled but he did not ask any questions. Instead, he nodded and said, "If that is what you wish, you may consider it done."

Afig reached into his shirt and withdrew the bundles of now sweat-soaked and crumpled file folders, and carefully tucked them beneath the man's harness. Once he was sure everything was secure, he said, "When you give these to Harris, tell him that the last time I saw Dr. Dicos was yesterday morning. He appeared to be going away and had a metal briefcase with him. I believe it contained the two vials of a substance he calls Zulfiqar. Four men, including me, were given Zulfiqar from one of the vials, and four women were given Zulfiqar from the other vial. Two of the men died within minutes and another man was driven mad. Two of the women were also driven mad and are now dead. The other two women and I seem OK but I..." The building shuddered as something inside it exploded. Knowing that they did not have much time left, Afig said, "We have run out of time. I will tell

Harris everything when I see him. Now you must go." The three soldiers had been standing nearby and had listened to what the two men had been saying. The team's ranking NCO, a tough-looking first sergeant said, "We'll get Colonel Singh and the documents to Colonel Bartnik." Afig looked at the man and replied, "Thank you." Afig was reaching to shake Colonel Singh's hand when another explosion ripped through a nearby section of roof. Flames leaped through the hole and shot upward, into the sky. The soldiers lifted the wounded man over the parapet and began lowering him. The two other members of the team had gotten down from the roof and were waiting to receive him.

As Colonel Singh disappeared from sight, Afig's thoughts went to Adelah. In the distance he could see the burning hulk of what looked like a garbage truck. Just to its right was where the Sewakla District Hospital access road intersected the gravel road that led to the town of Sewakla. As he traced the access road back to the hospital, it did not take long to spot two blue forms lying in the dirt. He was too far away to be sure, but it looked like two blue-burqa-clad bodies. Afig's heart stopped, and for a long moment it felt as if the world too had stopped. Seeing Afig's expression, the first sergeant said, "I'm First Sergeant Skity but if you want you can just call me Skity." He paused a moment and then continued, "It looks like something is bothering you?" It took several seconds before Afig could form words, but as his voice returned, he said, "Skity, do...do you know anything about those two...bodies?" First Sergeant Skity looked toward where Afig was staring, and answered, "Yeah, they're part of what kicked this whole thing off." The roar of the flames grew louder and the man was forced to raise his voice as he continued, "The plan was to hit this place hard and fast, at exactly 0700 hours. It was a coordinated operation with us hitting the hospital at the same time Predators were going to take out a three-vehicle convoy, about forty clicks south of here. We knew the two targets were in contact with each other, and those in the convoy were thought to be particularly skittish..." He was interrupted by the medic, who indicated Colonel Singh was down from the roof. One of their ropes had been used to make the sling, so there were only three ropes for the four of them. First Sergeant Skity had just ordered Afig to go next, when a hail of bullets slammed into the parapet. The gunfire caused all four men to drop down to the roof. No one had been hit but at the same time no one was going anywhere. In the next few minutes the soldiers made several attempts at locating the source of the incoming rounds, but every time they raised their heads they were greeted with another barrage that tore into the parapet and sprayed them with fragments of concrete and dust. Realizing they were pinned down and that they didn't have a lot of time, First Sergeant Skity radioed for assistance. Two five-man teams were on their way and an Apache gunship was about four minutes out. Told to hang tight, the men settled in and waited.

First Sergeant Skity took a position next to Afig and they both sat with their backs against the parapet. For the moment there was nothing they could do, so Afig hoped that Skity would continue telling him about what had happened to the two women. When the man just sat there, staring at the flames that were leaping skyward twenty meters or more, he decided the man needed some prompting so he said, "Skity, excuse me but it is very important to me to know what happened to those women so please, could you continue?" They were crammed together on the only section of the roof that was not completely engulfed in flame, they were taking fire from bad guys who had pinned them down, and if help didn't arrive soon they would have to choose between getting shot or burning to death. Considering their situation, First Sergeant Skity wasn't in much of a mood to talk. Yet, there was something about this young man that was curiously compelling, and a moment later First Sergeant Skity found himself saying, "At about 0610 hours we were advised that four Afghan Army choppers were inbound. This was about the same time we spotted the three women leaving the hospital building and starting to walk toward us. We kept an eye on them but didn't give them much thought since it wasn't that unusual to see women coming and going. Anyway, we came to find out that there was an Afghan colonel onboard one of the choppers. He was screaming over the radio for Colonel Bartnik to stand down. He claimed the operation had not been sanctioned and if we didn't 'back off' we were to be considered 'hostile.' Colonel Bartnik was in a shouting match with this Afghan colonel when the first chopper flew over the compound and drew a burst of automatic weapon fire. Best I can figure is that the bad guys weren't supposed to shoot at the Afghan chopper, but somebody screwed up because it was only one gun that fired, and then only one burst. Nevertheless, when the women heard the gunfire, they decided to make a quick exit. I saw the three of them running toward us, when some asshole with an AK-47 came charging out of the building. He started running after the women but when it looked like they were going to make it to the road, he started shooting. Two of the women were hit and went down, but the third woman stopped running, pulled out a small pistol from beneath her burqa, turned, and fired two quick shots. I gotta say it was some damn good shooting. She had to be out of breath and the guy was at least thirty meters away, yet she managed to place the first shot 'center mass' and the second shot in the middle of his forehead. The guy dropped like a sack of potatoes, right over...there." The first sergeant pointed to the body of a man, lying off the side of the access road. Continuing, he said, "We knew that Colonel Bartnik wouldn't take kindly to them shooting down women, and sure enough, my team was ordered to bring in the third woman even if it meant we had to break cover. From there on everything went to shit. First this beat-up old garbage truck comes driving up the road. Sergeant Janda's team tried to stop it but the driver rolled right past, and even after its tires were shot out the damn thing didn't stop until it was right in front of the hospital. The Afghan choppers and the bad guys must have had a thing for old garbage trucks, because they opened fire on it.

So there we were, our view of the woman and the hospital was blocked by this garbage truck that was being ripped to shreds, and even worse, we were taking stray rounds and ricochets. Having no choice, we began repositioning but we didn't have a lot of places to hide, and it wasn't long before we were spotted and started taking direct fire. I guess Colonel Bartnik figured that we had lost our element of surprise, so he gave the order to attack, and the battle for the Sewakla District Hospital began. Soon we were blasting away at the bad guys, the bad guys were blasting away at us, at the garbage truck, and at the Afghan choppers. The Afghan choppers seemed determined only to obliterate the garbage truck and most every cactus and thistle within fifty meters of it.

To make things even more messed up, two of the Afghan choppers touched down and unloaded about a dozen foot soldiers, who charged right into the middle of this 'shit storm.' About five minutes later, two of our Apache gunships showed up and the Afghans hightailed it out of Dodge. It took another twenty minutes to take out the bad guy gun positions, but by then the hospital building was ablaze." First Sergeant Skity shook his head and apologetically said, "Sorry man, we didn't think there was anybody left alive in the place. Anyway, when the dust settled, we checked on the two women and found they were both dead. We tried to locate the third woman but she was long gone. It was about then that we were told to go and get you and Colonel Singh down from this roof."

Afig was now sure Adelah was alive. She was the one who had the pistol and it had not failed her. Caught in the middle of the chaos Skity had described, Adelah had had no choice but to run, and she had likely headed to the Sewakla mosque.

About an hour had passed since he had first heard the gunfire, and Afig remembered telling Adelah to wait at the mosque for no more than two hours. If he wasn't there by then, she was supposed to...disappear. Running, it would take him between fifteen and twenty minutes to reach the mosque, but that meant nothing since he still had to get down from the roof, and even then, making it to the mosque without someone stopping him was unlikely. Afig was trying to figure out what to do next when he felt a rumble come from deep below. The roof shuddered and an instant later it dropped. He felt himself falling into a dark, smoke-filled abyss, and the next thing he knew, he had slammed against a concrete slab. The slab tilted downward, and Afig had to grab hold of an edge to keep himself from sliding off. Through the smoke he could see Skity had managed to grab hold of a piece of rebar sticking out from a section of floor that was still intact. Below them was a gaping chasm that spewed columns of black, oily smoke and hungry red flames. As Afig scrambled to try and get a foothold, the slab shifted and then it began to slide toward the chasm. The air was thick with smoke and the heat was unbearable. Flames reached out for Skity and in seconds fire enveloped him, and his clothing burst into flame. The man hung there, gripping tightly to the rebar as fire consumed him. Unable to watch, Afig looked away and when he looked back, he saw First Sergeant Skity's charred body drop from the rebar and fall into the inferno below.

The air burned his lungs and Afig could no longer take in a breath. The flames now crept toward him and soon they surrounded him. A moment later, he watched as his clothing burst into flame.

Unseen

Afig could still taste the oily black smoke and he remembered watching helplessly as the fire devoured the first sergeant. He remembered smelling the burning flesh, he remembered the hot air searing his lungs, and he remembered the flames that had come for him. What he could not remember was how he had gotten out of that hellish place. Maybe he had somehow gotten his strength back and had the power to... to do what? Even if he had the strength of ten oxen...he didn't know what he could have done. And why couldn't he remember?

Looking around, Afig found himself in what must have been the hospital foyer. The place had long ago been abandoned, and was strewn with garbage and dead leaves. Fine sand had drifted in through the missing windows, and the entry door was now only a mangled metal frame. The sand had coated everything and a dust hung in the air, illuminating beams of sunlight that shone in through the openings. So far, the foyer had been spared from the fire that Afig could still hear raging nearby. The obvious way out was through what was left of the entry door, but he could hear the distant thumping of helicopter blades and the sporadic chatter of small arms fire. If he came out through the front door, someone was certain to shoot him or at least try to detain him.

A few seconds later, Afig had crawled out one of the side windows and was heading for the brush that bordered the access road. Though gunfire sounded nearby, he felt drawn to the bodies of the two women, and found himself running in their direction. He had traveled about 50 meters when he saw the body of the man who had chased after the women and shot them. He was lying on his back and his arms were splayed out to his sides. There was a Kalashnikov lying next to him. Afig immediately recognized the man as Merzad. His shirt was bloody and he had a surprised expression on his face. Just as Skity had described, he had been shot once in the center of his chest and there was a small, round hole in the middle of his forehead. Adelah had made sure that Merzad would never again be a problem for anyone.

A few seconds later he reached the two burqa-clad bodies and stopped, but found that he could not look down. Though he was nearly certain that Adelah had not been killed, there was still a chance that he was wrong, and if he was wrong, seeing Adelah's body would utterly destroy him. Summoning his courage, he forced himself to look. The women's head covers had been pulled back and he immediately saw that Adelah must still be alive. The woman to his right was Mirah. He knew this because, like her sister, she possessed a unique kind of beauty, a beauty that had transcended even her death. Her eyes were open and Afig could see that they were the same blue color as Adelah's. Her hair was darker than Adelah's but the line of her jaw, her nose, and even her chin strongly hinted at them being sisters. Mirah was two, maybe three years older, and Afig wondered whether she had always been the protective one. Remembering what Adelah had told him, he knew that Mirah had tracked her sister thousands of kilometers and across three countries – countries that were dangerous for a man to travel, and many times more so for a woman. She was the one who had come up with the plan that had made it possible for Adelah to escape, and she was the one who had paid such a dear price. On seeing Mirah, his heart felt heavy and he could now more appreciate the terrible sense of loss that Adelah must be feeling.

Quietly he whispered, "Thank you, Mirah. Thank you for taking care of Adelah...and I'm ...sorry, I'm sorry that I was not there to help."

Turning to Shamail, he saw that her eyes were also open and she was staring vacantly at some point in the sky. The sight of her squeezed at his heart until it hurt. He...cared for this pretty young woman even more than he had realized. He had wished for her happiness, he had wished for her a long and full life. Shamail had been a kind and decent person, and had not deserved to die like this.

Afig wiped away his tears with the back of his hand. Adelah would be waiting for him; he did not have much time.

Afig ran as fast as he could but quickly realized, too late, that he had been careless. Rounding a corner, he ran right into a road block manned by a half dozen American soldiers. But instead of stopping him, they paid him no attention, and he was soon past the road block and again running. It was not long before the mosque was in sight, and Afig quickened his pace. Arriving, he immediately began searching for Adelah. He made his way around the outside of the building but did not see her. Thinking that she might have sought shelter, he went into the mosque. The mosque was not large and he soon had looked into every corner and every pantry, but had failed to find her. Leaving the mosque, he expanded his search to nearby streets, alleyways, and back yards. He looked inside sheds and through open windows of houses, but Adelah was nowhere to be found. Disheartened and emotionally drained, Afig returned to the mosque, where he stood, looking toward the smoke rising from the distant Sewakla District Hospital. He was wondering what had happened to his Adelah when a noise...no, a voice startled him. It was the amplified voice of the Imam calling the faithful to prayer. Less than an hour ago, a battle had raged just outside this little town, and yet people were coming out of their homes to pray. Afig stood there watching as people passed him on their way into the mosque. They were mostly old men and a few old women, yet not one of them looked in his direction. It was as if they did not see him. Something was...wrong; it had been wrong ever since he had found himself in the hospital foyer. Afig looked down at his hands and felt oddly relieved that he could see them. This relief dissipated quickly, though, as an old man passed so close to him that Afig could feel him brush against his leg. The man had also sensed something, and stopped. He looked in Afig's direction but showed no indication that he actually saw him. Appearing confused, the man glanced down at his leg, paused a moment longer and then continued into the mosque. This encounter had disturbed Afig and he called after the man, but the man did not appear to hear him. Nearing panic, Afig yelled as loudly as he could, "I am here, do you not see me!" But his yelling had no effect. Not a single person looked in his direction.

Trying to make sense of what was happening, Afig reached down and picked up a pebble, thinking that he might throw it at someone. Holding the pebble in the palm of his hand, he stared at it. A second went by, then two seconds, but before the third second had passed, the pebble fell through his palm and to the ground. Not believing what he had seen, he picked up a second pebble and before he could count to two, the pebble again passed through his palm, and fell to the ground. On his third try, Afig could not get hold of the pebble. His fingers simply passed right through it.

CHAPTER FORTY

Contact

Harris needed some time to think, so he walked the battle-scarred grounds next to the smoldering ruins of Sewakla Distract Hospital. The mission had not gone well. An hour ago, two soldiers had reported witnessing Afig and their first sergeant fall through the roof of the burning building. They were convinced that no one could have survived that inferno. Another four of his men had been killed in the fighting, and three more had been seriously wounded. Dr. Dicos had....vanished and they had not captured a single doctor or technician. There was almost nothing left of the hospital structure. The only bright spot was the stack of medical files Afig had salvaged. Though Colonel Singh had suffered serious wounds, he had refused to be medevacced until he had personally handed Harris the documents, and told him what Afig had said.

On top of everything else, someone high up in the Afghan Government was pissed, and was sending troops in to take control of the site. Harris and his entire operation were given six hours to leave the country.

Tonight, in some Quonset hut in Uzbekistan, Harris would be writing six letters...but the one he would write to Afrah would be unquestionably the hardest. His head down and his shoulders hunched, he was passing what was once the Sewakla District Hospital foyer when he thought he heard someone calling to him. At first he thought it was his imagination, but he heard the voice a second time. Curious, he stepped through the twisted framework of what was once a door, and entered the foyer. The walls were still standing, but not much else was. Looking around, he saw nothing...well almost nothing. He thought he might have seen something behind a column that had once supported the roof. Unslinging his M4, he began cautiously approaching the column when he heard a voice that was only a whisper, say, "Harris, it is better that you do not come any closer." Harris immediately recognized the voice as Dawud's, and was about to call to him when the voice continued. "Yes, Harris, you have known me as

Dawud. My time with you has come to an end, but there is still much that must be done."

For the next hour, the voice spoke, revealing to him the past and the future, and then the voice told him what he must do. Harris was taken aback by all that he had heard, and did not know how to respond. At first he thought it was some kind of a trick, but as more and more was explained to him, he began to believe what he was hearing. He did not want to know these things. Maybe if the future was fixed he might be able to get his mind around it, but it was not. It was more like a massive keyboard with seven billion keys on it. You could push tens of millions of those keys every day, for the rest of your life, and little would happen. Yet if you pushed just a few of the right keys and in just the right order, the world might not go...*BOOM!* The voice wanted him to be the one pushing the keys. He was a soldier, he liked being a soldier. He had a career and in just a few more years, he could put away his gun and take up ......something that didn't require him to kill. Yet, Harris now knew that his life had just changed.

The last words he heard Dawud's voice say were, "Now go and find Adelah, see that she is kept safe, for she bears a child that will change the world." After saying these words, the voice went silent, but Harris did not want the voice to go silent. He had so many questions and there was so much he did not understand. He called out to the voice, but it did not respond. For the next half hour, Harris repeatedly called to the voice, but was met only by silence. Confused, bewildered, and exasperated, Harris slowly stepped toward the column. Looking behind it, he saw the charred remains of a human being. Much of the flesh had been burnt away, leaving a blackened skull with empty eye sockets, and a jaw that hung wide open.

THE END – BOOK I

ABOUT THE AUTHOR

The author was born to Polish immigrants in Winnipeg, Canada. He and his family came to Long Beach, California when he was fifteen years old. Graduating from high school and then City College, he married his high school sweetheart and took a job as a flight-line mechanic.

At this same time the Viet Nam war was raging and in 1966 the author enlisted in the U.S. Army and in 1968 he shipped off to Viet Nam.

After a three year stint, the author left the army and returned to college to earn a Bachelors of Science degree. On graduating the author would spend the next dozen years in various professions and occupations before he, his wife, and their two children moved to Santa Barbara, California, where he has now lived for over three decades.

Retiring in 2006, the author discovered he had no interest in golf or gardening, and was convinced that he had much left to accomplish. For the next several years the author focused his effort on developing an idea that would automate healthcare data collection and its analysis. Eventually, the United States Government would grant him two patents.

Wanting new challenges, the author's wife encouraged him to write a novel which led to the Sword of Zulfiqar. He is currently working on the second book in the Zulfiqar Project series.

www.ingramcontent.com/pod-product-compliance
Lightning Source LLC
Chambersburg PA
CBHW031939260626
47157CB00016B/276